NOT YOUR AVERAGE BRITISH ROMANCE BOOK 1

KERRY HEAVENS

Dear Karen
Thanks for reading
PRINCESS!
love Kerry Heavens x

Published by Kerry Heavens.
© 2015. Kerry Heavens.
Spencer
All Rights Reserved.

No part of this book may be reproduced or transmitted in any form or by any means, electronic or mechanical, including photocopying, recording, or by any information storage and retrieval system without the written permission of the author, except where permitted by law.

ISBN-13:978-1512149319
ISBN-10:1512149314

Published by Kerry Heavens
Editing: Ellie at lovenbooks.com
Cover Design: Rebel Graphics
Model/Photographer: Justin Charles Reed
(Image used under license)

For
The good ship Twitter
And all who sail in her.

You crazy, crazy bastards!

FRIDAY 19TH JUNE

Man, it's been a long morning.

I actually like my job. I'm good at it. My position as manager over two guys with far more experience than me, is hopefully a reflection of my hard work and not the boss' hard-on for me. I keep telling myself that. It's the only way I can get through the day.

I bury myself in paperwork and pace my phone calls so that I'm conveniently engaged whenever I see him come out of his office. My stomach growls, reminding me that I skipped breakfast, but I like to wait a little longer to take my lunch otherwise the afternoon drags.

When it finally comes time for a lunchtime escape, I cross the road with a group of assorted office workers and walk straight through the sliding doors of the supermarket opposite our shop. Standing in front of the sandwiches I stare blankly as usual, trying to get inspired by the same old selection. I step around two guys in suits to see what there is on the other side. Ugh, I'm so bored with these sandwiches. I lean forward to pick up a tuna and sweetcorn, just when the guy beside me does the same.

He reaches across me and the first thing I notice is that he smells FANTASTIC!

"Oh, sorry," he offers when he realises we were going for the same sandwich.

Holy cow, he smells fantastic AND he has a great voice. Deep, not Barry White deep, just sexy, you know?

I take the sandwich he has politely left for me and glance up at him for the first time.

Damn.

I blink.

DAMN!

How have I been standing next to this vision for three minutes, staring blankly at sandwiches and not noticed him? How have I even noticed the sandwiches? Where am I again? Tall, dark and handsome, three words that have finally found their purpose in life. God he looks good in a suit, not that I have any point of comparison. I bet he looks good in anything...or nothing. Is it hot in here?

I bet I look like shit.

And I'm still staring. Fuck!

He smiles at me. One of those, 'I know you're checking me out' smiles. I flush what I'm certain is a neon shade of mortification and turn to leave. Mouthing 'Oh my God!' to myself as I walk away.

Naturally, I trip and stumble on the edge of that stupid carpet thing they have around the fresh flower section.

Damn. These. Shoes.

I glance back, yep, he saw. And yep, he sees me checking whether he saw.

Fuck. My. Life.

When I get back to my office, I close my glass door and

slump down in my chair. Pulling out my phone, I do the only thing a girl can do at a time like this. A BFF SOS. Opening our text conversation, I type.

'Total Hottie McHotstuff in the sandwich section. Obviously I went all out and completely humiliated myself.'

'Pictures please.'

'Seriously? You think I could have coordinated a covert snap? This is me we're talking about here Mags, the flash would have gone off, let's be realistic. I was incapable of brain function. Lost all motor skills and barely made it back to the office.'

'I'm gutted I missed that!'

'It was ugly Mags.'

'He wasn't by the sound of it.'

'No. No he wasn't.'

SATURDAY 20TH JUNE

"Did you hear that Kate found a load of dirty photos on Nick's phone? She threw him out." Mags says casually sipping her iced latte.

"Porn?" I ask, hardly surprised. "Kate needs to get a grip, everyone looks at porn."

"No, of a girl he was doing on the side."

"NO!"

"Yes!"

"Shit, I didn't think people really did that."

"What? Cheat?" She looks puzzled.

"Please. I know too well they cheat. I mean the pictures thing."

"You've never sent a dirty picture?" She narrows her eyes with a sly smile, she thinks I'm playing innocent.

"Um, no."

"Not even to the arsehole?" She never says his name, they despised each other. "You never texted him to let him know what you wanted to do to him?"

I blush.

"What's that face?"

"Nothing."

"Liar!"

"Ok, I've done that. Just never to him."

"See! I told you he wasn't the one for you."

"Oh, please! Just because I never saw fit to text him a picture of my left nipple does not mean he wasn't the one for me, Mags."

He wasn't the one for me. I knew it deep down. But I wanted him to be, he had so much potential. Will I admit that to Mags now, even after all this time? Hell no!

It was doomed to fail from the start. I was the steady girlfriend with marriage prospects that he needed so he could start getting taken seriously at work. He is far too single for the kind of promotions he wanted. Those jobs go to the people with home life responsibilities. The kind of people who need the job so badly, they tow the line. He was nowhere near ready for that kind of commitment.

What was I doing, allowing myself to become the token live-in girlfriend, you ask? Being lazy, I guess. Too lazy to admit I deserved better, too lazy to fight moving into his flat because it's what he wanted and kept pushing for it. And just stubborn enough to try and prove I knew what I was doing, despite Mags' protestations that he would screw me over.

She always said he would mess around. He was the type apparently. She watched him like a hawk and not surprisingly, he didn't take kindly to it. I always thought she was just being over protective, but you should listen to your gut and if that has nothing productive to offer, then you should listen to your best friend. If your best friend hates the guy you're with, ask yourself why?

I look up at Mags and she is waiting for an admission. I

don't offer it.

"You knew he was all wrong for you," she says, with a hint of triumph.

I sigh, "Yeah ok, he was wrong for me. Happy?"

"Happy that you saw the light. Not happy about how it was shown to you. You'd better hope the little shit continues to keep well clear of me."

"Mags, he knows damn well you hate him, he's not stupid." As the words leave my mouth I realise how laughable that is.

Mags throws her head back and laughs. "Jazz, please! He got caught, didn't he?"

I shake my head, unable to help a little chuckle. He was caught out big time, there's no getting away from it.

"Maybe I don't give him enough credit, maybe he wanted to be found out," she muses.

"Maybe…" I consider. "Or maybe he was just the stupid fuck you always thought he was."

"I do have an impeccable fuckdar, " she giggles.

MONDAY 22ND JUNE

I just want a cup of tea, is that too much to ask?

I glance around the shop floor from behind the safety of my glass office wall. I can't see him, but that doesn't mean he's not there. James, the creep who lays in wait for me to pass his door, is a first class douchebag.

He thinks for some reason that he has a chance with me. The fact that, as far as he knows, I live with my boyfriend, seems to make absolutely no difference. I split up with my ex three months ago, but I'm not admitting to that at work. James will think it's game on.

My supposed lack of availability aside, I think I've been perfectly clear there is no reciprocation. Sure, I like being inappropriately groped as much as the next girl, but I have done nothing to encourage his advances, so why he thinks I'll suddenly be unable to resist his relentless 'charm' after all this time, I'll never know.

He likes the way I dress, I know this, but I refuse to change who I am because of him. I don't dress to provoke, I dress for me and it is by no means indecent. But I'm a girl who has curves and I love fashion. Should I have to dress like a nun because the office perv can't keep it in check? Nope.

Unfortunately for me, the office perv also happens to own the place. Steeling myself, I text Mags.

'Teatime. *Cringe*'

'You need to quit Jazz.'

'Sure, I'll get right on that.'

'Kick him in the balls :)'

'One of these days Mags, I just might.'

'Haha! James and his giant peaches wouldn't fuck with you again if you did.'

'I love you.'

'Love you too chick, now go get your arse groped...I mean tea. Go get your tea.'

Wiping the grin off my face, I suck in a deep breath and drag myself to the kitchen.
"Good morning, Jasmine."
My back straightens at the sound of his voice. Of course he followed me in.
"Good morning, James," I reply in my controlled tone. Not rude, he is my boss after all, but not warm, because if I give him an inch, he'll take a mile. He slides in behind me to reach

for a mug, he and I both know there is a more convenient position right beside me for reaching those mugs. He presses himself against me as he leans and I shudder. I'm not letting him know he is getting to me though, so I quickly finish making my tea and hightail it back to my desk, to keep myself from kneeing my boss right in the baby maker.

I know, I know, I could do something, but it's not like there is anyone I can report him to. It's just him, me and three other sales assistants. As I said, two of the other guys have far more experience than me and yet James promoted me to manager, so they aren't exactly my buddies.

They're jealous and they too think that James promoted me to get in my underwear. In fact, they probably think he's already been in my underwear and this is my reward. Twats. I have the most consistent figures and they are both so old school they are alienating much of our new business. So I know I earned this. But that leaves me with no one to turn to.

I could take it outside the company, hire a lawyer. I could just quit. The fact is, I like my job and he never takes it too far. Mainly because he is deluded enough to think he's still working towards breaking me.

That protects me. If he took it too far, even he must know he would have no chance of having me. His methods are screwed, but he isn't that bad.

When I get back to my desk and plonk down in my chair with a sigh, I see that there's another text from Mags.

'You know you'd be happier making chocolates…#JustSayin'

I lean on my elbows and rub my temples. She's not wrong. I love chocolate more than...than...shoes, there I said it! But what I really love more than anything is making chocolates. It relaxes me and makes me happy. My dream is to open a little shop, where I can quietly play with chocolate all day and share my love with other people.

Selling swanky kitchens is not my dream. It's what I do. I took this job after university because it was local and the money was ok. I didn't stop to think that I would still be doing it three years later. Or that I'd be good at it. I had loans to pay off and it was easy. I am good at it though. Damn good.

I have personally landed some very lucrative contracts with developers that have taken us beyond our shop front. We now have teams of fitters capable of huge jobs, fitting kitchens in new build developments and upmarket apartment complexes. So while my old school colleagues deal with the walk-in trade from the local moneyed city workers looking to keep up with the Joneses, I am better at negotiating the bigger deals. Which is why, I hope, James values me as an employee.

'Ignore me if you like. You know I'm right.'

I let out a long sigh.

'Oh, and speaking of...don't think I don't know you made truffles last night and didn't share!'

Laughing, I type.

'Use your eyes and you'll find the box I left you beside the toaster.'

There is a long pause. Then she's back.

'I'm telling you Jazz, you're wasting your talent in that bloody place. Why the hell are you selling kitchens? This, THIS, is what you need to be doing with your life. Supplying ME with this heavenly goodness, day and night."

'You're biased Mags, you'd eat a boot if it were covered in chocolate.'

'Yes, yes I would and that's why you need to listen to what I'm saying. If not for you, then for me, you need to quit that job and follow your/my dreams.'

I totally forgot about Hottie McHotstuff from the supermarket, until I'm back here doing the obligatory sandwich stare and I become aware of his height beside me. He seems to be talking quietly to himself so I risk a glance up at him and see he's on his phone. He's deep in conversation and is oblivious to me, so I take the opportunity to have a little stare.

Yep, I didn't dream it. He's just…wow!

He really wears that suit. It's well cut and bang up to date. Every detail is perfect. His physique is visible through the expensive fabric. You can see he takes good care of himself. He's not bursting through his clothes or anything, but I'd bet my granny there's at least a six pack under there. Ok, maybe I should return my gaze to the sandwiches.

Maybe in a second once I've studied his strong jaw and dark features for a moment more. And those glasses, the heavy black framed, old school type...he looks like Clark Kent. I wonder if he looks unrecognisable when he takes them off and rips open the shirt.

Shit, concentrate.

I stare right through the sandwiches for a few moments, then my gaze wonders back to him. I like his hair. All smart for work, to go with the suit and Clark Kent glasses. But I bet it looks great all messed up...My mind drifts off to some delicious hair wreaking scenarios...

Ok! Sandwiches. Focus. Roast beef and horseradish, chicken and chorizo...

God he smells good.

Damn it, Jazz.

BLT, tuna...I'm not taking any of this in. I hope he goes away soon or I'll starve to death.

He reaches across me for a BLT and the sleeve on his suit rides up slightly. Holy sweet baby Jesus! He has tattoos around his wrist. Not a tattoo - singular, on his wrist, no. His wrist is wrapped in tattoos down to his cuff, leaving me in no doubt he is hiding a full sleeve up there. My knees actually wobble. Bloody hell, this guy is something right out of my inappropriate dreams. I need to move away now or I'll embarrass myself...again.

He's still looking at the selection, so I move around to the next aisle to look at wraps and salads. It's cooler here, the air doesn't smell of him and I can concentrate. Shall I have a salad or a wrap? Salad or wrap? Salad or wrap?...Bloody hell, I can still smell him! He should not be allowed to smell so good in public that it permeates two supermarket aisles. It's dangerous to my health...and possibly to his. That's when I realise he has changed aisles too.

Fuck it, I'll just have fruit.

TUESDAY 23RD JUNE

"So let me get this straight," Mags says, reaching across to take a slice of cucumber. "You're making lunch so that you don't have to cross paths with the ridiculously hot guy who has got you all in a fluster?" She frowns. "Jazz, did you bang your head recently? Get in there, girl! You should be in your room picking out your deadly outfit, not out here making lunch. What is wrong with you?"

"Nothing's wrong with me. He's just too perfect, that's all, I can't function around that much perfection."

"He can't be that perfect, I bet he's a right arsehole."

"You hush your mouth," I scowl, waving the tin foil at her.

"Oh, come on, no one is that perfect. Either he knows he's amazing and he's an arsehole about it, or he's all front with nothing to back it up. You can't be that pretty and not have a flaw. Maybe when he takes off his Clark Kent glasses and rips open the shirt, he's 'Super-Disappointment.' Slower than a speeding bullet, nowhere near as powerful as a locomotive, able to deliver a less than satisfying sexual experience in a single thrust."

Her laughter echoes around the apartment as I plug my ears and call out, "I can't hear you!" I head off to my room to get ready. Not that I like to admit it, but she is right. I should be in here choosing a killer outfit in case I bump into him, but that kind of killer outfit just gives James an excuse. Plus, I'm avoiding the supermarket.

I slip my feet into today's choice of footwear. Louboutin, Bianca, in red patent. Slightly over the top for a normal day at work, but I have a meeting later for a big development contract and I want to look my best.

I close my wardrobe, once again thanking my lucky stars that Mags is a lucky bitch and I'm a lucky bitch's friend. Margot's dad has more money than Trump (and terrible taste in names), so Mags is rich.

We live in a riverside penthouse with a spectacular view, we spa, we lunch, she gets me into exclusive clubs, casts off more hardly worn designer fashion than I can stand to count and never makes me feel like the poor friend. She doesn't need a roommate, she refuses to take my rent.

Clearly I do very well out of being her best friend, but actually, our friendship was established before I knew this about her. She was very secretive about her money when we met. We lived together in a very average student house. I had no clue until the first summer when she took me home to her Dad's place.

So our friendship is mismatched in the material stakes, but we are equal in every other way. I just benefit from us being the same size, shoes and all. I'm slightly more, shall we say, 'ample' than she is, so the fit of her clothes is different on me. A little more 'ampleness' reveals itself...That is not equal to an invitation to feel me up. Something James needs to learn. Speaking of the douchebag, I'm going to be late.

As Mags and I turn out of our complex and start the short walk to work, I stop dead. I had been rummaging in my bag to check I had my keys, but I looked up…I have no idea why. Probably because the god of 'well isn't that just typical' wanted me to see that that's right where Mr. McHotstuff parks his car.

Yep, there he is being all hot.

Yep, here I am, staring.

Mags turns to look at me, "Did you forget something?" Her gaze follows mine and settles on the target.

"Oh." She says in a low voice. "Wow." She turns her head in my direction, but doesn't take her eyes off him. "Is that…?"

"Uh huh."

Once he locks his car with the clicker, he looks up and I quickly go back to rummaging in my bag so that I'm not just gawping. Mags has no shame and says, "Morning" as he passes.

"Morning," he replies in his luscious voice.

I put my head further inside my bag and pray for a natural disaster. Nothing major, I don't want to take anyone else out. Just a small sinkhole will do.

"Fuck, Jazz, you weren't kidding," she says too loudly, considering he's only a few feet away.

"Sssshh!"

"Come on, let's follow him."

"Oh, no, you don't." I grab her arm to stop her. She just reaches forward and knocks my bag out of my hand and when I bend to pick it up, she's off like a shot. "MAGS!" I hiss, to no avail, she's going after him. She turns and gives me an 'oh no, look at the naughty thing I'm doing' face. So I grab my things and head after her.

"What are you doing?" I whisper when I catch up with her a few paces behind him.

"Research," she replies, as if that's ok.

"What?"

"Don't you want to know where he works?"

"Why do I want to know where he works?"

"So you can find out who he is."

"Again, why do I need to know this?"

"So you can get to know him."

"I…" I close my mouth. She has a point. But no, she is not forcing me to stalk a guy no matter how pretty he is. Just then he turns into the big office complex at the top of the road where I work. "Oh, well," I shrug. "I guess we'll never know."

"What do you mean?" asks Mags, incredulously.

"I mean, there must be fifty companies in that place, there's no way of knowing which one he works for."

"Well, if you're willing to quit that easily, maybe you don't deserve to know. Hmmmm?" She looks at me and folds her arms, waiting.

"Mags, I am not going in there, I'll be late for work."

"Fine. Looks like a job for detective Mags!"

I stare at her, open mouthed for a second. "You wouldn't."

"Wouldn't I?" She grins and then with a dramatic flourish, she flings open the door to the building and disappears inside. As it shuts, I stare helplessly. For a second I contemplate going in after her, so she doesn't do anything ridiculous. But when I look at my watch, I only have three minutes and with a resigned huff, I continue my short walk to work.

An hour later, I'm sitting at my desk in my glossy office separated from the shop floor by a glass wall and fortunately from sleazeball, by the entire length of the shop. James wanted me to have the bigger office next to his, but that has a solid wall and I wanted this office because it is close to the front and I like being able to watch the world go by. Plus James has a tendency to visit often and with a glass wall, he never has any true alone time with me. I prefer it that way.

I'm just thinking about running the gauntlet to the kitchen for a cup of tea, when my phone vibrates with a message.

'Spencer Ryan. x'

'Huh?'

'His name is Spencer Ryan. You can find him on Twitter under @TheSpencerRyan. THE Spencer Ryan!! Haha! Do you think he fancies himself a bit?'

'Ok, firstly, have you SEEN him?? He is welcome to fancy himself as much as he likes. Secondly and most importantly, how the actual hell do you know this???'

I wait for a couple of minutes, but she doesn't reply. My mind is racing with all the possible embarrassing things she could have done in the last hour.

'Tell me you didn't talk to him.'

'Or get arrested.'

'Negative. I just put my sleuth skills to good use, it wasn't difficult. I saw which company he went in to.'

'And?'

'He works at an architectural firm. I checked out their website, but his face is not on their associates page. So I picked a guy he looked like he could be friends with and searched him on Twitter. Went through his followers and BINGO! @TheSpencerRyan. He uses a great picture of himself, you should check it out!'

'Mags, you have way too much time on your hands.'

'You're welcome.'

I laugh, and turn back to my screen, trying for a second to get back into this quote. But the temptation is too much and before I know it, I'm opening up Twitter. I type his @ into the search bar and wait.
Oh my.

There he is.
I click on his full profile and read his bio.

Spencer Ryan
@TheSpencerRyan
I am unable to quit, as I am currently too legit.

Oh my God, he loves himself. But scanning through his timeline I can see why. He is pretty perfect. He's funny, charming, sexy and, of course, he has a timeline full of girls. The really obvious types trying to outdo each other and be noticed.
My phone vibrates again.

'Are you going to follow him?'

'No, I'm not going to follow him!'

'Wimp!'

'He'll think I'm a nutter.''

'Please. He has about 4k followers. About half of them are girls throwing themselves at him. Do you think he will notice you? You don't even use your face as your avi. He will never know…DO IT!'

She has a small point.

'FINE.'

Before I change my mind I hit follow.

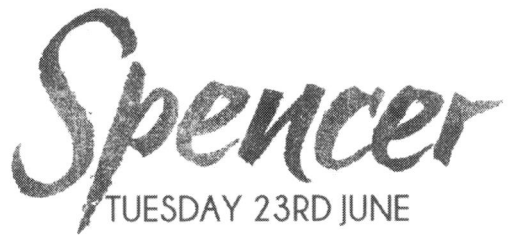
Spencer
TUESDAY 23RD JUNE

That drive is not fun. It's not that far, but rush hour traffic makes it a real ballache. I groan, pulling at my tie. I'm glad I won't be doing it too much longer. I like the work, but it does piss me off that I can't do it nearer to home. I chuck my keys on the kitchen table and grab a bottle of water from the fridge. Taking the water and my phone, I head upstairs to get out of this suit. I check the app I use to track my Twitter followers on the way up. Daily tweet stats, 19 new followers, 5 unfollowers. Not bad. Skimming through the new follows, I click on the ones that look interesting and follow back after a quick scan of their bio and tweets.

@NaughtyNat69 - Hot avi, let's see how naughty you are.
...Follow
@_Gets_You_Hard - Hmmm, how can I say no to that?
...Follow.
@Bea_have1 - Looks like she could be fun.
...Follow.

Yawning, I glance at the remaining list of new followers and I decide I don't have the energy for Twitter right now. I'll go through the rest later. They can wait.

I can't be bothered to go through my mentions either and even though my direct message light is on, I ignore it for now. I'm too wound up from crawling home in a hot car. Time for the gym, I think.

I pass the big mirror on my dresser and catch sight of myself. A bit dishevelled, but still looking good. Tie loosened, top button open, but waistcoat still in place. Pretty sharp for the end of the day. I snap a selfie before I strip it all off. I'll post that when I get back.

Oh, screw it, no time like the present.

SPENCER @TheSpencerRyan
Evening ladies. Gotta love a suit pic.twitter.com/kEy6s823rg

Jazz
WEDNESDAY 24TH JUNE

"Have you tweeted him yet?" Her voice rings out from the living room.

I roll my eyes and put my bag down in the hallway. "Hi Mags," I call back. "My day was shitty, thanks for asking. How was yours?" I stop in the doorway and see her sitting cross-legged on the floor at the coffee table, with her laptop open and loose pages of notes all around her.

"It was good, now why haven't you tweeted him? Hmmm?" She's not even working, she's stalking my timeline and checking up on me.

"Because, oh, mistress of mayhem," I sigh, strolling in to the room and depositing myself wearily on the armchair, "I've been busy."

"Feeble excuse! Next!"

"Because I don't know him?" I try.

"Pft."

"What? Is that not a reasonable excuse? I don't know the guy."

"Well there's only one way to get to know him, genius."

"Maybe I don't want to get to know him."

"Lies." She dismisses me with a wave of her hand.

"Even if I did, I'm not competing with all the slappers. I mean, have you seen them?" I put on a husky seductive voice. "Hey sexy, I've missed you. Where have you been?" I wrinkle my nose in disgust. "And there's no need for guessing either, they're blatant about it." My mock sexy voice comes back as I recall something I've seen today. "'I've been thinking about you baby…you know where to find me ;)'…Classy. I'm sure he knows exactly where to find you, but thanks for clearing it up for the rest of us."

Then I recall another one. "Oh, and my personal favourite… 'I sent you a DM gorgeous'…REALLY? He gets a notification for that dumbarse. You don't need to let him know! It's so obviously the, 'I've got him, so back off,' warning to everyone else." I shake my head. "Like anyone else cares. Silly cows."

"I know," she agrees, scrolling through his feed. "There's a bunch of them."

"Yeah, a herd," I giggle. "A herd of silly cows."

Mags laughs. "He probably needs a cattle prod to keep them under control."

I raise my eyebrows, "I think he has one of those, Mags."

"But I think he's poking them in the wrong places." Her cackle has me laughing too.

THURSDAY 25TH JUNE

MAGS @Magspie1
@OMGJazzyP How is work going? And by that I mean, how many times have you thought about tweeting a certain Mr.Hotstuff?

JAZZ @OMGJazzyP
@Magspie1 It's Mr. McHotstuff actually and I haven't been tempted at all.

MAGS @Magspie1
@OMGJazzyP Liar

JAZZ @OMGJazzyP
@Magspie1 Oh hush! I'm busy #VeryHardAtWork

MAGS @Magspie1
@OMGJazzyP I wonder if @TheSpencerRyan is #VeryHARDatWork

Oh.
My.

God.

She just tagged him!

JAZZ @OMGJazzyP
@Magspie1 :-O WHAT DID YOU JUST DO???

MAGS @Magspie1
@OMGJazzyP Oh relax will you. I'm just getting things going a bit.

JAZZ @OMGJazzyP
@Magspie1 Relax? You are such a shit stirrer Mags!

SPENCER @TheSpencerRyan
@Magspie1 @OMGJazzyP Hello ladies. This is an interesting conversation to be tagged in.

JAZZ @OMGJazzyP
@TheSpencerRyan Er, hi :) Mags I'm going to kill you! @Magspie1

SPENCER @TheSpencerRyan
@OMGJazzyP @Magspie1 No fighting now, I'm glad we were introduced.

MAGS @Magspie1
@OMGJazzyP @TheSpencerRyan See Jazz, he's glad you were introduced.

JAZZ @OMGJazzyP

@Magspie1 @TheSpencerRyan Sorry about her, I can't control her!

You were followed by @TheSpencerRyan.

Oh, fuck! A text comes through from Mags.

'Did he follow you?'

'Yes he fucking did!! Did he follow you too?'

'YES!! This is brilliant!'

SPENCER @TheSpencerRyan
@OMGJazzyP @Magspie1 So where are you ladies from?

Oh, shit! I need to answer this before Mags says something disastrous.

JAZZ @OMGJazzyP
@TheSpencerRyan @Magspie1 The UK

SPENCER @TheSpencerRyan
@OMGJazzyP @Magspie1 Me too, just outside London

I jump on my phone to text Mags again.

'I swear if you say one word, there's no more chocolate for you. Ever.'

'*Covers ears and sings la-la-la-la-la*'

MAGS @Magspie1
@TheSpencerRyan @OMGJazzyP What a coincidence, we aren't too far from London either.

SPENCER @TheSpencerRyan
@Magspie1 @OMGJazzyP Uh oh! Do I need to lock my windows tonight?

JAZZ @OMGJazzyP
@Magspie1 @TheSpencerRyan It's ok, you're safe.

SPENCER @TheSpencerRyan
@OMGJazzyP @Magspie1 That's a shame ;) Where are you?

JAZZ @OMGJazzyP
@TheSpencerRyan @Magspie1 Didn't anyone ever teach you not to give out your details to strangers on the internet?

MAGS @Magspie1
@OMGJazzyP @TheSpencerRyan Don't listen to her, she's just cranky because she's been single for a while. #DickheadEx

JAZZ @OMGJazzyP
@Magspie1 @TheSpencerRyan Oh wonderful, tell the world…

SPENCER @TheSpencerRyan
@OMGJazzyP @Magspie1 Sounds like one loser's loss is our gain.

MAGS @Magspie1
@OMGJazzyP @TheSpencerRyan Very much so, Jazz is a great girl, she was too good for him.

JAZZ @OMGJazzyP
@Magspie1 @TheSpencerRyan Um, Hello!!!! I'm still here!

MAGS @Magspie1
@OMGJazzyP @TheSpencerRyan Ssshh! I'm chatting!

SPENCER @TheSpencerRyan
@OMGJazzyP @Magspie1 Hmmm, so what I'm getting from this is, great girl, single, not too far from me…gotcha! ;)

JAZZ @OMGJazzyP
@TheSpencerRyan @Magspie1 Oh for the love of God! *Hides under desk and rocks*

SPENCER @TheSpencerRyan
@OMGJazzyP @Magspie1 Haha! Relax; I'm just teasing you.

MAGS @Magspie1
@TheSpencerRyan @OMGJazzyP But its all true #JustSayin

SPENCER @TheSpencerRyan
@Magspie1 @OMGJazzyP Noted.

JAZZ @OMGJazzyP
@Magspie1 I hate you. Not you @TheSpencerRyan

MAGS @Magspie1
@TheSpencerRyan @OMGJazzyP Eh, you'll get over it.

SPENCER @TheSpencerRyan
@OMGJazzyP @Magspie1 Well I have to run ladies, some of us are HARD at work ;) Don't be strangers.

MAGS @Magspie1
@TheSpencerRyan @OMGJazzyP Nice to meet you, Spencer.

JAZZ @OMGJazzyP
@TheSpencerRyan @Magspie1 Yes, nice to meet you.

SPENCER @TheSpencerRyan
@OMGJazzyP @Magspie1 Likewise.

JAZZ @OMGJazzyP
@Magspie1 I seriously HATE YOU right now!

MAGS @Magspie1
@OMGJazzyP What? For introducing you to your future husband? No you don't.

JAZZ @OMGJazzyP
@Magspie1 I have work to do.

MAGS @Magspie1
@OMGJazzyP Ok, but you'll thank me one day. Pick up salad on your way home.

JAZZ @OMGJazzyP
@Magspie1 Bite me!

MAGS @Magspie1
@OMGJazzyP <3

Spencer
THURSDAY 25TH JUNE

JAZZ @OMGJazzyP
@Magspie1 I seriously HATE YOU right now!

MAGS @Magspie1
@OMGJazzyP What? For introducing you to your future husband?
No you don't.

JAZZ @OMGJazzyP
@Magspie1 I have work to do.

MAGS @Magspie1
@OMGJazzyP Ok, but you'll thank me one day. Pick up salad on your way home.

JAZZ @OMGJazzyP
@Magspie1 Bite me!

MAGS @Magspie1
@OMGJazzyP <3

Interesting…Future husband, huh? Somebody has a little Spencer crush. Sweet!

Clicking on her profile, I decide to learn a little more about OMGJazzyP. Obviously, the first thing I noticed when I saw her tweet was the shoes. Enlarging the picture, I get a rush. They're fucking incredible. Black, shiny, red soled orgasms waiting to happen.

Yeah, I have a shoe thing.

Nope, can't explain why.

I just do.

These are probably just a stock image of shoes she wishes she could have, but it sets an image up, for me anyway, of the kind of girl I think she is. Long legged and curvaceous, mmmmm. I wonder if she's tweeted any pictures of herself. A quick scroll through her images reveals that she has not. There is nothing. She has a few of shoes. In fact, all she ever tweets are pictures of shoes, cocktails and food. No faces, nothing personal. She is an enigma.

Looking through her timeline, I can see that really, the only person she ever tweets is the friend I was talking to just now. No guys, no obvious flirting. She's different from most of the girls that tweet me, that's clear. I click on the friend and run the same checks. Same deal, nothing revealing, just a back and forth between them.

So according to the friend, I'm the future Mr. Fuck-Me-Heels, am I?

Well, marriage is a fate worse than death as far as I can see. No woman is getting her claws in me anytime soon. But if she was wearing those heels on the wedding night, I could think of worse ways to go.

I think I'll have to keep an eye on shoe girl. Yeah, I like that...Shoegirl.

Jazz

SATURDAY 27TH JUNE

I answer my phone on the second ring.

"When are you coming home?" Mags whines.

"I won't be long, I just had to email off a few things from the office while I was passing."

"Jazz, it's ridiculous that you bail early on a Friday to avoid being left alone in the shop with sleezeball and then have to creep back in to finish up on the weekend because James won't be in. You don't work weekends anymore, remember? It was a perk of your promotion."

"I know," I sigh. "But it won't be forever."

"It could be never again if you just took the money I'm offering."

I don't respond straight away; it's so tempting. I know at the right time I could really make a go of it, but the economy has gone to shit and being completely responsible for that kind of success or failure is daunting, to say the least.

"I'm not going to keep taking no for an answer, so think about it seriously."

"Yeah, ok," I say softly.

"Good, now when are you coming home? I'm bored and a bored Mags gets up to no good."

"I just have to finish up a few things, an hour maybe? I'll pick up some takeaway on the way home."

"An hour! Come on Jazz, I'm going to do something naughty to ease my boredom if you take another hour."

"You'll just have to entertain yourself, now let me get on or it'll be longer than an hour." I hang up and shake my head, returning to my inbox to finish up.

I'm tapping away when a Twitter notification comes through. I click it and a tweet from Mags pops up. I almost choke.

MAGS @Magspie1
@OMGJazzyP I wonder what @TheSpencerRyan is up to tonight?

That bitch! What is she doing? I'm opening our text conversation when another tweet comes in.

SPENCER @TheSpencerRyan
@Magspie1 @OMGJazzyP Going to the pub with my mates, what about you two ladies?

Freaking hell!

MAGS @Magspie1
@OMGJazzyP @TheSpencerRyan I don't know yet. Jazz is working. On a Saturday! Tell her to wrap it up, she'll listen to you.

I hammer out a text to Mags.

'WTF do you think you are doing?'

'Entertaining myself while I wait for you! Be quick, then I can't do much damage...'

'I'm going to kill you Mags!'

'No, you're going to come home like I wanted ;)'

SPENCER @TheSpencerRyan
@OMGJazzyP @Magspie1 It's Saturday, get your arse home and get out in the sunshine! Go to the pub!

MAGS @Magspie1
@TheSpencerRyan @OMGJazzyP If she is still talking to me, I'm taking her to a club.

JAZZ @OMGJazzyP
@Magspie1 @TheSpencerRyan I'M NOT!!!!

SPENCER @TheSpencerRyan
@Magspie1 @OMGJazzyP Ladies, ladies, is there a problem?

JAZZ @OMGJazzyP
@TheSpencerRyan Nothing unusual, @Magspie1 is just being an arse.

SPENCER @TheSpencerRyan
@OMGJazzyP @Magspie1 Now, now, why don't you kiss and make up? I'd love to see that btw!!

MAGS @Magspie1
@TheSpencerRyan @OMGJazzyP I just bet you would, come home Jazz, we can send him a pic!

SPENCER @TheSpencerRyan
@Magspie1 @OMGJazzyP *waits by the phone*... :)

JAZZ @OMGJazzyP
@TheSpencerRyan @Magspie1 Ok, enough! I'm on my way!

SPENCER @TheSpencerRyan
@OMGJazzyP @Magspie1 Have fun tonight girls. Don't forget to drunk tweet me later, yeah? ;)

I arrive home with Chinese food and slam it down on the kitchen counter.

"I'm not talking to you, Mags!" I yell down the hall.

She giggles from the living room and then wanders into the kitchen and starts opening the food containers.

"Yes, you are. You love me and I did a good thing."

"A good thing? How is making him more aware of my interest a good thing?"

"I'm sure he is pretty aware by now, he doesn't seem bothered."

"Well, leave it alone now, please."

She smirks and pulls a huge mouthful of noodles out of the box and scoffs it down like she has never seen food before.

"So, where are we going tonight?"

"I got us on the list for the new club that's opening tonight. You remember that DJ from the Blue Room?"

"How could I forget? You two were scratching out a beat on the kitchen counter when I came home!" I laugh.

"Yeah, him, well he's playing tonight and he wants me to come down."

"Taking orders now, are we? He must be good."

"You pretty much saw what he was working with, how could I say no?"

"Fair point. So, do I need to find a sofa to sleep on tonight? I cannot listen to that again all night."

She looks sheepish. "Actually, he lives close to the club..."

"Oh! So you've made plans? Taxi for one then, I guess."

"Not plans exactly, he just wanted to make sure I'd be there and happened to mention that his place is nearby. You don't mind, do you?"

"No, of course I don't mind."

I watch Mags looking for some sign that she is excited about it. Like always though, she looks pleased with herself, but there is no emotion there. It's always the same. I know she has fun, but in the whole time I've known her, she has never shown so much as a hint of that giddy, girly excitement we all get when we know that someone we like, likes us too. In fact, I can never even tell if she really likes them. Mags' emotions are a closed book.

Don't get me wrong; she's not a cold hard bitch. She is warm and caring and she enjoys herself. She's perfectly happy with her sex life and let me tell you, there is nothing boring about it! She just doesn't look for that emotional connection. The total opposite of me.

I want all the feels.

Jazz

SUNDAY 28TH JUNE

SPENCER @TheSpencerRyan
Remind me never to drink again!

    I chuckle even though it hurts my head. I wonder whether to respond. I don't know the guy. Sure I've talked to him a couple of times, but it's usually instigated by Mags. Is it ok to comment on a stranger's tweet?
    Of course it is. If I wasn't so obsessed with the guy, I would have no hesitation. If it was a girl, I'd be typing by now. Screw it!

JAZZ @OMGJazzyP
@TheSpencerRyan OMG me too!

SPENCER favourited
OMG me too!

    I get a thrill that sparks through my entire body.
    He favourited my tweet!
    He favourited my tweet!
    Then I groan as I turn over in bed. Never. Again. Every

inch of me is complaining about the abuse I gave it last night. It's so bad, Spencer McHotstuff is quickly forgotten.

Spencer

MONDAY 29TH JUNE

Taking a deep breath and a bite of my uninspiring sandwich, I perform my usual lunchtime ritual of reading through my Twitter mentions.

BETH @Luvs2BeNaughty
#HATESBeingIgnored @TheSpencerRyan

Ugh! What do I have to do to get the message through to that one? No, I'm not 'your man' as you put it. No, you don't get to tell me who I can and can't talk to. No, there is no chance on this earth I am meeting you. And YES, I am ignoring you, you crazy person. Sheesh!

Ok, we had some fun times, she has a dirty mind and a filthy mouth, but she got too clingy, which is where I draw the line. Then she started telling people I had promised to meet her. Whatever, love, like I'm going to tell you where I live! I'm 99% sure we live on different continents, but I'm taking no chances with that one. She needs to get over it or I'll have to block her.

This is all boring me right now. I think I could do with having a bit of an unfollowing spree. My timeline just needs an injection of fresh blood. It's all just the same shit. I deal with the tweets I'm sent, fend off the 'ladies' in my DMs...ok, I enjoy some of them before I start fending them off, but then this vicious cycle starts. It's just supposed to be harmless fun, but some of them take it way too seriously.

Leaving my list of notifications, I scroll through the timeline. It's all the same old, same old. Maybe it's me? Maybe I'm just bored of it all? Then I spot those two girls I talked to last week. Yeah ok, they're probably more of the same, but they actually seem like fun. They didn't seem to have that agenda you can feel from the others. I didn't get the impression they are only here to fuck guys. They seemed different.

Watching them tweet back and forth, they're funny. It's a refreshing thing around here to see two girls just having a laugh. All I ever see is competition, bitchiness and that special thing girls do to each other, faking friendship with a smile, while slowly inserting the knives in each other's backs. I just don't get it. I will never understand women. They would be simply unstoppable if they stopped screwing each other over.

These two are genuine friends though, it shows in their banter. Maybe they are the kind of fresh faces I need around here. Hmmm, perhaps I'll get to know them.

Just when I start typing out a tweet to them, my phone rings...Oh, well, maybe later.

Jazz

TUESDAY 30TH JUNE

MAGS @Magspie1
@OMGJazzyP Where are you?

JAZZ @OMGJazzyP
@Magspie1 Half a mile in your freaking Gucci skyscrapers isn't easy, you know. Neither is walking & tweeting! Be there in 5! #ImpatientMuch

MAGS @Magspie1
@OMGJazzyP You're always more than welcome to buy your own shoes, Jazz.

    Pft! I pick up the pace. I can see the restaurant now and it isn't much further. I'm definitely getting a cab back to work; these shoes are a joke and it's bloody baking! My phone whistles when I am only a few feet from the door and I glance down thinking it will be the 'hurry up' from Mags again.
    Then I see his name.
    It's a tweet TO ME! I'm tagged in it.
    I didn't tweet him, he was thinking about me all on his own!

All fingers and thumbs in my excitement, I try and click to open the tweet. While I'm fiddling around with my phone, the ridiculous shoes I am wearing become unmanageable, they catch together and I'm down.

Woman down!

Thank the lord that Mags always books us at upscale places, the kind with doormen. Because I am miraculously caught milliseconds from impact. My phone skitters across the pavement, which I am equally relieved to note, is covered with a large welcome mat emblazoned with the restaurant's name.

The doorman sets me back on my feet and bends to pick up my phone, my handbag and the small gift bag I was carrying. NEVER have I been happier to have a rich best friend. Had this been a Starbucks quickie, I would have face-planted on the pavement and probably smashed my phone and my face to smithereens.

I thank the doorman profusely and make my way inside.

Mags and her dad are already seated and have been watching my usual chaotic entrance with amusement.

George stands, always the perfect gentleman, and with his hands on my shoulders, kisses me once on each cheek. "Jasmine my darling, you look lovely as always," he says, as he pulls my chair out for me.

"As always George, you can thank your daughter's wardrobe for my lovely appearance," I reply, sitting down.

The waiter fills my glass with iced water and I take a welcome drink, while George orders for the three of us. Mags and I don't even cast a glance at the menu; he never fails to get it right. George is amazing at everything.

"Mags tells me you aren't planning to come to the house

with her while she stays."

"Oh, George, I'd love to but I have to work, and I live just around the corner. If I come to you, I'll have a forty-five minute drive through evil traffic, all so I can park at home and walk my usual 5 minute walk into work. It just makes no sense." I really wish I could. George is travelling on business for three months over the summer, right when there is lots of work scheduled on his estate. Mags is going to stay so that someone is there to oversee. "I will come on weekends, I promise."

"Good." He smiles. "And work? Is that still going ok?"

I sigh.

"It's the same Dad, she's just in denial."

"Jasmine, sexual harassment in the workplace is a very serious matter. I would be more than willing…"

I stop him before he starts telling me how he could call in a friend to represent me and sue James into oblivion. "George, really, I'm fine. It's hardly sexual harassment. It's more unrequited infatuation. I enjoy my job. Really."

"Have you thought any more about Margot's idea?"

Mags giggles. Damn her for dragging him into this debate too.

"I'm not a professional chocolatier, George, I just like messing around with flavours, that's all."

"Well, you know I think your chocolates are amazing and I fully support you. You have a talent, Jasmine, you should follow your dreams."

"Talent is one thing, I'm not sure I have what it takes to be responsible for everything it would entail. Health and safety, premises, staff. I love doing it, but on my terms. I just don't know if I could make it work professionally. It's a big decision."

He gives me that overly concerned fatherly look and says, "We just worry about you, that's all. As long as you're happy, that's all that matters."

"I am, thank you. Oh, that reminds me, I brought you these." I hand him the little bag containing a selection I have been working on.

"That's my girl!"

"Hey!" Mags strops. "Where's mine?"

I roll my eyes at George, before turning to placate her. "There's some for you at home."

After lunch is eaten, George excuses himself, kissing us both. I wish him safe travels, and, as always, he promises to keep in touch.

As soon as he is out of the restaurant, I delve into my bag for my phone.

"What did I miss?" asks Mags watching me.

"I got a message, just as I arrived."

"And it has been killing you, hasn't it?"

"Uh huh." I finally locate it, where it had slipped right to the bottom of my oversized bag. George is a big time lawyer. He is greatly in demand, but he's old fashioned. When he makes time for his girls, his phone is off and he is unreachable. He expects the same from us. This tweet has seriously been burning a hole in my pocket.

I open Twitter.

SPENCER @TheSpencerRyan

It's beautiful where I am, @OMGJazzyP I hope you are enjoying the sunshine too.

> Wow, he tweeted me. Just me! He remembered who I am, that I live in the same region as him and tweeted me about the weather. Aaaahhhh!
> Mags is laughing beside me as she peers in to see.
> "Oooh! Someone was thinking about you."
> I laugh with her. I'm ridiculous, I know I am.
> "Are you going to reply?"
> "Maybe later, I need to get back to work."
> "Treat 'em mean and all that."
> I scowl at her, but yeah, basically.

I was good; I kept him waiting until I got home.

JAZZ @OMGJazzyP
@TheSpencerRyan It was a gorgeous day, shame I missed most of it stuck in my office.

SPENCER @TheSpencerRyan
@OMGJazzyP Yes me too. Still, there's plenty of sunshine left, time to sit in the garden with a beer, I think.

JAZZ @OMGJazzyP
@TheSpencerRyan Definitely, or roof terrace in my case.

SPENCER @TheSpencerRyan
@OMGJazzyP Sounds good babe, but don't forget the beers.

Babe? Hmmm, interesting, not sure how I feel about 'babe.'

JAZZ @OMGJazzyP
@TheSpencerRyan Got it covered, the fridge was stocked last night ready. I'm enjoying my first wine as I type.

SPENCER @TheSpencerRyan
@OMGJazzyP Good girl.

Good girl...now that he can call me whenever he likes.

JAZZ @OMGJazzyP
@TheSpencerRyan Not just a pretty face.

SPENCER @TheSpencerRyan
@OMGJazzyP It's hard to tell when all I see is a pair of shoes!!

He is referring to my avatar, which is currently my feet, wearing my favourite pair of Mags' cast off black patent Louboutins. I never have my face on my Twitter.

JAZZ @OMGJazzyP
@TheSpencerRyan Well, you'll have to take my word for it! ;)

SPENCER @TheSpencerRyan
@OMGJazzyP Hey now. You've seen my face it's only fair you show me yours...

JAZZ @OMGJazzyP
@TheSpencerRyan Oh, no, no. No faces, I like anonymity

SPENCER @TheSpencerRyan
@OMGJazzyP You gotta give me something. Are they your shoes at least?

JAZZ @OMGJazzyP
@TheSpencerRyan Oh yeah, just one pair of MANY!

SPENCER @TheSpencerRyan
@OMGJazzyP Shit! Heels are my weakness...show me some more.

JAZZ @OMGJazzyP
@TheSpencerRyan Demanding, aren't you?

SPENCER @TheSpencerRyan
@OMGJazzyP You have no idea how demanding I can be. I want to see more shoes.

Shaking my head at his nerve, I stroll in through the doorway to my room from the terrace. Sipping my wine, I move over to my wardrobe and open the doors. A wealth of shoe porn greets me, but I'm not just going to submit to his demands. Am I?
No.
He wants me to model them for him. Instead, I snap a wide angle of a number of pairs in a row and send it.

JAZZ @OMGJazzyP
@TheSpencerRyan How's this…
pic.twitter.com/hsoUgTHsAg

SPENCER @TheSpencerRyan
@OMGJazzyP Not what I meant. I want to see them on your feet. But bloody hell, that's quite the collection.

JAZZ @OMGJazzyP
@TheSpencerRyan I don't just put on shoes for anyone, you know.

I take another long drink of my cool, crisp wine. I need the courage.

SPENCER @TheSpencerRyan
@OMGJazzyP Put the ones with the studs on, Jazz. You know you want to. Go on…do it

Maybe I should just play his game? Where's the harm?…Or maybe I should play a game of my own?

JAZZ @OMGJazzyP
@TheSpencerRyan Sorry, no can do. I'm jumping in the shower now.

SPENCER @TheSpencerRyan
@OMGJazzyP No fair! First the shoes, now the shower…you're killing me!

JAZZ @OMGJazzyP
@TheSpencerRyan I'd send you a pic, but I don't want to get my phone wet. You'll just have to use your imagination! :)

SPENCER @TheSpencerRyan
@OMGJazzyP.............*groans*.............no words!

Spencer
TUESDAY 30TH JUNE

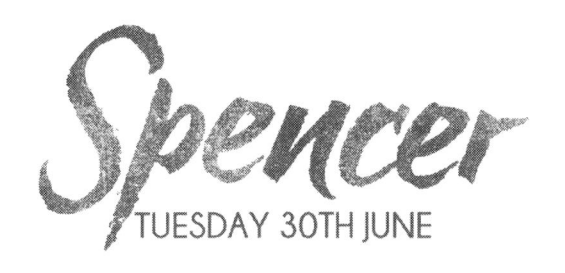

My cock twitches at the thought of her naked, in the stud heels, walking into some swanky bathroom, stepping out of the heels and into the shower. I don't know why the bathroom has to be swanky in my vision, but let's face it, she's a fantasy. You don't fantasise about a shabby bathroom that needs a clean, any more than you fantasise about a less than perfect girl wearing the shoes of your wet dreams.

Yeah.

I know.

I'm an arsehole.

That's life.

And now she's going to leave me with the image of her getting all wet and soapy.

I glance down at the slight bulge in my shorts.

Opening up a fresh DM to her, I know what I want to say. In the back of my head, a little voice is telling me, "Don't start back here with another one, you have enough trouble with the ones you have." But fuck it, this one isn't like the others. So I type out my message. I have nothing to lose.

'Set the shower head on the jet setting and

> have some fun. I hear it's just like a skilled tongue. You can think of me!'

A few moments pass. I think I was too late, she's already in the shower. Then, just when I'm about to close the window, a message appears.

'The head on this thing is way better than any tongue. Trust me…and I'll be thinking of me!'

Damn! She's not shy about showing her feisty side. I love it! Still, despite getting shot down, all I see is the word 'head'. My cock is already straining and that doesn't help. I know it's juvenile, but no matter how old a man gets, his dick always thinks like a teenage boy. I run my hand over it, feeling it thicken. I'm going to have to take care of that.

> 'Then we will both be thinking of you and that shower head. I hope it lives up to expectations. If not, you know where to find me.'

I wait.
Too long.
I should have put her out of my head already, but she's still there. My phone tells me I have another DM and I can't open it fast enough.
Then I realise it isn't from her.
Fuck.

'Hey Spencer, where you at, baby? This girl is lonely.'

Ugh! Why now with the neediness? I'm in the middle of something here. I don't answer.
I wonder if she's in the shower yet?
Another DM comes through.

'I miss our fun times…:('

Dear God! Not now. Still, my cock tries to tell me that she'll do. Shoegirl clearly isn't coming back. I've got this one waiting, or nothing from the Shoegirl…Hmmm, what to do?
I open the conversation to reply.

'Sorry babe, busy.'

Then I close down the app.
Damn.
What the fuck just happened?
I just dismissed a sure thing because a less-than-sure thing is occupying my head.
Never thought that would happen.
Maybe things are changing.

Jazz

WEDNESDAY 1ST JULY

"Maaaags!" I yell from the kitchen.

"Hold on," she yells back.

I huff and wait impatiently.

"What's going on?" she asks, as she comes from her room. "What the hell are you doing up there?"

I giggle, trying not to fall from where I'm standing on the kitchen table in some of my highest heels. "I need you to take a picture of my feet." I hold out my phone for her to take.

She smirks. "This is for him, isn't it?"

"What? No! I want to change my profile picture that's all."

"Sure." She aims the camera at the studded black suede platform heels and snaps a couple of different angles. "Bend your knee so that your heel lifts." I comply and she takes a couple more. "He'll like that," she mutters under her breath.

"Hey! I don't know what makes you think this is for him."

"Ooooh, show me yer shoes, Jazz...show me the studded ones...do it...wear them for me, Jazz!" She laughs handing me back my phone, "Yes, that's right, I read your timeline...'Can't right now, Spencer, I have to go and get all soapy in the shower...you can imagine that for a bit if you like.'" She finishes her taunt and laughs.

I scowl and snatch my phone back from her, stepping down carefully onto the chair and then the floor. "Everyone's a comedian," I grumble, annoyed that she busted me and stalk back to my room.

"Oh come on, it's funny!" she calls after me.

I shut the door and kick my shoes off, no way I'm wearing the studs to work. I might be tempted to use them on James, as he seems to have less and less regard for my personal space. Almost all of our discussions now seem to require him to have an arm draped across the back of my chair, leaning in to look at my screen, or a hand on the wall, blocking my path. Twice yesterday, while he was talking, I zoned out and actually started running through routines from the kickboxing classes Mags and I took for a few years. No…studs are a bad idea.

I look at the pictures on my phone and pick one for my avi. Then once it's changed I realise, there is no guarantee he will see it. I'm not tweeting him, 'How do you like my picture?' How desperate would that make me look? So, instead, I favourite one of his tweets and just hope he notices. Look at me! Shaking my head, I force myself to get ready for the day.

I'm at my desk for three full minutes before he finds an excuse to come in and discuss something he could have emailed to me. He is getting on my nerves this week. I think it's all Mags' talk of leaving and starting my chocolate shop. It's a pipe dream, but that carrot dangling is making me progressively more dissatisfied with life. James is my biggest gripe right now.

When he finally removes himself from my desk, I treat myself to a little check of Twitter. Hmmm, no notifications. I guess he didn't notice. I wonder if he's even been on? I type his name into the search bar and click onto his profile. Scrolling down, I can see he has been tweeting, talking to girls mostly, bleugh! Hussies. Then I get down a few to his first tweet of the day and my heart skips.

SPENCER @TheSpencerRyan
Day made…*wonders what else I could get her to do*

Holy shit! That's for me. A huge smile spreads across my face. Yay me!

Jasmine, will you just look at yourself.

No, fuck off!! *Internal happy dance.*

I want to reply, but I'm not going to, I'm staying strong. I managed to shrug off his blatant attempt to goodness-only-knows what last night in that private message he sent. Who knows where he thought that was going. We'll overlook the way I rolled over and posted a picture just for him. Nope, I'm staying strong. He can make the next move.

Although…I wonder if he is paying as close attention to my timeline as I am to his? I guess I could try and find out. What would I like to see him post? Hmmmm…

JAZZ @OMGJazzyP
I think people with great tattoos shouldn't hide them away.
#Tattoos #ThingsThatMakeMyDay #JustSayin

Lets see if he gets that.

Spencer
THURSDAY 2ND JULY

"Will you just take the picture!"

"My God, you're such a diva."

"Just do it."

"Have seen yourself lately dude? I think this Twitter lark has gone to your head," scoffs Will.

"Shut up and do it."

"Tell me why I'm doing this again?"

"It's for the followers."

"For the fucking followers? Listen to you. You're not Justin Bieber!"

"What? I have followers."

"Aren't there enough photos of you on there for your followers already? You post at a rate of twenty selfies an hour."

Scowling, I shift uncomfortably. "Shut it. If I take a selfie, I can't get my left arm in…and they want to, er…see the tattoos," I mumble in reply…I'm going to get some stick for this!

Will pauses and then a light comes on, "Hang on, this is for one follower in particular, isn't it? You dirty dog! What's she like?"

"Just take the fucking picture."

"Fine, smile...or whatever shit you do."

I lift my tea to my lips just as he takes the shot and wink over the rim of the mug.

"For fucks sake dude, it's bad enough that I have to do this, but if you wink at me again, I'll rearrange your pretty face."

Now it's my turn to scoff. "Yeah, like that'll happen." I grab my phone and look at the image; it's great. She'll eat it up. They all will.

"So this follower of yours, is she hot?"

"Dunno, she doesn't use a picture of herself."

Will spits out his tea. "That means she's a dog!"

"Not necessarily. She has these shoes, man, they're those fuck me kind of shoes. Dogs don't own shoes like that; fuckable, curvaceous goddesses own shoes like that."

"...Ooookkaaaayyyy..." He does an 'awkward' look and backs away.

Shit. Ok, maybe I should keep my curvaceous goddess thoughts to myself.

I'd beg her to wrap those shoes around my neck while I fuck her into oblivion, if truth be told, but best keep that thought to myself too. This morning has been weird enough.

Will snaps me out of my fantasy. "So, are you working on her? This goddess with the fuckable shoes?"

"I'm just keeping myself entertained," I smirk.

Will shakes his head. "You need help, man."

"What? I'm just giving them what they want."

Will rolls his eyes.

"Oh, forget it, I don't expect your tiny brain to understand, let's just get to the gym. I don't want to be late this morning. I have shit loads to do, it's my last day tomorrow."

"What do you care? You quit."

"Yeah, but they didn't want me to go, and freelancers make a fucking fortune. It might come in handy if business is slow, so I'm keeping them sweet."

I change my avi to the photo Will took as we walk to the car and tweet an early good morning to my timeline. That'll get her going.

Jazz

THURSDAY 2ND JULY

SPENCER @TheSpencerRyan
Morning peeps, hope you all slept well, I had sweet dreams of sexy shoes. The sun is out and I'm showing some skin. Off to the gym, BBL

I roll over in bed and squint at my phone, I blink a few times and yep, I read it correctly. He basically referred to me in his good morning tweet...AND he's changed his avi to one of him in a T-shirt, showing tattoos. Oh the tattoos! Both arms…amazing. Oh and some muscle too, a little more than I expected.

And damn him, he's winking! Fucking butterflies, go away! I will not go stupid over this guy. No way.

I drag myself out of bed and plod down the hall to put the kettle on.

"Morning," says Mags.

"Morning," I yawn.

Filling the kettle, I put it on its base and turn to face her. "I can't believe you're leaving me tomorrow," I whine.

"I told you, come with me," she says casually.

"We don't all have your charmed life."

Mags rolls her eyes, "It's not that charmed, I'm just house sitting. I'll be working too."

"Yes, but house sitting your dad's country estate while writing your next novel isn't the same as the shit I have to deal with." We have been over this; I can't just uplift and go for weeks of fun with her, even if it is only forty-five minutes away. I have responsibilities and a dick of a boss to handle here. Unlike Mags, what I don't have is a rich daddy.

"Jazz, I know you like your job, but it's surely not worth the regular feeling up from the boss. Get out, start up on your own. Follow your dreams. You know you can do it."

I shake my head. It isn't really that simple. It will take time to get going, the outlay will be huge and the responsibility scares the shit out of me. Mags has offered repeatedly to front up the cash so I can just do it, but it isn't that easy. Aside from the obvious fact that it's too much, I don't know very much about owning a small business.

"You know the money is waiting," she says, reading my mind, "and I'm getting seriously impatient. Soon, I'll give up waiting and open a chocolate shop of my own. I'll hire someone else, and then you'll have to stay working for James forever!" She grins.

I shake my head. She would too. That is what is both great and frustrating about Mags; she isn't flashy in a horrible way, but nothing is too much trouble where her friends are concerned. She will keep pushing me until I do it.

I'm starting to wonder why I'm resisting.

Jazz

FRIDAY 3RD JULY

My alarm shatters the very pleasant dream I was having where Spencer was worshiping at my Louboutins and working his way up my legs with his tongue. I groan. Why do I always wake up just as it gets to the good bit? I am getting more and more frustrated everyday. If I don't get some relief soon, I'm going to turn into a complete bitch! Maybe I should just go and jump in the shower…take the edge off.

As I grin and start to lift the covers off, Mags bursts in.

"Wake up, sleepy head! I have tea waiting. I'm leaving in fifteen minutes, I have to meet with some window guy at ten."

"Ugh! You pick your moments, Mags!"

She screws up her nose. "Ew, you weren't…were you?"

"No," I sigh.

"But you were thinking about it, weren't you?"

I shake my head dismissively and crawl out of bed and stumble into my bathroom.

"You need to get laid. Preferably by a hot young architect with a tattooed body to die for, who smells amazing."

"You live in a dream world," I call out from the bathroom.

"But it's nice here, you should join me."

There is no way I can shut her up, so I jump in the shower

to drown her out.

After lunch, I receive a text from Mags.

'Drinking champagne and having a pedi! Wish you were here. x'

'You're making me sick, I have to go with James to a meeting at the Hilton.'

'The sleaze is taking you to a hotel, are you serious? Why not lunch?'

'It's a big account; apparently the client is at the hotel for a week holding meetings in their suite. Don't worry; I can take care of myself. If he tries anything, I'll take him down! Haha, x'

'Let me know how it goes, I'll worry.'

'There is nothing to worry about, it's a meeting. x'

She has a vivid imagination. However, I still have to steel myself with a quick Spencer fix before I go.

In the cab on the way over, James is unusually quiet and respectful of my personal space. It's almost unnerving. We cross the hotel lobby and James calls the elevator, seeming twitchy. He gestures for me to go first when the doors open and doesn't place his hand in the small of my back like I had expected. This is very unsettling; maybe he is stressed about the meeting.

As we ride higher and higher, I mentally go over all my favourite kickboxing moves. No matter what James throws at me, he is no match for me. He is a few inches shorter than me, although he wears Cuban heels to look taller and thinks no one notices. And even if he were taller, Mags and I took kickboxing classes for three years. I can take care of myself, he has no sense and no skill, and I fight dirty.

I internally roll my eyes at myself. It's a business meeting not a date gone wrong. I've let Mags make me all jittery.

When the doors open, we step out and cross the wide hall to the double doors of the suite. James produces a key from his pocket...strange. He opens the door and ushers me in. I don't see anyone else here and alarm bells start to ring. He walks over to an ice bucket and pulls out some champagne. Thinking quickly, I click the screen of my phone and select the dictaphone app I use a lot for work. I press record. Slipping it into my pocket as James turns to face me.

"Where's the client, James?" I ask in an even tone.

"There is no client, Jasmine. This is all for us." He smiles his deluded smile. "You just need a little nudge to see I'm serious. We'll be great together if you stop denying me."

I draw in a deep, steady breath and keep a cool exterior, even though my stomach lurches and my heart starts racing. "James, I've said it as many ways as I know how. I'm not interested in you." I'm calm, even though the situation is volatile. I don't know how determined he is, but I know I'm ready for him.

He steps towards me and I tense involuntarily. "I think you like playing games with me," he says softly. "But haven't we played enough?"

"I'm not playing any games, I'm just not interested in you that way. You're a great boss, I love my job, but it's not going to happen," I say firmly. My hands start to shake slightly. I'm still convinced I'm not afraid, but my body is telling me otherwise. I take a deep breath.

James closes the space between us and hands me a glass of champagne. On autopilot I take it, not thinking that I am leading him on, or giving in. He sips his slowly while keeping his eyes on me.

Then he moves in and I go cold.

Trailing the backs of his fingers down my arm as he steps close is the creepiest thing he's done by far, my skin breaks out in goose bumps. The stench of his cheap aftershave as he swamps my personal space is enough to make me choke and yet I remain still.

"I've been very patient," he breathes against my neck. "I won't let you keep toying with me," he gently places a kiss just beneath my ear. I shudder. I should have pulled away, but my brain is working too slow.

Wake the fuck up, Jazz!

I think about turning on him. Ten different scenarios flit through my head, each ending with him bleeding on the floor, but a twisted side of me takes over as I turn my face towards his. I feel him smile against my cheek as he realises I'm not fighting him. As he seeks out my lips with his, his eyes meet mine, I smile and soften my eyes and I watch as relief and triumph cross his face.

I suck in a breath and remind myself this is just a means to an end, as his lips finally find mine. His tongue sweeps across my lips and I allow its entrance. This is nothing. I've kissed plenty of creeps.

A means to an end.

A means to an end.

He moans as he deepens the kiss and finds I am still not denying him.

Then he groans and whispers, "Oh God Jasmine, I want you so much," as he takes my hand and slides it over the growing bulge in his trousers. "Feel how hard I am for you."

Resisting every urge I have to yank my hand away and run, I nod slightly. Then I make my move. "I have told you repeatedly, NO!" I growl as I grip his package tightly, making sure I dig my fingernails in for anchorage.

He makes a strangled sound and fights for a lung full of air as he lurches forward and leans on my shoulder with his forehead. I tighten my grip and yank down.

He shrieks and staggers.

"Now get it through your thick head. I'm not interested in you." I deliver the final blow as I twist my handful sharply. He drops to his knees and I finally let go. He gags from the pain and almost throws up. He moans and curses. I push my stiletto into his chest and shove him back. He falls to the floor, rigid in the fetal position, still cursing through clenched teeth.

"You bitch!" he chokes, and then he turns his head to the floor and whimpers.

I stand over him and grab hold of his tie. Pulling out my phone and showing him the screen I want him to see that I have evidence. He doesn't see, because his eyes are tightly closed, so I yank his tie tighter to get his attention.

"Now you listen to me, I am going back to the office to clear out my desk. You are going to take the rest of the day off, because I think you'll need it. You will not stand in my way and you will not make things difficult for me, or I will sue you for sexual harassment. I have plenty of evidence and a big lawyer in the family. I won't need to fight, I have this," I tell him, thrusting my phone in his face. He whimpers again and nods. "I'm taking a vacation and when I get back, I'm going to take the generous redundancy pay you'll be giving me to start my own business. If you try to get in my way, I will ruin you." He just stares at me and then closes his eyes as a fresh wave of pain sweeps over him. "Do you understand me?" I yell. His eyes snap back open. He nods vigorously, and then chokes on his pain again.

I am getting way too much of a kick out of this; I need to get out of here before I go too far. I have the upper hand right now I mustn't ruin it. "I'll be in touch to let you know just how generous my redundancy package will be." His eyes widen, but before he has a chance to argue, I lean close to his ear. "Before you object James, I should just tell you that I know about the file of me you have on your computer. It's not nice to take photos of people without their permission, it's called stalking and the law takes a dim view. You're lucky I'm so understanding. I took a copy a while back. Remember when you were sick and you needed me to access some files for you to work on at home? It was pretty careless of you. But I'm glad I found it. It will make this transition so much easier, now that we both understand each other."

I let go of his tie and stand up. He groans from the floor.

"You should put some ice on that, it's going to bruise." I laugh as I walk out of the door.

By the time I'm sitting in a cab on my way back to the office, I'm shaking. I can't believe what just happened. I never thought he would take it that far. I still don't believe he would have actually forced me into anything, but enough was enough. I wasn't about to just sit back and find out. Mags is going to freak. She is in the middle of a pampering session right now, I'll fill her in later.

I never told her about the photos I found on his computer; she would have over-reacted. I never thought I'd really need it as evidence. Mags was insistent enough that I should get out of there. She was right of course, I've been really lucky. Who knows what could have happened.

"Miss!" the cab driver barks at me.

"Sorry," I mutter, thrusting the fare at him. We have arrived back at work, and I'm in my own world. I open the door to the shop and take a quick look around. I'm not expected back right now, and who knows if James was able to scrape himself off the floor and make a call. Quickly I go into my office and close the door. I only need a few things. I won't be coming back.

Opening the small cupboard, I pull out a file box and fill it with two spare pairs of shoes and the jacket and umbrella I keep there. Then I go to my desk and empty out all the things I have personally bought. I'm not supplying this office with so much as a paperclip unless I have personally inserted it somewhere rather unpleasant in James' gentleman's region.

Then as I'm making sure I have signed out of everything, there is a light knock at my door and I look up to see Justin, my only friend here.

"Are you ok?" he asks, concerned. "James said you'd be out all afternoon. Then he just called to say he wasn't feeling great and to not disturb him for the rest of the day."

I nod and force a smile.

"Jazz, did something happen? You look terrible and he sounded like shit."

I glance out onto the shop floor and when I'm sure no one is paying any attention, I tell him to sit and I tell him everything about James.

"Holy shit!" He gasps as it all sinks in. "I can't believe that, why didn't you tell me?"

"There wasn't anything really to tell until today."

"You should call the police."

"No, I'm not calling the police, I took care of it and James will be paying me full redundancy so I can start my own business and not have to put up with any more sleazy bosses."

"The chocolate thing?"

"Yeah, the chocolate thing. When I'm ready."

"Awesome, will you stay in touch? I don't want to stay here with you gone, it's going to suck."

"You'll be fine. You can probably muscle your way in to this job. Those two idiots out there wouldn't know how, they're far too old school. Stick your neck out, offer to pick up some of the work load and I bet James will go for it. He can't handle all this development stuff on his own. But you hold out for decent money, don't just let him dump the work with no reward, you hear me?"

"Yes, I hear you."

He helps me gather the rest of my things, and then we carry

them out together to the cab he called me. It's a short walk, but I'm not lugging this stuff on my own.

Back at the apartment, I dump the boxes on the coffee table and notice an envelope. Ripping it open, I pull out the papers and laugh. A hand written note from Mags sits on the top.

I am rich and stubborn and I will win!
M x

Underneath are the details of a retail unit in a great little location nearby. I giggle and pull out my phone.

'You don't know when to quit do you?'

'I'm used to getting my way.'

'We'll talk about this at the weekend.'

She hasn't twigged that I should still be in a meeting. Before she does, I switch off my phone and go to my room to pack for a long stay.

I pull up to the gates of George's impressive estate and enter the code in the keypad. Mags doesn't know I've even finished for the day and she isn't expecting me for a couple of hours. I had just planned to spend the weekend so when she opens the door to my two suitcases and me, she looks at me like I grew an extra head.

"Surprise!"

"Is this for real?" she asks, grinning.

"Yep."

"What about work?"

"It's a loooong story, and I'm going to need a drink to tell it."

"Shit!" she says, sitting down beside me, clutching the two margaritas she has just made us, while I give her the low down on my sucky day. "Why the fuck didn't you tell me how bad it was?"

I reach for my margarita and take a sip, sinking back into the overstuffed sofa in the beautiful living room. "It really wasn't that bad."

"Come on, you said he had pictures of you on his computer, and you felt threatened enough to record your conversation on your phone. That sounds pretty bad to me."

I sigh. "Yeah, I guess. But at least now he won't make me work a months notice and I'm going to make him pay. I told him he had to give me a fat redundancy. This was the perfect outcome."

Mags throws her head back and laughs. "That's my girl."

"It will become start up money, if I decide to go through with the chocolate thing."

"Uh huh, and I have the rest."

I ignore her. I know she's serious, and I will take it if I need it, but let's just see how it goes first. I can't believe I'm thinking about this, but now I have no job and no boyfriend holding me back; I'd be a fool not to try.

"Another drink?" I ask, changing the subject. I'm on fucking holiday and intend to enjoy myself. I feel more relaxed already. In fact, with all the excitement this afternoon, I haven't even checked Twitter and had a Spencer fix. In fact, I think my phone is still off from earlier.

It's probably not a bad thing.

Spencer

FRIDAY 3RD JULY

"So how's the fuck-me-heels girl?"

"Shut up," I snarl, stressed from working late on my last day. I could have walked away at five like most people would, but I like my bosses and enjoyed the work. I'll have no trouble getting freelance work from them if I need the cash, so it paid to be conscientious right until the end. I'm taking a big risk now, but I know I'll be happier. I just didn't want to leave anyone in the lurch. So, I've had a bitch of a last day.

"She's got under your skin, hasn't she?"

"Do me a favour, she's just a girl on Twitter, no different to the five thousand others."

Will almost spits out his water. "You have five thousand followers on Twitter?"

"Yeah, ok, it's four thousand and something, but they aren't all girls."

"Fuck me, no wonder your ego is out of control!"

"My ego is just fine, thanks. Are we going to chat all day or are we going to the pub?"

"Alright, God, what's up, didn't she tweet you today?"

I narrow my eyes at him. He's going to pay for that. And why has she completely ignored the fact that I did as she asked and posted a picture of my tattoos? That was yesterday morning and she hasn't even reacted. I don't do shit like that for everyone, you know. I thought we had a nice little game going on. I was looking forward to where it would lead. Maybe she thought it was a weak effort? Maybe I didn't show enough flesh?

Oh, well, it's a gorgeous evening, I don't want to waste any of it wondering what I can do to get one girl's attention, when I could be out there getting attention for real. But that doesn't stop me from daydreaming. I pull a bottle of water from the fridge and think about the shoes. I don't know what she even looks like, all I have to go on are the shoes, but it's enough to have me fantasising. Will is right, she could be hideous, but I just don't see it.

I know there are plenty of women who go out of their way to message me and flirt with me, but this one has my attention. Even her name is sexy; Jazz…ok, I'm losing my mind! Shoegirl is making me crazy, WTF? I need to go out and get laid.

I take the stairs two at a time, stopping by the bathroom to turn on the shower before I head to the bedroom. I drink down some water, then strip off my shirt and tie and chuck them in the basket. I am happy that I won't be putting them back on for a while. I look damn good in a suit, but it's nice to take it off and relax. I turn and face myself in the mirror. My eyes run over my abs and I flex to improve the view, I turn to inspect my rear as my phone tells me I have a tweet.

Looking at myself in the mirror is usually one of my favourite activities, but I'm straight on it. Yeah, ok, I hope it's Shoegirl. Fuck me, this is getting out of control. Especially as it's not her, so now I'm disappointed.

Fucking get yourself together, Ryan, it's a chick. One you'll never meet. Just melt her knickers off and get on with your day, the shower is running and this is ridiculous. She isn't the only girl that tweets me, why is she getting to me? I glance back at the mirror. If she wants a better look at my tattoos, now is the time. I snap a quick selfie. It's shameless, I know, but she's playing hard ball and if she doesn't appreciate it, hundreds of other girls will.

SPENCER @TheSpencerRyan
It's good to get out of that suit! #TGIF
pic.twitter.com/2iey2o8rqd

Jazz

SATURDAY 4TH JULY

The first thing I did this morning, was switch on my phone. I was wondering if maybe James had recovered enough to get nasty, but there were no messages at all. Then my next thought was, of course, my daily fix of the loveliness of Spencer...and I got a treat! He had posted a topless selfie last night, and I missed it. Although what can you really say to a hot selfie and still maintain your dignity? I don't know? Hot damn, was all I could think of. PHWOAR! Maybe? Not really my style. Besides, I missed the boat.

I could have commented this morning, but that just makes me look like a stalker who creeps around his profile. Yes, yes, I realise I am, but I don't want to draw attention to it.

Having had a cup of tea and looked at it a few more times though, I'm thinking maybe I should acknowledge it in some way. After all, that's the second picture he's tweeted to satisfy my demands, and I've said nothing. I should show my appreciation, just not be too obvious about it.

JAZZ @OMGJazzyP
After a shitty day that kept me away from here, what a gorgeous view to wake up to this morning!

Maybe that's a bit too vague, but I'll check in later. At least he will see from that that I wasn't around yesterday. Anyway, I need to get up and get out for a bit of exercise this morning, to clear out the cobwebs. It's unusual for me, but I occasionally get the urge. Of course, Mags' dad has a state of the art gym, but since it's so beautiful around here, I think I'll explore properly.

I pull on my trainers and call out goodbye to Mags. I have a reasonable idea of where I'm going, so I just head out onto the road and try not to make any unnecessary turns. It feels good to be out; it's gorgeous here. It's mainly country roads and fields, with the odd large house tucked behind huge gates. The road eventually leads me into the small village. It's beautiful, quaint and really tiny.

Although I've spent quite a bit of time here, usually I'm here for an evening or a breakfast. Sometimes both. But I've never ventured down here to explore. I stop at the window of a patisserie shop and stare at the works of art in the window.

"Go on, you deserve it after your run," a deep voice startles me. I flinch and then turn to the source.

Holy…wow!

I have to work hard to compose my face and not let my breathing bust me. This guy is all kinds of hot, and he is staring very intently at me.

"I…errr…I shouldn't, I'm in the middle of my, err, run." It was a brisk walk, but he doesn't need to know that.

He smiles an extremely disarming smile. "You're not from around here, are you?"

I laugh and look down at myself. "What gave me away?"

"I've lived here all my life and would certainly have

noticed you before," he grins. This guy is confident, but just looking at him, I know why. He is tall, fair haired and as handsome as they come. His eyes are the boldest blue I've ever seen, and you can tell he's going to be charming just by looking at him...aaaaaand now I'm staring. Great! I should get on with my 'run' before I embarrass myself.

"Can I buy you a cup of tea?" he asks, nodding his head towards the door of the patisserie.

No, I should get on my way...Except I don't say this aloud, do I?

No.

I think it, but what comes out of my mouth is..."Sure, ok, that would be lovely."

"Excellent," he smiles and holds the door open for me.

"Two teas, please," he says to the lady behind the counter.

She glances at me, then looks back to him with a smirk, and turns to make the drinks.

"So, where are you from?" he asks, as we sit down.

"Aren't you going to ask me my name first?"

He thinks for a moment. "I should, I just like this perfect stranger thing we've got going on."

I blush. Yeah, my cheeks definitely changed colour! WTF?

"How about, I ask you your name on our second date?" he says.

I am just thinking how a sane person answers a question like that when the lady who is still smirking delivers our teas to the table. Am I the only one who thinks this is a weird situation? Why is this woman so amused by our having tea together?

"Two teas," she says, placing them on the table. Then she

hovers for what I believe is an inappropriate length of time. "Aren't you going to introduce me to your friend?" she finally asks.

He sighs. "Mum, this is my friend, friend this is my mum."

"Hmm," she says in response. "Well 'friend,' it's nice to meet you." Then she smiles sweetly and goes back to her counter.

"So, this is your mum's place?" I ask him.

"Yep...and now I feel you know too much about me. You'll have to tell me what your mum does to keep things even."

I screw up my nose, "Do I have to?"

His face drops. "Not if it's an issue. I didn't mean to..."

I laugh, "It's ok, she's alive and well, and we get on fine, she just embarrasses the hell out of me! They both do." I sigh and put my face in my hands in embarrassment, just from thinking about them and their 'work.' I look up at him. "My mum and dad are a singing, keyboard playing duo, who make their living playing in hotels along the coast." I cringe.

"That sounds quite glamorous to me."

"Well, it's not. It's the lowest of the low. It's mortifying. They haven't updated their set since probably 1982. It has scarred me for life!" I sigh. Awesome. I meet a gorgeous stranger and the first fact he knows about me is the truth about my parents. Something I tell no one. "Hey, now you know too much about me. I don't know about your dad. No fair."

Again, his face falls.

"Shit...I—"

He laughs. "I'm kidding! He runs the post office across the road."

I heave a sigh of relief. "Wow, you weren't kidding when you said you'd been here all your life, and you would have noticed someone new."

"Actually, I said I would have noticed you," he corrects...and there's not even a hint of shyness about the way he says it.

Once again, I blush. Jesus! What is it about this man?

"So, second date, huh?" I ask clumsily changing the subject to territory that's no safer. "Does that make this our first?"

He shrugs, "I held the door open, I bought you a cuppa, and we are talking about ourselves...ish! This is very much a date."

I laugh. I can't argue with that. In fact, I can't argue with anything; his confidence is disarming and his eyes never leave mine. They're hypnotic. I could stare at them all day.

"So, shall I be mum?" he asks.

"Huh?" snapping out of my trance.

"Shall I pour the tea?" he laughs.

"Sure." I shake my head at my cocky stranger and laugh, sliding him my cup.

I don't even know his name. This is truly bizarre, but I kinda like it.

He pours my tea and slides it back, and then we sit in semi-comfortable silence and take a sip.

"Not bad," I grin.

He smiles triumphantly, and twiddles his spoon between his fingers. "So, where are you from, then?"

"I thought we're saving this until our second date?" I laugh.

"Ah, yes, but you already know where I'm from. Just keeping it fair," he smirks. God what a smirk!

"Ok, that's fair. I'm from Bournemouth, originally, but I moved up here for college and stayed." He watches me intently. I want to know his name, but I'm intrigued about this second date. So I move the conversation away. "It's beautiful here; you've always lived here?"

"Yeah, I have," he replies, looking out of the window. "It's ok, I guess."

"No, it's gorgeous."

We finish our tea and I check my watch. I have no idea why; I have nowhere to be. Just habit, I guess.

"I'm keeping you from your run," my stranger says. Then he stands and holds out his hand for me. I take it and get to my feet even though my knees threaten to buckle at the contact from this beautiful man.

Pull. Yourself. Together. Parker! He is just a guy.

He pays his mum, even though I can see her waving him away, then he holds the door open for me. We step onto the pavement and face each other. I hope he asks me for a second date. I really want to know his name.

"So 'friend,'" he says, taking a step backwards, ready to walk away from me. "What are you doing this evening? It's my birthday today, and I'm having a drink in the pub tonight with some friends. I'd love it if you came."

"It's your birthday?"

"Yeah."

"You should have said something."

"Why? Would you have ordered a cake and had the staff sing to me? Would have been interesting when you got to, happy birthday dear…frieeeend! Happy birthday to yooooou!" He sings the last part.

I can't help but giggle, honestly, I'm acting like a teenager. "I…um…can I bring a friend?" I manage.

"A friend I would like? Or a friend I would have to watch touching you?"

I do a worse, blushy, girly giggle thing…WTF??? Composing myself, I manage to respond. "A friend you would like, I think. I mean, she might touch me, but I don't think it would upset you."

He smiles a broad smile, like I just answered his prayers. As he takes another step away from me he says, "Excellent, eight o'clock at The Duck then."

"The Duck?"

He grins and points over my shoulder. I turn and see the 'The Duck on the Pond' pub. It is the last building before the beautiful village green with a picturesque pond. It looks charming. When I turn back he is already walking away from me, backwards.

"So eight, then?"

"We'll be there."

"Great," he replies. "See you then 'friend.'" Then he turns and walks away.

"Mags!" I call out as I walk up the sweeping staircase of her father's home. "Mags?"

"In here," she yells from her bathroom.

"What shall I wear to the Duck on the Pond?"

I hear her laughter as I walk through her room and into her bathroom. She is shaving her legs in the bath.

"That depends on who you're trying to impress."

"Well, I got us a date."

"Fast work, you were only gone an hour. What's his name?"

"I don't know," I laugh. "We're saving that for our second date."

"Second date?"

"Yes, tonight. Long story, just come be my wing-man."

She shakes her head. "Sure."

I head back to my room. It's eleven am and already I'm thinking about what to wear tonight. I laugh at myself. I don't know what's up with me lately? This is as bad as the obsession with a guy I've never met. Oh! Speaking of...I wonder if he saw my tweet? I look at my phone and am surprised to see a message. Maybe it came through while I was out, and I didn't hear it.

It's a tweet.

From him.

SPENCER @TheSpencerRyan
@OMGJazzyP A shitty day huh? Tell Spencer all about it...

Well, well. So he saw my tweet.

JAZZ @OMGJazzyP
@TheSpencerRyan Nah, you don't want to hear about it.

SPENCER @TheSpencerRyan
@OMGJazzyP You sure about that? I'm a great listener.

JAZZ @OMGJazzyP
@TheSpencerRyan No really, it's boring. Thanks though. I left my job that's all.

SPENCER @TheSpencerRyan
@OMGJazzyP Really? Me too! I finished yesterday. I'm going into business for myself.

Hmmm, I wonder what he'll be doing? Architecture?
It sucks I won't see him around at lunchtimes any more, but then I realise with a wave of shock that I don't work around there either anymore.
Damn!
No more potential for running into him.
While I'm thinking that I won't see him anymore, another tweet comes through.

SPENCER @TheSpencerRyan
@OMGJazzyP Something I've wanted to do for a while. I hate the commute. Don't want to do it anymore.

He's awful keen to share. I don't see him being this chatty with other girls who hang around waiting for his attention.

JAZZ @OMGJazzyP
@TheSpencerRyan That's brave of you. It's something I'd love to do. How long was your commute?

SPENCER @TheSpencerRyan
@OMGJazzyP Less than 30 mins on clear roads, but since

they don't exist, 45 mins to an hour. It sucks!

SPENCER @TheSpencerRyan
@OMGJazzyP Correction, It suckED! Starting Monday, I work locally.

JAZZ @OMGJazzyP
@TheSpencerRyan Sounds like you did the right thing. I like to work close to home.

SPENCER @TheSpencerRyan
@OMGJazzyP Ah yes, close to home. Where is that again?

I laugh at his brazen attempt to find out information I've already avoided.

JAZZ @OMGJazzyP
@TheSpencerRyan the UK

Instantly, my DM light goes on.

'The UK isn't that big Jazz, I'm good at getting information!'

'Sorry. No personal info. Not even to people who may or may not live near me. ESPECIALLY not to people who may or may not live near me.'

'You know, if you tell me, you might end

up with a treat."

        'Oh really? And what's that then?'

'Me, duh!'

        'Silly me! Of course. Is this a treat you offer to all your 'ladies'?

'God no! This is a first. I just want to see those shoes in person.'

        'Just the shoes? Give me your address, I'll post them to you.'

'I'd prefer your feet in them.'

        'I'm rather fond of my feet, sorry. I'm going to need to hang on to them. Call me selfish.'

'That is rather selfish, Jazz! How about a picture to ease the pain?'

        'You had a picture the other day, Spencer, this isn't Instagram you know!'

'I want more! More you in the picture.'

        'No chance! Sorry! Rules are rules.'

'Rules are made to be broken.'

'Not these ones. Go meet one of the other girls. This girl won't give it up!'

'I don't want to meet one of the other girls. I like you.'

'You don't know me!'

'I'm trying to change that.'

'I could be anyone.'

'Yes, you could. That's the fun part. Lighten up, Jazz, I'm just trying to get to know you.'

'Ok, you're right, sorry.'

'Good. So, what are you up to tonight, got anything fun planned?'

Typical! of all the 'getting to know me' questions he could have asked, he asked that one. Now, do I answer ambiguously, or say I have a date? I guess I don't owe him an explanation…

'Just going out for a drink, what about you?'

'I think I'll just have an early night tonight. It's been a long week.'

'That sounds good to me.'

'You can join me if you like. Stay home, we can get to know each other.'

'Can't sorry, I've made plans. Maybe another night, though? I'd like to get to know you better.'

'Sure, sounds good.'

I have an outfit to plan for the strangest second date in history. I can't sit here all day chatting! Spencer Ryan and his ego will have to wait until tomorrow.

I feel slightly guilty as we approach the pub. Spencer was sweet enough to suggest a night in getting acquainted and I blow him off for a stranger whose name I don't even know! But this is at least real, I guess. What has my life become when these are my two options for a Saturday night? #FirstWorldProblems

Mags holds the door of the pub open for me and I step in. The small bar is full of people, and at a quick glance, I can't see my stranger. No way am I going on a desperate search for him, so I stride to the bar with Mags in tow and wait to be served.

"So, is he here?" Mags asks, once we have our wine.

"I don't see him," I reply, still scanning the bar. Then from an area tucked away behind the bar, male laughter erupts. I look at Mags and nod towards the sound. "Could be them, shall we see?" Mags nods and follows me. I move with confidence into a larger room, full of people. There is a second smaller bar in here and standing between two guys watching their shots being poured is my stranger. Without pausing I walk up behind him, and as he slams his empty glass back down on the bar, I tap him on the shoulder.

He turns around and his face lights up. "You came!" He shouts and throws his arms around me. He must have had a few shots already!

"Of course I came," I reply. "I couldn't miss our second date, I want to know your name."

"Will?" Comes Mags' voice from behind me.

"Mags?" My stranger says, releasing me. He is no longer looking at me and his expression is serious. He is intently focused on Mags, who for some reason looks like she has seen a ghost. "What are you doing here?" He turns to me. "Is this the friend?"

"Er, yeah. This is Mags." I'm totally confused.

"I'm staying at Dad's," Mags says.

Now, I've seen Mags handle a million guys, but this guy has her completely rattled. Remember when I said there is never any emotion when it comes to guys? Well I definitely see some now. She's working hard to hide it, but it's there.

"Oh," my stranger says. "I didn't know." He looks worried; what is going on here?

"I didn't think you'd be here. What happened to Australia?" she says, staring intently into his eyes.

"I came home," he says quietly.

Silence envelops us as Mags and my stranger, who is apparently not a stranger to Mags, stare at each other. It is abruptly broken by one of the other guys at the bar.

"Fuck me, Will! You gonna introduce us or are these all for you?"

Ugh, gross! THESE? Jesus, objectify much? I turn to give this delight a dirty look and bam! There he is in all his glory.

I try to take it all in. The suit is gone and in its place, as you'd expect, is an equally spectacular vision. Just jeans and a slim fitting T-shirt, which shows off his toned body underneath. But like with the suit, this guy turns the ordinary into the extraordinary. That's before I even acknowledge the ink on his arms, screaming "Lick me! LICK ME NOW!!!"

Spencer. Fucking. Ryan.

He's had a shot or two, that's obvious. He's practically drooling at Mags and I. Classy!

'Hey babe,' he lifts his chin in a nod to me.

Sorry, am I in the fucking Twilight Zone? I'm here to meet my stranger. Now, in the space of thirty seconds, he is no longer my stranger, he is 'Will' and 'Will' is clearly 'something' to Mags. Now, his total douche of a friend is only my current reason for living…Spencer Ryan. Who, if I remember correctly, is supposed to be having an early night somewhere 'near London'! The Liar!

Spencer. Fucking. Ryan!

Mags and Will continue to stare at each other, and I'm just looking back and forth at them, hoping in a minute something will make sense.

Then the vision of perfection I have in my head of Spencer

Spencer

Ryan shatters into a million pieces, when he says to me, "Looks like you've lost out there! Still, more for me!"

What. A. Jerk!

"Aren't you going to introduce us?" The jerk says, elbowing Will.

"Sorry," says Will, snapping out of his daze. "This is Mags. Mags, this is my cousin Spencer."

This is the moment where Mags finally realises the magnitude of what I'm dealing with and struggles to control her expression.

I shoot her a look.

"And this is…I still don't know your name!" Will laughs nervously.

"Parker." I blurt. Mags raises a questioning eyebrow and I give her the 'just go with it' look. It's not a total lie, is it? I just can't handle this shit right now.

"Parker, it's nice to meet you," Will says softly, still glancing between Mags and I.

"Yeah, very nice. I'm Spencer," the idiot to my right interrupts.

Ugh! Take my dreams and stomp all over them, why don't you! I may be overreacting here, but I've had a pretty tough week. I've lost my job, come close to being assaulted, met a very nice guy who, it now seems, is off limits and found out that my virtual crush is in fact a bit of a douchebag! The pressure is getting to me all of a sudden and I can't stand it a minute longer.

"Where are the loos?" I ask no one in particular.

"Just there," points Will.

"Thanks, excuse me." I bolt for the door, glass of wine still in hand. I stop in front of the mirror and mouth, 'what the fuck?' at my reflection. Shaking my head, I begin to down the entire large glass of wine. Halfway through my self-medicating, Mags joins me at the mirror, my eyes meet hers, but I don't stop drinking until the glass is empty.

"What the fuck just happened?" I ask her, setting the glass down.

"I have no idea!" she laughs, and then her expression turns serious. "I, um, I have history with Will."

"I got that!"

"I'm sorry."

"Hey, you didn't know. What's the deal anyway? I've never seen you like that."

"It's not important, really. We just go way back. Do you like him?" she asks, her voice wavering a little.

"He's nice, but we just met. If you have history, you know I wouldn't ever go there."

She smiles tightly. "Thanks."

"But you have to fill me in; this is a big deal, I can tell."

"Ok, but not here." There is a silence for a second then her eyes widen. "So, THAT was Spencer Ryan?"

I sigh. "What are the fucking chances?"

"I know, right?" She shakes her head in disbelief. "And he's Will's cousin!"

"Have you never met him?"

"No. I didn't even know he had a cousin. When I knew Will, it was only him, his sister and his parents in the village. I guess his other family never came up."

"And he's a douche!" I fake sob!

"Totally."

"Oh God, Mags, why did this have to happen?"

"Maybe he's just drunk. Why did you give him your last name?"

"Really? You think I want to have the whole 'Hey, you're OMGJazzyP' conversation with THAT guy? No thanks!" I sigh again. "He's just so…disappointing!"

"Yeah, I know." She rubs my arm. "You could use another drink, I'll go get us one. Just take a minute and come back out there with your game face on. We'll set him straight."

I nod and she smiles at me in the mirror before she leaves. I sigh. What a day! I start out debating on whether to go on a bizarre second date with mystery stranger No.1, or have a night in with my fantasy man. And just like that, I'm left with no mystery man and my fantasy crashed and burned. That'll teach me for hedging my bets.

I cannot believe I fell for the 'night in' routine. He was full of shit. He never planned to stay in for a second. What do you suppose he'd have done if I'd said, 'ok then.' He's an idiot. I feel stupid for thinking otherwise.

I wash my hands, no idea why, just habit. Then I take a deep breath and make my way back out to my personal hell.

"Parker?" Oh, wait that's me! I turn and find Will leaning against the wall.

"Hi."

"I, er," he shifts nervously and ruffles his hair.

"It's ok," I assure him. "You have history with Mags."

"Sorry," he sighs. "I'd like to be friends though."

"Sure." I smile. He seems really sweet and I love that this 'history' he has with Mags has put an instant stop to furthering our relationship. As Mags' friend, this is just the kind of thing

I want to see in a potential guy for her. I like him already.

"Friends."

He grins. "So, Parker, I'm Will. Nice to meet you."

I laugh. "Hi Will, it's always nice to make a new friend."

"Shall we go and rescue Mags from my friends?"

I raise an eyebrow and laugh. If by friends, he means Spencer, then we should get out there!

Jazz

SUNDAY 5TH JULY

"How do you feel this morning?" Mags asks, setting a tea down beside me and sitting on the edge of the bed.

"Ugh! Don't be so loud!" I groan, my voice gravelly and weak.

"Last night wasn't pretty."

I sigh and pull my pillow over my head.

"I think you left an impression on the locals!"

I whip the pillow back to shoot Mags a glare. "Was I that bad?"

She laughs. "No, its fine, everyone was wasted. But I think Spencer sobered up pretty fast when you threw your drink in his face!"

I sink my head back down and groan at the memory. "I was hoping that part was a horrible nightmare!"

"No, that happened…He totally deserved it though. What a dick!"

I groan. "It's so unfair. How can THAT really be him? He is so nice on Twitter. His bio should carry a warning…'Total douche in real life.' Thank fuck he doesn't know it was me."

"I know. What are you going to do?"

"Do? I'm going to do nothing. My Spencer Ryan fantasies

are over."

"Oh, please, like it's that easy."

"Mags, trust me, the Clark Kent glasses were off last night and Superman he ain't. Did we even get to the bottom of what the hell he's doing here?"

"He lives here, with Will. That's all I know, there was a lot going on last night. But I'll try to find out."

Her phone vibrates, and she smiles when she checks the message.

"Ok, spill!" I demand, as I sit up and get my tea. "You and Will have history…tell me how I don't know anything about this."

"There's nothing to tell," she replies unconvincingly.

"Crap! For one thing, I've never seen you so jittery around a guy, I saw that look on your face. His was the same."

Mags sighs and flops back onto my mattress.

"Spill." I sip my tea and wait.

"It's nothing, it's over." She waves her hand dismissively in the air, while staring at the ceiling.

"Uh huh, sure. It looked totally over. Now get over yourself and tell me what the deal is."

She props herself up on an elbow and glares at me. "We dated."

"And...?"

"And nothing. We dated, it was ok."

"OK? Wow, sounds really special." I roll my eyes. "Mags, please, this is me. I know you and that reaction was not for someone you dated and it was 'ok.' You liked him."

"Fine I liked him, satisfied?"

"Getting there. Slowly. So you liked him and he liked

you?"

She huffs. "Yes, I liked him and he liked me."

"And they lived happily ever after," I smirk, my words heavy with sarcasm.

"Jesus, Jazz," she sits up, turning to face me so that I can feel the full force of her frustration, but she doesn't scare me. This is a big deal and really it's her that should be scared that this is the first I'm ever hearing about it. She glares at me and I offer her an unwavering determination that this conversation will continue, in return.

She sighs, defeated. Pushing her fingers through her hair, she gives in. "It was good, ok? I liked him, he liked me, we had a good time, obviously we didn't live happily ever after and now it's in the past. I haven't thought about him in a long time."

"But you're thinking about him now."

"Not in that way. It was just a bit of a shock seeing him."

"So that's it?"

"In a nutshell."

"When did this all happen?"

"The summer of the year we started college."

"So you broke up right before we met?"

"Yes."

"How long were you together?"

"A little over a year, maybe more, I can't remember," she shrugs.

"Mags, no girl that age fails to recall exact dates and anniversaries, so don't give me that crap."

She rolls her eyes, shaking her head, but without a moments hesitation replies, "Seventeen months."

"SEVENTEEN MONTHS?!"

"What?"

"I've never known you date anyone seventeen days, let alone seventeen months!"

"Well there you go. Are we done here?"

"Not quite. Why did you break up?"

Mags' shoulders slump.

"Come on Mags. I can't believe I've known you six years and I don't know this stuff. Tell me."

"Money."

I frown.

"I have it, he doesn't."

My frown deepens. "He doesn't seem that shallow, at least that's not the impression I got anyway."

"Yeah well, it drove a wedge, what can I say?"

"Shame. I didn't have him down as the superficial arsehole type. He seemed very sweet."

Mags snaps her eyes back to me. "No, he is sweet, it wasn't his fault, I made it an issue, I made him feel not good enough." She looks so full of regret.

I shake my head. "The Mags I know wouldn't make someone feel that way."

"I learned the hard way."

"Is that why you were so cagey about it when we first met?"

She shrugs, studying her nails. "I guess."

"Why did you never try and sort it out with him?"

"Because he left. I went to see him, to try and fix things and he was packing."

"Where did he go?"

She looks up at me and pauses for a moment. "Australia."

"Wow. That's pretty final."

"Yeah."

So you haven't heard from him since?"

"No, so I let it go."

"Now he's back."

"Yeah, now he's back," she sighs.

"Did you talk last night?"

"No, I think we were both in shock."

"Why was he in shock? You technically live here, he must have expected to see you again."

"I haven't been here though have I? I went from our student house to our apartment. I only visit here now, overnight at the most. I have my own life now."

"But he wasn't to know that."

"Jazz, this is a small village, nothing goes unnoticed."

"So you think he thought it was safe to come back, knowing he wouldn't run into you?"

"Yep."

"Hmmm, well if that's the case, which I doubt, it truly backfired, didn't it? Anyway, that was him texting you just now, I know it. You don't get that look for anyone."

Mags finally smiles again. Uncontrollably.

"Come on, what did he say?"

Looking at her phone again. She grins. "He just said it was really good to see me last night."

"Bullshit, I saw your face, you blushed." Despite my hangover, I leap up and grab her phone from her hand.

"Hey!" She objects, but she doesn't put up much of a fight, as I look at the text.

'Hey you. It was really good to see you last night. Do you fancy breakfast and a proper catch up? W x'

"See! He wants breakfast! And you know, a good morning text doesn't just mean good morning. It also means, 'you were the first thing on my mind when I woke up.' That's not someone who was hoping never to run into you again. How did he even know your number?"

"I wrote it on his hand as we were leaving," she blushes.

"Shit, you're blushing. You have it bad!" I groan and sink back onto the bed as the full force of last night's drinking hits me. I cover my face with my hands.

"I do not!"

"You so do," I reply from behind my hands. "And," I continue, peeping out, "you got the 'hey you'!"

"That doesn't mean anything."

"Oh, it does and you know it. 'Hey you' is flirtation. It's...'I know you too well for 'hello' and I care about you more than 'hi'.' It's intimate."

"Seriously, where do you get this stuff?"

"You have to trust me."

"Yeah, ok," she mocks, but quickly changes the subject. "So, you're not going to tell Spencer it's you?"

"Hell no!" I frown.

"He'll keep tweeting you," she warns.

"Let him, I don't care. That ship has sailed."

"Oh God, Jazz, you're a nightmare sometimes. We both know it's not going to be that easy. Just tell him and get it over with."

"No." Sitting up, but not meeting her eyes, I mutter, "I'm going to take a shower."

I hear Mags sigh as I walk away.

My stomach lurches when my phone tings with the notification. Yes, yes...I have notifications set so that I know when he tweets, so what? I guess I should turn them off now that I know what he's really like.

SPENCER @TheSpencerRyan
SHOTS ARE EVIL!

I drop my phone on the bed and head to the wardrobe to decide what to wear. I don't plan on doing anything today besides sulking, so I just throw on my trackies and a vest. What I wouldn't give to be able to tweet him back and tell him to feel better. Careful what you wish for is all I can say. Yesterday, I lived in a beautiful fantasy where I thought meeting him would be more than I could handle.

It turns out I was right, but for all the wrong reasons. Maybe I could pretend I don't know the truth and just continue my Twitter fantasy? Hell, half of Twitter aren't who they say they are. He is only playing a role like the rest of them, I guess. It doesn't need to change things. He is still beautiful and funny online, it's just there are some things you can't unsee. Like when he ran his hand up the back of my thigh last night and didn't find it necessary to stop at the hem of my skirt.

I threw my drink in his face without thinking, I was so shocked. Ugh! He's disgusting. After James, he's lucky he could still walk. Seriously, what is it with men who think they can just help themselves? It wasn't even his predatory nature; under other circumstances, I might find that strangely appealing. It was just his entitled attitude. He didn't know who I was, and yet, he seemed to think I'd been provided for him to paw.

Taking my tea with me, I find myself a quiet spot to sit outside and mope while Mags is at breakfast with Will. It's so tranquil here; I almost prefer it to the hustle and bustle that I so love. Then suddenly the peace is speared by the buzz buzz of my phone's vibrate against the patio table.

SPENCER @TheSpencerRyan
#SelfieSunday pic.twitter.com/wiDeqO3uy2

Huh. I should really turn those notifications off at some point. I don't want his face on my timeline anymore. I don't want to keep being reminded that he is so much less than I dreamed he would be.

I put my phone back on the table and sip my tea. I haven't had a holiday in so long, except to see my folks and we all know how relaxing that can be. I had been longing to get away to somewhere hot, with a pool, but it turns out, this is exactly what I needed. We are in the lap of luxury, I won't deny it. Mags' father doesn't want for anything, the house is historical looking from the outside. I have no idea which period, architecture isn't exactly my thing. But it's old and stately looking. However, on the inside it's cool, modern and sophisticated. Everything is very sleek and grown up, like a beautiful boutique hotel. Oh, and a pool? Got one! Indoors, of

Spencer

course, but still the very best. I'm planning to spend my day reading beside it, or in it.

A little while later, when I'm finally relaxed and not feeling like death, the buzz buzz interrupts the silence again...

A direct message, from none other than Mr. Ryan. Hesitating, I wonder if I really want to know what it says. But curiosity wins over stubbornness, so I hit open.

Holy fucking shit!

Spencer
SUNDAY 5TH JULY

Oh God it hurts! Why? Whyyyyy? I roll over in bed and wince. Why the hell would I do shots? Why?

Never again.

I reach for my phone to check the time, ugh! Its 9.30, no wonder I feel like crap. I've usually been to the gym by now. I should get up. I swing my feet over the side of the bed and groan as they sink to the floor. My head hurts. I pull my phone closer and type out my prevailing thought.

SPENCER @TheSpencerRyan
SHOTS ARE EVIL!

I hear Will crashing around in the kitchen and decide I'll feel better if I get up and moving.

"Really?" I groan, as a stack of pans clatter to the floor while Will is rummaging around in the cupboard.

"Sorry dude, I'm making breakfast."

I open the fridge and pull out an energy drink. Electrolytes, that's what I need. "How very domesticated of you, but I'm just going to grab some cereal and head to the gym."

"It's not for you, shithead, Mags is coming over."

"Well, well! The 'nothing' is obviously 'something' after all."

"I never said she was nothing. I said there's nothing going on."

"Yeah, now maybe, but there has been."

" A long time ago."

"And from the way you're making out like you're Gordon-fucking-Ramsey this morning, I'm guessing you want a repeat performance." I take a long drink. "She must have been good!" Will shoots me a 'don't fuck with me' look and gets back to his ridiculously loud breakfast preparations.

Smirking, I head for the shower.

My phone chirps beside me as I finish working the product into my hair, so I wipe my hands off on the towel wrapped around my waist before checking it.

BETH @Loves2BeNaughty
Hey @TheSpencerRyan where have you been lately? I miss you sexy…

Damn, I thought it might be Shoegirl.

I wander into the kitchen and smile at Will's friend who is drinking tea at the kitchen table. "Morning. Mags, right?"

"Put some fucking clothes on, mate!" Will snaps.

I look down at my towel, slung low on my hips, as I pick up the kettle. "I'm wearing a towel." I roll my eyes, then wink at Will's friend, who by the way is a fucking stunner. Even after a heavy night, she looks fantastic. How did I not notice this last night? Oh, yeah, the distracting megabitch friend. Bloody hell, how could I forget that psycho?

What was her name again? Precious...Princess...Piranha? That girl has an attitude problem. She threw her drink in my face! God knows why? I was just showing her some attention - girls love that. Don't they? Normal girls do. Whatever, she's obviously got issues and she wasn't that hot anyway; her mate is way hotter. Shame she seems hung up on Will, I'd definitely nail her otherwise. She's fit.

"Spencer."

I turn in the direction of Will's voice. "Huh?" I was staring.

"Are you going to put some damned clothes on?" Will's eyes are narrowed on me. Sure, of course he needs me to cover up, he doesn't want his girl getting a look at the other goods on offer, does he?

"Don't get your knickers in a twist, I'm making a cuppa, then I'll be out of your hair."

It's possible that I take a little longer than is needed to make my tea, while Will and his hot friend return to their conversation. I stop and browse in the fridge pondering what I should have to eat, seeing as I didn't get invited to breakfast.

I can feel her eyes on me.

I can feel it pissing Will off.

I love it!

After taking an eternity to make a bowl of cereal and a cup of tea, I leave them to their whispers, grabbing a banana on my way out the door.

I sit on my bed and munch on my cornflakes, flicking through my phone. I scroll through my timeline and star a few things, then, as has become my habit, I type OMG into the search bar. I can hardly even admit to myself that I've done this enough times now that her name appears top in the drop down list. I click on the name and her profile loads up. What is it about those shoes? I want them digging into my arse while I drive into her.

Aaaaand, now I'm hard! Fucking get a grip Ryan. They're just shoes! You don't know what she looks like. She could be old, or a dude! Or an old dude!! I shudder and look down as my cock retreats in terror. It's enough to put me off my cereal, so I put the bowl down on my bedside table.

I look at my phone again. It's not true, she's a knock out, I know it. For a moment I consider tweeting her, but I really need to sweat this alcohol out of my system. I just need to get moving and clear my head of crazy bitches with attitude problems and fuck-me-heel-wearing sex bombs.

Maybe I'll just tweet something to get her attention before I leave for the gym.

SPENCER @TheSpencerRyan
#SelfieSunday pic.twitter.com/wiDeqO3uy2

By the time I'm home from the gym, she still hasn't commented. Maybe she hasn't seen it? Even if she has, it was a bit tame I guess, just my face. Stripping my sweaty clothes off, I glance in the mirror and smile. Maybe I should give her something more to look at?

Aiming my phone at the mirror, I flex and shoot. The dresser that the mirror sits on cuts a neat line across my pelvis, it's just slightly less than decent, but hey, I don't give a shit, she'll love it. This isn't for timeline though; I open up a direct message and add the photo.

> 'For your eyes only!'

That's it. I'm not saying any more. I throw my phone on the bed and head for the shower, smirking as I try to imagine the reaction that picture is getting right now. I step beneath the steaming hot water and sigh, that feels so good. For a minute I just let the water run over me. As I rub soap over my body, I wonder if that picture turned her on. I wonder if she's touching herself right now? I groan, what am I doing? Thinking like that can only lead to…too late!

I run my hand down my stomach and over my hardening cock. Grasping it in my hand and stroking up and down the growing length. Just the thought of this girl in her heels has me hard, I don't care that I don't know what she looks like, she's hot, I know she is. My wet hand slides easily up and down my now rock hard cock, in long, slow strokes. The slick feeling of the soap has me imagining her mouth around me. I increase the tempo, imagining my Shoegirl on her knees, taking me deep. I close my eyes and lean my forehead on the tiled wall. With my free hand I feel my balls as they begin to tighten. I imagine grabbing her hair and holding her still as I fuck hard into her mouth. I thrust into my hand, once…twice…three times…"Fuck!" I moan as I come long and hard and shoot my load all over the tiles.

With a towel around my waist, I stroll back into my bedroom. The first thing I do is check my phone. Fucking nothing! Fine, whatever, I'm not going to beg.

Jazz

MONDAY 6TH JULY

SPENCER @TheSpencerRyan
I'm beginning to think @OMGJazzyP has been abducted by aliens!

"For the love of God!"

"What?" Mags looks over her book with an amused expression.

"He tagged me in a tweet."

"So tell him who you are and he'll back off."

"No, I'm not telling him. He'll get bored eventually."

Mags stifles a giggle.

I narrow my eyes at her. "What's so funny?"

"Nothing, I was just thinking how three days ago you'd have loved it that he won't stop tweeting you."

"Yeah, well, things change."

"Really?" Mags replies with a knowing look. "He didn't morph into a two-headed monster since I last checked, did he?"

"Hey! I'm not that shallow. He may be pretty, but he's still an ARSE."

"Maybe it was just the drink?"

"Oh, come on, you don't believe that was just alcohol, do you?"

"All I'm saying is, you don't fool me, you can't just switch it off like that when you like someone."

"I don't like him, like him. He's hot, but the guy's an idiot. Sorry but it's game over. Moving on. If I ever see him again, it will be too soon."

"Well," giggles Mags. "That's going to make this morning a little awkward!"

I snap my head up to meet her eyes.

"What?"

"I don't really know the best way to tell you this, but, it turns out the building firm we've got starting today…it's Will's." I watch her closely, thinking that soon she will steer the subject away from the awful turn I think it's about to take. "I didn't know, Dad didn't tell me. But there's more."

I sigh. "Spit it out,"

"Spencer is his partner."

"Spencer is his what?"

"You heard me."

"No, no, no! Spencer is an architect, he wears a suit. He's not a brickie."

"I got the scoop yesterday. He is a structural engineer. But he doesn't like commuting and he likes to work outside and get his hands dirty. Office life was making him miserable. He and Will used to work together in Australia, they enjoyed it, so they decided to start doing it again here. Soooo…starting in thirty minutes, he'll be working here."

"And you're just telling me this now?"

Mags nods.

"What the hell? Why didn't you tell me when you found out?"

"Because you'd have been out of here like a shot."

"So you were keeping me here under false pretences?"

"No, I'm just not giving you the time to run away." She shrugs. "Who knows, maybe you'll get on when he's not plastered."

"No thanks."

"Just relax and see how it goes."

"Mags, it's not happening."

"Oh, you know it will, so save your breath."

"I'm serious. I am not spending an hour with that man. Not one."

I hear the van pull up on the gravel driveway. My heart sinks. This is going to suck. But I don't want to be stuck upstairs all day just because I'm avoiding him. I'll be better off getting it over with and then ignoring the arsehole. Taking a deep breath, I make my way down the hall to the top of the stairs. That's when I see him through the big picture window that runs the double height of the stairway.

I've seen him in his to die for suit, and dressed for a night out. But this...dressed for a day's hard graft...rawr! Ok, I can't look at him like that anymore. He's a dickhead.

But look at his T-shirt, so tight over his body, screaming for the attention he so desires. His tattooed arm rests on the side of their van. I saw some of that ink on Saturday night, but to be honest I wasn't in the mood to appreciate it. But here, where I can stare without being seen. It's as good as I hoped, if not better.

God, I want to lick it.

Pull yourself together woman! He looks like sex, but he'll taste like jackass! I just need to keep my head and remember to kill Mags later.

Like a condemned woman, I walk down the stairs, watching him chatting to Will, trying not to notice how his hair looks in the morning sun. As I reach the bottom of the stairs, Mags opens the front door and they both look up, right as I come in to view.

"Oh, fuck me," he glances at Will and from the look of shock, and the way Will stifles a laugh, I can tell this was just sprung on him too.

Spencer
MONDAY 6TH JULY

I'm going to kill him.
Look at her. She can't even look at me. As I suspected, she wants me and fuck if she isn't smoking hot. This is my problem; I have the opposite of beer goggles. When I drink, I don't really register how hot girls are. I mean, I see that they're hot, but they are just that and nothing more. I don't see their beauty when I'm drunk, I don't see how desirable they are, until I see them in the light of day. Sometimes it makes it that much harder to leave in the morning, but sticking around really isn't my thing.
This girl is amazing though; curvy, beautiful and she hates me. The deadliest of combinations. She has clearly made no effort whatsoever, maybe she didn't know I'd be here, or more likely, she just didn't care. She's wearing old fraying denim shorts that show off her thighs and fuck me, what thighs they are. Her lived in T-shirt hides the rest, but I can tell she has one of those ripe, juicy bodies that make me want to bite. She's incredible, even with her hair all piled up and hardly any makeup. If she wasn't such a bitch, she'd be in big trouble.
I realise I'm staring and she gives me a look of disgust and disappears into the vast house. Typical rich girl, too good for

the help. Mags on the other hand, comes out and wanders over to Will. They have a quiet chat while I start to unload with the rest of the boys.

"I assume you knew about this?" I grumble at Will as he joins us to finish unloading.

"Obviously I knew who the job was for. But I didn't know Mags and her friend would be here for the summer."

"For the whole summer? Fucking hell."

"What are you complaining about? She hates you, she'll keep as far away from you as possible."

I look back at the house. Yeah, she will, won't she? Shit, that's going to make it worse.

"Oh, no! Spencer, you keep away from her as well. This is a huge job for us, you will not screw it up because some girl with a great arse hates you and you can't resist a challenge."

I grin at him and carry on moving tools.

Once we're settled and had a short meeting so everyone knows what they're doing, Mags and her apparently unwilling assistant bring out a couple of trays of tea.

"Do you mind?" she snaps.

"Huh?" Fuck, I was staring.

"Don't you know it's rude to stare?"

"I was not staring."

"You're looking at me like I'm your next meal. I believe I already wasted a glass of Pinot telling you to keep your hands to yourself, don't push me again." Some of the guys try to hide their amusement.

What is with this chick? She doesn't even know me; it normally takes them way longer to hate me this much.

"Oh, calm down, Princess, I have no interest in getting my

retinas burned out again. You're nothing special, you know."

She laughs and shakes her head. "Back at ya."

"Well, we both know that isn't true," I smirk.

"Oh, my God!! You are unbelievable!"

"Hey, just telling it like it is. I'm hot and you know it." I try to take the tray of tea from her, but she has it in a vice-like grip.

"I can manage," she snaps.

"Calm down, precious, I was only trying to help," I step back and let her put the tray down and when she looks up, I smile and wink.

She lets out an exasperated "Ugh!" Then storms off.

This round goes to me.

I flop down on my bed after a tough first day on the job and check my phone again. Still nothing from Shoegirl. It's been a couple of days. I'm not bothered, I can talk to other girls, but I don't want to. Not even the couple that I still play with in DMs occasionally. I wonder if Shoegirl DMs with anyone? The idea of that has me scrolling through her timeline, looking for clues. She doesn't talk to that many guys, but she's quite flirtatious; there are a couple who encourage it, I bet they take it further…Yeah, ok. I'm a little bothered.

Screw it!

SPENCER @TheSpencerRyan
@OMGJazzyP Where are you? I had a long day, I need you to make me smile…

I wait and wait and wait. I'm starting to wonder if it's something I've done to upset her, because I'm good at that. I've never been anything but nice to her though. But I notice she has been tweeting for the last few days, just not to me. I want to ask her, but not only would that make me a complete pussy, I don't know her well enough. I'll try something else...

SPENCER @TheSpencerRyan
MISSING SINCE FRIDAY - Have you seen the owner of these shoes? Reward offered for her safe return @OMGJazzyP pic.twitter.com/kleeufeg34

I grin, then catch myself. What the fuck am I turning in to? I'm no better than these girls who stalk me. Fuck this! I switch on the TV and distract myself. I finally find a good film and try to forget about Twitter for the night, when my phone chirps beside me. I pick it up straight away.

I know. Pussy.

JAZZ @OMGJazzyP
@TheSpencerRyan Wow! I'm here. I don't know whether to be flattered or freaked out? Do you stalk all your women like this?

Do I stalk all my women? Cheeky bitch! What has got up the female population's nose today?

SPENCER @TheSpencerRyan
@OMGJazzyP I was just concerned that's all. I thought maybe you needed urgent medical help.

JAZZ @OMGJazzyP
@TheSpencerRyan Just because I'm not tweeting you does not automatically mean I must be sick. I do have a life you know!

SPENCER @TheSpencerRyan
@OMGJazzyP I don't doubt it sweetheart. I just miss your shoes on my TL.

God, her too? Why are they all so moody today? I could have let rip, but it isn't her that pissed me off.

JAZZ @OMGJazzyP
@TheSpencerRyan My shoes or my adoration?

SPENCER @TheSpencerRyan
@OMGJazzyP Both.

JAZZ @OMGJazzyP
@TheSpencerRyan That's quite an ego you have there.

She's feisty tonight.

SPENCER @TheSpencerRyan
@OMGJazzyP Thanks I think it suits me.

JAZZ @OMGJazzyP
@TheSpencerRyan Of course you do.

SPENCER @TheSpencerRyan
@OMGJazzyP Oh don't you start with me.

JAZZ @OMGJazzyP
@TheSpencerRyan Haha! Please, you'd know if I was starting with you. What's up? I thought you had a quiet, relaxing weekend.

SPENCER @TheSpencerRyan
@OMGJazzyP I did. How about you? How was yours?

JAZZ @OMGJazzyP
@TheSpencerRyan I went to the pub Saturday night. It was rubbish. The pub was full of douchebags!

SPENCER @TheSpencerRyan
@OMGJazzyP That sucks babe, but it can't be as bad as what I've had to deal with today, I promise you!

JAZZ @OMGJazzyP
@TheSpencerRyan Oh? Tough day?

SPENCER @TheSpencerRyan
@OMGJazzyP You could say that, I had the bitchiest client ever, total pain in the arse.

JAZZ @OMGJazzyP
@TheSpencerRyan Maybe you just didn't click.

SPENCER @TheSpencerRyan

@OMGJazzyP Or maybe she is just a spoiled little princess. Either way, I hope she keeps her distance.

JAZZ @OMGJazzyP
@TheSpencerRyan Maybe it's you?

SPENCER @TheSpencerRyan
@OMGJazzyP Seriously, is there a global PMS warning I missed? What is up with women today?

JAZZ @OMGJazzyP
@TheSpencerRyan Don't get your knickers in a twist!

This is going down hill fast, I don't get my knickers in a twist. I glance down at my black boxers and my bare legs stretched out on the bed and smile.

SPENCER @TheSpencerRyan
@OMGJazzyP Relax babe, my 'knickers' are smooth, see... pic.twitter.com/oy90a86JK3

I laugh out loud at the thought of her and half the girls that follow me, taking a screenshot of the image.
You're welcome girls!
Then I realise what I should have said and kick myself for not thinking fast enough. It might be a bit much for her anyway; I don't know how far I can push it with her, especially on the timeline. But in private might be different, I guess there's only one way to find out, I open up a direct message

'They're a little too smooth, maybe you want to help me change that?'

'OMG are you serious?'

'No one in here but you and me, it could be fun'

'You're for real!! Is this something you do a lot?'

'Not really'

Fucking ages goes by, I guess that's a no then. I close the app and relax back into the pillow. After the day I've had, am I really surprised? They're nuts, the lot of them.

'So Mr. 'Doesn't really do it a lot,' how does this work?'

Holy shit! She's up for it.

'Have you never had phone sex before? It's just like that.'

'I'm not even going to ask how often you have phone sex.'

'It happens.'

'I'm sure it does.'

'If you don't want to, that's fine.'

'I didn't say that, did I?'

'No, you didn't.'

'But I think the moment has passed now, don't you?'

'*Grabbing your hand and pulling you close* I don't think it has. *I kiss your neck, breathing in your scent and feel you shiver*'

'Wow, um, ok…'

'You don't like?'

'I haven't done this before and clearly you have.'

I don't want her backing out now, I need to show her it can be fun. It's annoying that Twitter makes you stick to their 140 character limit, even in private messages, but oh well, here goes...

'Shhh, I'll talk, just go with it. *Kissing your neck and running my hand up into your hair, I wind it into my fist and use it to ease your'

'Head back. Licking and sucking my way up your throat until I finally reach your lips. I graze them with my teeth, then slide my tongue'

'Between them as they part for me. You taste perfect, I want to taste all of you. I break the kiss, just to lift your dress over your

'Head and discard it on the floor. Stepping back I take in the sight of you in your underwear and those fuck-me-heels of yours. You go to'

'Step out of your heels and I tell you to leave them on. They look INCREDIBLE! Moving closer I press myself against you so you can

'feel what just looking at you does to me. I groan at the contact and I fight the urge to bend you over my bed and take you right now.'

'Fuck!'

'Jazz?'

'Yeah?'

'Are you touching yourself?'

There is a really long pause.

'Yes.'

'Good'

'Kissing you again, this time with more urgency, I walk you backwards to the bed and guide you to where I want you, my tongue still'

'exploring you. Moving lower I tease your nipples through your bra, but I don't stop there long, because I need to taste you again. I lick'

'my way down to your underwear and pause, you look so sexy in them but they've got to go. I work them down your hips and lift your legs'

'to slide them off. I can't help but want to lick those heels on your feet and you moan with pleasure when I do. Smiling down at you laying'

'before me, I pull your arse to the edge of the bed and wrap your legs around my shoulders so I can claim my prize. I feather my tongue'

'across your clit and your hips buck in response, you taste so sweet, I need more of you.*'

'Oh God!'

'You ok?'

'Uh huh'

'Keep going?'

'Uh huh'

'You still touching?'

'Uh huh'

I grin with satisfaction as I stroke my hard cock again through my boxers. I can't touch and type, but it's going to be good when I do. I need to finish this so I can get to it.

'*I slip my tongue between your folds and

lick a long trail through, back up to your clit again, over and over I lap up your juices'

'teasing your clit with each stroke. Your thighs tighten around my head and I feel your sharp heels digging into my back. This is what'

'I've been fantasising about. You moan with longing each time my tongue reaches into your depths so I slide my hand between us and ease'

'two fingers into you, turning my tongue's attention to your clit. Your fingers slide into my hair and tighten as you pull me even closer.'

'you grind yourself against me, desperate for more friction so I suck hard on your clit and work my fingers faster into you. Your back'

'arches off the bed as you moan my name. I'm rock hard and hearing my name like that makes my cock ache. I stroke it with my free hand,'

'knowing it won't take much to finish me.*

Please...*you gasp as I lap harder and faster at your clit. You pull on my hair and your whole'

'body tenses around me. I feel the bite of your heels in my flesh and hear your cry as your orgasm rips through you.*'

Waiting for her to say something, I push my boxers down and ease myself out, slowly stroking my cock and thinking about whether she came or not. Finally my phone chirps.

'You really have done that before'

'Maybe, did it do the trick?'

'Wouldn't you like to know?'

'I would actually, I could do with the visual so I'm not left hanging.'

'Hmmm, maybe you need more than that...'

'Oh?'

'Maybe it's my turn to turn you on?'

'I'm already turned on babe'

'Alright, to finish it'

           'Knock yourself out sweetheart, I'll be here, I just need my hands!'

There is a long pause, I assume while she works up the nerve to try this. Then finally she's back.

'I come down from the high of the fantastic orgasm you just gave me And focus on you. Your eyes are full of need as you rise above me and'

'kiss me deeply. I taste myself on your tongue, it's sexy, you taste like lust and it makes me want you more. You stand, maybe to make your'

'next move on me, but I halt you with my shoe on your chest. You look at my Louboutin pressing into your skin and continue to stroke'

'yourself. I push forward and ease you back a step. Your eyes close and you sigh with pleasure as my heel digs in'

           'Damn'

'You like the shoe thing, don't you?'

'You have no idea. Keep going'

'I get slowly to my feet and stand before you. Unhooking my bra, I hold it out to the side and let it slip from my fingers and fall to the'

'Floor. Your eyes are heavy with desire as you watch me twirl my fingers around my nipples. I step towards you and press my naked'

'body against yours as I take your mouth in a deep kiss. Your hand moves between us, still stroking your length and I trail my kisses'

'down your neck, determined now to taste you. First, I run my tongue over the ink on your skin, something I've wanted to do since I first'

'laid eyes on you. I groan, it's so damned hot, but I don't linger, your hand is moving faster and your breathing is strained, you won't'

'last long and I want you in my mouth. I consider getting to my knees, but isn't that what good girls do? Bad girls bend at the waist right?

'Fuck'

Bloody hell Shoegirl, you sure can talk the talk. My hand grips tighter and moves faster, keeping up with her story. The image I had in my head of her now enhanced by knowing how her dirty little mind works, I bet she's an incredible fuck. I moan at the thought.

'I lower myself until I can lick the glistening head of your cock, you groan as my tongue makes contact and curse under your breath as'

'my lips close around the head. I place my hands on your hips and your hand falls away as I take you all the way in, in one slow smooth'

'motion. Cursing again, you sweep my hair into one hand to get a better view and cup my chin with the other. With a firm grip on me, you

'start to move, cautiously at first, but as I accept you deeper and deeper, you abandon your caution and take your pleasure from me.'

'A tear runs down my cheek taking with it a streak of mascara as I fight my urge to gag, but just when I worry I can't take any more of you,'

'you erupt into my mouth, shouting my name and staggering from the force of your orgasm.'

I'm so close, I can hardly take a breath, I can feel it coming as my balls tighten, then she sends me over the edge with her final comment

'I greedily swallow every drop as you hold me tightly in place.'

My cock jerks in my hand as I come, I moan as I shoot onto my chest in thick strands, pooling in the grooves of my abs. I shudder. Fuck me, that was amazing. I've done it before, got worked up with a girl in DMs, but I usually store it in the wank bank for later. That's definitely the first time I've come along with the story. Fuck she's good!

'Are you still there?'

Still panting, I type…

'Just about.'

'Sorry'

'Don't be, that was fantastic!'

'So, did you?'

'Come? Hell yes I did, but did you?'

'Yeah'

'Good.'

'I can't believe we just did that.'

'Next time, I want inside you ok?'

'Next time?'

'Trust me, after that, there will be a next time'

Oh, yeah, we're doing that again. My hot little Shoegirl will be getting me through working around the princess of bitches.

Jazz
TUESDAY 7TH JULY

I whimper into my pillow and pull the covers further over my head. I still can't get past what I did last night. Seriously, what was I thinking? I was just so mad at him for being all cocky and the ongoing disappointment of him not being how I hoped. He drives me crazy. It's worse than I thought, actually having to spend time near him, because I want to do nasty things to him. I can't help it. He's all I've been thinking about, and however much of an arse I now know he is, when I see him, smell him, I want to bite him. But I also want to strangle him, and not in the good way. I'm so angry.

In many ways, that's not his fault. He didn't know I had high expectations; he doesn't even know who I am. But seriously though, where does he get off faking a decent personality for the sake of followers when he's really a walking dick? Which brings me back to the question, what the hell was I doing last night?

I was so irritated by him, I had to go for a long walk to calm down. Then I had to hide out upstairs and stay away from the window until they left. And later when I had practically forgotten about him, he started tweeting me, acting like nothing had changed. For him, though, nothing had, and I was so jealous. I miss our tweets, I wanted that again. It was so stupid, I'm no better than him really, but I just thought screw it, I'll pretend. Then when he direct messaged me, oh God, I should have told him no. I should have walked away. I thought it was a ridiculous idea. But then he was good.

I felt like I deserved just one time with my fantasy. I know, I know, it wasn't real; that's the worst thing about it really. Cyber sex??? Really? I mean, come on, that's not me. Apparently I'm not above it though, and it's pretty evident that he makes a habit of it. So now, not only have I sold out for some virtual action with 'THE Spencer Ryan,' I'm just one in a long list.

I feel dirty.

Having come to my senses after it was over, I showered for an hour, so I can't really be dirty, but it sure feels like I'll never get this shame off my skin.

I need to clear my head, so, reluctantly, I haul my arse out of bed and throw on my workout gear. I don't think it's ever seen this much action, but I'm not working. I have to do something other than sit around eating biscuits.

It's late, I slept in, so I let myself out quietly. I don't want to attract Mags' attention. I really don't want to have the 'what's up with you this morning?' conversation. I can NEVER tell Mags what I did last night. She won't get it, it makes me look like a freak. I am a freak. Doing that stuff is all very well, but doing it with someone you know you hate, just because they are acting like someone you like…it's just fucked up.

After ensuring I am out of view and won't run into him, I do a quick warm up, then I put my headphones in, jog down the long drive and turn out onto the street, settling quickly into my stride. The cool of the morning and the lush green everywhere settles me and I decide to take a different route than last time. I'm pretty certain it will circle around the village and bring me back through the centre of it. But I really don't care where it takes me as long as it looks like this.

Thirty-something minutes later, I smile with satisfaction as the pond comes into view. Slowing my pace to a walk as I reach the edge of the green, I stop for a few minutes and stretch out. I want to buy a few things at the shop and I may stop for a cup of tea. Anything to prolong my time away from dickhead. I am starting to think I should just go home. There's no point in me being here if I'm not enjoying myself. I should look for a job, my savings won't last forever.

Mags would freak if I did that, she hasn't even started working on me about this shop she's seen, I think she's trying to give me a little break to relax first. I'm sure I can learn to tune him out and enjoy myself; I just need to let it go. With my hair re-tied so that I don't look a sweaty mess, I head for the shops.

Of course he's here, of course. Getting lunch, right this second, while I'm here avoiding him at the house. Because the universe hates me and I have obviously done only evil in my previous lives. I can't turn around and choose a different aisle because he's seen me; all I can do is ignore him. I stop to look at the yoghurt, hoping he'll pass me by, but instead I feel his presence behind me like a drooling, snarling monster in a horror movie, breathing down my neck. Except he smells fantastic. Fuck! A shiver travels silently down my spine as I wait for him to make his move or go away.

"Been for a run?"

A glance down at my sweaty running gear, "Wow, nothing gets by you."

His lascivious gaze falls to where I have just drawn his attention, his grin widens. "You cold, or just happy to see me?"

Mother. Fucker.

My nipples are just begging for attention. Why me? Why here? We're in the refrigerated aisle and I'm all sweaty, of course they've reacted. Now he thinks it's for him! "Don't flatter yourself, jackass."

"Uh huh," he grins a stupid, crooked grin that makes me want to slap him, because it makes me want to kiss him. Ugh! I really can't be around him.

"Trust me, it will be a cold day in hell before I have this reaction for you."

He shakes his head and begins to turn away, "Sure thing, Princess."

"Hey!" I yell, I didn't mean to, but rage just boiled over. "Don't call me that."

"Well, you are, aren't you? Spoiled little rich girl, bad attitude, the name fits you perfectly. Prin-cess." He irritatingly enunciates both syllables.

"You know nothing about me."

"Ha! I know you're a princess, Princess."

"Go to hell," I snarl, and I turn and stomp away.

"Good chat," he calls out after me. Shaking, I toss my empty basket back onto the pile as I storm out of the store and onto the street. I'm so mad I could cry. I break into a jog and head for home.

Running up the big stone steps at the front of the house I open the door and let it shut loudly behind me. I hear Mags call out my name from the kitchen, but I take the stairs two at a time and go straight to my room. I'm already under the hot shower when Mags makes her way into my bathroom.

"Jazz?"

"Yeah?" I try not to sound like a crazy person who didn't break stride from her jog until she was under the shower and is still out of breath.

"You ok? I was calling you."

"Yeah, I was just really gross from my run, I wanted to shower."

"Ok, I'll um, see you in a little bit." I can hear in her voice that she thinks something's up, but I don't have the energy to discuss it. I wouldn't even know what to say. I'm so ridiculous letting him get to me like that. The truth is I loved that man. Not LOVE loved, I've only known who he is a couple of weeks. But total infatuation loved.

So, finding him to be how he really is feels like I've been played. I know I haven't, not really, but I don't know how else to feel. He led me on. He let me think one thing, when something else is the reality and I feel stupid and disappointed. Then there's the rage I feel when he shows his true self. Totally disproportionate, I know, but I can't help it. He didn't promise me anything, it was just a little online fun, but I'd give anything to go back a week and not come here. I'd have been happy not knowing the truth and worshipping him from afar.

I turn off the water and step out of the shower. All I want to do now is go back to bed. I can't face Mags and her questions and I can't face going out there again, knowing he is around. I hear my phone as I wrap the towel around myself. It is still zipped inside the running gear I shed as I ran into the bathroom. I'm irritated by the excitement that flutters in my belly. I can't do this any longer; I'm going to have to tell him. It's either that, or treat him as two different people. Have fun with him on Twitter and avoid him while I'm here.

I laugh at myself as I gather my clothes and carry them to the laundry basket, taking out my phone as I do. As if it could be that easy to separate the two. I'd still know.

No, I need to tell him to leave me alone. I look down at the screen. Shit, he's tweeted me.

SPENCER @TheSpencerRyan
@OMGJazzyP Get your shoes onto my TL

I sigh. This is a shitty situation. I've just got to get it done and move on. I take a deep breath and open up my direct messages. I open my previous night's conversation with him. My stomach lurches a little when I see the last few messages.

'Next time, I want inside you ok?'

'Next time?'

'Trust me, after that, there will be a next time'

I don't think so buddy! I type a message.

'I'm here.'

A few long moments pass and I start to regret looking so eager, then a message comes through making me jump.

'Straight into DMs, sweetheart? You're making my day! *Grabbing your arse and pressing you against me, kissing you urgently*

I sit on the bed and blink at the screen, holy shit! No, no, this isn't how it's supposed to go, I start typing words to that effect, when another message comes through.

'Miss me babe? *Slipping my hand inside your underwear and sinking my fingers into your soaked pussy* I think you have.

As my head is saying 'fuck no,' my traitorous clit comes alive. I can feel the aching throb starting. I need to get rid of him; I can't do this again.

'We can't do this again.'

'Says who? We're just having fun aren't we? *Circling my thumb around your aching clit*

Fucker!

'*Plunging two fingers inside you* I can stop if you want me to.'

I…I, fuck! I don't want him to stop. I'll loathe myself afterwards, but it's still going to happen.

'*Feeling your growing cock pressing against me, wondering how it will feel inside me* No, don't stop.'

'Babe, you had me worried for a minute. *Pulling my fingers out of you, I pick you up and carry you to the bed, throwing you down*'

'*Crawling over you.* I've had a hell of a morning, how about you help me work out my frustrations?'

I sink back against my pillows. Though I hate to admit it, the thought of him crawling over me, sends a thrill through me. His muscled arms, the tattoos, fuck it…

'*Running my hand over your cock through your underwear* These need to go. *Tugging at the waist band*'

'Hmm, They're gone…but yours too, yeah? Off! But leave the shoes on'

'*Shimmying out of my underwear as you do the same, I reach down to stroke your hard cock* You love the shoes don't you?'

'*Stifling a moan when you touch me, I swallow hard* God that feels amazing and, yes, the shoes are fucking hot.'

'Hahaha!'

'What's so funny?'

'You don't even know if I'm wearing fucking shoes, and you're carrying on about how hot they are.'

'Hush you! I'm imagining a lovely image, don't ruin it with all this talk of reality. *Closes eyes and brings back the image.*'

'What are you imagining?'

'That'd be telling.'

'Tell me!'

'Ok, you asked for it. I'm imagining black suede, high, really high. The kind with the platform…and a peep toe.'

Oh my God, I have some just like that. I leap up and go to the wardrobe praying I brought them with me, I can't remember what I packed, as I was in the middle of an adrenaline rush. I pull back the sliding door and there they are!

Spencer

One of many pairs I brought with me, which in hindsight is ridiculous, as I have only worn trainers or socks since I arrived. Well, there was that one night I wore heels, the night I met the jackass. There he goes creeping into my head again. I push him out so I can focus on the shoes. Picking them up, I head back to the bed and check my phone again. There's another message.

'In my head you're wearing them with black stockings and suspenders and nothing else.'

As I'm reading it, another message drops through.

'Don't go quiet on me. You asked to hear what was in my head.'

'I'm not quiet, I was looking for something.'

'What?'

I take a deep breath, here goes. I slip the shoes on, feeling a little silly in a towel and Louboutins. I let the towel fall and sit on the edge of the bed. I don't have stockings, but my legs are smooth, so I select the camera on my phone and take a picture. Once I have a shot, I open up his message again and reply, adding the picture to the message.

'These.'

A few moments pass.

'Damn!'

'I mean, DAMN!'

'You have the exact shoes I was imagining.'

'Shit, that's unbelievable.'

'Will you marry me?'

'Lol, Careful. You can't just go saying that to random girls. Someday, someone will take you up on it and then you'll be fucked.'

'Babe, I'm serious, this is some Cinderella shit. You have to be mine, fate is telling us something here.'

Oh God, this is nice and all, but we're losing sight of what we're doing here. I want the fun. I type out a reply to get things moving.

'Sure, well you can think that, but I'm no Cinderella and this ain't no fairytale. Now, weren't we in the middle of something?'

'I'm enjoying talking about your fucking hot shoes for a minute. What else are you wearing babe?'

'Nothing.'

'STFU! Now I know you're fucking with me.'

'It's the truth.'

'You're just laying around in the middle of the day, naked, in heels?'

'No, I just showered and I put the heels on to show you.'

'Show me.'

'Show you that I'm naked? No goddamn way!'

'Oh, come on, just a peep.'

'Yeah, I don't think so.'

'Tease.'

'This was a bad idea, I'll catch you later.'

'Jazz wait.'

'What?'

'Don't go, you're right, I shouldn't have asked.'

'Ok.'

'Now where were we?'

'I'm kinda not in the mood now.'

'No problem babe, *moves in beside you on your bed* I can help you get back in the mood.'

'No really, it's gone. Maybe we should just talk later.'

'*Trailing my fingers over your bare hip and down to where your warm wet pussy is still waiting for me* Don't go Jazz, I want to have some'

'Fun with you. *Watching you closely as I slide my fingers back to where they were when you decided you wanted me inside of you.'

'How does this feel?' *circling your clit*'

Damn, just when I was going to walk away. Sighing, I close my eyes and imagine his fingers slowly stroking me, his muscled arm around me...

'It feels good.'

'It feels amazing, babe, you know it does.'

I bet it would feel amazing; I sink into my fantasy, before I can judge myself again.

'You're so wet babe, you want me, don't you?'

'Yes'

'Is that the best you can do? Tell me what you want.'

'I want you to fuck me.'

'*Moving in closer behind you, my cock presses against your pussy from behind.* You want this?'

'Yes.'

'*Whispers* Tell me.'

'I want you to fill me.'

'You can do better than that.'

'I want you to fill me with your hard cock. I want to feel you.'

'Good girl. *Still rubbing your clit, I slide inside you, just a little.* Like this babe?'

'Uh huh.'

'You want more?'

'Yes. I want it all.'

'*Pulling back, I push forward and fill you with my whole length, pausing all the way inside you, whispering in your ear* Like this?'

'*Gasping as you thrust fully into me and stop, still playing with my clit.* Yes like that, do it again.'

'This? * Sliding out almost all the way and pushing back in.'

'Yes, more, don't stop.'

'*My fingers still working your clit, I wrap you tight in my other arm and start to fuck you with deep long strokes.* You're so wet.'

'*Groans*'

'You like that, do you?'

'Yes.'

'You like to hear how wet and tight you are?'

'God, yes.'

'How I'm going to fuck you every way I can?'

'Uh huh.'

'*Pulling at your hard little nipple. I whisper.* I'm gonna do dirty things to you, every chance I get.'

'*Pumping faster into you now, I feel you begin to tense around me.* Come for me, Jazz'

'Oh fuck, *I'm right there and your words

trigger it. I come hard and my pussy tightens around your cock, I can feel you tense behind me'

'and hold me tighter so you can slam into me one last time.*'

'*I bite into the perfect skin on your shoulder as my release rips through me.*'

My legs tremble as I slide my fingers away from my over sensitised clit. God, that man's words do something to me. I can't believe what I'm doing here. I can't believe he's made me come again, only an hour after I wanted to smack him face to face. But I want this. I want this to wash away the rest of it. I can pretend meeting Spencer Ryan never happened and that other 'thing' I met is just the local jackass. I never thought I'd do something like this, but in my fantasy of what he was really like, this guy, the one with the words, is what I was hoping for. I'll be damned if the local jackass is going to spoil my illusion.

There is a light tap on the door and I leap up and grab my towel. Kicking off the shoes and securing the towel around me, I clear my throat and call out, "Come in."

Mags appears in the doorway. "Are you ok?"

"I'm fine." I glance guiltily at the rumpled bed and run my fingers through my damp hair. "I was just deciding what to wear."

"Ok, I just wanted to let you know that I made us some lunch, whenever you're ready."

"Thanks, I'll just throw something on and be down in a

minute."

Mags smiles at me, but I can tell she still thinks something's up. "Ok," she says and leaves me to get dressed.

I pick up the discarded shoes and put them back on the rack in the wardrobe. Staring at the rest of the collection I brought with me, I smirk; Spencer would love all these. Shit! Spencer! I dash back to the bed and grab my phone. I've missed a couple of messages.

'That was hot Jazz.'

'You still there?'

'Sorry, my roommate came in. I'm here.'

'Oh ok, I thought you bailed on me.'

'No, but I do have to go.'

'Sure, well maybe I'll catch you later?'

'Sure.'

I go back to the wardrobe and pull out some jeans and a sweater, it's a nice enough day, but I feel like some comfort. Mags came in and shattered the illusion. It's not her fault, but now I just feel weird. I feel bad that I just ditched him like that too. This is a fucked up situation.

Spencer
TUESDAY 7TH JULY

She seemed to bail on that pretty fast. Maybe all the talk was too much, my mouth always seems to get me into trouble. Still I got a picture out of it, I think, glancing down at my phone again. Pity it's just the feet, but fuck me! Those shoes are straight out of my wet dreams and there they are on my dirty little Shoegirl's feet...while I'm making her wet. For real.

She is pretty much my ideal woman. I almost don't want to know what she really looks like, it might ruin my fantasy.

Yeah, I know, I'm shallow.

I'm just heading back to work at the house after a slightly prolonged lunch when I hear my phone in my back pocket.

It's from her.

A picture.

Fuck me.

It's not her, but damn, she gets it. It's a girl with those 'go-on-forever' legs, leaning against a dirty brick wall. Hands on hips. You can't see her top half, but the bottom half, wow.

Barely there stockings, with blood red tops, black suspenders, luscious curvy hips, mile long legs and red platform stilettos. Shiny ones.

The message reads, 'Sorry I had to go, I had fun. Here's something to keep you going until next time x'

Fucking GET IN!!!

Spencer
WEDNESDAY 8TH JULY

After laying here in a semi-sleep for what feels like forever, my eyes finally open, damn. I glance at the clock, 4am. Shit. I'm never going to get back to sleep. I don't know what disturbed me, but I know what's on my mind, preventing me from switching off. Shoegirl.

She won't agree to meet me, won't tell me where she is, and I don't want to push her away by pressing the issue, but it's driving me mad. Fuck, every time we talk, driving is all I can think about. Not driving her away, driving into her tight little hole. And wondering how close she is is making it worse. I don't ever want to meet them, most of them don't even live in this country, but something about this one is different.

Reaching down, I wrap my hand around my morning wood. Pah! Morning, that's a joke. It's not even dawn, but unlike the sun, my cock has risen at the thought of my Shoegirl in my bed. I wish I could just pull her to me and sink into her right now. I'd do her slow, like the stroke of my hand. My breath catches as an idea forms. She needs to know I think about her. I need to share this with her.

Jazz

WEDNESDAY 8TH JULY

Returning from the bathroom, I check the time on my phone and frown when I see lots of messages from Spencer, the last one two hours ago. What the hell? It's barely even light out. Too intrigued to be annoyed, I open them and scroll back to find where they start.

'It's 4am, I don't know what woke me, maybe I was dreaming about you? I guess I was because my cock is wide awake and ready for you.'

'I take it in my hand and work it in long slow strokes. I want you. Right now, reaching across I feel for you, your soft breathing,'

'the only sound in the room. You're facing away from me, sound asleep. My hand falls on your hip and I stroke the soft skin there,'

'before sliding in behind you carefully.

You sigh sleepily as I slip my hand between your legs. You're so wet and ready for me.'

'Maybe you were dreaming too? About me, I hope. Gently lifting your leg and hooking it over mine, I position myself at your slick entrance.'

'You're stirring as I press forward and slide into you from behind. You moan in your sleep, but I can tell you're very close to the surface,'

'so I wrap my arm around your waist and stroke your clit as I start to move. You awake to all the sensations. I'm pressed into your back,'

'holding you tight against me as I thrust my hips in a slow rhythm. Your body starts to move with mine as you become more aware and I moan'

'when the rotation of your hips tightens your pussy around my hard cock. Your whispered "Fuck" as I drive deeper is the first sign I have'

'that you're fully awake. I nuzzle your neck

and lay some kisses there before biting the delicate skin. You sigh and push back into me,'

'your hand reaches round and grabs my hip, encouraging me to work harder. My slow strokes were to wake you gently but that's not what you want'

'now. You want me to welcome you into the day in a way that you will think about every time you walk. I smile, happy that we are in tune that'

'way. Faster, I pound into you, stroking your clit until you're begging for release. I slow my touch to stop you getting there, but drive'

'deeper into you to keep you tantalisingly close. Your little gasps as I bury myself deep are so fucking hot, my little reward for hitting'

'the spot. I circle your clit and you clench around me. With that, I can't wait any longer to feel you come undone. I allow my fingers to'

'give you what you've been waiting for and

when you let go, calling my name, I cum deep inside you.'

'Good morning Jazz, I hope your dreams were as sweet as mine.'

I'm speechless.

How can the person that wrote that be the same person that I met? How? I want him to do that to me, I want to be able to say, "You know what? We should meet."

But I've had a special preview, and the feature performance does not live up to the trailer. In fact, it's a fucking let down. Still, that was amazing to wake up to. I should respond. I don't know how, but I should. Slightly dazed from being confronted by that hotness so early in the day and unable to decide how to respond, I go down to find Mags.

She is up and buzzing around the kitchen. All I can smell is coffee, lots of coffee. She must have been up early too, must be something in the air around here.

"Morning," I yawn.

"Morning."

"Why are you up so early?"

"Don't know, I couldn't sleep. Coffee?"

I giggle, "You sure you haven't drunk it all?"

She rolls her eyes. "I've only had two cups, want some?"

"I'll have tea."

Mags busies herself making the tea while I scroll through the barrage of messages from earlier. She places a mug in front of me and goes back to her laptop with hers. Three times I read through Spencer's messages, still not sure what to do. I'm shocked at how good he is with his words and by the fact that he was thinking of me at four in the morning. And I don't know how to respond to that. It's been ok so far because the conversation has been back and forth. But as this conversation was over and done with before I woke up, I don't really know what to say. 'Thanks?' I wrinkle my nose at the thought. I can't think of anything which isn't patronising or insufficient.

I'll think of something, I hope.

"Come on," Mags says abruptly. I look up to find that while I've been in my own head, she has cleared away the cups and put away her laptop and is standing there looking at me expectantly.

"Come where?"

"We can't just sit here and veg out every day," she says, throwing my gym towel at me.

I catch it and frown. "Speak for yourself, I've been for two runs since I've been here." Mags raises her eyebrows. I sigh. "Fine, they were mostly brisk walks. But the point is, I haven't been vegging out."

"Please Jazz, just come down and if you don't feel like working out, you could swim."

"Fine!" I sulk. "But you can deal with Jackass. He's working for you. I'm not going to even look at him."

"We'll see," she smirks.

"I fucking hate you sometimes, you know?"

Mags throws her head back and laughs her evil laugh. "No you don't, you love me. Now get your arse into the gym."

Mags' dad takes his fitness very seriously. His gym is better equipped than the one I pay to attend (occasionally).

Their pool and hot tub are my idea of heaven and he's even got a sauna and a steam room. I have to admit, it's the perfect way to spend the morning, but damn it, there he is working and of course we have to walk straight past them to get to the pool.

They are just breaking ground on a large extension to the former stable block which now houses the pool, gym and a games room. Once they are done, a series of rooms and a covered indoors/outdoors area will join the block to the main house and complete the extensive renovation to the house.

For now, though, we have to walk past the dickhead. The same dickhead who blew me away this morning with his smooth words. This is so fucked up. But I see him and my hackles rise. I immediately want to be vile.

I make eye contact with him as I approach and wait while he ramps up his ridiculous shit-eating grin. Then, when he's at full megawatt, I put my headphones in, and walk right past him. I catch the fall of his smug-arsed smile and laugh to myself as I walk away. I can hear Mags saying, 'morning' but I drown the rest out with some great running music courtesy of Thirty Seconds to Mars.

In the zone ten minutes later, listening to Mr. Leto tell me he's going to wrap his hands around my neck with love…yes fucking please…I become aware of the jackass watching. He isn't even trying to hide it. He's just staring through the glass wall from where he is working. He really has no shame, I want to get off the treadmill and move to where he can't see me, but my stubborn streak kicks in and I won't allow him to win.

Slowing to a walk because I'm distracted and accident prone, which is a terrible combination, I try to reign in my

Spencer

anger. I don't know who he thinks he is. For a second, I don't even associate him with Spencer; it's becoming frighteningly easy to separate the two. But the reality again creeps in, accompanied by the feeling of disappointment.

I pound the treadmill in a brisk stomp; I'm out of the zone now, thanks to him. Opening up my phone to change my music, I then go to my Twitter app without thinking and open our private conversation.

Those words!

I feel an involuntary clench just thinking about them. Scrolling back I read through our conversation yesterday, he loved that picture I sent him.

'DAMN! You can keep them coming babe.
Throw in some of yourself, don't be shy.'

'We'll see.'

I had no intention of sending any more of me; I sent him something in apology for rushing off so quickly. It wasn't of me, just one I thought he would like, knowing his thing for shoes. But last night after a few glasses of wine with Mags, then a long hot bath, I tried on a few pairs of heels and took a few shots. I shudder now at the thought, there's no way I can send any of them. I don't even know why I took them, it's just not who I am. I just felt brave and sexy and got carried away.

But I'm kinda proud of them, which is, of course, why they're still on my phone, taunting me. 'Oh, Jaaaazz…this is you now…this is what you've become…someone who sends sexy photos to strangers…go on…send him one…send him the one where you can see your freshly shaved pussy behind his favourite shoes…go on…do it.'

No! Oh my God, I can't believe I even thought the words 'freshly shaved pussy,' never mind took a picture of it with the idea of sending it to him of all people, in the back of my mind. I won't do it. I need to delete them. Now.

But as I watch him working, imagining him doing the things he said, I can't quite bring myself to hit 'delete.' He would love them, there's no question.

He's so beautiful when he's not being a jackass. But then he glances my way and catches me watching him. Damn. His face says it all; he sees me watching him, he thinks I want him. But I don't. It's not him I want. It's his damn fine body and a personality about as far removed from his as it's possible to get.

As is now my habit, I click on his name, but as soon as the page loads, I'm pissed off. There he is chatting it up with all the girls. I wonder how many of them have had the pleasure of his verbal skills? Just the thought makes my blood boil. I have no claim to him, but this whole situation is bad enough without thinking I'm sharing him.

I look away and try to focus again, but I'm too annoyed. I don't want him! Why do I have to keep reminding myself of that? I just want a fictional character that looks like him, that's all and I'm ok with that. He's no different. He wants OMGJazzyP.

I look on his timeline and my heart sinks, girl after girl with their 'Morning, Sexy' and their 'Hey, Gorgeous.' He just laps it up, answering each one, being all charming and sweet.

I stand corrected. He wants OMGJazzyP, when he can tear

himself away from all the other girls he entertains.

Maybe she should surprise him at work and refocus his attention?

Hmmm.

I slow the treadmill down a little and glance around to see where Mags is. She is facing the other way and is heavily into what she's doing. Deciding it's safe to open up my photos, I scroll through to see what I have. I can't send him the money shot, I have some dignity, but there are a few here that would set his pulse racing without a full frontal. I pick one that shows me sitting on the floor, knees bent and my feet crossed and drawn close to my body. You can see my feet, legs and the curve of my bottom; it was the next shot when I uncrossed my feet that you could see…everything. But this is just provocative. I took it in front of the full-length mirror and cropped it nicely so that it's anonymous. And I made it black and white. What? So I played with it a little, doesn't mean I planned to send it! Everything looks better in black and white.

Glancing out of the window, I see that he is actually focusing on his work for a moment, it's a good time to send it. I just don't know if I can…

People do really do this. I could be one of those people if I wanted to. It's not like it's hurting anyone…

And it is a great way to thank him for what I woke up to…

Fuck it.

I open our conversation, add the photo, type 'Good morning, Spencer. My dreams were sweet, thank you. x' and hit send.

I quickly put my phone back in the cup holder on my machine and turn it up to a run, so I look busy. I watch him from the corner of my eye; he stops what he's doing and pulls his phone out of his pocket. His face is a picture. I'm so happy that I got to see it. His smile is out of control, and he mutters something under his breath that I can't make out. Then he types something with a grin and puts his phone back in his pocket. I look away, just as he looks around, he doesn't see that I was watching him, he turns his attention back to his work, but I'm happy that for a second I got to see MY Spencer and he has no idea. I glare at my phone, knowing that there is a response waiting, but I'm not checking it now. It can wait.

I don't even allow myself to look at his message until I'm safely back in my room, where the Spencer I lust after still exists.

There is a message.

'O.M.G…JazzyP…I'm speechless!'

I laugh aloud, that's cute.

'It's unlike you to have no words.'

His reply is instant.

'It's not every day a girl sends me a picture like that of herself.'

'What makes you so sure it's me?'

'It's you.'

'And damn. DAMN!'

I grin like an idiot. What. Am. I. Doing?

Spencer
THURSDAY 9TH JULY

The first thing I do when I wake up is look at the pictures now saved on my phone. The first one she sent of her feet, the one from her avi, yeah ok, I know that's sad...and now the one she sent last night.
Wow.
Just wow.
I still can't believe she sent one like that of herself.
She tried to make out like it might not be her, but it damn well is her. Those shoes, I will never forget. But it's that sexy little anklet that gives her away. I noticed it when she sent the first picture. It's fucking sexy. Adjusting myself, I put my phone away before it's too late. I'll be late if I don't get up now. The last thing I want to do is be late. How will I be able to find a way to piss off Princess if I'm not there on time?

Jazz
THURSDAY 9TH JULY

I'm not used to having this much free time. Now I'm starting to see why Mags is always up to no good. I'm bored. Mags is writing and I feel like I've distracted her enough, so I'm trying to stay out of her way today. I don't deal well with having nothing to to do…so I'm thinking of tweeting him. Checking my phone to see if he has been on this morning, I smile.

SPENCER @TheSpencerRyan
I took a hot shower this morning. It's like a regular shower, but it had me in it.

Dear God, the ego on that man. I favourite the tweet though. It's bloody funny.

I can see him working from the window seat in my room. He's sexy when he sweats. I find myself willing him to take his shirt off, but it isn't going to happen all by itself. He needs some gentle persuasion. It's a shame our roles aren't reversed. I'm sure if he was up here and I was down there, he would casually lean out the window, wolf-whistle and yell, 'Show us yer tits!'

I chuckle to myself. As tempting as that sounds, I think I'll just send him a message instead.

JAZZ @OMGJazzyP
I wonder if @TheSpencerRyan is HARD at work today?

I can see from his face he hears or feels his phone in his pocket, but he has his hands full, so it takes him a minute to get to the message.

SPENCER @TheSpencerRyan
@OMGJazzyP No that was yesterday, thanks to you. Evil woman.

JAZZ @OMGJazzyP
@TheSpencerRyan Sorry, it will NEVER happen again.

SPENCER @TheSpencerRyan
@OMGJazzyP Now, let's not be hasty.

Laughing, because it's that easy and feeling a thrill because it's exciting, I open up a direct message.

'So you want me to get you hard at work? I'm confused.'

'Well hello there, Trouble!'

'Hi.'

'How's your day going?'

'Pretty good. How's yours?'

'Better now that I know you were thinking about me.'

'So arrogant!'

'Hey, you tweeted me. You can't deny it.'

'I was just wondering if you were working hard, that's all.'

'Lies. You wanted to get me all horny.'

'And is that a terrible thing?'

'Normally no. It's easy to hide a boner under a desk, but I'm working out in the open at the moment.'

'Good to know. So, what is it that you do? What am I going to get you fired from for lewd behaviour?'

Of course I know what he's doing, I can see him. But he doesn't know that, so the more I can get him to tell me the easier it will be. I may as well find stuff out while I get the chance.

'Haha! It's really boring.'

'Really? I find that very hard to believe.'

'Well I enjoy it, but for most people, it's boring.'

'Try me.'

'I'm a structural engineer.'

'Oh.'

'See, dull as shit, I told you.'

'No, not at all, but why aren't you working in the office right now?'

'Because even I got bored! I'm back building again. I love the physical side of engineering. The desk job and the commute were killing me.'

'Now I get to do the part of the job I love, on site and be out in the fresh air, ten mins from home.'

Wow, some honesty for once! This is new.

'So you're working outside right now? You

must be hot.'

Shameless, I know, but I'd love to see that shirt come off.

'Sweetheart, I'm hot wherever I'm working.'

Damn, I walked into that one.

'There's that arrogance again.'

'You love it.'

'Uh huh.'

'Oh please, you wouldn't be in here otherwise.'

'Maybe.'

A little while goes by. I watch him doing his thing. Then he stops to take a drink of water, so I move in.

'So, no shirtless selfies then?'

I watch him smile as he reads, then chuckle to himself as he types out a reply.

'I'm hurt, Jazz. I feel objectified!'

'Oh please, you live for female attention.'

'It pleases me greatly that I seem to have yours.'

Damn him. There's not really much I can say to that, and it irritates me that he's right.

'What? No sass?'

'Oh I have plenty of sass, don't you worry.'

'So I've discovered. But I can think of a better use for your smart mouth.'

'Is that right?'

'Uh huh'

I want to see what he'll do if I play with him. There's nowhere for him to go.

'*Licks my full lips*'

I watch him smile and then shake his head.

'Damn.'

'*Bites my bottom lip.*'

He is silent for a moment, he's just looking at his phone.

> 'I want to know where you want this smart mouth.'

'You know where I want it, Jazz. But I'm working'

> 'Awww, poor Spencer, can't handle teasing at work.'

'You haven't seen where I'm working. There's nowhere to hide out here.'

> 'Oh I don't believe that, there must be a bathroom.'

He glances up at the house, and I pull back from the window.

'There's probably 17 bathrooms in this place. But they aren't for the help.

> 'Not for the help? Sounds harsh. What is it? Buckingham Palace?'

'Haha! Almost. But it's not the queen that lives here, it's the Wicked Bitch of the West.'

Bastard.

'Oh really? Well wouldn't it give you some satisfaction to defile one of her bathrooms?'

'It would be funny, but I'm not in the mood for a run in with the bitch today. Maybe later?'

My shoulders sag…and then I get an idea…

'Fine, you get back to work, I'll catch you later. X'

'Laters.'

I watch while he puts his phone away. Then I continue.

'I'll just be here keeping myself entertained…'

'*Licking my finger and circling my nipple, watching it tighten and beg for more attention. I give it a pinch, sending a shiver through my'

'body, before sliding my hand down my naked body to the silky smooth skin of my pussy.*'

I wasn't even watching to see if he checked his phone again so when the message comes through it surprises me and makes me evil laugh.

'Bitch!'

I peer out of the window and see him typing.

'Do you know how HARD it is to work while you're doing this?'

'I can imagine. Don't mind me, you carry on!'

I laugh to myself. This is brilliant.

'*Sighing as my finger lightly strokes my swollen clit, taking my time, savouring the feeling.'

'Gasping as I slide it inside and feel how wet I am thinking of you.*'

'Jesus Jazz! I'm struggling big time here, go easy on me.'

'*Groaning as I start to stroke two fingers over my sweet spot, wishing it was your cock in their place.*'

I watch him try and adjust himself and look around to make sure no one else has noticed. He is in big trouble if I carry on. He starts typing.

'Damn you, no fair!'

'*Knowing how hard you'd feel inside me as you took me, turns me on. My free hand strokes my clit in time to my fingers inside.*'

'Fuck! Ok, ok, I give in, just stop for a minute so I can think.'

My laugh is so loud, I worry he will have heard it from outside. This is hilarious, what the hell is he going to do? They have an outhouse for their tools. It's one of several garages, but really it's like staff quarters. You could live there. They have a kitchen and a toilet. But as well as a ten strong crew, in and out for tools and tea, the gardener uses it and right about now, he'll be parked up in the kitchen reading his paper with talk sport on the radio. Hardly an ideal situation for a quick fumble in the loo.

I'm starting to think he might actually sneak in here and find a bathroom. I look to check what he's doing but he's nowhere to be seen. Shit. Where is he?

'What are you doing?'

'Locking myself in one of the palace's

bathrooms. You're going to get me in so much trouble, Jazz... Now, carry on.'

Holy fucking shit! Where is he? I get up and open my door, looking up and down the hall. I don't know what I'm expecting to see, he said he was in a bathroom. There's no way he'd be up here either, he probably found the closest one to where he was working. The one down by the laundry room most likely. I close my door again, sitting back on the window seat.

'Hey, where did you go? You can't tease me like that.'

'I cannot believe you're in there, did anyone see you?'

'The bitch isn't around. She's probably off torturing kittens. Now I have a tent pole situation here, are you going to help me out or not?'

'Haha! Ok...where was I? Oh yeah, I had two fingers in my soaking wet pussy and I was stroking my clit, wishing it was you I could feel.'

This is so fucked up. I doubt this is what Mags meant when she said people do the sexting thing. I bet nowhere in her imagination did she have me talking dirty to him while he scratches his itch in the guest bathroom downstairs. But hey, it is what it is; I wanted to toy with him, I guess it's game on.

'*Pressing my fingers harder against that magic spot, I can already feel the urge to come for you. My finger circles my clit in the same'

'motion and my back arches. Knowing you're touching yourself makes me so wet, I wish you could hear it. The sound I make as I fuck myself'

'slowly with my fingers. It's so hot. Rubbing my clit harder, moaning as the pleasure takes over, start climbing higher and higher.'

'My eyes tightly closed, imagining your toned abs moving above me as you bury yourself in me, over and over. I can't hold back any longer'

'stroking harder and faster until I feel the hot flow of my juices as my body shudders with release*'

I sit and wait, I can only imagine what he's doing. I want to know if he makes a sound. I want to know what he sounds like when he comes. But if I leave this room, the illusion is shattered.

Curiosity gets the better of me though and keeping my phone with me I tiptoe out into the hall. The tiptoeing is a bit much, I'll look like I'm up to no good. Get a grip, Jazz, just act normal. The house is quiet as I make my way down the stairs. I can see Mags on the veranda at her laptop as I pass by the huge open plan living room.

'Are you there?'

I type as I enter the kitchen. Across the room is the door to the laundry room and beyond it is the small guest bathroom I believe he is in. Quietly I get a glass and pour myself a juice so I look like I have a reason to be lurking in the kitchen. My phone screen lights up.

'I'm here. You are a bad, bad girl. You know that?'

'You asked for it!'

'You're going to get me sacked.'

'From your own business? I don't think so.'

'I mean from this job when I'm caught with my pants around my ankles by the wicked bitch!'

'Then be very careful leaving. You don't want to get caught.'

'Roger.'

                                                'Spencer?'

'Yeah?'

                              'Was it worth it though?'

'Fuck yeah! Next time it's my turn. I'm going to blow your mind.'

                                 '*Waits by the phone!*'

'SMH, I can never tell if you're being serious or not.'

                                '*Keeps you guessing*'

'Ha! Well it's been fun, but I have to get back to work.'

                                  'Ok, have a great day.'

There is a flush from the bathroom and I hear water running, then the door to the laundry room opens and out walks the jackass, looking far too pleased with himself. I give him a disapproving stare, and he freezes for a millisecond when he sees me, but then he just acts like it was no big deal he was in here using the toilet.

"You have your own bathroom facilities, You shouldn't be

in here," I snap, eyeing him critically.

"We do," he shrugs, not offering any more.

His audacity gets the better of me and my occasional fiery temper makes an appearance. "Well, what do you think you're doing in here then? Use the facilities you were given and stay out of the house."

He looks completely unfazed, amused even. It pisses me off. "It was occupied. I couldn't wait," he replies casually. "I'm sure Mags won't mind. I'll tell her if you like. Admit my crime." He smirks, "Do you think she will let me keep my job?" Then he pulls a mock terrified face.

Ugh! Only he could turn this around on me when I had the upper hand.

"Just get out."

"Sure thing, Princess."

I open my mouth to retaliate, but I realise I'm not going to win. So, I turn away and start cleaning the immaculate kitchen and putting the juice away. When I glance back. He has gone. I sigh, defeated. Fucking wanker, ruins all my fun.

"You ok?" asks Mags as she enters the kitchen.

I turn to face her. "Yeah, I'm fine. How's the writing coming along?"

"Good today, I might hit my target." She goes to the fridge and pours herself a juice. "Do you fancy pasta tonight?" she asks, looking at the contents of the fridge.

"Yes, but I'll make it; you write."

She smiles. "Thanks. I'll get as much done as I can, and then we can have a chilled out evening."

"Ok, sounds good."

She takes her juice and starts to leave. "Oh, before I forget,

Will has invited us to the pub tomorrow night, if you want to go."

My stomach lurches, "Will he be there?"

"Spencer? I don't know, probably. But you can't hide from him forever. It's a small town."

If only she knew. "Fine," I sigh. "I'll go, but if he's there, I can't guarantee I'll be nice."

Jazz

FRIDAY 10TH JULY

I time it so that I'm down in the gym before they start this morning. I don't fancy a run in with him, I just want to read by the pool and relax. I push back the huge bi-fold doors that look onto the gardens and pull a couple of the loungers out onto the deck a little. Mags joins me with a tray of breakfast, and we settle onto our loungers. Pouring the tea and handing one to Mags, I see the work crew arriving out of the corner of my eye. Damn it.

"This is the life," sighs Mags.

"This is your life, it's like being on holiday for me."

Just then, the peace is interrupted by the sounds of work starting for the day.

Mags laughs, "Yeah, like one of those holidays on that "Holidays from Hell" show. Where you show up and your balcony overlooks a building site."

"It's a little better than that, Mags. It's free, it's beautiful. The weather is unusually good and there's no broken glass or used condoms in the jacuzzi."

"Yet!" she giggles.

I laugh out loud and look up to see I caught Spencer's attention. He looks over at us with barely masked contempt.

He must think we are a pair of pampered princesses, but he knows nothing about us. Yes, Mags' family is wealthy, and, yes, she has had a privileged upbringing and has money of her own that she hasn't had to kill herself to earn. But, she is also a successful writer who has had three books published and she is currently working on her fourth. Even if she weren't a rich kid from the Surrey hills, she'd be doing ok. And I work for a living. Or at least I did. This is just a holiday, I'll be working hard again soon, he'll see. He doesn't know me.

Then I realise that I'm mentally justifying myself to him. Fuck it. Let him think what he likes.

"It's fine, Mags, we both have our headphones on, the noise doesn't bother me." The arsehole making the noise bothers me, but the noise is fine. I can tune it out, my head is so full of thoughts anyway, I can barely hear it. I'm too busy detesting myself for yesterday. I need help, that's all there is to it. I can't stand the guy, and yet I'm lusting after him and playing illicit sex games with him…and he doesn't even know it. He would freak. Which is why he can never know who I am.

Self loathing or not, it doesn't take long for thoughts of him to start eating into my relaxation. I wonder if he has thought about me at all since yesterday. I haven't even checked my phone, I was so focused on getting down here before he arrived.

Well, would you look at that, I have a message.

'Good morning.'

'Morning. How are you?'

'I'm god, how are you?'

GOD! I stifle a laugh, I don't want him to see and I have Mags beside me.

'Bahahahaha! Either your ego is worse than I thought, or that is the best typo ever!'

I actually hear his laughter from where I'm sitting.

'Haha! Typo? I don't see a typo.'

'That'd be right, you think you're rather special, don't you?'

'I am rather special, Jazz. I don't think, I know.'

'Oh, God!'

'Yes! I love it when you say my name.'

I giggle out loud.
"What's so funny?" Asks Mags, looking up from her writing.
"Nothing, just one of those funny autocorrects.'
"Oh." She goes back to concentrating.

'So no plans to try and get me sacked today?'

'I thought today was my turn? You were going to blow my mind. Or were you just blowing hot air?'

'I'd love to, but the Wicked Bitch of the West has taken up residence where she can see me today. I wouldn't want to give her the'

'Satisfaction of thinking I was HARD at work because of her in her little shorts.'

'Oh really? Is she hot?'

'She would be if her mouth zipped shut.'

'And you, I suppose, are the perfect gentleman?'

'I'm never anything but perfect, Jazz.'

'Suuuure!'

'My God woman, you would benefit from a good spanking.'

'Oooh, promises, promises. I'm still waiting to have my mind blown. Or should I just entertain myself again?'

'Oh no! Not today. I'm not going through that again while she can see me. Behave, you.'

'So meet me halfway. Send me a picture and I won't torture you.'

'I'll see what I can do. Now let me work, will you? I'm falling behind.'

'Ok.'

'BBL.'

As the sun reaches the highest point in the sky, Mags gets up to re-position our umbrella.

"I think I'll go and make us some lunch," she says, stretching.

"No need," I tell her, getting up and going to the little bar area in the corner of the pool house. I produce plates, knives, bread and from the fridge, a little platter of meats and cheeses we bought at the deli.

"Wow, look at this. You were up early."

"I just thought it would be nice not to have to move," I grin. Actually, I thought it would be nice not to have to walk past him, if at all possible, so I came prepared, but let's not dwell on that.

We sit and munch on our lunch, while Mags tells me about the plot of her book. It sounds great; I can't wait to read some.

Despite the fact that I can see him if I turn around, I haven't really thought about Spencer for a while, so I am surprised when my phone buzzes with a message from him. It's a selfie of him grinning with sunglasses on. His T-shirt is tucked into the waistband of his shorts and his biteable body is on display. I physically have to fight with my reflex to turn around, which is difficult, but for the best because I don't know if I can fight the urge if I see it in the flesh.

I message him back.

'Careful, the Wicked Bitch might want a piece of you if she sees all that on display.'

'Pft! She's got no chance. Besides, she's too busy eating lobster and caviar, or whatever rich people eat these days.'

'You do make me laugh, she might be a nice girl.'

'Yeah and I'm a monkey's uncle.'

He goes quiet then and when I get up to put the plates back in the pool house I look over to see it's because they've had a big delivery of materials, and they are all busy.

After a quick work out, I finally make my way back to the house for a shower when I think the coast is clear, but my heart sinks as I round the corner and find him working just out of sight.

"Are you off?" he asks as I walk by.

I ignore him.

"You must be exhausted, Princess, go and have a lay down."

Fucker! I continue walking. I'm not letting him have the satisfaction.

"Ok then," he continues cheerfully as if I replied. "I'll see you tonight," he says behind me with a laugh.

I stiffen, but carry on walking, muttering, "perfect" under my breath.

We've been in the bar an hour and so far it's been very nice. Three guesses as to why.

I place my order at the bar.

"I'll need to see some ID," says the bartender. I roll my eyes, no one else has asked me. I don't know whether to kiss the guy or be insulted.

"Sorry, I have to ask. I made a mistake recently and I'm on a warning."

I laugh and look for my driving licence in my purse.

"Don't serve her, she's dodgy." I stiffen as his voice cuts my good mood in two. Tonight was going so well.

I hand over my license and stare ahead, refusing to acknowledge him even when he settles his elbows on the bar beside me and leans towards me. He sniffs and I fight the urge to smack him.

"What do you think you're doing?"

He sniffs again. "Just checking you showered." He smirks. "When I saw you earlier you were a bit ripe."

I turn to face him and open my mouth, incensed. When I catch sight of his stupid grin, I close my mouth, I'm not rising to it. I turn back to the bar. The bartender starts to hand me back my licence, and I watch as the dickhead plucks it out of his fingers. I try to grab it from him, but he laughs and holds it over his head.

"Ah, ah, ah. Not so fast, Princess. Let's have a look, shall we?" He continues to hold it out of my reach, but tilts it so he can read it. He busts out laughing at my picture and I lunge at it, but he easily holds me back with his free hand. Then his mirth fades and a frown forms as he reads. "Your name isn't even Parker!"

"No, it's not," I snap, grabbing for my licence. "It's also none of your business." I finally catch a break and snatch it from him, putting it away as quickly as possible.

Shit! Shit, shit!

I glance back at him, but he doesn't seem to have joined the dots, he's still too pleased with himself. I grab my drinks and retreat to the safety of our table before he can say anything else.

It's a nice group, well at least it was until he showed up. Mags and Will are looking cosy. He's a great guy, from what I've seen. She has been texting him constantly, but I've been a little wrapped up in my own nonsense. I really must ask her what's going on there. There are a few others, a few of the guys from Will and Spencer's work crew and a couple of girlfriends. I was chatting to this really interesting girl about her charity work, which made me feel about an inch tall. Especially when she asked me what I did and I had to face facts and tell her, at the moment nothing, but I'm working my way up to opening my own chocolate shop. Could I feel anymore shallow? Tell me again about building schools in Tanzania…*face palm*.

The dickhead comes over with his beer and pulls up a chair. We are at two tables pulled together, and I am sitting in the gap between them on one side. So, when he dumps his chair opposite me on the other side of the gap, I feel like screaming. Now, here he is in my face without even so much as a table between us for protection. I sip my wine and try to focus on the conversation beside me.

"So, JASMINE, tell us about yourself," he says, loudly.

I turn to face him, catching Mags' wide-eyed expression as I go. Arranging my face into what I hope looks like mock sincerity and finding a patronising tone to match, I reply, "Thanks for your interest in someone other than yourself, Spencer, and while your personal growth should be celebrated, I'd just really prefer to enjoy my drink."

"Easy, Princess. I was just asking," he holds his hands up in surrender. "I was just wondering why you use a FAKE NAME?" He says the words loudly, so that everyone can hear.

I sigh. "It's not a fake name, it's my real name. Plenty of people don't go by their first name, you know. I just chose to go by my last name, that's all. I've never really liked Jasmine."

"What's the matter, Princess, is it not regal enough for you?"

Narrowing my eyes, I snarl, "You're a real jerk, you know that?" Then I turn back to Mags and try to forget he is there.

The awkward silence at our table seems to dissipate and conversation begins to flow again. A little while later, I see that he is on his phone typing away and in a lull in conversation, I check my own phone out of interest. Sure enough, he's on Twitter. Flirting with some skanks. I shouldn't be surprised.

SPENCER @TheSpencerRyan
@SassySinner Where have you been, sweetheart? I've missed your sexy smile.

TIFFANY @SassySinner
@TheSpencerRyan I've been around baby, you just aren't looking hard enough.

The sickening pleasantries go on and on. Clearly they're familiar with each other in more ways than one, and after a few tweets, I've seen enough. I come out of the app and drop my phone in my bag. I get up and throw my bag over my shoulder, before heading to the bathroom. As the door swings closed behind me I slam my bag on the counter and pace.

Shit.

I cannot be pissed at him flirting on Twitter with some skanky whore.

I cannot be calling random women who talk to him on Twitter skanky whores!!

I need to get a grip.

I need to get a fucking life.

Despite all these revelations, I still reach for my phone in my bag and check again.

Her last tweet says,

TIFFANY @SassySinner
@TheSpencerRyan Well, sexy, you know where to find me if you want me ;) I'll be waiting.

Awesome!

And just look at her picture. It's not her, that's for sure. Just some model, boobs out in invitation, no shame.

Well, Miss Boob-avi, you can put the girls away, because I have the shoes that he craves, and I'm not afraid to use them. Without thinking too hard, I open my DMs and find the picture I'm looking for. It's the one I swore to myself I'd never send. Shoes, legs, and shaved pussy, all on display. I promised myself this would never be seen by anyone, but I'm in a rage and who fucking cares? You can't see my face. I hit send. No words. Just a reminder.

I take a minute to get myself together and then head out to rejoin my group.

When I sit down, dickhead is still looking at his phone. He is deeply engrossed.

Will comes back from the bar and hands me a glass of wine. Thanking him, I take a sip and sit back crossing my legs. Quietly and with smug satisfaction, I watch him. I know he's seen it. With any luck he will have forgotten all about Little Miss Sassy-Boobs and be fantasising about my Louboutins. There might even be a reply waiting, I'll have to find a moment to check.

Abruptly, Spencer gets up. I turn to see what he's doing and catch his eye. He looks at me with an expression I am unable to read. There is almost nothing there, yet something deep all at the same time. Then without a word he turns and stalks away to the toilets.

Weird.

I open my bag and pull out my phone, the screen is lit from a message just having come through. I quickly open it and read.

Beneath my picture says...

'Babe that is beautiful. I want to taste it.'

Then a second message...

'Have I told you how much I love that sexy little anklet?'

Of course. My anklet.
I always forget I wear it, because I've never taken it off since I was 17. It was my grandmother's necklace and I had it made into an anklet after it was left to me. It is a fine silver chain with a small key pendant. It was her 21st birthday present, she wore it for years and I always loved it. But the chain was broken, so rather than replace it, I had it made into an anklet. That way I'd still have part of her with me.
Another message comes through. He must be sending them from the bathroom,

'It's so hot. I especially love how it looks with those blue shoes.'

I frown at my phone. I wasn't wearing blue shoes in that photo. I was wearing the black peep toes, the ones he fantasises about.
Then another message drops through.
A photo.
It's a photo of my anklet and the blue shoes I'm wearing right now. Here. Tonight.

Shit.

Just as I'm taking this in, the door to the men's toilet bangs open and he steps out with that same look, which I can now see is confusion and anger and it is getting worse by the minute. He stops and glares at me for a moment and then turns and storms out of the bar.

My heart is pounding. I have no idea what to do. He is mad as hell and a crazy part of me wants to run after him. That's obviously not the part that detests the jackass. It's the part that still wishes she could believe in Santa.

"Jazz?" Mags breaks through my thoughts.

I blink at her. "He knows," I tell her, swallowing hard. How did this all happen?

"How?"

How? How? Because I've sent him naked pictures of myself and he recognised my jewellery, that's how!! I think to myself.

Out loud is a different matter though. "He just does." That's all I can give her. There are no words for everything else that happened.

Mags frowns. "Are you ok? You look upset."

"I'm fine." I take a long, long drink of my wine. I think what I really need is tequila, but as I look around at my present company, they are all oblivious. They just met for a nice drink and were kind enough to accept Mags and I into the fold. None of them really look in a tequilla-y place. I really don't think I can just sit here; I need to get drunk, or get out of here, possibly both.

"I think I'm going to go," I mutter to Mags as I pick up my bag and my phone.

"Wait, I'll come with you," she replies.

Will looks disappointed.

"No, no, you stay, I'll be fine," I insist.

"You're not walking home alone."

"We'll all go," Will suggests, standing up and putting an end to the discussion. "I'll walk you both home."

Will and Mags say goodnight to the group, I'm already out the door. Great first impression, Jazz. Nice. But I don't care. I just needed to get out of there, I need to get out of this place, this county, my own skin, if at all possible. I feel like screaming. How could I do something that was so not me; I knew it would blow up in my face, I just wasn't hearing my own warnings. He's pretty, but he wasn't worth all this. I feel sick...Over a total jackass.

Mags and Will join me in the car park and I just start to walk. I really don't feel like talking and I didn't ask them to leave, so I set off ahead of them, setting my own pace. I can hear parts of their hushed conversation. Mags telling him that I already knew Spencer from Twitter and that us meeting was coincidence, but as he is 'different' in real life to how he is on Twitter, I was a little disappointed. He's still confused and Mags tries to explain in more detail, I don't hear it all.

Then, "Wait, you're Shoegirl?" Will says loudly.

I stop in my tracks and turn around. Will looks shocked and now I need to know just what he knows. "What has he told you about me?" I demand.

"Nothing...I..." He stutters. "He just talks about the girl with the shoes. I thought you'd be..." He catches himself.

"You thought I'd be what?" I snap.

"Jazz!" Mags chides.

"No, come on, what did you think I'd be?" I realise I'm not being fair, snarling at this poor sweet guy, but I can't stop. "Tell me!"

"Ugly," he murmurs. "I thought you'd be ugly."

Mags shoots him a glare.

"What? I thought because she uses the shoes as her picture, that she wouldn't be much to look at." He shrugs a holds up his hands. "I'm a guy, ok? I'm sorry, we don't think."

I hold his apologetic stare for a few seconds and then turn on my heel and continue on my way home.

"Spencer knew you'd be a knock out," he continues almost to himself. Mags must have glared again, because there's a pause, but then he continues. "He said you had the 'fuck me' kind of shoes. The kind only knock outs wear…" He tapers off as I round on him. "I'll shut up now."

"That's it, where do you live?"

"Jazz, let's just—"

I cut Mags off with a hand. "No, I need to deal with this Mags, so either Will here directs me to him, or I'll have to have a chat with him at work tomorrow." I fold my arms and wait.

Will sighs. "Fine. It's this way," he says, reluctantly turning around and leading us to his place.

When we arrive, he opens the door and calls out for Spencer. There is no response at first and he walks down the hall. "Spencer?" He calls out again.

"What?" Comes the grouchy response from the room at the end of the hall, which I can see from the open doorway is in darkness.

Will hits the lights and Spencer curses. He is sitting at the kitchen table with a beer, head in hands, his back to us.

"You've got a visitor, mate," Will says cautiously, and Spencer whips round to see us all standing in the doorway.

"What is she doing here?" He snarls.

"I think we should leave them to it," Mags says to Will.

Will nods, "I'll walk you home."

Then they're gone, leaving me standing in the doorway to the kitchen watching him down a beer. The silence rings in my ears. Maybe I shouldn't be here. Spencer drains the last of his beer and scrapes back his chair. Getting up, he moves to the fridge and pulls out another beer. He pops the cap on a wall mounted bottle opener and the cap drops straight into the bin beneath. Total bachelor pad, figures. "What do you want?" he asks, with his back to me.

What do I want? Hmmm, that's a very interesting question. What do I want? Well let's see, I want tonight not to have happened. I want to have not sent him those pictures and not whored myself to a beautiful stranger on the internet. I want the last month to rewind and preferably to never have known about the existence of the most beautiful, annoying man I've ever met.

"You knew." His accusation cuts through my thoughts. I look up and he's staring at me. Anger rolling off him, the confusion in his eyes is gone now that he has had a chance to think about it. "You knew and you made a big show of how much you hate me, while you played me. Is this your thing?"

"My thing?"

"Yeah, you pretend to be one thing, when really you're another."

"ME??" I yell. "What about you?"

He laughs a bitter laugh. "You knew what you were doing.

I had no clue. I didn't know who you were. You know my name, my face," he raises an eyebrow, "my body." He shakes his head, disapprovingly.

I scoff. "It's just a shame you're not the full package, isn't it?"

"Babe, you don't know the first thing about my package."

"Suits me just fine. As if I'd want you now that I know who you really are."

"Hasn't stopped you, Princess, has it?" He frowns. "So, what's the deal here? Do you get your kicks from pissing guys off and then virtual-fucking it all better? Is this what you do?"

"Fuck you!"

"No thanks, Princess, I think I'll pass."

"Huh, seems like that'd be a first."

"That's rich coming from you. 'Oh I've never done anything like this before,'" he mocks, doing a stupid girly impersonation. "You seemed to know just what you were doing, if you ask me."

"As opposed to your tried and tested 'It's just you and me here babe, you'll love it' technique? They all fall for your charming pretense, I suppose."

"I've never pretended to be anything I'm not," he says defensively.

"Other than a nice person, you mean?"

He growls, moving closer, putting his beer on the table. "You don't know me." He's right in front of me now.

He smells amazing.

Dammit.

"I don't want to know you."

He lets out a clipped laugh. "Liar."

"You arrogant piece of shit!" I raise my hand to slap his smug face, but he catches my wrist and pins it against the wall above my head. He leans into me until I can feel his breath against my cheek. It sends unwelcome shivers down my spine. I hate him and I hate what he does to me.

My breathing is rapid, but so is his.

"Why do you have to be so fucking irritating?" he hisses, through clenched teeth.

"You bring out the best in me. Now get the fuck off me before I hurt you."

He sneers. "That, I'd love to see, Princess."

"Try me," I dare him, turning my face ever so slightly to look in his eyes. I want him to see how angry I am, to see that I really can't stand him. Unfortunately, he is looking at my lips, why is he looking at my lips? Just then his eyes flick up, and for a second, I see just a hint of confusion, before his lips crush against mine with such force an involuntary moan escapes.

His tongue forces its way into my mouth and begins exacting its revenge on mine for the nasty things I've said.

What the fuck is happening? I hate him, but my God I want to fuck him. This is so bad. I need to stop this now. His hand is still pinning my wrist to the wall, so with my other hand I shove at his shoulder, he breaks contact with my mouth for a second grabbing my other wrist and pinning it along with the first in one strong hand.

"What do you think you're doing?" I gasp, fighting to breathe. I badly want to fight him, but I need to feel him.

"Figuring this out," he murmurs as his mouth begins to travel to my neck. He bites my earlobe and I cry out. Pleasure and pain, passion and fury, surge through me and I start to fight.

Yanking at my hands held securely in his firm grip, I can't help another moan as his hot, breathless kisses work their way down my neck. His free hand snakes into my top and yanks down the cup of my bra.

"Figuring what out?" I pant. "I hate you and you hate me, it's perfectly easy to understand. Ah!" His fingers pinch my nipple hard.

"If you hate me, why are you panting like a dog in heat?" he says as he sinks his teeth into the soft skin of my neck and bites hard enough to leave a mark.

"Fuck!" I growl, the pain just increases the damned pleasure. I fucking hate my body for its betrayal. "Don't flatter yourself," I spit. His head dips lower and my top is lifted up, then his mouth is on my nipple. At this point I'm screwed; my nipples are my weakness. I moan loudly and lose myself for a second in the sensation. He bites down and I cry out. Then realisation floods back in. I wriggle to get out of his grasp again, but he holds me tighter. His hand stills my hips and I freeze as it slides around my arse and up, under my skirt. I try again to get free of him as his busy hand pushes my skirt up around my waist.

"Why fight me?" His fingers travel around my thigh.

"Why? Because I hate you, that's why."

"You want me, you can't deny it."

"In your dreams," I start to protest, but his fingers find their way to the front of my knickers and slip inside. All the air leaves my body as his fingers slide across my clit and then sink inside.

"Liar!" he purrs, working his fingers.

I whimper. I've never been so turned on, or so at odds with myself.

"If you hated me," he pulls his hand away, leaving me to sag with disappointment, "you wouldn't be this wet." His fingers force their way into my mouth, coated with my need.

This display of dominance has a shiver running through me, and without thinking, I suck at his fingers and groan.

He smirks. "Face it, Princess, you want me."

I do.

No.

Shit.

I don't.

He lets his fingers slip from my mouth and stares at me with a look of triumph, like he has me right where he wants me.

"You're a pig," I whisper, "you make me sick."

"Yeah?" he challenges.

"Yeah," I breathe.

Then, he presses himself against me.

Ho-ly fuck.

Everything is forgotten in that instant. His grip on my wrists loosens and my hands fall free. I grab his face and kiss him deeply, aggressively, winding my fingers into his hair.

While I devour him, he works quickly, tugging at his jeans until they release him. Then he hitches me up, slamming me into the wall and roughly pulls my knickers aside. Just when I'm expecting to feel him, he looks me in the eye. That same look I keep seeing flashes across his face. Anger and confusion, but there's something else. Need, maybe? Then, after a split second of fiery eye contact, he pushes into me.

We both moan. He's big. I didn't get the chance to see him before I felt him, but my God, he's everything I hoped the great @TheSpencerRyan would be. He pulls out a fraction and then pushes back in, this time all the way. I draw in a long breath on a hiss as I'm stretched around his full length.

Forgetting himself for a second, his eyes close and he sighs almost with relief. It's just a moment, then he snaps back into life, grunting as he draws back and slams into me. My legs wrap around him, pulling him in tight, and I grasp the back of his neck to hold on. His pace is punishing, his breath, hot and fast against my ear.

"You're so fucking wet," he gasps.

I moan, grinding against his thrusts. I want to argue, deny that I'm wet, not give him the satisfaction of thinking it's for him. But I can't fight this. He shifts me up a little, effortlessly in his strong arms and I can't help the sound I make as he hits a different spot inside of me.

"Yeah," he growls, in response to my hum of pleasure, "you like that, don't you?"

"Yes…" The word is out of my mouth before I can stop it. It sounds more like an impassioned plea. Just hearing it from my lips causes a jolt of guilty pleasure to pulse through me. Knowing I'll hate myself later only seems to make it more intense. Like the fear of getting caught, only this is like catching myself. I choke on the word as it tries to escape for a second time; it barely makes it out as a whisper.

He begins kissing my neck again. The smell of him is all around me and I want to bite it, lick it and push it away all at the same time. He's making me crazy. I fist his hair, trying to bring him closer, but he pulls back and looks in my eyes.

My eyes!

While. He. Fucks. Me.

Seriously?

All I can do is watch him watch me, while he slams into me; his intense stare is almost my undoing. Then he leans forward and takes me in a hungry kiss. I close my eyes and for a moment I'm paused on the brink, feeling only pleasure, then he bites on my lip and release crashes through me.

My body contracts violently, pulling him over the edge.

"Oh, fuck," rumbles from him as he rides it out for both of us, and I cling tight to his shaking shoulders. He rests his forehead on the wall above my shoulder and he sighs heavily.

It's then that realisation sets in for me.

Suddenly the smell of him surrounding me, the weight of his body pressing me against the wall, which seemed so erotic seconds ago, now feels suffocating. I act without thinking, shoving him off me. He stumbles back in surprise, pulling out of me in the process. As he lets me go, I don't even look at him, I straighten out my skirt and knickers, grab my bag from where I must have dropped it on the floor and on freshly fucked, trembling legs, I leave.

Spencer
SATURDAY 11TH JULY

BANG, BANG, BANG.

BANG, BANG, BANG.

What the hell? Stretching, I try to focus on the sound that has disturbed my sleep.

BANG, BANG, BANG.

Why is there banging?

BANG, BANG, BANG.

Where the fuck is Will?

BANG, BANG, BANG.

Jesus. "Ok, ok, I'm coming," I mumble, hauling myself upright and scratching my head. I reach out to my underwear drawer, still sitting on the edge of my bed. My eyes have barely opened; it's fucking early. Picking a pair of pants off the top of the pile in the drawer, I lift one foot to start putting them on and it happens again.

BANG, BANG, BANG.

BANG, BANG, BANG.

Motherfucker!

"ALRIGHT!" I bellow, "I'm coming!" I yank the pants on as I stand up and stomp down the hallway to the stairs. I'm barely halfway down when it starts again.

BANG, BANG, BANG.

BANG, BANG, BANG.

"For fuck's sake," I grumble loudly, yanking the front door open. "Where's the fucking fire?" That's when I'm confronted with this sexy, annoying ball of rage, in running gear.

"We need to talk," she demands, pushing past me.

"Good morning, come the fuck in, why don't you?"

"Put some damn clothes on," she demands.

I watch her retreat to the kitchen and glance down at my all but naked body. Adjusting the package slightly and smirking, "Nah, I'm good like this," I reply and follow her.

"Well, I don't want to see it," she throws over her shoulder.

"Babe, don't kid yourself. If you didn't want to see it, you'd have stayed at home."

"Hey!" She snaps, turning to face me, just inside the kitchen. "I don't want to be here."

I step a little closer, watching her, aware that this is exactly where I had her last night and I could have her again right now if I wanted. She is thinking about it too, her nipples are begging again. It's a great habit they have and I know how much she hates it. "Well then, Princess, I'm a little confused about why you are."

"Because you..." She yells, pointing to the wall beside us, then dropping her voice to a hissed whisper, "because WE did that without a..." She once again trails off.

I stare at her blankly, what is she going on about? "It's early, Princess, you'll have to spell it out."

She sighs. "Because we had unprotected sex!"

Oh.

That.

"I'm sure that's just a regular Friday night for you, but I'm freaking out!"

I was so angry last night after she walked out, I didn't even think about it.

Let's face it, I just didn't think, full stop.

"Aren't you on the pill or something?"

"That's none of your business," she snaps.

"I think you just made it my business, don't you?"

"Yes, jackass, I'm on the pill, but I think you're missing the point. You need to be tested."

"I need to be tested? What about you?"

"I'm clean!"

"So am I."

"Oh please, you're probably banging your way through the south-east."

"Who I 'bang' is none of your concern."

"It is when you force yourself on me and share whatever you've picked up from them."

"Force myself?" What the actual fuck? She is NOT accusing me of that. I may have taken control, but I would never take what wasn't on offer. "I didn't hear you say no," I growl. She can't deny the need was mutual. Regret is her problem, not mine. She needs to be reminded of how lost in it she was when she had me inside her. "I did hear you moan though, Princess. I watched you come, felt you wet for me."

She visibly shudders. "You didn't hear me say yes though, did you?" She counters, her eyes narrowed, calculating how far she can push me.

I throw my head back and laugh. She's so in denial, it's ridiculous. "No, it was more like this, 'YES!...yesssss.'" I whisper the second one, stretching out the sound, just like she did last night as she clung to me, desperate to come.

Her palm connects with my face before I see it coming, I'm so busy laughing.

Son of a bitch.

I close my eyes as my head turns away from the force of the slap. Stunned, I touch my stinging skin as I turn back to glare at her. I stretch my jaw as I size her up; I think she's done for now. After only a second or two she shakes her head in disgust and marches out the door.

"Get a test," she yells over her shoulder as she slams the front door.

Fuck this shit, I run after her. Pulling open the front door, I see her jogging away. "That goes for you too, Princess," I call after her. "And I want to see results too."

I slam the door shut and take a deep breath. What. A. Bitch. My only thought is how my Shoegirl is worth a thousand of her.

Then it hits me.

FUCK.

I slam my fist into the wall and growl in pain as I hear the plaster cracking along with my knuckles.

Shit. Pulling my hand back, I tentatively flex it and wince. I don't think anything is broken, but fuck it hurts. Great move, Spencer, really great. I need ice. Ignoring the dented wall that I'll have to explain to Will later, I head back to the kitchen to make an ice pack.

Sitting at the kitchen table with a bag of peas on my hand, I tap my phone. I go for the Twitter app without thinking and realise what I'm doing too late. I'm already in our DM chat.

Fucking hell.

How can that bitch be MY Shoegirl? How? What did I do to deserve this? Shoegirl is my go to, she's where I relieve my stress. Stress which has recently been mostly caused by the spoiled princess.

I scroll through the DMs. She's filthy and confident. I love that. I imagined she'd be smoking hot, and, fuck, she is, but her personality leaves a lot to be desired. I fight the need to message her and need is the only word for it. But as I look at our final words, where I had busted her for lying to me last night, I realise that whatever we had is already dead and gone.

And now I've got last night to deal with. What the hell was I thinking going bareback? I never do that, this girl is messing with my head. She has seriously screwed with my senses, I broke my golden rule because she had me so fucking wound up. And now she's acting like I'm some disease-ridden whore. She can stomp around as much as she likes. I'm clean and I'm not sitting in a bloody clinic staring at the waiting room floor with a bunch of irresponsible teenagers, then getting something shoved in my dick, to prove it to her. No way. I don't owe her anything. She's the liar, she can deal with it

Jazz
SATURDAY 11TH JULY

"Do you want to talk about it?" asks Mags.

"Nope."

"Are you ok?"

"Yep."

"Jazz?"

"What?" I look up to see her concern and stop slamming around the kitchen.

"What happened?"

"I'm sorry," I sigh. "It's just such a mess."

"Come on, it doesn't have to be a big deal. You fancied him and he turned out to be a giant douche. It's not the end of the world."

"It's a little more complicated than that."

"Yeah ok, you didn't tell him that it was you straight away, and you threw your drink in his face. I'm sure he'll get over it."

I look at Mags, and she reads the silence and the problems weighing on my shoulders.

"That is all, isn't it?"

I slowly shake my head.

Mags' mouth drops open. "Did you sleep with him?"

Spencer

I close my eyes and hold back a groan.

"Oh my God, Jazz. You slept with him!"

"No, I didn't sleep with him. He fucked me right where you left me standing in his kitchen, and I didn't stop him. Big difference."

"Whoa! I need details now!"

"I really don't want to talk about it. I think I'm just going to go home."

"Oh, no, no you don't," she warns. "You aren't going anywhere. Maybe we should go out for the day?" She ponders for a moment, "Yes, let's do it, get yourself ready, we'll get out of here."

She looks at me with such unreserved enthusiasm, I just automatically do as she suggests.

Plonking herself down on the chair opposite me with our second round of cocktails of the afternoon and a table number, Mags whispers, "There's a seriously hot guy in there!"

"Really?" I strain to see inside, but it's darker in the bar and so bright out here in the garden that I can't see a thing.

Mags picks up her conversation where she left off right before she went to order our food. "So do I get to see these naughty pictures?"

"No!!"

"Damn. You're no fun. I'll have to see if Will can get hold of Spencer's phone."

"Holy fucking shit! They're on Spencer's phone!" My hand rakes through my hair in despair.

"Well yeah…you sent them to him."

"How did I not think of this? He has them…and he's a

dickhead. How did I not think it through to this point?"

"Don't freak out, it's no big deal."

"No big deal? That's easy for you to say. The biggest idiot in England doesn't have naked pictures of you on his phone, does he?"

"Ok, calm down."

I rub my forehead, trying to deal with this revelation. "Oh my God, what do you think he will do with them?"

"Nothing probably. Have a wank over them occasionally. They don't have your face in them, do they?"

I grimace at the idea of him using them as wank material, but relax slightly. She's right. "No, my face isn't in them."

"Well then, he's got nothing, they could be anyone."

Sighing heavily, I reach for my glass.

Mags is quiet and reflective for a few minutes. "I can't believe you did that," she says, shaking her head slightly and laughing.

"What? Only a few weeks ago, you were telling me it was the thing to do!"

Mags laughs hard. "I didn't tell you to do it with a stranger, Jazz. I merely said, it was more common than you were thinking."

"Is it really, though?"

"Yes! People do it all the time…Ha…look who I'm telling!"

I narrow my eyes at her, but I can't help laughing.

As we're giggling, the waiter comes over with our food. Good, I'm bloody starving!

"Two cheeseburgers with everything?" he asks looking at us expectantly.

I forget words for a second as his California accent makes me look up and when I do all I can think is wow.

"That's us," Mags steps in and he puts the plates down.

"Can I get you ladies anything else?"

"No thanks, Danny," Mags drawls, causing me to frown. How the hell does she know his name?

He smiles a shy smile, showing that he may be drop dead gorgeous, but unlike some, he's not a dick about it. As he turns I see that his uniform emblazoned with the bar logo, has his name embroidered on it, 'Danny.' I roll my eyes at Mags. She always does this; she's such a flirt.

Once he is out of ear shot, I look at Mags in awe. "Wow!"

"Told you." She shrugs picking up her burger. "Married though." She takes a huge bite.

"Damn it."

I shake my head incredulously at her. She doesn't miss a thing.

"So, was he good?" She just casually throws out there.

"Huh?" The waiter? How am I supposed to know if he's good?

"Spencer. Did he make your toes curl?"

"Mags!"

"Sorry, but you knew I was going to ask," she laughs.

Bitch! Of course I knew she would ask eventually, I'm just not sure how I can answer it right now.

"Well?"

"Well what? I don't know what to tell you, Mags."

"Tell me everything." Her expression is greedy and she quite literally rubs her hands together.

"This is not a situation I've laid on purely for your

amusement, Mags." I shake my head, chastising her, but can't quite hide my smile. "I'm dealing with this shit for real."

"But come on! I need some details. Was he…you know…packing?"

"I didn't exactly inspect it, Mags, it happened kinda fast."

"Jazz." She gives me a withering look for being obtuse.

"Yes! Alright? He seemed to be doing ok in that department."

Her eyes light up. "Next time, you'll have to get a good look, I want to know everything." She giggles.

"Next time? Trust me, Mags, there won't be a next time. I have suffered my last lapse in Spencer-related judgement and I will not let it happen again. Ok?"

"Who are you trying to convince? You or me?"

"I hate you sometimes."

She blows a kiss at me.

Jazz

SUNDAY 12TH JULY

Zipping up my second case, I look up guiltily to see Mags standing in the doorway.

"What are you doing?"

"Mags, I can't be here when he comes to work in the morning."

"Don't be ridiculous. You can't let him drive you away."

"So, you want me to hold my head high and lounge by the pool so he can look on and judge me?"

"No, you'll be too busy this week for the pool, and let him judge all he likes. He doesn't know you."

"What do you mean 'I'll be too busy?'"

"Don't be mad…" she bites her lip. Oh God what did she do? "Come with me." She reaches out and takes my hand, and pulls me all the way down to the kitchen. There on the huge centre island is all my chocolate making stuff. I look at Mags, she shrugs. "I popped home to pick up the mail this afternoon, while you were having your pity nap. I just thought it was time you started figuring out what you're going to sell in this shop of yours."

I roll my eyes. "IF I have a shop, Mags. I haven't decided yet."

"Yeah, ok, whatever... You keep procrastinating, but in the meantime, make me some of the good stuff."

I can't deny that it would be a welcome distraction from dickhead, and I suppose if I'm going to think seriously about doing this for real, there's no time like the present. I run my hand along the cool marble top of the island. Perfect for tempering chocolate. I've always made do with a slab. Here I could really spread out.

"I need ingredients," I say, almost to myself.

"Make a list, get online, get everything you think you'll need to put a menu together. We'll have a tasting."

I nod, already thinking about fresh mint and raspberries and all kinds of things I want to play with. Mags turns to leave me with my thoughts and then stops.

"Oh, there's something else."

"What?" I look up, concerned. After everything that's happened the last couple of weeks, I dread to think what else there could be.

"This was in the mail box." She pulls an envelope out of her bag and hands it to me. Written in careful, clear letters, 'Jasmine.' Not his usual confident scrawl.

"It's from James."

"I know, hand delivered."

My stomach turns at the thought of him being where I live. At least he couldn't get beyond the mail boxes.

"Are you going to open it?"

"I don't know."

"Just do it. Here…" She holds out her hand, and I give the envelope back to her. She rips it open and I close my eyes and listen to her pull the paper out and start to read.

"Oh my God!"

My eyes open, "What?"

She hands me three pieces of paper and I stare at them. What the hell?

One is a cheque made out to me for £30,000. Holy Shit! That's far more than I was going to demand. The other is for £20,000 and it's made out to one of our suppliers. I frown and at first think he has put the cheque in the wrong envelope, then I read the third piece of paper. A compliments slip with the company name across it, then in James' handwriting, it says…

'To help you get started, some equipment with our compliments. Mike is expecting your call.

Good luck in your new venture, Jasmine.'

I'm speechless.

"Who is Mike?"

"He handles commercial equipment sales at one of the big appliance suppliers we use."

"Oh."

I still can't get over the figures.

"How did he know?"

"Huh?" I pull myself from my thoughts to concentrate on Mags' question.

"How did he know about your new venture?"

I didn't even think of that. "I don't know. Justin maybe? I should text him." My handbag is in the hall and upon retrieving my phone I realise that it has been off since I stormed home from Spencer's on Friday night. I switch it on, not knowing what to expect. As it comes to life a couple of messages come through. The first is from Justin. I open it as I walk back in the kitchen and hear that Mags is on her phone. Justin's message was sent on Saturday morning.

'Jazz, are you home? James has asked me
to deliver a letter to you. X'

Then there is another.

'I've just left it in your box. Hope you're
ok, call me x'

I feel bad for being AWOL, but I needed to switch off for a bit, I would have driven myself crazy. I'm quite surprised I haven't felt like anything was missing. Typing out a reply to Justin, I half tune in to Mags' conversation.

'Sorry, I was away. I'm glad it was you, I thought James had been! I was just wondering, did you tell James what I planned to do next? It's fine if you did, I just want to know he isn't stalking me.'

I look up at Mags; she's talking into her phone and studying the two cheques. I walk over to listen.
"Yeah ok, hang on…" She pulls the phone away from her ear. "Dad says the generosity is an admission of guilt and he can get you more. Way more."
I shake my head. "I don't even want this. It's creepy. I mean why is he buying me appliances?"

"She doesn't want to, Dad, but thank you."

"Ask him what I should do with them."

Mags listens while George talks, clearly he heard my question.

"Use them," she says. Then she listens again while he continues. "Ok then, Dad, love you too. Bye."

"He says that he was a fool to pay you off without legal advice, because you could wipe the floor with him now, but as you don't want to, just enjoy it. He says James has been considerate in paying you off like this because £30k is the maximum redundancy you can receive that can't be taxed and he has gifted you equipment because he can probably write it off somehow, or lose it in the books. Don't feel bad about taking it Jazz."

"Oh, I don't feel bad, he can afford it. I just worked my arse off on a huge contract with a developer that will see him right for a couple of years, this is basically a great big commission, I deserve it. But I feel weird that he is buying me equipment. Like he has some stake in my future business."

"Dad said it's just a way to hide it, or you'd get taxed. I'll let him know that you're worried and he can figure something out, but he says spend it, so it's fine.'

"Hmmm, ok." Just then my phone beeps.

'I'm really sorry. He kept going on and on about wanting to give you a reference for your next employer. He wouldn't drop it so I just told him you were setting up your own business. He thought you were going in to competition with him, so I had to tell him what you were doing to calm him down. Me and my big mouth. I'm sorry x'

I sigh with relief.

'It's fine, Justin, don't worry, I thought he was tapping my phone or something! I'm ok that he knows, it's no problem. x"

'Ok good. I'll catch up with you soon, you can tell me all about it. X'

"It's ok," I tell Mags. "Justin told him I was setting up on my own, then had to tell him what I was doing because he thought I was going to steal his customers," I laugh. "It's not a bad idea, I'd be good at it."

"Oh, no you don't! I demand chocolate!"

"Yeah ok. I guess I'll start making a list."

"After you've unpacked, ok?"

I sigh. "Ok."

Jazz

MONDAY 13TH JULY

After a very haphazard trip around the supermarket, looking for anything I could experiment with, even though I'm still not really sure what I'm doing, I'm loading the car, when I notice a sign stuck to the lamp post. 'Farmers' Market - This Sunday'. I walk over and at the bottom of the poster is a phone number. This could be great for me, so without thinking too much about it, I dial the number. Five minutes later I have a spot this Sunday, just like that. My stomach turns over, there's so much to do. I jump back in my car and drive home faster and more determined than I was on the way here, when all I needed was a distraction.

When I set out this morning, it was to get out of the house while the builders all arrived and give my mind something to focus on, other than you know who. I never thought I'd be committed to my first retailing venture by the time I returned.

"Mags?" I call as I crash through the door with the first bags. "Maaaaags!" I drop the bags on the counter and go back for the rest. When I return to the kitchen, Mags is snooping through the things I bought.

"Blimey, who lit your fire?"

"You did." I grin, panting from the exertion and the

adrenaline rush. "I've just done something crazy?"

"Define crazy."

"Did you know there is a farmers' market here on the weekends?"

"Yes."

"Well guess who has a stall this Sunday?"

"That's brilliant," she squeals.

"Yes it is brilliant but it's also terrifying. I need your help."

"What can I do?"

"Help me decide what to make." I grit my teeth. This is crazy!

About half an hour later, we have a list of which of my tried-and-tested chocolates I'm going to make, and I'm going to work on three new ones to see if they make the cut. While Mags sorts through the random shopping I did, I get online to the chocolate supplier I like and start placing a proper order. Until now, I've been playing, buying small quantities, now it's for real.

"Oh my God, Mags, I'll have to decide what I need to charge."

"You'll be fine, we'll work it all out."

"I'll need scales." I didn't think of all this. "And packaging! Shit, what was I thinking giving myself six days?"

"You weren't thinking and that's a good thing because now you're finally doing it."

Yes, she's right, I am. And what's more, I haven't thought about dickhead at all.

Jazz

TUESDAY 14TH JULY

SPENCER @TheSpencerRyan
#ToplessTuesday pic.twitter.com/cojKPwdU7r

 Mother of GOD! Is he for real? Yes, yes, I know I shouldn't look, but it was just a peep. Seriously though, he's taking attention seeking to a whole new level. He has his top off, ok I'll allow that, it's bloody hot. But his shorts hang off him to an indecent level, even before he undid the button to get even more attention. But I'm left in no doubt that he is not wearing underwear, because I can see all of the 'V' along with some neat manscaping and the base, for want of a better word, of 'stuff' that should not be seen by all the girls that fight so hard for his attention on Twitter. Just looking at the number of replies the picture has already got him proves that they are all over it like flies on shit. Ugh!

 I want to march out there and tell him to put it away; of course, then he'll win because he'll know I was looking at his tweets. Instead, I make a glass of juice for Mags and take it out to her on the terrace.

 "How's it going?" I casually ask, while I try and eye up the workers without being noticed. He's totally into his work, so I risk a better look. Oh good, he may still be topless, but his shorts are at least back where they should be. I don't know what I was expecting to find, he's not going to be working with his bits all hanging out. I just wanted to check…not look. I certainly don't want to look!

I look back to Mags' laptop, to try and feign involvement in the conversation. But it's difficult to concentrate. Honestly, I need to be away from here. I should have left while I had the chance. He's trying to get to me. He has no shame, doing that where he could be seen by any of about a dozen people and then just going back to work like it's no biggie.

"Jazz?"

"Huh?"

"You were away with the fairies," she laughs. "I said, it's going very well, how's the planning?"

"Oh, sorry. Yes, it's fine. I'll feel a lot happier when this delivery gets here though."

"Give me a shout when it does, and I'll come in and help you."

"Thanks," I reply, glancing again at Spencer. He has a beard coming in. It really suits him.

God dammit!! This is the first time I've seen him since it happened. I studiously avoided him yesterday, now I bitterly regret breaking my resolve. It's much easier to hate him when he's nowhere to be seen. Now, I can't help staring.

Will looks up first, but his expression quickly has Spencer turning around. Maybe he tries to keep an air of indifference, but if so, he fails. There is a smug satisfaction to his cold stare. I quickly turn to go back to the kitchen. I have so much to do, I don't have time for his shit.

Spencer

I stalk back into the kitchen, furious with myself for making it obvious I'd seen his little plea for attention. Who does he think he is? I ask myself for the umpteenth time since I met him. It's all I do lately, ask myself who the hell he thinks he is, or where he gets off. I glance again at the picture, still open on my phone. Then let out a frustrated growl and stomp my feet.

STOP LOOKING!

It's driving me crazy. He's plastering his bits all over Twitter, and I'm letting him win by letting it get to me. I should just tweet him to pack it in. I should actually tweet that clearly someone who needs to flaunt their attributes like that is obviously lacking downstairs. I smirk, but then I have a flashback of being pressed against the wall while he made me feel that he lacked nothing whatsoever downstairs. No his flaws are not physical, they're far, far worse. It saddens me, but it does give me an idea.

JAZZ @OMGJazzyP
It's a shame when the beauty on the outside masks the horror that lurks underneath.

I slam my phone into the drawer beside me and go back to dusting my new lime and mint flavour mojito truffles with cocoa powder. Aggressively.

From inside the drawer, my phone sounds with a tweet and I sigh. Why am I doing this to myself? I'm only kidding myself, when I claim that I keep forgetting to turn the notifications off. I'd be checking it every five minutes even if I did. The fact is, I want to know when he tweets, what he says, how he flaunts his body. I want to know as much as I don't want to know, and when I see it, I love it just as much as I hate it. Spencer Ryan is eating me up from the inside, and my best bet was to run, but now I'm stuck for the week and he's right outside the door.

Another tweet sound. I roll another truffle through the rich dark powder. This is going to be a long week, but once it's done, I'm going home.

Another tweet sound. I'm definitely going home. I need to be as far away from here as I can get.

Another tweet sound. What the hell is he doing? I yank the drawer open and open the notification.

SPENCER @TheSpencerRyan
#23 Big enough that you'll still feel it the next day sweetheart

What the fuck?

SPENCER @TheSpencerRyan
#69 You know full well I'm an arse man! Haha!

SPENCER @TheSpencerRyan
#123 First I'd take you to dinner, then I'd take you to a place where you don't even know your own name. Sound good?

Oh my God! What is going on? I scroll through his timeline and find that he's playing a game

SPENCER @TheSpencerRyan

Spencer

Got a question? I've got answers. #DMgame Ask me anything and I'll answer truthfully on TL. Don't forget to leave a # number for a reply.

Holy shit! What are these 'ladies,' and I use that term loosely, asking him?

SPENCER @TheSpencerRyan
#17 the position doesn't matter darling, I can hit the spot from any angle. #Skillz

Oh my God, I've had just about all I can stomach of this. These little skanks need to back off! It sickens me thinking how many of them have sampled his '#Skillz.' Ugh! Suddenly, despite never wanting to speak to him again, I have the urge to play his silly game.

I take a deep breath and open our direct message conversation. Swallowing hard when I see that the last words he said to me were when he caught me out at the pub. I feel a sinking sadness, I actually feel bad that I upset him. Did I upset him? It's difficult to tell. But then I recall what happened next and the sadness is replaced by the all-consuming heat that spreads through me and pools in my aching clit.

Angry desire raging inside me pushes me on as I start to type.

'I have a question. How many of these pathetic skanks has it taken to hone your so called '#Skillz.'

I wait and wait and no answer comes through. Then it hits me that I'm supposed to look on his timeline for the answer. But is there one? No. He's still answering people's questions, just not mine. Fucking charming. I scroll through his other stomach-churning replies and then I come to,

SPENCER @TheSpencerRyan
For the social media challenged among us…You have to leave me a number if you expect me to reply.

I huff. I should know better than to feed his ego any more than I have already, but I'm too mad. I go back to our conversation and reply.

'Arse.'

Then just as I'm about to type a number, a message comes through from him.

'You're supposed to leave a number. Don't worry, Princess, I assigned you a number myself…'

I switch back to his timeline and there it is. I actually laugh, it's a begrudging laugh, but it's there.

SPENCER @TheSpencerRyan
#4/10 The skills come naturally, no practice required. Why? Jealous?

Four out of ten? The cheek of it! I'm shaking my head and conceding silently to myself that this round might just have gone to him. I should never have risen to it, now he's one up and he'll be intolerable. Then another tweet comes.

SPENCER @TheSpencerRyan
#4/10 Arse...is that an offer? Because if it is, I might have to bump you to 5/10

That Fucker. I go straight back to our conversation and type a response. I'm not plastering this all over the timeline.

> 'I wouldn't touch you again if I was hanging by my fingernails from a cliff and yours was the only outstretched hand for miles.'

'Ok babe, whatever you say. What if it wasn't my hand that was outstretched? I seem to recall you weren't so averse to my cock.'

> 'You are such a pig. I don't know what came over me on Saturday, but trust me when I tell you that it will NEVER happen again.'

'Oh please don't say that, I'll cry myself to sleep tonight...Oh wait, no that will be you.'

'Don't flatter yourself, Spencer, just quit the attention seeking and leave me alone.'

'Babe, you feel free to unfollow me at any time, but if you stick around and see something that offends you, tbh…I don't care.'

'Oh I see plenty that offends me, just looking out the window.'

'Sorry, Princess. If the help is bothering you, maybe you could move to the west wing until it's over?'

'Fuck. You.'

'No. Chance.'

This is getting me nowhere, I rest my palms on the cool marble of the counter and sigh, sending a wisp of cocoa powder into the air. I look at my phone between my hands and contemplate my options. Unfollow, block even…that's the only sane thing to do. Otherwise I'm just as much a willing part of this fiasco as he is, no matter what I tell myself.

My finger hovers over the unfollow button. But the child in me cannot let it drop. If I unfollow, I'll still be able to see what he says, it achieves nothing and I'm not giving him the victory. No. Not happening.

SPENCER @TheSpencerRyan
When I say Princess, I mean intolerable, spoiled brat with a tiara. #JustSayin

    Oh, for fucks sake! Now you're going to airtweet about me? What are we, twelve? FINE.

JAZZ @OMGJazzyP
Since narcissist is probably too big a word for you, lets try arsehole. Do you understand arsehole?

SPENCER @TheSpencerRyan
I'd rather be an honest arsehole than a lying bitch.

JAZZ @OMGJazzyP
Honest? It's cute how you want the world to think you're a nice guy. Maybe you should work harder on being one than you do trying to sell it

SPENCER @TheSpencerRyan
NEWSFLASH! I don't give a shit what you think about me, I don't think about you at all.

JAZZ @OMGJazzyP
For someone who doesn't think about me, you seem to spend a lot of time on my TL.

SPENCER @TheSpencerRyan
Princesses in glass houses shouldn't throw diamonds. Seems like it's you stalking me.

JAZZ @OMGJazzyP
You keep telling yourself that, whatever gets you through the night, jackass.

SPENCER @TheSpencerRyan
Don't worry Princess, if I have trouble sleeping I'll just lay there and count the reasons you're such a spoiled bitch.

JAZZ @OMGJazzyP
It's funny how the people who know the least about you always seem to have the most to say.

SPENCER @TheSpencerRyan
1. Entitled
2. Rich
3. Superior
4. Judgmental
5. Snobby
Yawns I'm half asleep already… #Zzz

JAZZ @OMGJazzyP
You know nothing about me, so why don't you introduce your top lip to your bottom lip and shut the fuck up

SPENCER @TheSpencerRyan
You should take your own advice. But I reckon that mouth of yours needs something more substantial to silence it.
#GotJustTheThingRightHere

JAZZ @OMGJazzyP
Big talk for a little boy

SPENCER @TheSpencerRyan
LITTLE? Do you have trouble judging sizes as well as all your other flaws?

JAZZ @OMGJazzyP
Nope! I just don't remember any details. Can't have made much of an impression #Unremarkable

SPENCER @TheSpencerRyan
Seems you need a refresher

JAZZ @OMGJazzyP
All mouth and no trousers

I wait for the onslaught to continue, but it stops. Just like that. Did I shut him up? Did I win? I huff out an exasperated laugh, who am I kidding? I lost the moment I replied. That jackass has me playing his game, and I'm so busy trying to one-up him, that I'm ignoring what I'm becoming. I look towards the door that leads out to the side of the house from the kitchen. He's probably only feet away on the other side. I could just go out there, like a grown up, and ask if we can put an end to all the childish games.

I walk cautiously towards it, my stomach turning at the thought of talking to him. I pause, knowing that if I do this, he could laugh and throw it back in my face. Let's face it, he's going to laugh and throw it back in my face. There's no way he'll just roll over. I sigh and turn back in to the kitchen. Looking at all my chocolates lined up on a tray. THIS is what's important, not Spencer Fucking Ryan.

The door opens abruptly behind me and bumps the door stopper that protects the wall. I turn, expecting to see Mags, but his deep brown eyes, hungry and fixed on me are what I find in her place. He steps inside and closes the door behind him, never breaking eye contact. I can see his chest rising and falling; my breathing picks up to match his.

His tanned, inked skin, all on display looks absurdly out of place in this kitchen, not like it did out in the open. Here, the definition of his toned body feels indecent, up close and personal. Is it suddenly hot in here? He prowls towards me and I instinctively back up, until I meet the island counter.

"What are you doing?" I barely whisper, clearing my throat in the hope that the next thing out of my mouth is audible.

"Backing up my mouth," he smirks. "with my trousers."

He is now standing before me and his scent is once again surrounding me. It's intoxicating. How can someone who does a physical job, outside in the sun, smell so good? He smells like man, sexy man. I take a deep breath in, inhaling him.

What. Is. Wrong. With. Me? Two minutes ago I was in a rage, slinging insults at him. Then I catch one whiff and I'm gone. "Don't bother," I mumble.

"Did you just sniff me?"

Oh, fuck, busted. It's bad enough I can't resist breathing him in, the last thing I need is for him to get a big head about it. "No! I did not just sniff you!"

"Yeah, ok," he says sarcastically.

"Why would I sniff you? You're not that irresistible." Even I don't believe me, but I pursue it regardless. "Sweaty man is a smell I can live without."

He lifts his arm and takes an exaggerated sniff. "Smells pretty good to me. It's ok, I know you can't resist me, I'm not holding it against you."

He can barely contain his amusement and I want to smack him again, but that's becoming a bit of a thing with us, and I don't want to give him more ammunition. "Your arrogance is out of control," I tell him instead.

He ponders this for a second and then shrugs. "No I think it's about right."

Ugh! He's so infuriating! "You need to leave. We need to stop the games."

He leans in, coming even more into my personal space and takes my hand from where it's gripping the edge of the counter for safety, or comfort, or maybe just to stop me launching myself at him. I flinch and pull away, but he keeps his grip on me and watches my face as he lowers my hand and presses it into his hard cock. "Does this feel like a game to you?"

I gasp and try to wriggle my wrist free. He's got me pinned again, and the annoying thing is, I like it. "Yes," I swallow hard. "I think you like playing with me."

"Funny," he says, as he moves my hand up and down. "I think I'm the one who got played." I'm silent; I have no comeback. He's right. There I said it. I'm not going to say it out loud, but I can admit it to myself. I played him, I can't argue and the size of him is too distracting to try.

Holy shit, Mags would dine out on this forever, I think to myself as I realise my hand has started to curl around him while he continues to guide it up and down his length. I want to see it...Damn him.

"Got nothing to say?" he says softly...too softly.

I look up and meet his intense gaze. It's a mistake. My resolve evaporates. "I thought you wanted to shut me up?" I whisper. A clear invitation.

He quirks his eyebrows and presses himself harder into my hand to test the water. I respond by bringing my other hand to his shorts and finding the zip of his fly. With the sound of the zip, the eerie calm we had for a moment disappears.

He frees my hand so I can undo his shorts and almost without my noticing, he pushes on my shoulder and encourages me to my knees. Before I can control it, I have complied with his cocky insistence and find myself kneeling, pulling open his shorts. His eager cock springs out, not hindered by underwear as he is going commando.

My fire returns and I scoff, "No underwear? Figures."

"Took them off for a selfie," he smirks.

"Attention seeker."

"Worked though, didn't it?"

I open my mouth to argue, "I..." but he grabs my ponytail firmly and surges forward into my mouth... He pushes in deep, far deeper than I'm prepared for and I gag and push him back. He withdraws completely, and I look up at him, my breathing heavy. He still has my hair in a firm grip and when I part my lips again to object he does the same thing. Slower this time, then he pauses.

"Told you I had just the thing for that mouth of yours, Princess."

He keeps my eye and waits for me to push him away again,

but I relax. Then he nods slightly and eases forward a fraction. It's a gesture that almost says 'Good girl, you can do it' and it sends a shiver down my spine. I accept him as far as he demands, even though he's a lot to take.

Rational thought has all but left me as I allow this man I hardly know, and frankly despise, to use my mouth. I don't know what's come over me. I like to be in control and I especially don't like pushy arrogant men, but as he withdraws and slides his big, hard dick into my throat, so deep I struggle, the pain from his grip on my hair, simply heightens the experience.

The way he leaves me no choice, has heat spreading through me like wildfire. I'm so wet and aching for relief, but I don't touch myself. Somehow I know he'll object. He's in control now, and as much as I hate that, it feels so good.

The moan that reverberates from him snaps me out of my stupor. While I've been lost in the physical and psychological thrill of letting go, he has found his pace and I'm just taking it. He's paying close attention to where his glistening cock disappears into my mouth. Studying it closely and tightening his hold on my hair as he drives in and out. He moans again and his eyes close, with pleasure.

"Fuck," he growls and pulls out. He lifts me up by tugging on my hair; I comply willingly and whimper as he whips me around to face away from him. He grinds himself against my arse and his hand creeps around to the front of my waistband. He slides his hand straight in and moans when he finds how wet I am.

His insistent fingers quickly bring me close, and I manage to bite out, "Yes!!"

Almost like it won't do that I'm close, he pulls his hand away, leaving me ready to beg. But before I allow the feeble plea to leave my lips, I'm roughly bent over and pushed down onto the cool marble, sending utensils scattering. He still has my hair in his hand and he's using it to hold me in place while he yanks my shorts and underwear down.

He presses against me and I moan in anticipation. I hold onto the counter and brace myself for him. My body is pleading, my clit throbbing and between my thighs is slick with need. I want him now. He grinds again. I can't bring myself to say it. He may have me under his control, I may secretly love it, but I can't bring myself to beg.

"Do it," I growl, taking back some of the control.

He laughs and grinds his hips, yanking my hair back and leaning in to my ear. "Oh, you want it, do you, Princess?"

I sigh.

"Say it," he hisses, "I don't want any confusion later."

I swallow, he's a dick, but with my hair in his hold, his cock pressed against me and his breath against my neck, I can't fight it. "I want you to fuck me." He growls at my words and rotates his hips. "Now," I add with a frustrated tone.

"Ah, ah, aahh! Princess, aren't you forgetting something?"

Oh, don't tell me he expects me to say 'please?' That is where I draw the line. I try to push away from the counter, but he holds me down. "What?" I demand.

He fumbles around behind me, what the hell is he doing? Then his hand appears before my face, a condom packet between his fingers.

"Safety first, Princess, don't you agree?"

Twat.

He releases my hair to open it and roll it on, but the loss of contact damn near breaks the spell, my sense floods back in and I feel ridiculous. What am I doing? The guy is an idiot, then he pulls my hair and I become weak for him. What the hell? Part of me wants to call an end to this right now, but the ache in my pussy emphatically disagrees.

"Hurry up," I snap. I won't beg.

His hand is back in my hair, and I sigh with relief. That bite and pull has me complicit, and I don't have to fight my thoughts while he's got me in his grasp.

"What's the rush, Princess? Do you want me?"

I stay silent, earning myself a hair tug. My skin tingles all over with pleasure.

"Tell me," he growls.

A slight twist of his wrist, pulling my head back towards him, has me moaning.

"Say you want it, Princess." He lines himself up and makes me aware that he's ready and waiting to give me what I need. "All you have to do is say the words."

He presses a fraction inside, and I try to surge back, but the palm of his hand presses me firmly against the counter. Totally in his grasp, I let it all go. "I want it."

"Good girl," he moans as he seats himself fully inside me.

I cry out. The sudden fullness, his words, the painful, wonderful way he has me in his hands, it's all too much. He pulls back and abandons his measured approach, slamming into me over and over.

It all becomes a sweaty, loud, breathless blur. He never lets me go; I'm rooted to the spot, while he pounds into me. Only feeling, not thinking. Our moans mix together, unconcerned with our surroundings. I am close to the brink as he kicks my legs further apart and lifts his hand off my back.

I feel its absence immediately, but it is quickly replaced with the weight of him as he leans over me. His breathy sighs against my ear has the blood rushing down to where he owns me completely. His hand brushes my thigh and I gasp, but when his fingers touch my clit I jump. "Oh God!" I moan.

He circles it, while slamming into me, making me whimper and then he increases the pressure.

I can't hold it back any more and I explode around him, my pussy clenching against his hard cock.

"Fuck," he whispers. Then with one more stroke he comes, pressed deeper in me than anyone has ever been. He rests his weight down on me and continues to thrust slowly into me as we both milk every wave of pleasure we can from each other.

Panting, I become more aware of my surroundings. He pulls away from me and my pussy contracts one last time as he slips from my body. He releases my hair and steps back, leaving me free and exposed.

I try to force myself not to immediately go back into bitch mode with him. I straighten up and pull up my shorts, not looking at him. I don't honestly know what to say. I've been a bitch, I played him, he's right to be angry. But that was incredible. I want to do it again. How can I tackle it in a way that won't make him gloat?

Be humble, Jazz, I tell myself, I think it's the only way. Taking a deep breath, I risk a glance at him. He's watching me. Clearly not having the internal battle I am, just cool as you like, watching me, with his cock still out and everything. Bloody hell, he's something else. He smiles his cocky smile, pulls off the condom, in no hurry to cover himself.

He holds it up and smirks. "Better safe than sorry, hey Princess?" Then I watch as he tosses it onto my tray of freshly made truffles and turns and heads for the door, doing up his shorts and laughing.

He stops when he reaches the door and looks back at me standing in stunned silence.

"Same time tomorrow?" he laughs.

I see red and grab for the nearest thing to my hand. A whisk, it will do. I launch it at him as he closes the door and watch it hit the place where he stood and clatter to the floor.

My hands are shaking with rage, and I turn to look at my beautiful chocolates lined up on the tray with the condom full of his nasty spent seed lying among them.

I let out an exasperated growl and grab the tray, yanking the bin open and tipping the whole tray in. Humble, my arse! I should have fucking known better. I look at the empty tray in my hand and shudder. "Ugh!" It has got to go too. I dump it in the bin and slam it shut.

"You ok?"

I jump out of my skin at the sound of Mags' voice and turn guiltily to face her. She frowns and comes towards me.

Her eyes are on my hair, which must be all kinds of messy. I try and straighten it. She reaches out and touches my temple, then brings her finger close to inspect. It is covered with cocoa powder. Therefore so is my face. Awesome.

Spencer
TUESDAY 14TH JULY

SPENCER @TheSpencerRyan
Lunch was…Empowering. Now back to work I go.

I smile to myself putting my phone back into my pocket. "Where's lunch?" asks Will, with a frown. Oh, shit. While I was taking my break, I was going to get lunch, and now I have nothing to show for it other than a smear of chocolate on my arm and a deep satisfaction.

"I'm just going, I had something to take care of."

Will rolls his eyes at my procrastination, and then as I turn to head for my car, I see him glance at the direction I had come from. "Wait a second," he demands. I pause, grin and keep walking. "You didn't?" He calls after me, but I don't stop. "Did you?" He can't hide the cringe in his voice. I keep going until I'm in my car, chuckling to myself.

What I love about a physical job, is that I don't have to go to the gym. I do like the gym, when I'm in the habit of going, but if I have work that keeps me in shape, I'd far rather relax. That is why I love this work. I get to keep fit, be in the sun and not worry about the mathematical problem solving of my office job. I still get to apply all my practical engineering skills, but I can leave the desk and all the dull stuff behind and get a tan in the process.

My skin still damp from my shower, I recline on my bed in only my boxers. With the windows open, I can hear Will and Mags sitting in the garden having a drink and enjoying each other's company. This is the third time he's had her over. I don't think in the three years we've lived together he's ever entertained a girl here. Not in daylight hours anyway. He must actually like her.

I made a big thing of saying, 'fine, I'll give you some space' and stalking up here to have a shower. But the truth is, chilling out with the cool evening air filtering in through my window and getting an early night is just what I needed. I haven't slept well the past few nights, and I have a feeling tonight I'll sleep just fine.

I smile to myself. That was a result today. I managed to shut the spoiled princess's mouth and got some pretty sweet head out of it too. My cock twitches at the thought.

"SHUT UP!" Will's voice carries up to my window. Mags has just told him something he obviously can't believe.

"No, I'm serious!" she replies.

"Fuck!" He sounds astonished. I move over to the window to eavesdrop a little; they've piqued my interest.

"She's livid. He kind of just did it, no discussion. Just you know…took it."

Oh God, not this again, she was totally into it. I won't have her saying this stuff about me.

"What?" He slams his drink down so hard on the glass table I'm surprised it doesn't shatter. I'm trying to stay out of sight, but I need to hear this conversation. He better not buy this bullshit.

"Oh, no, not like that. In a hot way. She loved it, that's why she's so mad with herself."

Huh. Interesting.

"So, was this today?" Will asks, still in disbelief.

"Friday, when we brought her back here."

"It happened HERE?"

"Yes, why?"

Yes, Will, why?

"Because I think I saw him come out of your kitchen with that 'cat that got the cream' look today."

Damn him.

"No way!" Now it's Mags' turn to be stunned. "No she wouldn't go there again; she's too stubborn."

Don't bet on it, love.

"I don't know," Will says. That's my boy, backing me up. "He seems to thrive off the ones that hate him," he laughs. "I think he's a glutton for punishment. I bet he can't get it up if they aren't hurling abuse at him. It's a bit like bear baiting, he gets off on the anger."

HEY!

Will roars with laughter.

He'll pay for that later.

Mags laughs too. "Jazz is perfect for him then. She's extremely fiery, she's no one's little plaything, that's for sure."

My cock twitches again. Plaything, what a perfect description for her. Mags might think Jazz is no one's plaything. Hell, Jazz might even think it. But that's exactly what she was today. Blood flows south when I think how willing she was. That girl pisses me off, but she has me hard whenever I think about her.

"So, you think it wasn't just a one off?" Mags asks.

"He definitely had that look today. I assumed it was a first, I didn't know about Friday. How did Jazz seem?"

"I don't know, she was all covered in chocolate when I saw her, looked like she had been hard at it."

Laughter erupts and I decide to step away. It was handy to hear some of that, like how she loved it when I took it. But I can't be arsed to listen to them laugh it up.

I flop back down on the bed and think about today. She was so annoyed, it was hilarious. I had her right where I wanted her. She admitted she wanted it and she loved it. Despite being a royal pain in the arse, she's so fucking hot. Especially when she's fighting her hatred for me because she wants me so bad.

I wonder what she's doing right now?

Glancing at my phone, I contemplate finding out. She won't be happy to hear from me, I'm sure. Do I care?

Nope!

'Evening, Princess.'

Why beat around the bush out on the timeline? I hear she likes it when I take it, so I do just that and go straight into our private conversation. After waiting a couple of minutes and getting nothing back, I decide to poke.

'Aren't you feeling chatty this evening?'

'If you don't want to talk, I could just tell you how I plan for my lunch break to go tomorrow.'

'Fuck off.'

'That's not nice, Princess.'

'Just leave me alone, Spencer.'

'You can unfollow me if you don't want me in here you know.'

I watch my follower count for a couple of minutes. Funny, it stays the same.

'I'll take that as the ok to be here then, Princess.'

'Do what you like, I'm getting off here for the night.'

Sure she is. She'll still be lurking to see what I do, we both know it. I'll just have to give her something to watch. I'll just amuse myself describing in detail what I plan to do. I'm typing out a message, when an evil idea pops in my head. How would she like it if I took it out of our private chat. Put it on my timeline where everyone could see. Describe in great detail what I'd do to my Shoegirl. I stifle a laugh at the thought of her freaking out, and the rest of the girls falling over themselves to comment. I think it's a great idea.

SPENCER @TheSpencerRyan
There you are at the kitchen counter, where I left you yesterday. Busy with something or other. I don't care what, because you're going

SPENCER @TheSpencerRyan
to drop it all when I tell you and be busy with me. You know I'm behind you and you pause, waiting. I eye you, standing with your back to

SPENCER @TheSpencerRyan
me, breathing heavy in anticipation. Your thin sundress skimming your ample curves, and finishing beautifully high on your thigh. I lick

SPENCER @TheSpencerRyan
my lips. You sent me a picture of something I want to taste and I'm going to. Right now. Closing in on you, I feel your heat. You turn as I

SPENCER @TheSpencerRyan
reach you and start to speak. I silence you, sliding my hand up your thigh and under the short skirt of your sexy little dress. I quirk my

SPENCER @TheSpencerRyan
brow when I find nothing beneath it. You bite your lip, knowingly. You knew I'd come for you. You were waiting.

My fingers slip into your

SPENCER @TheSpencerRyan
velvet pussy and you sigh, relaxing instantly because it's what you need. I slide them out and circle your engorged clit, feeling you

SPENCER @TheSpencerRyan
tremble. But I came here to taste you. Withdrawing my hand and lifting you onto the counter behind you, I sink to my knees. You

SPENCER @TheSpencerRyan
watch me with hunger and I hold your gaze as I slide my tongue through your folds. Your eyes close as you gasp 'Oh my God.' Yes that's me,

SPENCER @TheSpencerRyan
Princess. Your God. And I'm going to take you to heaven. The sweet taste of you is even better than I had imagined and I bury my tongue in

SPENCER @TheSpencerRyan
you so it coats my face. You prop yourself on your elbows watching where we are joined and when my tongue swirls your clit your head

SPENCER @TheSpencerRyan
drops back as you whimper. I suck it in, pulling at it, grazing it with my teeth, which has you jumping and crying out. I

flick my

SPENCER @TheSpencerRyan
tongue over it lightly, and as you relax, I push two fingers inside you. You draw in a sharp breath and your pussy grips my fingers. I

SPENCER @TheSpencerRyan
curl them towards me as I give your clit a hard suck. Putting pressure on your sweet spot. Your body tenses, your feet dig into my

SPENCER @TheSpencerRyan
shoulders, and as your hips buck, I increase the pressure and your juices start to flow. 'Spencer!' You cry as you gush, coating my face

SPENCER @TheSpencerRyan
and your thighs. I love the taste of you and lick greedily, making you jolt and moan. You are completely overcome from the intensity and

SPENCER @TheSpencerRyan
you don't see me stand, keeping my fingers inside you and drop my jeans to the floor. My cock is hard and begging for some action. You

SPENCER @TheSpencerRyan
can barely contain your ecstasy when I fill you. Your pussy is still contracting from your orgasm and by pushing my thick

cock into you

SPENCER @TheSpencerRyan
without warning I set you off again. Moaning 'yes' and grabbing at my t-shirt to pull me closer, you can't get enough. I lift your legs

SPENCER @TheSpencerRyan
and use them as leverage to get as deep in you as possible, you tighten around me even more when I press them together and hold both your

SPENCER @TheSpencerRyan
ankles in one hand. Wrapping my other arm around your thighs I slam into you, pulling you against me with each thrust, getting as deep as

SPENCER @TheSpencerRyan
possible. Your moans are now pleas and I answer them, dropping your ankles onto my shoulder and leaning over you, pressing your

SPENCER @TheSpencerRyan
legs against your chest and making you somehow tighter. Like this I'm gripped so tight, I can't stop myself seeking release. As I push

SPENCER @TheSpencerRyan
into your vice-like pussy and growl, holding you there. Your pussy responds, contracting and milking my load from me.

You are still lost in

SPENCER @TheSpencerRyan
your moment when I let your legs down and sit you up. I don't need to ask if you enjoyed that. Of course you did. Besides, I doubt you can

SPENCER @TheSpencerRyan
speak right now. I pull up my jeans and fasten them, noticing as I do, the sheen of our combined pleasure on your pussy. I dip my

SPENCER @TheSpencerRyan
fingers between your well used lips and get them nice and wet. Bringing them to your lips to taste. You suck them willingly,

SPENCER @TheSpencerRyan
purring with pleasure…Tomorrow, this will happen.

    My notifications have been going crazy through that, but I was too focused on getting it out to read them. I know dozens of the girls have reacted. I see nothing unexpected as I scroll through. The general gist is that they'd all love me to do that to them, and they're waiting should I decide which one of them will be the lucky candidate.
    Pitiful, really.
    And not one word from Shoegirl.
    Fine.
    I know she saw. I'd bet my last penny on it.

Still, I'm not waiting around, just one more thing before I sign off.

SPENCER @TheSpencerRyan
I'm glad you all enjoyed my story ladies, unfortunately the one person I hoped would enjoy it is the one person who has said nothing.

SPENCER @TheSpencerRyan
So until tomorrow, I wish you goodnight.

Jazz

WEDNESDAY 15TH JULY

Ok, today it gets real. I made a couple of batches with ingredients I had already. Then yesterday, after the, umm, lunchtime incident, my delivery came. So last night, I did a lot of prep and squeezing things in fridges and making notes, and this morning it's all systems go. I have four days.

"Tea?" Mags says from behind me as she enters the kitchen to see me with my hands on my hips, staring at everything all lined up ready.

"Please," I reply, smiling that she's up. She wants to help and although I've insisted she doesn't have to, and I don't want her to get out of her writing zone, I am extremely grateful that she is. I'm absolutely terrified about what I have to do in such a short space of time.

There is one other reason I'm glad she's going to be around. And right on cue, he pulls into the driveway. My body and my brain react in opposite directions, watching him step out of the car. Heat sweeps through my lady parts, I can't help it. My pussy is a slut. The rest of me recalls his presumptuous performance on Twitter last night. 'Tomorrow, this will happen.' Bleugh! Who does he think he is? Oh, yes, that's right, God! Pft! In his deluded dreams.

Mags places a tea beside me and stills my hand. "You're slamming around," she says gently.

I pause and sigh. I was. He just gets to me. I glance out of the window again. He's there, leaning against his car, looking at his phone and laughing to himself. My hand goes for my phone on instinct. I might be able to see what's making him laugh. But I catch myself. This is why I'm glad Mags is here to help me. She will stop me obsessing over Spencer and keep me focused on the job. And should he attempt to make his lunchtime fantasy a reality, he will be cock blocked by a pro.

No obsessing. Work to do. This is just what I need right now to stop this situation getting any messier. I just have to concentrate, and when this weekend is over, I'll go home.

"So, where do we start?" asks Mags, surveying the sacks of chocolate and equipment.

"Ganache!" I reply brightly, snapping into action. "Lots and lots of ganache."

"Oh my God I've died and gone to heaven," sighs Mags, stirring the dark chocolate ganache I've just showed her how to make. "What are we putting in this one?"

I laugh, she's like a kid in a sweet shop. "This one is Dark and Stormy."

Her eyes light up. "Ooooh, that sounds gooood!"

"Uh huh," I laugh. "It's one of the new ideas I had. Based on that cocktail I had at Lady Luck's the other day. It's ginger, rum and a hint of lime."

"Yuuuum!"

"Let's add the flavours, then it can cool."

Mags huffs. She really isn't great at waiting for things to

cool, so I get her on the next batch, setting some cream to boil. Once it comes to the boil, she lifts it off the heat and waits a minute before she pours it over the chips of chocolate in the large bowl I've given her. While she waits she swipes one of the plain 70% truffles I've just finished.

"Hey!"

Mags moves quickly back to the stove giggling through a mouthful of chocolate. "You know Will's parents are moving?" She casually drops in.

"Are they?"

"Yeah, they're moving down to the coast," she says with a conspiring look. "It means the patisserie is on the market…"

Pausing for a second to figure out her logic, it suddenly hits me. "Oh, hell no!"

"Jazz, hear me out."

"No, uh uh, no way."

"It's perfect for you. The set up is mostly in place. You can start off slow. The customers are already there, it's busy. You could just take it over as a running coffee shop and slowly introduce your chocolates. The staff are trained, and I'm sure they would all stay on. All you need to do is focus on gradually making changes."

"Mags, when George gets home, we will be back home and living far too far away to have a shop in this village. I mean, with that kind of business you need to be there at the crack of dawn and…" I pause and catch that look on her face. I roll my eyes. "You have an answer for that too, don't you?" I put my spoon down and wave my hand dismissively. "Go on, just get it out of your system."

She cringes visibly as this is clearly not going how she

wants it to go.

"Go on," I demand, folding my arms.

"Jesus, Jazz, could you be any more closed off?"

"Spit it out, Mags."

"Fine. Their house is also going on the market."

I laugh. Loud. There's nothing else to do really. Other than turn and walk out of the room, which suddenly seems like a great idea. Move here? What is she thinking?

"You're not keen? It's beautiful here."

"Keen? Mags, I'd rather staple my eyelids to my arsehole! Not that this isn't a beautiful place, it is. But there are a thousand other beautiful places, and they don't come with Spencer Ryan. Nope. Not happening."

"But…"

"Stir, Mags!" I tell her sternly as she pours the hot cream into the bowl. "You're good at that."

She gives me a 'really?' look.

"Oh, please, you're the queen of stirring."

"Is that so?"

"Yep. You can't resist."

"If that were true, don't you think I'd have been talking all morning about how Will swears he saw Spencer come out of here yesterday with that look of pure satisfaction?"

I freeze. Not turning to face her.

"I KNEW IT!"

I shake my head. "Just keep stirring, Mags."

"Oh, don't worry, I will." She laughs.

I add more rum and contemplate swigging from the bottle.

"So?"

I sigh and put the bottle down. The temptation is too great.

"Oh my God, you DID!"

I cover my face with my hands, feeling mortified, depositing chocolate on my brow. Mags leaves her stirring and comes over.

"Jazz, what is it?"

I peep out of my fingers and look at her.

"Don't do that!" she smacks my shoulder, "I thought you were crying." She goes back to the ganache.

"I should be crying, Mags. Look at me!"

"What? All I see is you finally getting on with something you should have been doing for years." She pauses, "...and maybe having it away with a hot arsehole," she mutters.

My shoulders sag.

"Sooooo?"

"OK! Yes. We did. I didn't want to, but…"

"But?"

"But he's impossible."

"To resist?"

I screw up my face, but a laugh escapes.

"But I saw you on Twitter yesterday having a go at each other."

"Yep. Then he came looking for me and…"

"Your underwear burst into flames?"

I wince.

"Jazz, it's ok if you like him, you know. You aren't hurting anyone."

"I don't, though. He's a dick. It's THIS!" I point at my rebellious crotch. "This is the bit that likes him. The rest of me is fucking pissed off, Mags!"

"Pissed off about what?"

"That he's so fucking smug, and that I can't stop the bloody rush of desire when I'm around him. I feel like I'm living in the Twilight Zone. Except it's just this bit right here," I draw an invisible square in the air around my bits. "This is the zone where nothing makes sense. It's the Spencer Zone!" Mags laughs and I try to keep a straight face. "Every other bit of me is quite aware that this is insane."

"So what? You yell at each other over social media and then fuck? Is that how it goes?"

I cringe. "No, that's how it went yesterday."

"And now, he's taken to telling the world what he will do to you next?"

"You saw that?"

"Jazz, everyone saw that."

I let out a long breath.

"Well, it's not happening. I can tell you that now."

"Ok."

"It's NOT."

"Okay."

"Oh God, he's going to try though, isn't he?"

"I guess so. Is that so bad?"

"Yes, yes it is. I can't have him near the Spencer Zone." I gesture at the zone. "Bad things happen when he gets too close."

"Bad or really great."

"Really, really bad. I don't even know who I am around him."

"Ok," she says, taking my arms in her hands to bring my freakout under control. "Here's what we're going do. He thinks he will just waltz in here at lunchtime and find you unable to resist. So let's get one step ahead. Go and get changed, so you feel nice, and we will take tea out to them together and a plate of chocolates for them to try."

"Nooooo, no, no, no! I am not going out there! I'm safer in here."

"But he thinks this is where you will be. If you go out there, it's like you're saying, 'Not on your terms today, buddy.' It'll be fine, you'll see. Now go and get changed. If you're going to take control, you want to look good and you look like shit." She laughs wiping a smear of chocolate off my face.

"Cheers!"

"It's the truth, now go."

Reluctantly, I concede that she may be right. If I'm going to see him, I'd rather not look like a wild woman. And maybe leaving the kitchen, where he expects me to be, is a clear message to him that says, 'nope.'

I take my phone out of my pocket as I walk up stairs and can't stop myself seeing if he has tweeted. I pause on the landing.

SPENCER @TheSpencerRyan
Temptation is a dangerous thing. Especially when it's just on the other side of a kitchen door. #RollOnLunch

Oh, I'll fucking show him!!

Spencer
WEDNESDAY 15TH JULY

I glance at my watch for the third time. Almost lunch time. Almost time to see what I can make her do today. I look up and am surprised to see the two of them walking towards me. Huh. I'm a little disappointed, I wanted to find her alone. Oh, well, I'm sure I can work this to my advantage, too.

I smile, "Well, well, ladies. To what do we owe this rare pleasure?"

Jazz narrows her eyes, but she can't look at me.

Mags smiles, knowingly. "We just wanted to get out of the kitchen, you know how it is."

Uh huh, I'm getting the picture.

"We thought you'd like tea and maybe to try some of Jazz's handmade chocolates."

Hmm. Chocolate. Ok, I'm listening.

Will swoops in. "You made these?" he asks.

She nods.

'Cat got your tongue, Jazz?' I want to ask. But Mags jumps in again to save her.

"She did. She's setting up a business. You can be her guinea pigs. She'll be at the market on Sunday selling them."

I watch her shoot Mags a look and stifle a laugh. Looks

Spencer

like she's not happy Mags is sharing this information.

Will takes a ball of chocolate off the plate Mags is holding and shoves it in whole.

"Oh. My. God!" He rolls his eyes in ecstasy. "Dude, you have to try these."

The arsehole in me wants to decline in a less than polite way.

But it's chocolate.

And it looks good.

So good.

I reach out to take one. Then a thought crosses my mind. It's more of a flashback really. A tray of very similar looking chocolates was in the kitchen yesterday. It shows how distracted I was that I didn't register them at the time. But last time I saw the tray, I was laughing at the condom I'd dumped on it. I look directly at Jazz and ask, "Did you make these today?"

She finally meets my eye, puzzled.

"Yes, fresh this morning," Mags replies, oblivious to my reasons.

"Good, just making sure they're fresh." I smile an irritating smile and help myself to a couple. Jazz scowls. I think she caught my drift. Walking away so I don't do the orgasmic eye roll thing Will did in front of her, I pop one in my mouth and Oh. My. God. See, walking away was a good choice. I don't want to give her the satisfaction. Biting down on the second chocolate, I glance back at her in her little sundress, thinking, now she's given me two things I need to taste. That tasty looking snatch and more of these bad boys.

Then I double take. Wait there…little sundress?

Hmmmm.

Am I living in a dream world, or is that a clear sign that she approved of my story last night? I wish I could tell if there was underwear under there. That would confirm things, but as she's sticking to Mags like glue, it won't be possible.

For a lesser man, that is.

While Jazz is talking about her chocolates to the boys, I put my tools away for lunch and look around to see who is where. I start to walk towards the front of the house and pause by the kitchen door, looking back. Will sees me and narrows his eyes, daring me to go against the lecture he gave me this morning, but Mags, who is also watching, touches Will's elbow and asks if she can talk to him over by the tree we might need to remove. He gives her his undivided attention and follows her, she glances back at me with a slight smile.

I take that as, 'I'll keep him busy for you' and duck into the kitchen.

The sight and smell that greets me is just the same as it was yesterday. Bowls and utensils everywhere; and an incredible smell of chocolate and trays with neat lines of rolled truffles. Except today, I notice it. How did I miss all this crap yesterday, chocolate usually comes above everything!

Oh, but yesterday I was on a mission.

Drooling, I head around the counter and pick up a ball of chocolate from one of the trays, savouring it as the flavours explode in my mouth. Dark chocolate with some kind of boozy fruit flavour. God, it's good.

And she did this?

She's dangerous.

A woman who looks like her, thinks like her, wears those

shoes, gives me shit and makes stuff like this, is a danger.

If I had a heart, I'd be falling in love.

I come to a big bowl of soft looking chocolate goo with a spatula sitting in it. I dip my finger in the gooey goodness and lift it to my mouth.

Holy hell! That is fucking amazing. It's ginger and dark chocolate with some alcohol. Damn. I want to put my face in the bowl. I glance around, then shrug. Lifting the spatula out, with a decent scoop, I lean against the counter and take a good long lick.

"What the hell do you think you're doing?" she barks as she comes into the kitchen.

"Just having a taste, Princess," I reply, turning to let her see me take another lick.

She storms over, trying to grab the spatula out of my hand. Good luck with that sweetheart, this is me and chocolate. You ain't getting it back.

"You can't just wander in here whenever you feel like it."

"The door was open."

"Give that back!" she demands, catching hold of it. For a second we both pull at it, but then I see an opportunity and let go. Chocolate splatters her face, neck and chest and stops her dead in her tracks.

I choke on a laugh.

She looks at me, mouth open, "You did that on purpose!"

I shrug.

She glances down at the mess on her chest and my eyes follow, locking in on her begging nipples, visible through her dress. She looks embarrassed.

"It's ok, Princess, I know they like me even if you don't.

Happens whenever I'm around."

"It does not!"

"Mmmm-ok."

I step closer. She backs off, but I catch her arm and pull her close.

"What are you doing?" she gasps.

"I don't waste chocolate," I reply softly and then lean in and swipe my tongue over her temple.

She wriggles, but it's a weak effort. "Get off me," she demands.

"Hold still, Princess, it's all over you." I take another lick at her cheek and move down to her neck.

"Ok, that's enough," she snaps, her breath catching in her throat as I suck in her earlobe.

I lick her neck just below her ear even though there's no chocolate there and the way her head falls slightly back in surrender makes me swallow hard. "It's never enough," I murmur.

What the fuck?

I shake the sappy shit out of my head before I grow a vagina, and pluck the spatula out of her hand, painting a trail down her cleavage. Dropping the spatula on the floor, I grab her by the arse and lift her so that I can lick it all off. She yelps and struggles and I plonk her down on the kitchen counter, leaning forward and feasting on the stripe I painted between her breasts. Her dress is ruined, shame, I quite liked it. Which reminds me…

Moving my hand between us I feel what I could only hope for. No underwear! SCORE!

"Little sundress, Princess? No underwear? It all rings a

bell."

"You're so full of yourself."

"I can't imagine why?" I laugh. "You send me naked pictures, tell me in detail what you want to do to me. Then when I post an innocent story about a little fantasy of mine, you parade around wearing just what I've described."

"Innocent story?" she snarls, ignoring the fact that my fingers have begun to explore her folds.

"Absolutely," I skim my thumb across her clit and she gasps.

"You don't know the meaning of the word," she attempts to snap, her voice wavering as I push a second finger inside her.

"It's you who keeps showing me things I want to taste, Princess." I lick another splatter of chocolate from her neck, causing her to sigh. "This isn't even what I came here to taste, Princess. It's just the icing on the cake." I grin, licking my lips as I sink to my knees, just like I described last night. "This is what I'm here for. I warned you last night. You think because you ignore it, it won't happen?" I push back the fabric of her dress and feel the rush at the sight of her pussy. "You think because you ignore it, I think you don't want it?"

"I don't want it," she whispers.

"No, you don't want to want it, there's a difference, Princess."

She shakes her head at me. I nod.

I move my face closer, the smell of her is intoxicating. She watches me, I can feel her willing me, but she's too stubborn to say the words. I slowly continue to pump my fingers and stroke her clit again, feeling her tremble. "You want me to taste you, Princess?"

She nods her head but quietly replies, "No."

"You do give off some mixed signals, you know," I laugh, curling my fingers up towards me. She curses under her breath and her eyes flicker closed. "Let's start off small, shall we? Do you like this?" With her eyes still closed, she nods. "I thought so. What about this?"

I circle her clit and she moans. "Oh!"

"I'll take that as a yes," I smirk with a satisfaction she doesn't see. Finally, I lean right in so my breath can be felt against her glistening lips and breathe the words, "Do you want to feel my tongue, Princess?"

"Yes," she sighs, and to my surprise, uses her hand to close the inch between us.

The taste of her...

My cock has been fighting with my clothes for long enough and the taste of her makes it impossible to ignore. So while I bury my face in her, I undo my jeans and set it free, taking it in my hand.

I hum my relief as I stroke it.

My fingers are slick from her and my hand glides smoothly up and down. Her hand holds my head in place, her fingers flexing in my hair and she watches, just like I wrote. I suck in her clit, and keep the suction strong, teasing it with my tongue. She grips my hair tight and cries. I groan at the bite of her fingers and stroke faster.

Her hips have begun to grind as she's letting go of all her objections and just feeling it. Only one thing could make this better right now, I want to make her gush just like in my story. Reluctantly, I release her clit. She moans.

"Don't stop," she whimpers. I slide my fingers inside her, leaving my cock wanting. "Please, don't stop that," she begs.

"Relax, Princess, I want one more thing from you," I tell her, standing between her legs. She leans back on both hands and shakes her head.

"Don't spoil it, just finish it," she breathes.

"Oh, I'll finish it, Princess. Don't you worry. You're going to gush for me as you come."

"That doesn't really happen, it's a myth."

"Ok, Princess, if you say so."

"You watch too much porn. That stuff isn't real."

I laugh. She's for real. "Oh, Princess, I'm going to show you something really special."

She sighs, exasperated, "Please Spencer, you're ruining it now, just finish it without trying to be your usual cocky self. I was half enjoying that."

"Don't kid yourself, babe, you were in heaven. Now shut up and watch."

"I…" I cut her off with a vigorous rub of her G-spot. She gasps. I show no mercy and attack her sweet spot with determination. I'll show her it's no myth. She just needs someone who knows what they're doing to handle her right.

"Fuck!" she cries.

I place a hand just above her pussy pressing down so the pressure I'm putting on her from the inside is amplified.

I know when she is trying to back away from me; I've got it just right. She's begging and she doesn't even know what for. I increase the speed of my fingers and use my thumb to rub her clit.

Her orgasm hits her so hard, she screams. I feel the hot rush on my fingers I was seeking. I pull my hand away from her as soon as it starts and stand in shock as she soaks my T-shirt.

Holy shit!

"Holy shit!" she cries, still in the throes.

She can't believe what just happened. Hey, I can't believe what just happened. I was expecting a little gush. I've never seen a squirt like that in real life!

I'm so stunned, I almost forget myself and my cock begging for attention.

Grabbing her hips, I pull her back to the edge of the counter and rest her ankles on my shoulders, filling her in one thrust. She can hardly handle the intrusion on top of the avalanche of other sensations she's experiencing, she claps her hand over her mouth to prevent another scream.

Pulling back, my hips meet her arse again. She hasn't stopped coming yet, and she's moaning yes, over and over with each thrust, while she clenches down on me.

She feels so fucking good.

I watch her, still feeling every nerve lit up. She can't stop.

She has no idea how beautiful she is, not a single angle on her, just curves.

I can't hold it any longer, I fuck her hard and feel it coming.

It hits me almost as hard as hers.

"Fuck!" I manage through clenched teeth.

I stumble against her, hitting home again and pushing in further still.

"Fuck," I mutter again.

I'm breathing hard as I have to lean on the counter over her for support.

She has finally returned from wherever she was floating and is watching me when I open my eyes.

Jesus.

That was…

She's still staring at me. Breathing hard.

I'm still inside her.

It's way too intense.

Pulling out of her, I quickly fix my clothes. Then look down at my chest, drenched. I can't go out there like this. I think I have gym clothes in my car, I'll need to change.

Jazz sits dazed on the side. In shock, I think. It's all a bit too silent, I've go to do something to break it.

"See, I told you," I gloat. That's better.

She looks at me puzzled.

"I told you it wasn't a myth."

She opens her mouth to say something and then shuts it again like a goldfish.

"It's ok, Princess, you don't need to thank me," I grin. "You can make it up to me some other time."

"Ugh," she huffs, pushing herself off the counter. "Whoa," she exclaims, as her shaky legs almost don't hold her up.

"Careful," I steady her. "And watch out," I smirk. "It's a bit slippery around here."

She whacks me on the arm. "You're disgusting!"

Still laughing, I lean against the opposite counter. "So sorry to offend you, Princess, but it wasn't me who drenched the kitchen." I shrug. "Personally, I thought it was awesome."

"You would."

"You hated it, I suppose? Gonna tell Mags on me? Oh, Mags, you won't believe what he forced me to do this time!"

"Shut up!" she growls, knowing she hasn't got a leg to stand on, quite literally.

"Yeah that's right, I know you make out like I force myself on you."

"Don't you?"

"Oh, and you hate it, do you?"

She looks at me with a fire in her eyes, but nothing comes out of her mouth.

"Thought not."

She shakes her head at my gloating.

"Face it, Princess, my biggest crime today was making you come too hard." I hold up my hands in surrender. "Guilty as charged."

I notice a smudge of chocolate on my hand and lick it off. God, that's so good, I want more.

She sees me eyeing the chocolates lined up on trays on the other side of the island. "Don't even think about it! I'm trying to start a business here, and you keep coming in here like a walking food safety violation and cost me hours of work."

"What did I do?" I notice the bowl I was tasting when she showed up sitting beside her, I reach over and dip my finger in it and lift it to my mouth, sucking it clean. "Oh God, this is so good, Princess, what is it?"

"Dark and stormy," she sighs. "And you may as well take the bowl. I can't use it now you've had your dirty paws in it."

"Hmmm, dark and stormy…like you. I like it."

She looks at me. "Can you just do me a favour and stay out of this kitchen for the next few days. I can't afford the setbacks right now."

"No worries, we can find somewhere else tomorrow," I

laugh, knowing that isn't at all what she meant and it will piss her off to no end.

"There's no need, we won't be seeing each other tomorrow."

"You sure about that, Princess?"

"I guarantee it."

"Uh huh, we'll see."

"Just go."

I push off the counter and step towards her. She watches me, unsure of what I intend to do. I dip my finger in the bowl again. The same finger I sucked. Scooping out a nice big blob of the Dark and Stormy, I hold it high and let it drop from my finger onto my waiting tongue. "Mmmmm." I let it melt in my mouth and smile at her. Her face is full of contempt and it just makes me laugh. I dab my chocolatey finger on the end of her nose. "See you later, Princess." I suck the rest of the chocolate off my finger as I walk out of the kitchen with a spring in my step.

No utensils fly after me. That's progress.

I glance towards the boys working as I leave the house. I need to change. Actually, I need a shower. I'll probably be finding chocolate in weird places all afternoon if I don't. Mags looks up from her conversation with Will and sees me, but she doesn't give me away to him. Time to dash home I reckon. He'll kill me if he sees me like this.

SPENCER @TheSpencerRyan
Lunch…Just as I planned, but with chocolate.
#DarkAndStormy

Jazz

WEDNESDAY 15TH JULY

"Mags?" I ask tentatively after sitting for a while plucking up the courage.

"Mmmmm," she replies still typing.

"Have you ever…" Fucking hell, I can't just hit her with, 'have you ever squirted?' right out of the blue like this!

"Have I ever what?" she asks, finishing her sentence and turning to face me.

I bottle it. "Oh, never mind, you write. Sorry, I don't want to disturb you."

Her eyes narrow and she studies me.

"It's fine, honestly," I assure her.

Big mistake.

She grabs hold of that tiny shred of bullshit and knows there's more to the story. "Nope, this is too interesting, I'll get the wine!" she says, jumping up and heading for the kitchen.

"No, no, no," I call, following her when I realise she's ignoring me.

She has the cork halfway out of the bottle already by the time I reach her.

"Mags, you write, I'll read. It's too late for wine, I'm fine."

"Bollocks! Firstly, it's never too late for wine; and

secondly, you never have any trouble asking me things. This is juicy. Now, get the glasses and sit your backside back on that sofa."

I sigh, picking up two wine glasses from the cupboard and following her back to the lounge. I went about this all wrong. Now she's on high alert and I wasn't planning to tell her what happened today.

"So?" She demands before I've even sat back down.

I shake my head; what have I done?

"You fucked him again, didn't you?"

My mouth drops open.

"Oh, close your mouth, you'll catch a fly. I saw him come in here."

I close my mouth.

"Yeah, busted, missy! This is becoming a habit."

I close my eyes and cover my face with my hands. "I know," I whine. "I need an intervention." Then I look up at her, remembering our talk this morning. "Wait, you were supposed to be protecting me. Why didn't you stop him if you saw him?"

She giggles. "I thought you needed a little time in 'The Spencer Zone.'" She does the little square thing with her hand to clarify the location of said zone, as if we need reminding. "I kept Will busy for you."

"I can't believe you!" I hurl a cushion at her.

She catches it after it hits her head and bounces off to the floor. "Hey! You're welcome."

"Pft. Some friend you are."

And then it hits me. We did it again!

"What's the face?"

I look at Mags, ashamed with myself. "We did it again with no protection. I can't believe it! He has my brain so scrambled that I've only just realised."

"Ok, that's not good, I agree, but before you freak, I mentioned it to Will and..."

""You mentioned it to Will?" I interrupt, a few decibels louder than I intended.

"Yeah, we were talking about the two of you, and I mentioned that you were concerned that you'd got caught in the heat of the moment and he didn't, you know, suit up."

"Perfect." I drop my head.

"Oh, Jazz, we both know what's going on, you think we're not going to talk about it?" She stifles a laugh, "It's way too juicy not to talk about it, trust me!"

"Right, awesome. So what did he say then?" I sigh, resigned. I am now the main attraction obviously.

"He said Spencer never does that. That he has a reputation for being safer than Fort Knox."

"So, you're saying that he never, ever goes bareback? Oh well, I'll take Will's word for it then because, you know, it's only happened twice this week, so I can definitely believe that it's never happened before!"

"Ok, easy with the sarcasm there." She holds up her hand to stop me. "It's true, apparently his best mate made a girl pregnant with twins the night he lost his virginity at 16. Spencer was scarred for life. He is absolutely fanatical about it, apparently."

"So, fanatical that it's gone completely without consideration twice now?"

"Jazz, have you ever gone without protection?"

"No."

"Not even with long term boyfriends?"

"No."

"And you let it happen with no consideration twice with Spencer?"

"He fries my brain!" I cry in frustration.

"Well, maybe you fry his too!" She throws back in an equal tone.

I sigh.

"All I'm saying is that it's perfectly feasible that this is a unique situation for both of you, and that you shouldn't tie yourself in knots about it. You're on the pill, so you don't have that to worry about. No little Spencers running around," she giggles.

"Oh, fuck." I clutch my stomach, just the thought makes me want to hurl. "I'd seriously die."

"Look, you just need to make sure you talk to him about it. Be responsible. If you've both never gone without, then where's the harm?"

I look at her with a disapproving expression. "Have you ever thought of teaching sex education, Mags? I'm sure with your 'fuck it' way of thinking, you could be a breath of fresh air to all the STD campaigns. You should put a CV together and see if you can help in some way."

She laughs and I can't help laughing too.

"Just talk to him."

"There's no point, it's never going to happen again."

"Well, when you've returned from your trip up de-Nile, next time it happens, you should really have 'the talk,' that's all I'm saying."

My back stiffens. She's a sarky bitch at times, but she's right. If, and I mean IF, I ever allow him near me again, we should talk about it. It's unlikely though and yelling seems to be more our thing anyway.

"So, come on then…have I ever?"

"Have you ever what?" She pulls me out of my thoughts and I have no idea what she's going on about.

"That's what started this whole thing. You asked have I ever…?"

"Oh, that."

"Yes. That. Now spill."

I swallow.

"Because if it's have I ever taken it up the arse, you know the answer." She says and falls about laughing.

"Ugh, Mags," I laugh, screwing up my face. "I'm not listening!" I plug my ears and continue, "I don't mind hearing about your exploits, but you know how I feel about hearing details of you sleeping with my cousin. That's just toooooo much information!"

She recovers herself, she loves doing that to me. At the time I could have killed her for corrupting my cousin with her smutty ways, until I discovered that he was way more filthy than she is. I learned the hard way that you shouldn't let your friends near your family. Neither should you ask them to tell you about it, out of morbid curiosity. Some things can't be unheard. Christmas was awkward last year.

"Anyway, it's not that."

"So, come on then, cut the coy shit out, what is it?"

I look down at my fingers. "Have you ever…like, gushed?"

Mags shrugs a little and thinks. "I guess, yeah, a little at times. I mean, it's not like the fountain you see in porn. That's bullshit."

My face forms into a dead giveaway 'that's what you think' expression and her forehead crinkles as she studies me. "Ok, spill!"

I wince.

"Oh, shit, bad choice of words!" She laughs. "But come on."

Still not ready to regale details of a secret sex life with a guy I can't stand out loud, I hesitate.

"Jazz?" she pokes me. "Don't you hold out on me! We tell each other everything, remember?"

I sigh. "Fine, ok." I rub my face. "It's not bullshit. I thought it was, too, but it's not. It's really not."

"Spencer made you gush?"

"No, he did more than that. He was soaked!"

"Bloody hell."

"Seriously, I've never felt anything like it. It was…" I swallow, feeling that familiar rush of arousal, just thinking about it. "It was unbelievable." Then I catch myself doing a dreamy, misty, far away thing that just won't do.

"Wow," she says in wonder. "I want!"

I shoot her a look and she giggles.

"You'll have to see if Will has the skills."

"Hey! Will and I are not sleeping together."

My face clearly tells her I don't believe a word out of her lips.

"We're not, honestly. We're just friends."

"But you like him?"

"Yeah, but we've been there and it hurt us both. I don't think I can go there again."

"If it is meant to be Mags, it will be, you won't be able to fight it."

She frowns, then redirects back on to me. "A bit like you and Spencer, then? You think you hate each other but you still can't resist. Maybe it's meant to happen?"

I scoff. "Oh, please! No, that really isn't meant to happen and it won't be happening again."

"Really? Your resolve is stronger than it was this morning, is it? You remember this morning right?" She smirks. "When you definitely weren't going there again, ever. Just before you came all over him by the sounds of it."

"I really don't like you sometimes," I scowl.

"Yeah, but you know I'm right. Why fight it? He's hot, you're into it, and he certainly sounds like he knows which buttons to push. Just enjoy yourself and let it happen."

I roll my eyes and stand. "I'm going to hit the hay, I need to get up early tomorrow and find myself a new best friend. You're no use whatsoever."

Mags gasps, theatrically. "That hurts!"

I grin and head up to my room. Just as I'm closing my door, my phone receives a text.

'Was it loads?'

I laugh.

'Well, I was pretty out of it, but it felt like a lot and he was basically dripping!'

'Awesome.'

'Goodnight, Mags.'

'Goodnight, Shamu.'

I frown at my phone.

'No wait, that sounded wrong, I'm not calling you a whale, I was referring to the blowhole thing…you know what? It was a terrible analogy, forget this happened. As you were, nothing to see here. Goodnight, Jazz.'

I shake my head as I type.

'Go to bed before you hurt yourself.'

Jazz
THURSDAY 16TH JULY

    I don't know whether to be pissed off, or relieved. He was a no show at lunchtime, but then I did ask him to stay away. I just never really expected him to. A delivery of concrete came at midday, and I guess that's a pretty time-sensitive job, so he couldn't really just set down tools for a break anyway.

    Whatever. I didn't want to see him, I'm just surprised, that's all.

    My phone buzzes.

    That's another thing. He's been on Twitter all fucking day. Entertaining the ladies. I'm not even looking at this one, it'll be another selfie. Shameless attention seeker. I don't know why I'm remotely surprised. I liked all that stuff before I actually met him. Now, I just have to live with the reality.

    There's another buzz. Damn him, I can't help wanting to look.

    I'm surprised to see a message from him. I ignored it because I thought he was just tweeting. What does he want? I grumble as I wait for it to load.

    Oh my God!

    He's sent me a photo.

Of MY shoes in MY bedroom. He's in my fucking bedroom!

The message says,

'Holding out on me, Shoegirl?'

That fucker!

I'm running up the stairs before I even think about the consequences, bursting in my room, I find him sitting on my bed, like he owns the place.

The wave of desire hits me like I've walked into a closed door, but I shake it off. "Who do you think you are?" I'm shaking from the shock of his audacity. At least I hope it's that and not the sight of him looking so at home on my bed. I need to get him out of here. "Get the fuck out!"

"Relax, Princess, I'm just doing what I was told," he gives me that pseudo-innocent grin he does.

"What are you talking about?"

"You told me not to come to the kitchen for the next few days. I'm respecting your wishes."

"You? Respecting my wishes? That's a laugh. You don't respect anything."

"Now, now, that's just hurtful." He smirks.

"Oh, really? Sorry to hurt your feelings, but did no one tell you it's disrespectful to come into a house without permission and go up to someone's bedroom? Not to mention downright creepy."

"Whatever you say, Princess."

I let out a long sigh. I hate the way he says that. I tell him he's acting creepy and he just calls me Princess in that derogatory way, and I feel like I'm the one being judged.

"Please, just leave," I say quietly, pointing to the door. I'm surprised when he stands and comes towards me to leave. I was expecting more of a battle.

Then he takes my hand, the one that's outstretched, showing him the way to the door. I watch silently as he turns it over and looks at my wrist. Somewhere in my head a voice mutters something about pulling it away, but I'm mesmerised by the way he is gently holding it and studying it.

"What are we making today?" he asks.

Huh? For a second I can't make sense of his question. Then my brain kicks into gear just before it's too late. He bends his head and slowly licks up my wrist before I can stop him.

Oh. My. God.

"Mmmmmm. Not Dark and Stormy," he says, licking his lips. "This one isn't as fiery. Have you mellowed out, or is it just the chocolate?"

God, does he have to ruin every moment with his smart mouth? "I…" I start, but his tongue is on my wrist again, gliding over the sensitive skin there. The heat starts to spread and I badly want to pull away, but it feels too good. Is the wrist an erogenous zone? Someone needs to look into that, I think vaguely, as he licks again.

"Caramel?"

'What does it matter?' I want to ask. Lick me again.

Thankfully, I'm unable to form a sentence, because I don't want that to ever come out of my mouth!

Instead, I nod. Yes, it's caramel, and I wish I were covered in it.

I hate how he twists my determination. I came up to throw him out. It was creepy, remember?

Hello?

Jazz?

I'm sorry, Jazz can't come to the phone right now, she's busy losing her mind to an irresistible arsehole with personal space issues and a dangerous tongue.

His dangerous tongue removes itself from my skin again and I allow myself to breathe. He moves closer. "You know, I love that little noise you do when I stop touching you," he says, sliding his fingers into my hair, pulling me close. "It's like a sigh of relief mixed with a plea not to stop." He ghosts his lips on my neck and I sigh. "Do you think you'll ever just let yourself want me?"

Mags' words last night about just enjoying myself and letting it happen play on my mind as he takes a nibble of my neck. Shuddering, I try and think about what she said. Where is the harm? I guess that's her point. She might be right, I just can't let go of that need to refuse.

"I don't want you," I whisper. He begins to pull away and I stop him. "I want this though," I clarify.

He pauses and looks at me. His eyebrows raise. "Friends with benefits, eh, Princess?"

I scoff, "I wouldn't even say friends."

"Harsh," he says with a sly smile, then he shrugs slightly. "But, I can work with that." He leans in and kisses me, parting my lips with his tongue. Feeling less of a weight on my shoulders having admitted what I want, for the first time I really kiss him back. His hands on my body don't feel like such an intrusion; I welcome them slipping under my top and lift my arms willingly so it can be lifted over my head. Our lips are still locked and he pauses, my top up to my shoulders, my arms raised in anticipation and neither of us willing to end the kiss.

Eventually, he pulls away, whipping my top off. His hands go for my jeans, but I stop him. I want his top off too. This is the first time I have actively participated in this thing we have. If I'm going for it, I'm not just going to be along for the ride. He has a look of uncertainty; I guess he thinks I've changed my mind.

Smiling, I'm happy to convince him otherwise. I hook my finger in the hem of his white T-shirt. How does he keep a T-shirt white, working out there all day?

Why am I worrying about the whiteness of his T-shirt, when I could be ripping it off?

I lift it up, trying not to gasp at the sight before me. Throwing it on the floor, I stroke my hands around his muscular shoulders. He's incredible close up, the Clark Kent get-up he was wearing the first time I noticed him was indeed hiding something super. Maybe that 'S' on Superman's chest stands for Spencer? He allows me to gawp, completely unfazed. I guess he's used to girls staring at his body and he obviously loves it.

Before I have the chance to irritate myself with thoughts of all the others, he wraps me up in his strong arms and resumes the heated kiss. His hands find their way onto my bottom and he holds an ample handful in each hand.

My skin pressed against his feels surreal, I've longed to be pressed against him and rejected the idea simultaneously for a month now and it's finally happening. Everywhere he touches me leaves me aching for more.

The grip he has on my arse is released in favour of getting in my jeans, and in just a moment, he has them pushed down around my arse and his hands are back there. He growls, grabbing real flesh and kisses me hungrily. I fumble at his jeans and pull them open and we break apart to shed them.

When I look up, he is watching. The way he looks at me leaves me feeling vulnerable, he has this power in his presence that I can't help but submit to. It's not my style. But it feels right.

I want to draw his attention away from my body, not because I'm self-conscious, just because he's so bloody intense. I take a step back and catch my foot on the bloody rug, tripping myself backwards. It happens really fast, but he has lightening reflexes and he has me in his arms and back on my feet before I can blink.

Shit. He's really naked, I think to myself as I realise he's all pressed against me. Eye to chest, I take in the feel of him holding me to him. To all of him.

"Jazz?" He cuts into my thoughts.

I look up at him, "Yes?"

"Put some heels on."

I laugh and roll my eyes, relieved that he popped the bubble. "Really?"

"Really," he nods.

I hesitate; this is silly, it's the middle of the day, we both have work to do, but we're naked, debating my footwear.

"You know that's why I came up here. Just do it."

"Jeez, bossy, aren't you?"

He quirks an eyebrow, "And if I'm not mistaken, you seem to respond quite well to demands. Now go and put some shoes on. The ones I like." He releases me.

Giving a petulant huff, I turn towards the wardrobe. "Good girl," he says, smacking my behind.

I straighten up, shocked and turn and glare at him.

He ignores my attitude and nods towards the wardrobe, "Go on."

I turn back, shaking my head and go to the wardrobe. He left the door open after he took the photo and the pair he likes, the ones he described to me that first time I took a picture for him, are sitting at the front. I take them out and bend to place them on the floor, aware that I'm giving him a view of everything. I stand up and step into the suede peep toes, sliding the heavy mirrored door closed as I turn to face him.

He's stroking his cock, staring.

Feeling very exposed, I look away.

He walks towards me and uses a finger to lift my chin until my eyes meet his.

"I feel ridiculous," I admit.

Taking hold of my arm, he spins me to face the mirror.

"Does that look ridiculous to you?"

I look at him in the reflection.

"Don't look at me, look at yourself," he orders. "Tell me you look ridiculous."

I look at myself, up and down, then watch him do the same with a salacious smile.

"No, I don't look ridiculous."

"No, you fucking don't, you look incredible," he says, still stroking his erection, eyeing me from behind. He thinks I'm one of those self-conscious girls. That's not what I mean. I feel silly because I can hardly stand him, but I'm standing here naked in my shoes at his command. But I don't feel self-conscious. I feel desirable.

His eyes on me are not leering, they show his hunger and it's for me. It's empowering. After studying my reflection in the mirror until he's satisfied, his heated gaze falls on my arse. A slow smile spreads across his lips.

"Fucking incredible," he repeats under his breath, stepping forward so he's almost pressed against me. His fingers start at the nape of my neck and trail slowly down my spine. His eyes follow them intently as they make me shiver. His other hand at my shoulder bends me forward and I place my hands on the mirror, just as he parts my legs with his feet and slips his fingers inside me.

I don't know whose sigh is more pleasure filled. Mine, as his fingers sink into me? Or his at discovering I'm so turned on?

"God, Princess, always so wet," he murmurs, teasing me with light strokes.

Now would be a good time to tell him that it's only when I'm around him, but I can't do it.

His thumb brushes over my clit, I gasp at his light touch. Then he pulls away and stares.

"Keep your hands on the mirror."

I watch him behind me stepping back to get a better view and do as he says.

"You should see how hot you look."

Without thinking, I reply, "Take a picture."

His face lights up. "Really?"

I immediately regret the suggestion and start to stand up. His hand is on my arse so fast, leaving a print for sure.

"Ow!"

"Do you have trouble following instructions, Princess? Hands on the mirror."

I stifle a giggle and he flashes me a serious no-nonsense look that has me swallowing my laughter. Holy shit, that's hot! I resume my position, holding his stare.

He watches me for a moment, challenging me to try him again. I must say I'm tempted, just to see what he'll do. But then his eyes go to the spot on my bum that's stinging. His hand soothes it with a soft stroke and he admires the mark he's left on me.

Then he turns and goes towards his clothes. Panicking, I realise I can't let him have a photo of this…But I do want to see it. I want to see myself the way he is seeing me right now.

"With my phone," I tell him in no uncertain terms. Yep,

that's right, I can be bossy too, buddy.

He laughs and shakes his head, but still goes for my jeans instead. Patting the pockets to locate my phone. When he turns back, my heart pounds, what the fuck am I doing? To go from storming up the stairs to kick him out, to posing naked for a picture I told him to take, is madness.

He must see the concern in my eyes because when he comes towards me, my phone is in his hand but he's not paying it any attention. I watch him study what's on offer, in his hungry, self-assured way. I'm half tempted to call an end to this right now if he's going to get cocky about it; it was a stupid idea anyway.

But then he starts to murmur his version of sweet nothings and it stops me.

"Look at you," he says, running his hand over my arse again.

"Incredible, waiting for me to take you," he says, following its ample contours. "The way you take an order makes me wonder what I could get you to do."

My breathing hitches as I watch him kneel behind me.

"The way you offer yourself to me whether you mean to or not."

His breath makes me flinch; he's so close.

"I'm glad you've stopped fighting it, Princess."

I want to correct him, I'm not fighting it right now, this is not a permanent status. But my eyes close and words are forgotten as he licks. My legs tremble, this is no polite lick, I whimper as he drags his tongue right through my aching pussy.

"I'm going to have this whenever I want it," he continues. Licking again.

I moan.

"I'm going to do all kinds of dirty things to you."

He probes deeper, making me push back onto his tongue. He groans in pleasure and sweeps his tongue slowly, right through again. I jump in surprise when he keeps going and flicks it across a place that wasn't expecting to be licked.

He grasps my arse with both hands and circles his tongue around the tiny hole again.

Fuck.

I shudder.

"And I'm going to have this too, Princess," he says with an arrogance that should have me correcting him, but instead I'm mute. No way to argue when I can feel the evidence of my desire flowing.

Then he stands.

He picks up my phone off the floor and as I look him in the eye, he takes a picture of me, bent over, hands pressed against the mirror as I was told, wearing nothing but Louboutins, legs spread and my wanton desperate pussy on display. I'm so aroused, I sway my hips trying to find some relief. Reading my signals, he tosses my phone on the bed and stroking his cock, comes back to me to finally do what I'm silently begging for.

He feeds just the head into my pussy, still working it with his hand. I see a flash of hesitation on his face in the reflection; I push back, trying to encourage him.

"Shit, we're doing it again."

"What?" He can't back out now. I need this.

"No protection," he starts to pull away.

"Wait!"

He stops, we still have contact and I plan to keep it.

"I'm clean." I tell him. Looking him in the eye in the reflection of the mirror. I feel stupid having this conversation how I'm standing, but I daren't move.

"Me too," he shakes his head, "I never do this, you make it very hard to think straight."

"As long as I make it very hard, that's all that matters." I grin.

He tries to cover his smile with a frown and delivers a little smack on my arse, making me gasp. "This is serious, Princess."

"Sorry." I smirk. Adjusting my footing and grinding a little on him.

"I mean it, I NEVER do this," he says in a more serious tone.

"I believe you. Neither do I and I'm on the pill, so we're good."

He sighs when I sway again. "I promised myself it wouldn't happen again, but you're making it hard."

"How hard?" I laugh.

"So hard," he whispers, sliding the head back in.

"You're a bad influence on me," I admonish, trying to keep my voice from wavering.

"Oh, and you're a saint?" He grips my hips, ready to take me.

"Shut up and fuck me."

"Shhhh. All in good time."

He groans, stretching me as he sinks in slowly.

Until now, I've barely had the chance to register his size. I knew he was big, I even just watched him stroking it. But like this, from behind when he's taking it slow, making me feel every inch, I really know it.

I push back slightly, claiming more and he moans. "You feel amazing."

"It feels so good...with nothing between us."

"Fuck," he whispers on a shuddery breath, then he pulls back and takes over.

His hands on my hips holding me steady as he takes me slowly, watching me.

My mouth falls open, as I'm slightly overwhelmed by how incredible it feels.

It feels so good as he thrusts into me that I close my eyes, moaning. But he slaps my thigh and I snap them open, meeting his in the mirror.

"That's it, watch," he insists, thrusting into me again, as he places a hand on my shoulder, gripping tightly. His eyes travel all over my reflection, making me feel their heat on my skin.

"Watch me fuck you."

Oh my God.

He looks down to watch as he disappears inside me and for a minute is mesmerised, sliding in and out. I can't take my eyes off him. When he returns his gaze to mine, he's breathing harder and his eyes are heavy.

Leaning over me, he wraps an arm around my waist and when his fingers stroke my begging clit, my eyes begin to close. I can hear his laboured breaths close to my ear. "Watch, Jazz," he gently commands as my head tilts towards his. Reluctantly, I lift my head to look in the mirror and am treated to a sight. The way he's looking at me when my eyes meet his in the glass is such a rare moment. Just for once he is totally focused on someone other than himself. It's so intense and when he swallows, I know he thinks so too. I feel I want to look away, but I can't and all the while his slow, deep thrusts don't waiver. After an age, he tears his eyes away from mine, but only to straighten up and resume watching where we are joined.

"I wish you could see this Jazz." He purrs.

"I wish I could see it too." I sigh, disappointed that he stopped touching me.

"You want me to tell you about it? The way it slides slowly in and out of you."

"Yes," I whisper.

"It's quite a sight. The proof of what I'm doing to your body, shining in the sunlight on my hard cock."

I moan at the thought.

"You feel how stretched you are?"

"Yes," I whimper.

"Does it feel good?"

"Mmmmhmmm."

"Feels amazing," he sighs. "Looks incredible too, the way I fill you."

He withdraws and again slides his full length into me in one complete, long stroke. "So big," I murmur, losing track of which words stay in my head and which float out of my mouth.

A chuckle rumbles in his chest.

Shit.

Just when I think he's going to be all jackass-y about it, he surprises me.

"This body makes me hard," his eyes roaming my body.

He thrusts again.

"This pussy is so tight."

Thrust.

"Those fucking hot shoes."

He moans on that thrust.

Without warning, he pulls out, spinning me around and lifting me into his arms. I wrap myself around him as he feeds himself into me. He grips me with both hands and uses his impressive strength to hold me while he thrusts. He takes his time, not showing any sign of flagging. I moan as he reaches my limits again and again.

He carries me across the room, his cock still buried inside me, pulsing with every movement. He uses his foot to sweep our clothes aside and deposits me on my dressing table, sending my things scattering everywhere, never pulling out of me. I'm speechless. He barely misses a beat though, before he starts to move again.

I have to lean back on my hands to steady myself. His hands pull at my hips, bringing me too him as he begins to fuck me hard. The dressing table knocks against the wall and bottles and tubes of cosmetics continue to roll off the moving surface. I'm certain Mags will hear the banging, but I'm too far gone to care. He releases my hips and reaches behind him to grasp my shoes, moaning as his hands slide over my ankles and meet soft suede. He brings them in tighter around him and I'm aware that the sharp tips of my heels are digging into the muscles of his arse.

"Fuck," he groans, and pumps faster into me. I'm on the verge of letting go, I know he is too.

"Touch yourself," he demands.

Leaning my weight and the force of his thrusts on one hand, I slip the other hand between my legs. Gliding my fingers over my clit, I jump. I'm so damn close. My finger makes contact with his cock and I slide them either side of him and for a moment enjoy the slippery feel of our connection.

He growls, "Do it now. Touch yourself. I want to feel you come."

I willingly obey, sliding my wet fingers to where we both need them right now. Circling round, I feel myself building.

"Harder, come on," he insists.

I rub harder, moaning loudly as it's almost too much on my sensitive skin, but I don't stop until I'm there.

"Oh God!" I cry as I come.

He slams home and comes hard.

Spencer
THURSDAY 16TH JULY

"Got you rattled, hasn't she?" Will abruptly breaks the silence in the car.

I try to make a nonchalant, dismissive sound, but it comes out as a kind of splutter/snort. Crunching the gears as I choke, I glance at the dickhead beside me, as he stifles a laugh.

Dick.

She has not got me rattled. Does this look rattled to you? Yeah, I won't ask that out loud, because I know he'll twist it and say I protest too much...he's got me.

I'm not, though. Rattled, I mean. I was just thinking, that's all. About Shoegirl and how I left her utterly fucked just an hour ago, wearing nothing but her shoes and a very satisfied smile.

"Uh huh."

"Shut it, fucker."

He watches me. "I just haven't seen you like this in a while, that's all."

"Like what?"

"Like, I don't know, all daydreamy," he chuckles.

"I am fucking not all daydreamy!"

"Ok," he says, in the most unconvinced, humouring tone.

"Go fuck yourself."

"Oooooooh!"

I open my mouth to let rip, but close it again. I can't win this one.

"I'm just saying," he continues, undeterred, "You've been a bit spacey lately, and it's unusual to see one girl holding your attention for more than five minutes."

"Spacey? What the fuck does that mean?"

"Well, let's see, you look up at the house approximately four hundred and thirty eight times a day. You look at your phone constantly, and your actions say your head is elsewhere."

"My actions?" This should be good.

"This morning, I tipped my cup up to finish my tea and got slapped in the face by a wet tea bag."

"Oh, big whoop! Sorry, precious, I'll be more careful next time."

"It's not just that," he hesitates.

"What?"

"I, umm," he fidgets, "I hear you're going bareback these days?"

I snap my head to look at him, then turn my attention back to the road as I narrowly miss the curb. "Oh, 'you hear,' do you?"

"Yep."

"How sweet, quite the little knitting circle you're part of, isn't it? Learn anything else?"

"Just that you're breaking your golden rule and you can't make tea for shit."

I sigh.

"So, going back to my original point. She's getting to you, isn't she?"

"She is not getting to me, I'm just..." I drift off not knowing how to justify what I'm feeling. I'm just...what? I'm just not myself around her. That's the best I can explain it. It's not that she's getting to me.

"You're just...?"

I shrug.

He turns to face me in his seat. "This is what I think. You're attracted to her."

"She's hot," I concede.

"You piss her off," he continues.

"Hey, it's a talent."

Will laughs, "And when she's all fired up and can't stand you, she becomes irresistible to you. And then the bad stuff happens."

"There's nothing bad about it, mate," I almost sigh. Aware that I sound a bit like a girl, I clear my throat and concentrate again on driving.

He pauses, then pretends not to notice. "Anyway...that situation where you're both riled up, and she's irresistible to you..."

"I'm irresistible to her," I correct. I'm not the only one making these bad choices; let's not forget that.

"Ok," he continues. "You're irresistible to each other. But what I'm saying is, you get into a situation where neither of you is thinking and then you just do it."

"Yep."

"Which is how you've ended up in this position."

"Uh huh." Why do I feel like I'm getting a lecture from my

mother?

"You worried?"

I shrug again. "She's on the pill. I got lucky."

"I meant about the other stuff."

He's right, I know I should be worried about health stuff too, but it's not my first concern. I know that's bad, but I think I'd rather my dick dropped off than I knocked her up. I couldn't deal with that. But anyway, something about her tells me this is not how she usually behaves. I think she's normally the extra cautious type. I think that's why I love how she's begging. Because it's a shock to her. I guess I should find out more about her, I just don't think of it when she's in my hands coming apart.

Will interrupts my train of thought with the answer to my unspoken thoughts.

"She's just as careful as you apparently. So don't worry."

"Fuck me, just how much of this has been discussed in your mother's meetings?"

"Don't you worry your pretty face about it," he says, reaching over to scruff my hair.

I smack his hand away and turn into our driveway. "Yeah, well cut it out in the future. Maybe you and Mags should be discussing things that actually concern you. I'm surprised you have any time to chat; you can barely take your eyes off each other. I'm sure when no one's watching, it's not just your eyes you can't keep off each other."

He opens his door and climbs out of the car. As I step out and shut mine, he mumbles, "We're not sleeping together," then he stomps off down the path and has opened the door by the time I catch him.

"Whatever, dude."

"We're not!"

"Ok, you big girl. You're not 'sleeping together'…but what are you doing while you're awake? That's what I want to know." I glance at him trying to take off his work boots in the hall, preparing to push a major button. Here I go…"I bet she's a right dirty bitch. Is she into the same weird shit as you?"

His head snaps up and his face twitches slightly as he stares at me with as much restraint as he can muster. Choosing not to dignify my inquiry with a response, he looks away and yanks off his boot. Starting up the stairs without a word.

"Don't want to talk about it?" I call after him. "She must be pure filth then," I chuckle.

He pauses and stiffens at the top of the stairs, but shakes his head and goes to his room without looking back.

I laugh to myself as I head to the kitchen. I still don't know the exact details of whatever freaky shit he's into. I just know I borrowed his laptop one day when my battery died and I wish I hadn't. He hadn't shut it down, just closed the lid and when it came on the porn he had been watching filled the screen and my brain. Some guy in ropes with a ball gag, getting flogged. I couldn't shut the thing fast enough!

I mean, who leaves their laptop laying around if that was the last thing they were looking at? Admittedly, when I say laying around, I mean in his bedroom, with the door closed, on his immaculate desk, perfectly central as always. I swear he must bring his spirit level home to get everything spot on. The guy is obsessed with order.

Anyway, I can never unsee it and now I find myself watching his behaviour. I don't know what I'm looking for,

I'm no expert on this stuff. But was he really watching that, or was it a pop-up? He's a bossy bastard, a total control freak. I can't quite imagine a side of him that can be pushed around in the bedroom. Then again, I don't I want to imagine it either. He's my cousin. I shudder. Nope, don't wanna know.

I just know I could never give up the control. I like to be the boss, and I love it when they respond to that. Like Shoegirl.

There's so much about her I enjoy. Take today for example. You could say I did a questionable thing going into the house uninvited and going into her room. I know that, I did it to piss her off so I could watch her cave. Because that moment when she lets go of the fight is the highlight of my day. Really, she likes me, but she won't allow herself to admit it. I mean, of course she likes me, come on, it's me! But she won't give in without a serious fight and I like that. It makes me want to poke the bear.

It could have gone badly wrong. But I knew I could turn it around. The place is huge and the first door I opened was Mags'. I wasn't sure at first. It could have been hers; there was girly shit everywhere. But after checking in there I checked the one opposite and when I opened that door I knew. The smell of her hit me.

When she came running up the stairs, I had that thrill of seeing her fire and then as I walked towards her, she totally let go. One lick of the wrist and she was mine. She even admitted to wanting it. She wouldn't say she wanted me, but she admitted she wants us to fuck. We all know that's the same thing.

And then, once she gave in to it, it was fucking awesome. That sight of her waiting for me at the mirror was too much; I had to taste.

And she let me take her picture! I'm still amazed that happened, but she was totally into it. Maybe she just got caught up in the moment. I hope she doesn't delete it. I need that picture.

Making her watch was a genius move, I could see her getting all self conscious, I wanted her to see what I saw. How fucking amazing she looked right then with me fucking her. That look of utter pleasure and lust on her face. She's absolutely beautiful, she needed to see it, so she can stop denying it.

Then when I held her up so she could see me, hard as fuck sliding in and out of her...that was almost it for me. I had to take her away from the mirror before I lost it.

Now I'm fucking hard again. Awesome.

Jazz
FRIDAY 17TH JULY

I can't get my head around the fact that that's me. It's just so…shameless. But tilting my head and really looking at the picture, I wonder why I automatically feel there should be shame. It should be shame-less, I look beautiful. I almost wish I could show people, it's the sexiest I've ever felt.

"So, it's big you say?"

I jump out of my skin and clear my phone screen as Mags comes out of the laundry room with more boxes. "Huh?"

"Like, how big are we talking here?" She grins and does a gesture that leaves me screwing up my nose at her crudeness and in no doubt that she is referring to Spencer's bits.

"Oh, that."

"Yes, that. Don't hold out on me."

"Big."

"Pft. You're just giddy with lust, give me a number."

I roll my eyes. "Sorry, I didn't happen to have my tape measure handy."

"If you don't have a number, it can't have been that impressive."

Tutting, I turn to her, hands on hips. "I'm telling you, Mags, he lifted me up and held me there and fucked me for a bit. Then he casually walked across the room to the dressing table, put me down, STILL IN ME and carried on!! I felt like a fucking parrot on a perch!"

"Fuck me, he must be big." She smirks. "And built like a brick shithouse!"

"Cheeky bitch!" I shove her back as she laughs.

Putting the lid on the box of truffles we just finished making and taking it to stack with the others, I feign indignation. She just laughs some more and fills the sink to wash the utensils.

"But it was good though, right?" she says over her shoulder.

I think for a bit about the answer to that. It was better than good, but saying that he makes me feel more desirable than I ever knew I could feel is difficult. I know I told him in the heat of the moment I wanted it, but Mags knows all the ins and outs...literally. She knows all the things I can't stand about him. So, saying I want him despite that is just ludicrous.

"It's ok to say it was," she continues, knowing the reason for my hesitation.

"It's not really, it's weird...But yes it was great."

"So you're going to carry on?"

"I don't know about that."

"But if he tries, you won't say no?"

I shake my head.

"And from the sounds of it, you have a great time, and you don't want anything heavy from him, so it's likely he will try again."

I shrug.

"So you'll be doing it again," Mags chuckles.

"I don't know why you need me to say it so badly," I reply, sounding irritated.

"Because, my dear, you're in danger of falling in to some old habits."

I frown, "What on earth are you talking about?"

"You have a tendency to ignore what your gut tells you because your head thinks it knows better."

I watch her, looking pleased with herself, washing up. "Is that so?"

"Uh huh," she continues, unfazed by my irritation. "You always do this. Your head tells you what's for the best, completely ignoring your gut. Then you make these knee jerk decisions based on what you deem logical, and you end up in these situations that frankly stink."

"Like what?" I stop wiping down the counter to listen to this crazy logic.

"Like..." She swallows. "Like moving in with Arsehole."

"Oh, here we go."

"Your gut was telling you that he didn't really want to settle down, but your stubborn brain was telling you to move in with him because if you didn't, he would find someone else. So, you ignored the obvious signs that he wasn't ready, neither of you were, and went all in."

Sighing at the wasted months, I give in. "And your point is?"

"I think you're about to do it again."

"How?" I bark, now sounding infuriated.

"Your gut, or maybe in this case, your newly appointed 'Spencer zone,' is telling you to shut up and let him make you come, pretty much every time you're around him. But your head keeps getting involved and telling you it's wrong and weird and should be stopped."

"Are you telling me that it's right and perfectly normal and should be encouraged then?"

"No, I'm telling you to listen to the rest of your body for a change and tell your head to take a break. I mean, what does your heart tell you?"

I don't know whether to laugh or cry at that question. I shake my head like she's lost the plot and start scrubbing places I've already cleaned. "Don't even go there!"

She stays silent.

"My heart has no opinion on this matter and it never will. Spencer Ryan is not a man you fall in love with. He's a man who can rock your world for as long as you can resist the urge to stab him. And when the urge finally gets too much, you walk away before you get yourself a criminal record."

"You've cleaned that bit," she says as I scrub.

I glare at her. "Look, I listened to what you said the other night, I've given in to it, it feels good and there's no harm in it. But you can fuck off with all your heart talk. I can just about take the fact that I physically want him so badly when I don't even like who he is, but there's no way you're going to turn this into a 'what my heart wants' conversation. He's a means to an orgasm, that's all. As long as he shuts up."

"Well, I think you've got it all wrong. I think your whole attitude towards him is to stop yourself from getting hurt. You don't trust yourself because your last big relationship decision was a bad one. But you weren't listening to yourself then either. If you'd gone with your gut, then you wouldn't have moved out and got stuck in a shitty relationship and your heart wouldn't have got broken."

"It wasn't broken!" I jump in.

She holds up her hand to shut me up. "Dented then. Anyway, now you're doing the same bloody thing, but with the opposite effect. Instead of talking yourself into a shitty relationship, you're talking yourself out of a potentially good one. All because you won't listen to your gut. Again."

"A potentially good relationship? Have you been smoking something?"

"The point is Jazz, you don't know. He could be just what you need."

"No, the point is, Mags, you've lost your mind. And will you stop using the word relationship!"

We both look up and freeze when the kitchen door opens.

"Erm, Mags," Spencer says cautiously, probably because we both look shifty. "Can Will see you for a second?"

"Sure." She wipes her hand on a towel and throws me a 'go for it' look as she leaves us in the kitchen.

Alone.

Where we are most at risk...cue Twilight Zone music...You just crossed over into 'The Spencer Zone.'

I'm so infuriated by what she said, part of me is actually glad he showed up, because now I can maybe work out some of my frustration.

He sits on a stool beside the stack of freshly made chocolates and sniffs in their general direction. "Whatcha been making?" he asks, all excited looking.

Despite my annoyance, it doesn't escape my notice that he hasn't approached me, or done anything to piss me off and he's been here at least thirty seconds. It could be a record.

"That one is chai latte," I reply.

He screws up his nose, "I don't like coffee, got anything else?"

"It's not coffee."

"You said latte."

"Have you never had a chai latte before?"

"Err, no. Like I said, I don't like coffee." He looks at me confused as to why I'm not understanding him.

"Do you like cinnamon?" I walk over, caught up with educating him about possibly the best drink ever and not realising that I have voluntarily walked into his personal space, for the first time since we met.

"I love cinnamon," he grins, sitting back slightly so I can reach the boxes. I pull the lid off and he leans back in, resting his chin on my forearm to take a good sniff. "Mmmm," he purrs.

A shiver ripples from the point of contact, up my arm and down my spine.

"Try one," I offer, trying to sound normal. He is quick to take me up on my offer and has one between his teeth before I can blink.

"Oh my God," he moans. "It's like Christmas."

"Yep." I try to step back but he has me kind of surrounded.

"Why didn't you call me earlier when I could have smothered you in it and licked it all off?" He shoves the rest in his mouth and reaches for another, grabbing three before I can shut the lid.

Holy shit, just the thought has me tingling in ways I don't have time for right now. I shake my head, but otherwise ignore his suggestion. I have work to do, I can't be getting into it with him. Clearing my throat to snap myself out of it, I try to sound unaffected. "So, you've never tried a chai latte?"

"I've never even heard of one."

"Would you like me to make you one?" Brilliant Jazz, encourage him to stay.

He nods enthusiastically, popping another truffle in his mouth.

I've already steeped all the spices with some Darjeeling to flavour the ganache, so it's simply a case of steaming some milk. I fill the metal jug of the snazzy coffee machine with milk and froth it up. Then straining out the last of the chai from the pan and pouring a little into two mugs, I finish them by topping them up with the hot milk and dusting them with cinnamon.

"This is the wrong weather for this drink, but you have to try it." I bring the drinks over to him and I've been so absorbed in the task, I'm sitting on the stool beside him before I realise what I'm doing. This is very social, very normal...very not us.

He takes a sip and his eyes flutter closed. "Fuck me, that's amazing."

"It's my favourite. That's why I do it as a chocolate."

He is in heaven going between his drink and the chocolates. "I think this is the best thing I've ever tasted," he says through a mouthful. "Well, almost," he adds with a lascivious grin.

I feel the rush of heat as it first hits my cheeks then surges southwards, which instantly annoys me. But even though it annoys me, I can't fight the physical reaction I have for him, and I start to ponder if I would feel differently about it if I instigated it for once? Maybe it's the lack of control I have that pisses me off. Let's face it, I can't control the way I respond to him, but I could be the one who starts it.

He is just sitting, drinking. He doesn't seem to have any intention of starting something, perhaps this is a good time to try and take the lead. Right as I'm thinking this and my pulse kicks up a notch from the anxiety of making the first move, he knocks back the rest of his drink and stands.

"Right, I'd better get back to work. Thanks for that," he nods at his empty mug and winks. "Orgasmic." Then he turns and saunters out the door, like it's perfectly normal that he didn't touch me.

It's not perfectly normal.

It's fucking weird.

What is up with that?

Maybe he's over it.

Maybe I keep giving in too easily and he has lost interest.

Maybe I shouldn't care, but alas, apparently I do. Shit.

I pick up his mug and take it over to the sink, mumbling to myself and shaking my head.

"Well that was either disappointingly fast, or his mouth got him in trouble again," Mags says entering the kitchen.

"Huh?" I snap, still irritated.

"Mr. McHotstuff came back outside. I was going to give you two a bit of alone time in 'The Spencer Zone.' What happened? Did you guys fight?"

"No. What made you think that?"

"Well, he was only in here for like ten minutes…" She drifts off when she sees I'm in a mood. "What's the matter? Are you upset?"

I shake my head, huffing out a big sigh. "No, I'm not upset.

Spencer

I was just thinking about stuff that's all."

"About?"

"About taking control for once," I mumble.

Mags giggles. "Hmmm, I see my book has been rubbing off on you!"

"NO! Not that kind of control." Mags laughs even harder. "I mean of my life. I feel like I'm on a runaway train. I think it's time to take the wheel."

"Do trains have steering wheels?" Mags muses. "I thought they were just a forward and backward kind of…thing…" She feels my glare. "No, ok, I can see this is not the time to be picking apart your metaphors."

"I mean, who is he to always call the shots? He has forced his way in at every turn, refused to take my protests seriously and got me…" I sigh, "hooked." Mags chews on her lip to stop a grin from spreading, I know her. "So after treating me like prey every single time we've met, I finally come around and then he thinks it's ok to just make idle conversation and leave?"

"Jazz, I think you're…"

"I don't want to hear it." I stop her with my hand. "You and your 'listen to your heart' bullshit and Spencer Fucking Ryan and his egotistical 'I don't want it unless it's a challenge' attitude can fuck off. I've had enough!" I wipe my hands on my jeans and storm out of the kitchen.

"Where are you going?" calls Mags.

Ignoring her, I keep walking.

Twenty minutes later, Mags taps on my door and doesn't wait for it to open before she begins her apology. "Jazz, I'm sorry. You won't hear a peep out of me about it from now on, I promise. Just think about staying, please. This market is a great way for you to get started and no man should get in the way of that."

I open the door. "I'm not leaving," I tell her, watching her face drop.

"Whoa!"

Looking down at myself I blush a little. I'm wearing my favourite dress. A very simple, form fitting little black dress, with a low cut v-neck. There is absolutely no way you can wear underwear with this thing and anyone who knows anything knows it. This is a 'make no mistake, I'm feeling sexy' dress. And with my red suede platform pumps, smoky black eyes and red lips, its dangerous.

"Just taking some control back."

"You sure the hell are! Do you need a whip to go with that?"

"It's not too much, is it?"

"Depends what for."

"For showing him that he doesn't call all the shots."

"Then no, it's perfect."

"Good."

Then before I can change my mind, I set off down the stairs.

"Oh, now?" she says behind me in disbelief.

"Now," I tell her without looking back.

Striding across the lawn in a barely decent dress and red heels, I'm acutely aware that it's not just Spencer's attention I'm going to get. I need to make this swift and painless. As I approach, I can't see him, shit. I don't want to break stride, it'll draw more attention. Scanning the site, I spot him, working in one of the holes they've dug for something or other. Only his head is visible, perfect. I walk straight to the edge of the hole and stop dead. A wolf whistle behind me causes him to look up and come eye to toe with red suede.

He freezes and then looks up.

Slowly.

His expression is dumbfounded and he swallows as his gaze reaches my hemline. Before he can speak, I turn and walk briskly to the pool house.

I'm confident I hear him scramble out of the hole and as I near the door to the pool building, I can hear his footsteps behind me. I fling open the door and step inside. Turning to face the door, I stand with my hands on my hips, waiting. A few seconds behind me, he appears in the doorway and scans me up and down. Hungry in the way he devours the sight of me.

"Fuck," he whispers.

I draw in a breath as he comes towards me.

"What is all this?" he asks.

"I can't be the one who decides it's now?"

His lips curl into a salacious grin. "You can decide whatever you like dressed like that." He reaches out and wraps an arm around my waist, bringing me close. "So, this is for me?"

"No, this is for me." I rest my hands on his biceps, feeling them tense at my touch.

"Fair enough, Princess," he laughs, but then his face becomes more serious. "You look incredible."

"Thank you."

He leans in to kiss me, and I pull back slightly. "You're filthy."

"Yes, I am, thanks for noticing," he grins.

"No, I mean you just climbed out of a hole."

"And now, I'm hoping to jump into another one."

I sigh. "You and your mouth, Spencer!" I push back on his arms, to get him and his sweat off me.

"Uh huh," he comes right back. "Where do you want it?"

I shake my head. "Your clothes are filthy, this was a bad idea, I'm sorry. Maybe we should just…"

"The clothes are gone," he says pulling his T-shirt over his head. "And maybe we should get in that big shower together," he adds, nodding his head to the large shower beside me.

"But I'm not dirty," I protest.

"Don't worry, I plan to change that," he replies, pulling off his boots and stripping out of his shorts and boxers.

He stands before me naked. Hard. And completely unashamed. I can't help but feast on the sight.

"Well?"

"You should shower," I agree.

"And you should join me," he holds out his hand and waits for my response.

Spencer
FRIDAY 17TH JULY

She looks at me, thinking God only knows what. Her eyes roam my body, and I know she is hooked in, but that hesitation is still there. She needs a nudge.

She sucks in a breath when I step closer, as if I startled her. But she knew I'd be coming. This was her doing, she's not backing out now. Reaching her, I don't hesitate to try and find a way into that dress. My hands go around her back searching for a zip, but there's nothing there. I mean nothing. No zip, no bra and less dress than I realised. But it's made from very soft stretchy jersey. It will come off easily over her head.

I slip one hand down to her arse and grab a handful. Her body drives me crazy and I push my ever hardening cock against her to prove it. She sighs. She wants me so bad, I can feel it. I need to get clean so I can get her dirty. Stepping back, I decide to delegate undressing to her. I step into the shower and face her walking backwards.

"Strip," I tell her.

She gives me a sassy look.

"Now," I command, reaching across and turning on the water so it can heat up ready for us while I watch her.

She crosses her arms in front of her and grasps the hem of

the dress, where it clings to her upper thighs. Peeling it slowly up, she reveals that her bra isn't the only thing she seems to have forgotten. As she reveals herself to me, I stroke my cock. She drops the dress on the floor and walks towards me.

"Take the shoes off."

She looks at me puzzled. "I thought you liked them on."

"I do, but I'm thinking about the next time you'll be wearing them for me, and if we get them wet, they'll be ruined. Not happening. Off!"

She laughs. Kicking the heels off and joining me in the shower.

I grab her and tug her under the water with me, pressing my lips to hers, the hot water washing the dirt off my skin. She turns and pumps a little expensive looking shower gel into her hand from the fancy dispenser on the wall and smooths it onto my chest, working it into a lather with one hand, while her other hand drifts slowly down my chest, over my abs and spreads the rest over my cock. Fuck, it feels good as she builds a lather there! I push my tongue into her mouth and wind my fingers into her wet strands of hair. Moaning against her lips and closing my eyes, I just enjoy the feeling.

She's not fighting me, and as much as I love the fight with her, this is awesome too. Her hand leaves me and I open my eyes. She lifts the shower head from its cradle and she uses the spray to gently wash the suds away from my skin, which gives me an idea. I let her finish, then I take the shower head from her as she tries to put it back. She gives me an enquiring look and I just smile and push her back against the frosted glass, almost wishing I could see the view from the other side. Her lush, wet curves pressed against the opaque glass must look spectacular.

Bending to my knees I twist the dial on the shower head, finding among the settings what I'm looking for. The jet. I look up at her and she smiles.

"I bet you've tried this, haven't you?"."

"I haven't," she replies. "But if it's as good as the one upstairs then…" and she gasps and stills when I direct it at her soft folds. I slide my finger under the jet of water, to part her lips and give the water direct access to her clit and she jumps.

"Ah!" Her hands come to the shower and try to move it away to give her relief. I know it's intense, but I know what I'm doing, she needs to trust me. I move her hands away.

Within seconds they are back, she can't help herself.

I look up to see how I can occupy her hands to keep them out of my way. The top of the glass is too high for her to reach, the only thing available is the rail the shower sits on. So I stand up and move her so it's behind her.

"Hold the rail."

She watches me silently, but lifts her hands above her head and grips the rail behind her head as she was told. This stance pushes her chest out to me. She has great boobs. I touch them, weighing them in my hands, they're perfect. A nice big handful and soft and biteable like the rest of her. I can't stop myself bending to take a nipple into my mouth, sucking and grazing my teeth over the sensitive flesh. while she sighs.

"Don't let go," I tell her, falling again to my knees and once again revealing her sensitive hidden bud. This time, it is my tongue she feels attack it first. I suck it in, just like her nipple, nipping at it, causing her to gasp. I pull away, and after a pause, I go in again with the jet of water. Her body jumps and she lets out a loud moan, but this time she keeps her hands away.

Twisting and twitching against the spray, I can tell it's almost too much, but she holds on and lets me continue. Her teeth biting down on her lip to prevent screams. Soon her hips stop trying to escape the jet and start gyrating towards it.

"Please," she begs. Gripping the rail tight and coming up on her toes to try and get more of the jet. She wants to come desperately and she will, but I'm not giving her anything extra, she has to find it. She wants my fingers inside her, I can feel her willing me, but I want her to chase this herself.

I watch her, her eyes tightly closed, her teeth digging into her bottom lip. Her arms stretched above her, clinging on, her chest rising and falling rapidly. The water droplets rolling down her stomach, where they meet the cascade from the shower all focused in on that one point. Her legs tremble and I can feel how close she is to finding relief.

Suddenly her whole body jerks and she lets out a relieved cry. Her legs buckle and I rise, scooping her up in my arms. Trembling and panting, she barely notices when I replace the shower head and turn the water off. I carry her back out to the plush changing area to find a place where I can have my way with her. Stepping out of the shower, I look at the built in bench and then glance around for another option. That's when I notice the jacuzzi.

As I lower her into the warm water and settle onto the seat, she reaches over my shoulder and presses a button which starts the bubbles then turns in my arms and kneels on the seat with her knees either side of me, lowering herself slowly. She whimpers when my hard cock makes contact with her over-sensitised skin. I place my hands on her hips to guide her gently, needing to be inside her.

Face to face, she slowly sinks down, gazing into my eyes as her body accepts me. It's shockingly intimate.

I don't do intimate.

But as she starts a slow grind, her eyes never leave mine and I wrap my arms around her and hold her close, enjoying the feel of her pressed against me. Wanting more.

I barely do any more than flex my hips in time to her movements. She is in control. Her movements start out slow and minimal, she rolls her hips making my cock find her sensitive places. Back and forth, she rolls, grinding her clit where our bodies meet and moaning with each wave of pleasure. My hands roam her back, her arse, her hair, whatever it takes to pull her closer.

As we move like this for what feels like forever, our breathing becomes ragged, but totally in sync. She's riding me harder and harder with each thrust and I meet her like for like. The sound of our breathless moans are drowned out by the roar of the jacuzzi and it feels like nothing outside of the two of us exists.

When it comes, it takes me by surprise, but I can't stop, I need to come right now. Pulling her mouth onto mine, my tongue meets hers. I growl into her mouth as I come and feel her body start to shake. Stilling so I can feel her grip me, she keeps the waves of pleasure coming each time her tight little pussy pulls on me. I have to break the kiss so we can breathe, but she stays where she is with her forehead pressed against mine.

Then after a minute or so, without a word, she leans

forward and gives me one last slow, lingering kiss. Then she stands and climbs out of the water.

I sit for a second, slightly stunned, then scrub my face with my hands and push the wet hair back off my forehead. What the hell just happened?

We had this down. I piss her off, she puts up a show of fighting it, we have crazy hot sex, I piss her off again, you know, one for the road...and repeat. But that was out of this world and then she just walks away without a word? And I let her? What the fuck?

I rise up out of the water and walk, dripping, back to the changing area. Silently, she passes me a towel and I dry myself while she does the same. She puts her dress back on and then uses a cotton wool pad and some lotion from the well-stocked vanity area to clean the smudges of makeup under her eyes. I notice they have a couple of hairdryers and everything else you can imagine rich people need in their pool house. But she doesn't bother to dry her hair, she just winds it up into some sexy little twist using a clip she gets from a drawer.

She's putting her shoes back on before I know it and I want to say something to her, but I don't know what to say. I don't even have some dickhead comment I can hurl at her to save face. We just had really fucking intense sex and then she got up and got dressed and hasn't said a word.

Man up, Spencer. Say something.

I watch her, straightening herself out in the mirror and I open my mouth to speak, but she turns and catches my eye and gives me an awkward smile that I can't read. Anything I say will just make me look like a pussy. So instead, as she passes me to leave without so much as a word, I grab her wrist and pull her to me, taking her in a deep kiss, not giving her the option.

I release her and turn away to get dressed. I hear the door open, then close and I sigh.

What the fuck? I feel like the chick. Perhaps I should sit here and have a cry. That was all off. Until now it has been so wrong between us that it's been fun. But that was so right it felt wrong.

Shaking my head, I pull on my T-shirt and sit to put my work boots back on. Then as I drop my towel in the basket she put hers in and go to leave, I realise we left the jacuzzi on. I head over and press buttons until the rumble stops and as the water settles I run my fingers through it pondering what just happened here. Catching a glimpse of myself in the ripples I realise I'm being a fucking girl about this. I just had a great fuck with a hot girl at work. Does life get any better than this?

No.

So, I shake it off and head back out to go finish whatever the hell it was I was supposed to be doing.

"Where have you been?" Will demands.

"She had a problem with the um, shower," I nod towards the pool house. "She wanted me to look at it."

"Uh huh," he says eyeing me suspiciously. "Your hair is wet."

"It was a big problem," I laugh.

"Your dick is going to get you into trouble one of these days, you know that right?"

"I don't know what you're talking about," I grin.

Spencer
SUNDAY 19TH JULY

Pussy boy was out at the butt crack of dawn this morning. It's embarrassing how badly he wants in Mags' drawers. He needs to man up and make it happen, but instead he's being all nice and sucking up. Not just with Mags, but with the bff too. So he was out practically before the sun came up to help them with this chocolate shit this morning.

'You should come,' he bleated last night. 'It wouldn't kill you to help.' I told him straight up, I'm not getting up that early on a Sunday morning to impress a chick. He can do what he likes, but he can fuck off if he thinks he can make me feel bad. And besides, he doesn't know it won't kill me. It might, then he'd feel awful for making me go. Really, I'm doing us both a favour; I smile smugly to myself as I turn over in bed and get comfy again.

The bloody sun though, has other ideas. It's shining right on my eyes within minutes of me falling back to sleep. I shift but it's still way too bright and after turning over and fidgeting around, I know it's no use.

I'm wide awake. Ugh!

It's only half past eight, I wanted to sleep until lunch time. About two pm, to be precise, so that I can skip the whole market thing completely. I don't want to be laying here thinking about her. I don't want to wonder what she's wearing today, or think about the fact that she's just over the road surrounded by chocolate. And I certainly don't want to spend any time thinking about why, after she walked out of the pool on Friday, I have not seen or heard a peep from her.

Because I don't think. Thinking is for mugs.

Huffing, I sit up. Bloody hell. If I'm awake I may as well go to the gym. That would be a good use of a Sunday morning if I can't sleep in. Better than falling over myself at a stupid market trying to score points. I'll leave that to my cousin. I throw back the covers and yawn as my feet hit the floor.

I could even stroll to the gym. Hmmm. I peer out of the curtains. It looks like a gorgeous morning and it's not far. It has nothing to do with the fact that I'll have to walk through the Farmers' Market to get there. Nope, nothing at all.

Stretching, I walk naked to the bathroom, turning on the shower. I answer nature's call, then stand under the hot water and let it wake me up. Why am I showering before I work out, you ask? Well...because, going to the gym looking like shit is not an option. The place is full of hot girls for a start. That should be reason enough, right?

I check myself in the full length hallway mirror. Yep, perfect. I love this weather. I hate covering up all my hard work, so I love it when I can wear a sleeveless T-shirt and show off the guns. My grey trackies are soft from years of wear, but that is why they look so good on. They hang just so, almost like they might not stay up and I can feel the looks I get when I wear them. Perfectly finished with white trainers.

Hair is looking good, as always, a few days' stubble, neatly trimmed. A nice sun kissed look...Uh huh, I'm ready...for the gym. That's all.

The market is busy already; this is where locals buy a lot of their fresh produce. I haven't had breakfast yet so I stop by the fruit and veg stall and pick up a bunch of nice big bananas, breaking straight into one. Walking through the market chewing on my banana, I keep an eye out for Shoegirl and her chocolates. Avoidance is key here, but I can still have a look. When I spot her, I stand and watch for a second. She's all business, with a nervous edge. I don't exactly know her well, but I know that look she has when she's keeping her nerves in check and putting her game face on. I saw it on Friday in the pool.

It's who she's talking to that has me changing my plan to avoid her completely. That smarmy git photographer, I should have known he'd be there sniffing around. We don't get many new faces around here, and if we do, he's always straight in there with his 'oh you have a very photogenic face' crap. Look at him, he's probably asking if the cocoa is ethically sourced. He's that type. He probably learned all about it when he was off photographing village children in Venezuela or some shit. He has to be better than everyone else. He can step away from Shoegirl, she's way too much woman for him.

I circle in, listening, chewing my banana. She's telling him that she uses the finest something or other, he's hanging off her every goddamn word.

"I guarantee you won't have tasted anything like it," she tells him.

He smiles, some kind of expectant smile. He can fuck right

off if he thinks he's tasting anything other than her chocolates!

"Guarantee?" I interject from behind. "Careful mate, her guarantees don't mean much, I'm just sayin." I take a bite of my banana.

"What is that supposed to mean?" she snaps.

"Well," I say chewing my mouthful of banana and swallowing in my own time. I grin and she straightens. She knows I'm going to piss her off, she's braced for it, so I continue. "You've guaranteed me certain things wouldn't happen several times this week and yet…they did. So, I don't think you should make guarantees, you're clearly full of shit."

Her expression changes to fury, and I just smile. I've managed to piss her off AND let God's gift to philanthropy here know that I've been fucking her. So far it's been a good morning.

She rolls her eyes and turns on me, "Spencer, just Fuck. Off."

"What? I'm just trying to spare him from disappointment. It's a very bold claim. I mean I've tried this one for example, it's very good," I lean over and before she has chance to stutter her objections, pick one of the chai ones off the tray and put it whole in my mouth. I bite down and close my eyes, hamming it up as I moan. "But," I tell him through a mouthful of chocolate, "I couldn't tell you if they're all this good. Some, I've only licked off her naked body. I'm still working my way through the flavours. I'll have to let you know."

He looks at me with disdain and then turns to Jazz. "I'll come back later when you're less busy," he tells her. And backs away.

"Buh-bye," I tell him, giving him a little wave.

"What the hell is wrong with you?"

"Nothing, I was just helping you out. Banana?" I hold my half eaten banana right up to her face and she pulls away a little in disgust. "Go on," I push it further towards her, knowing I'm on very thin ice and enjoying the thrill. "Open up, it's good practice," I wink.

Her expression changes, she softens a little. God knows why I'm pressing every button I'm capable of right now. Her mouth slowly opens and she slightly shows her tongue, ready to curl around it as she accepts it into her mouth. I ease it in, watching closely; I can't believe she would go for this. Then she slams her teeth closed, making me jump. Brutally severing the banana.

Chewing, she smirks, "You're right. It is good practice." Then she smiles a smile so cold my cock tries to find a place to hide behind me.

"Is there anything else, Spencer?"

I clear my throat. "Nope, just off to the gym."

"Well, don't let me stop you," she says through gritted teeth.

In a last ditch attempt to annoy her before I leave, because I'm on a roll, I reach into my carrier bag and pick off the largest straightest banana of the bunch. "I'll leave this with you," I say placing it on her table, "to remind you of me."

"Oh, it's ok, Spencer, you can have that one," she says, bending to pick something up from under the table. She lifts up a much smaller curved banana with bruises all over it and grins. "I already have one that reminds me of you," she laughs.

Uh huh, very good.

Bitch.

"Well, I'll catch you later then."

"Can't wait," she replies, oozing sarcasm.

Retreating, I see Will and Mags returning to her with three teas and some bags of food, probably bacon sandwiches, and my stomach rumbles. I can see Mags ask her what's wrong and she shakes her head, not wanting to discuss it. Will simply looks up and scans the crowd for the source of her irritation, when his eyes fall on me, I give him a satisfied grin and salute. He shakes his head, but I know he's a tiny bit amused.

When I come out of the gym a couple of hours later, I take the long way home. Will texted me, 'Pub later,' while I was running. I'll go, but I'll go in my own time. I know she'll be there, and I don't want her to think I have nothing better to do. They'll probably be another couple of hours anyway with all the packing up.

Yeah, I know I could go and help. But I'm an arsehole, remember?

Once showered and dressed, I take my cuppa into the garden and sink down into my favourite chair. Ah, this is the life. A nice chilled out day and no long commute to dread tomorrow. I'm so far very happy with my change of career. This first job is really good for us because George is well known around here and will recommend us to everyone. Will has been doing work here and there for him for a couple of years. He has other properties, and he has known Will a long time, so he trusts him. I've been off doing my thing, so this is the first time we've put a team together and taken on a big job, but we all know what we're doing. It's going really well.

I wasn't expecting the distractions though. Will had no

clue that Mags would be staying here. It was arranged fairly last minute apparently, when George's business plans changed. I guess that's how the other half live. Able to change plans and uproot to a different house for the summer, with nothing bothersome like work to stop them. Nice for them!

I guess as distractions go, though, it could be worse. At least today I managed to put us back in our comfort zone of casual, slightly aggressive banter. After the last couple of days, it's a relief. It got all intense for a minute there. Yesterday I was even thinking about messaging her just so I could talk to her. What the fuck? I don't need that in my life. Fucking her is ok. Winding her up until she's ready to slap me, then fucking it out of her, that's fun. But sitting here wondering how she is, what she's doing?

No, just no.

I'm glad we are back on the right track now.

You slog your guts out selling your chocolates, Princess, and I'll just sit here and drink my tea. If you're lucky I might even fuck you later...Just as it should be.

Jazz

SUNDAY 19TH JULY

"Oh God, really?" I grumble at Mags as soon as I spot Spencer coming through the pub.

Seeing him makes the image of his face as I left him getting dressed at the pool flash into my head. Maybe taking control was the wrong thing to do. It felt great, it felt guilt free for the first time since it all started. Control was just what I needed. Not that I dominated, no, I just levelled the playing field by instigating and it felt great to enjoy the pleasure without that nagging feeling that I should be annoyed about it.

If only it had lasted. That feeling of control I mean. Since I walked out of the pool house, I have never felt less in control. Sure, I had the adrenaline rush that kept me going for a while and I still had loads of stuff to get done before today, so I stayed nice and distracted for the most part.

I had to stay busy or I'd have had time to think about it…and I really don't want time to think about it.

It was weird, ok?

I admit it.

It was way too intense and so fucking good that I can still feel him pressed against me if I close my eyes. That look as I got out of the jacuzzi, I could swear it was hurt, but I don't think he even has feelings, so I doubt I hurt them. It was more likely panic, that I would turn all clingy after such intense sex. Well, I've shown him that's not the case now and it seems he's gone right back to being his usual self if today's display at the market is anything to go by.

It's the kiss that confused me. Right before I walked out, he grabbed me and kissed me so damn fervidly that it was as if it meant something to him. I swear, he knows how to turn that shit on. But I didn't need a consolation kiss to make me feel better, I felt great, until then. Now I just feel weird. The kiss, the eye contact, the way he held me, it all felt so…special.

I shudder.

Nope. This is Spencer Ryan. Special is not in his repertoire, it was probably just the heat from the jacuzzi. It makes you feel funny at the best of times.

First, I realise Mags has gone silent and then, I realise she's watching me. I didn't notice at first because I'm watching him intently, lost in my head. Shit, now I'm busted.

"You knew he would come," she smiles.

"I just hoped he wouldn't," I murmur.

At least he didn't arrive earlier and spoil the lovely Sunday roast I insisted on treating Mags and Will to as a thank you. I'm really grateful to them, Will came over at seven this morning and helped us load the car. Then he stayed all day, handed out samples, got tea and went around the market inviting people to come and try. He literally knows everyone.

Without him, I'd have been the quiet new girl; hoping people would come to her. But he made sure they all came to me. Short of shouting 'Roll up! Roll up!' and ringing a bell, there was very little more he could have done. And he and

Mags are so cute together. That's the first period of time I've really spent in their company, together. I have a zillion questions for Mags, but the biggest one is, 'what the fuck is stopping you two?' They are adorable. I need to interrogate her the way she's been interrogating me. They need to get their shit together. They would be an awesome couple.

She laughs at my protests. "You're so full of shit! You light up when he's around, you just can't see it."

"Really? I don't feel very lit up right now."

"You are. In a grumpy sort of way," she chuckles. "But you can't deny he brings out a reaction in you. You just need to start seeing it and let it in."

I turn and glare at her. I'm not getting into that discussion again here. "It's your turn."

She shakes her head and returns to our game of pool. I'm relieved that Spencer spots Will at the bar and stops to get himself a drink, delaying the inevitable.

"Jazz."

"Huh?"

"It's your turn, if you can tear yourself away from watching Loverboy."

Another glare goes her way; I must be losing my touch, they're having no effect whatsoever. All off my game now, I fail to hit anything and have to wait while Mags takes her turn, potting two of her balls. I glance at the bar and he's watching over Will's shoulder while they chat. A slow smile spreads across his face when my eyes meet his. A triumphant smile because he knows I couldn't resist looking.

How the hell can he do this? I mean, I turned the tables. Didn't I? I had some of the control. Yeah, I had a little wobble afterwards, but he doesn't know that. So I don't get how he flipped it back so fast. He caught me off guard today, I wasn't expecting to see him. He humiliated me in front of that customer, and even though I didn't stand for his nonsense, I still feel on the back foot now. I mean, what was that? Jealousy? It was like he was marking his territory, and I am NOT his territory.

I scan the table for a shot, trying to put him out of my mind. He's here, I don't have to like it, but I've had a great day, I'm not going to let him spoil it for me. The market went really well. I sold far more than I expected to. We were giving out samples all day and response was really great. So much so, against my better judgement, I've signed up for next week. I know I wanted to get out of here, but the opportunity to do this just isn't available where we live. I could be stubborn and go home for the week, but the flat will be empty and lonely and the kitchen here is much bigger.

And I may as well just admit that if I go home, then there's no chance of any…whatever this thing is. I don't like the idea of leaving and that being it. I hate it, in fact.

Like he senses my annoyance, he comes over to the seats we have by the pool table and sits down so that he can watch our game. I take a deep breath. I'm not sure I want to do this with him watching. Sitting there with his smug face, I can feel his heated gaze burning into my arse as I lean over the table and take my shot. By some miracle it's actually a good one and I save face. I'm pretty good at pool, but I'm not used to this kind of pressure.

As I'm figuring out my next move, I see him stand out of the corner of my eye. He walks over and pointedly puts a pound coin on the edge of the table, just above the coin slot.

Bastard.

I was enjoying this game until he arrived, and now, not only has he spoiled it, he wants the table. Well, fine, he can have it. I think I want to get back to the house anyway.

"Play the winner?" he asks.

I look up as if in slow motion to see his grin and turn my head towards Mags; dumbstruck and fixed to the spot, I know just what she's going to say. In my head, I see me Sylvester Stallone style, throwing myself across the room, arms outstretched trying to stop the bullet, yelling 'NOOOOOOOOOOOO!' But in reality I just stare in horror as she says…

"Sure," then gives me a highly amused look.

Bitch.

Satisfied, he takes his seat and waits.

I'm winning and suddenly my usual competitive streak evaporates. I do not want to have to play him. But I won't give him the satisfaction of retreating with my tail between my legs, because he won. So I 'miss' an easy shot and let Mags take the lead. On her next turn she stands in front of Spencer to get lined up. As she pulls back her cue, he nudges the end, making her completely fuck up and barely even skim the white.

"You fucker," she laughs.

This is painful, I take the lead again, with only the black left to pot. But she can't make me win, I'll just keep missing. Of course, I could just say I don't feel like playing another game, but this is dickhead. He'll gloat. Mags goes to have a sip of her wine, and I watch Spencer say something which amuses her. When she returns, she is grinning and she gets in place to try and pot one of her two remaining balls. Then just like that, she misses and pots the black.

'Oh,' she exclaims, putting her hand over her mouth. "That means you win, right?" She looks back to the boys, "That means she wins right?"

She can fuck off with her dumb girlie act, she knows the rules. She did that on purpose! I narrow my eyes at her and she winks, retreating back to her wine.

"Well, Princess, looks like you and me." He stands and swaggers over.

"Ugh." I don't even try to hide my disgust. "Fine, rack them up, I'm going to the ladies." I stop before I walk away and look at Mags. "Wine," I demand. "A big one," and storm off to the toilets.

Stopping at the mirror, I take a deep breath and blow it out. Jeez, he annoys me. But this is hardly a disaster. I need to get myself together or all the progress we've made will be for nothing. We agreed, we like taking pleasure from each other. It's never going to be a romance, but I can certainly play a game of pool without blowing a gasket.

Ok, calm.

Sliding the lock closed on the cubicle door, I hear my phone beep. I take it out of my pocket and see it's from him.

'Take a picture.'

I shake my head, he's fucking something else. He really thinks he can just snap his fingers and I'll jump. Fine, he wants a picture, I'll send him one. Snapping a picture of the toilet roll dispenser, I attach it to the message and hit Send.

'Very good, Princess. Just send me the one I took in your bedroom.'

No way.

Finishing up, I let myself out and wash my hands. My phone beeps again.

'Don't make me beg.'

Ignoring it, I stare at myself in the mirror. Come on, Jazz, get it together. He is only on top because you let him be. You've got to just show him he doesn't get to you and stand your ground. Psyched up, I push through the door, back into the pub. Mags is returning from the bar with my wine, which I take from her before she can even put it on the table and take a big gulp.

"Ready for me?" he asks, wiggling his brow to emphasise the innuendo.

"Sure, why not?" I say, game face on.

"What are we playing for?" he asks.

"Uh, to win obviously."

"And what do I get when I win?"

"Pft!" I laugh. Oh, look, my competitive streak is back, with bells on. "You wish. What do I get when I win?"

"Name it," he says. Cocky bastard, thinks I'm no challenge.

"Mmmmm," I consider my options. I don't really want anything from him, at least nothing I'll admit to here.

"I know what I want," he says, handing me a cue.

"What?"

"If I win, I get that photo."

"No fucking chance."

"Don't lose then," he says, completely serious.

I have no idea how good he is. But with a prize like that on the table, I'll have to take him down. Cursing myself for being the most stubborn bitch in existence and not being able to back away from a challenge, I act like I'm considering it, then answer, 'Fine. But if I win, I want a photo of you."

A laugh rumbles from his chest. "Sure thing, Princess."

I sigh, I wish he'd stop calling me that.

"You break," he says, keen to get on with winning. He wishes.

A few turns in, holding my own, I have a shot I can barely reach. Every shot I take, he's right behind me perving, or across the table, staring down my top. This time I really have to lean over the table, and as I come back up, my phone beeps.

'You have no idea how badly I want to fuck you on that table."

I put my phone back in my pocket and don't look in his direction. He takes his turn and pots a ball. We're both really playing to win. The stakes are high, I really don't need or want a photo of him, I just need him not to have the photo of me. He has enough of those already, and in this one, you can see my face. It's not happening. He, on the other hand, probably sends his dick out to all his little Twitter playmates; he'll think nothing of it. He just wants that photo.

After he's taken his second shot and comes up empty, I weigh up my options. Choosing my target, I lean over the table. A beep from my pocket breaks my concentration, and I mess up, pocketing nothing and leaving him with a clear shot. Grinning from ear to ear, he steps back and has a drink, letting me sweat. I've barely noticed Mags and Will at the table, they're watching it all unfold and laughing quietly about their private jokes. Ignoring them, I check my phone, I know he's going to keep doing this.

'I want to bite that arse.'

Then another message beeps and I can't help but look at him. He smiles and puts his phone in his pocket. Picking up his cue and circling the table, making a real meal of assessing all his options, when we both know I handed him an easy ball.

'What would it take to get you naked and
on a pool table?'

I'm holding it together, but each message sends a frisson of excitement through me. If we weren't in a busy village pub on a Sunday evening, I'd be sprawled across that table by now, I have no doubt. Thank heavens for the general public.

He stops at the other end of the table and eyes up his shot, or rather eyes me up, under the guise of studying angles. Heat spreads. His greedy eyes firing the need I had under control. Is it hot in here? I need to get out of this hoodie. Slowly unzipping it, I don't realise I have his full attention until the zip is halfway down, but once I do, I keep it. Dispensing with the zip, I open the front pulling it off both arms simultaneously in a way that pushes my chest forward. Slowly. Then I straighten out my fitted black tank top, pulling the hem down, in turn lowering the neckline slightly. Revealing a peep of bra lace.

Spencer swallows.

Satisfaction sets in as I rest both hands on the edge of the table and bend slightly to come down to his eye level, affording him a great view of my cleavage. "Are you going to take a shot, Spencer?"

"Huh? Oh, yeah."

He takes the easy shot I left him and pots the ball, although a child could have pocketed that. The second shot is not so easy, he needs to work for it, and while he is figuring it out, I type a message.

'Buy a pool table, don't keep it in a busy pub, I'll think about it.'

He finishes his turn and checks his messages. I see him smile. Happy with myself I push on. I can win this.

'You'll think about it? I need a promise, Jazz. If I get a pool table, I need a promise that I get to fuck you on it. It's a big investment. Fair's fair.'

Between shots the messages continue.

'If you get a pool table, you can fuck me on it. Promise.'

Like that will ever happen.

'Sweet.'

'You could have pocketed that one.'

'You're distracting me.'

'Good.'

Finally we're left with just the black. It's his turn. He takes a drink, he knows what is riding on this. He considers it for ages. Too long. I mean this picture can't be that important, can it? I walk over to get my wine and take a long drink, placing the empty glass back down. "Ah, that's better," I tell everyone and no one in particular. "My throat was so dry." Turning to watch Spencer try and take the all important winning shot with the thought of how wet my throat is on his mind. He chokes!

"Oh, dear." I try not to gloat, but I can't help it. Moving around the table, I have the perfect shot. He's watching me. I line up and when I'm sure, I look him in the eye and take it. I don't take my eyes off his, the white ball connects with the black and the black falls into the corner pocket. The white drifts back towards the centre of the table and I keep my eyes locked on his.

"Better luck next time," I almost whisper, my heart banging in my chest from the sexual tension that suddenly amped up in here.

He feels it too because he says nothing, just stares.

"Want another drink?" I ask him, clearing my throat when

my voice sounds weak.

I turn to Mags and Will to extend the offer to them. "Actually, we were thinking of heading back to ours for a drink and maybe watch a film, want to come?" says Will looking to Mags who nods her agreement.

Damn, so my choice is to stay here with Spencer or go back to their house -- with Spencer. Yes, yes, I know my third option is to say, "no thank you," and go home alone. I'm a big girl. But I'm not looking to explore all the logical options right now. The choice I'm presented with is stay here and get more and more sexually frustrated, or go HOME with Spencer Ryan. Willingly. That's basically what it boils down to.

"She'll come," he says. Cocky git. I watch him almost drown downing the rest of his pint. He can't drink it fast enough.

"Yeah, she will," says Mags with a giggle.

Rolling my eyes, I look only at Will. "Apparently, I would love to come. However, we will need to stop and buy wine. All of a sudden, I'm really thirsty."

Will laughs and stands up, holding out his elbow for me to take. "As you wish, my lady, allow me to show you the way."

Spencer frowns, Mags laughs, and I throw caution to the wind, grabbing my stuff and taking his arm.

Will squeezes my arm with his and grins, "Good choice."

"I mean it, Will. Wine."

"I know you do, Jazz," he laughs, weaving me through the tables and out into the evening air. "I'm on it."

It's now that I realise I've had a few already, the fresh air always does that. But if I'm going back there, I need some fortification of the fermented grape variety.

We walk along the village high street, calling into the convenience store with Spencer and Mags in tow. Will steers me straight to the wine section and waves his hand at the selection. "As my lady wishes," then he bows.

I laugh for the first time tonight. I don't know what I'm so uptight for. I'm supposed to be having fun.

"Why, thank you, kind sir," I reply, kissing his cheek.

Will releases my arm to pick up a case of beer, and I grab a couple of bottles for Mags and I. We realise that Spencer and Mags have gone off elsewhere, and we start looking for them, then my phone beeps. Tucking a bottle under my arm, I retrieve it.

A picture message is waiting....of the lube shelf in the toiletries section.

'Need anything?'

I laugh out loud, causing a man looking at peanuts to sidestep me as I pass by. All of a sudden I feel too drunk to be in public. I'm not drunk, but I feel it here. Giggling, I respond as I head down the aisle towards Mags, where she's looking at sweets, clutching an armful of popcorn and crisps.

'Not for me, thanks.'

I could have said something cutting, but I've got nothing. The fact is, right now, lube is the last thing I need. It's a couple of minutes before he replies.

'I see, wet enough already.'

I smile and clench my thighs together. Very much so. A wave of need washes over me.

'Always.'

'I've noticed. Hurry up.'

I look up from my phone feeling the need to get out of here. Will joins us with his beers, and I turn to see Spencer waiting outside on the pavement holding a carrier bag and eating a packet of crisps. His slow smile does nothing to ease the throbbing which has begun since he drew my attention to how wet I am already. I need some relief.

Mags is still choosing between Minstrels and Malteasers. Seriously Mags? With all your money I think you can splash out and have both. I lean over her and grab a bag of each and head for the till before she can argue.

He watches us pay from a few feet away through the open door. I can't look at him, but I know he doesn't take his eyes off me. I can feel them like hands on my body, caressing me as they roam. Then we finally hit the fresh air again. It's such a warm evening; it's warmer out here than it was in there and I was hot enough already. Will and Mags chat away and I keep up with them. Spencer walks behind, but I can't trust myself to walk with him. There is so much tension between us right now, I'd probably agree to let him fuck me on a parked car. Luckily, the walk to their house is short.

Mags goes straight into the living room, dumping her bags out on the coffee table. It's nice in here, I've never seen it. I've only ever been in the kitchen and...well...it's dangerous in there. Kitchens in general seem to be an issue for us. The living room is nice. Very homely considering two guys live here and one of them is Spencer. I collect up the empty carrier bags and the wine and take them to the kitchen, handing them to Will as he loads the fridge. Spencer knocks the caps off two cold beers from the fridge, and Will opens a wine and pours two glasses. I perch myself on the kitchen table and watch. I'm sure Will must be able to feel the crackle of electric tension in the room. No one speaks.

Will hands me one of the wines he is holding, I smile in thanks. Then picking up one of the beers, he leaves, without a word.

And then there were two.

Spencer takes a drink, leaning against the kitchen counter.

"What do you think they'll watch?" I ask. I don't know what else to say. He seems perfectly content staring.

He shrugs. "Who cares? We aren't going to watch it. I'm going to be too busy getting you naked on my furniture."

I shiver.

Looking around, I smirk though, trying to cover up my desire. "I don't see a pool table anywhere." I look down at the kitchen table I'm sitting on and tap the surface. "This might not be the same."

"We'll get to that. I want to show you something first," he says, stepping forward and nodding towards the back door. "You game?"

I have a rush of nerves, but I try not to show it and reply, "I'm game," following him. He leads me down the side of the house into a beautiful garden with a little deck covered with a pergola and climbing plants, comfy seating and a big BBQ.

Beyond that, a well kept lawn leads to a double garage at the end.

We keep walking until we reach the garage door and he stops, turning to me all serious and says, "This is usually a no-women-allowed space. I'm ONLY letting you in right now because my life right now depends on it."

I open my mouth to give him a serve about how sad it is he needs to have a no-girls club house at the bottom of his garden like he's eight. But he said his life depends on it, which has me intrigued. "Ok," I manage to croak.

He proceeds to unlock the door, and then he switches on a light and steps aside to let me in.

Wow.

To say that this is a boys' den is a massive understatement. This is a Man Cave of epic proportions. The outside gives no clue. It's carpeted, decorated and furnished. A huge well-worn leather sofa faces a TV with game consoles beneath it. A punch bag is hanging in the corner, a dart board on the wall, a bar with stools, a fridge…and there, with pride of place, a pool table.

I laugh.

In fact, I get a fit of giggles.

Turning to look at him, laughing, I see he's looking at his phone, then he looks at me, holding up the screen. "You promised."

I shake my head, still laughing and admit, "Yeah, I did."

He walks towards me, backing me up. I'm still laughing a little until my bum bumps against the pool table and his strong arms cage me in. I look up into his serious face and gulp.

"Take your clothes off," he whispers.

"Care to make it interesting?"

He looks at me quizzically.

"I'll play you for clothes."

He considers it for a second. "Ok, but make it quick, I've been wanting to get you naked for the last hour."

He racks up the balls and insists on breaking to get things moving. He has a lucky break due to brute force and pots something. Stalking towards me, he pulls my top over my head, bending to kiss my neck. I sigh as it sets off a shiver. He places two more kisses on my neck close to my ear, before capturing my mouth in a deep kiss. He pulls away and I breathe. "Your turn," he smiles.

I blow a strand of hair off my face, damn I can hardly think, let alone hit a ball. Nevertheless, I want his body. I don't pot anything though and he wastes no time taking his turn, potting a stripe.

"Hey, you were spots."

"Don't care," he growls, coming at me and unhooking my bra in a flash. He pushes me back, so that I have to lean back on my hands and sucks in my nipple, making me gasp.

"My turn." I push him off, turning to take a shot, but find him pressed against me. His hand runs down my bare back and he grabs the back of my jeans to pull me close against the hard straining bulge in his jeans. He flexes his hips, pressing harder against me, an ache starts between my legs. God, I need him to touch me. I have a failed attempt at hitting something and end up picking up a ball and shoving it down a hole, to get things moving. His chuckle is muffled by me turning suddenly and yanking off his T-shirt. "Mmmmmm," I purr, running my hands down his defined chest until they reach his jeans. I quickly slide the button through its hole and pull so the zip slides down.

"Hey!" he swats my hand away. "It's my turn." He moves out of my reach to the other side of the table, but he doesn't do up his jeans, and I can see now that he's wearing no underwear. I am treated to the perfect view of his delicious happy trail starting just where his abs finish and running down between the pronounced V of his…whatever that is. The little piece of heaven on earth that's made to be worshipped.

He easily pots a ball, "Shoes," he demands.

I kick off my black and purple Air Max.

"And socks," he adds.

"I bet you wish I'd worn heels tonight," I mutter, as I pull my socks off.

"Actually, I'd have made you leave them outside."

"Oh?"

"The temptation to fuck you in them would be too strong and no stilettos are getting on my pool table. Nuh uh."

"I see, precious to you is it?"

"A bit."

I take my turn and actually pot something. I look up to find him taking off his shoes and socks. That peep of happiness is too much to resist, I climb up on the table and start to crawl across it.

"Crawling on the table is frowned upon," he says quietly, as he straightens up and sees me coming towards him.

"I can live with that," I say, reaching his side and pulling him close by the corner of his open fly. I ease them down slightly letting him break free from the fabric that was barely holding him in. As I'm moving closer, I nudge some balls and a couple go in. "Lose them," I tell him, just as I take the head in my mouth.

He groans and tries to wiggle out of his jeans, but he isn't having much luck. He stands, stuck in his half-down jeans and lets me tease him, knowing from this angle I can't take him all in. Then I hear a ball go down a hole and I know he doesn't want teasing anymore.

"Yours. Off. Now."

I come up on my knees and watch him lose his jeans and stand before me completely naked. Getting to my feet on the blue cloth surface, he looks like he really wants to object, but as I slowly shimmy out of my jeans, he watches mesmerised and says nothing. Tossing them on the floor, I walk to the edge and he strokes the sides of my legs, hooking his fingers in my underwear and sliding them down. I step one foot out of them and as I step the other out, he captures it, almost knocking me off balance. I steady myself on his head, the only thing I can hold on to up here and he guides my leg over his shoulder.

I have to hold on for dear life as his mouth closes in around my aching lips. His suction starts my standing leg trembling immediately. His tongue flicks at my clit and my hands grip tight in his hair, both for balance and so that he can't pull away. A loud moan tears from me and my leg threatens to buckle. He eases my other leg down and releases me, then his strong hands lift me down. He sits me right on the edge of the table and wraps my legs around him as he surges into me.

The way he fills me is such a relief, and the way he kind of sighs shows me he feels the same. He lays me back across the table and stares for a moment, his fingers tracing my lines as he studies me.

"Finally," he whispers and leans over me, pushing his hard length further into me and his lips meet mine.

As soon as our mouths connect he starts to move, long deep claiming strokes. He wants me to know this is his turn. I feel it. I feel like I'm his. His arms resting either side of me, encase me, and his hands toy with my hair as his tongue caresses mine and he swallows my moans. Driving into me over and over, he's simply chasing his pleasure, the fact that he's bringing mine is just chance, but there is no way I can avoid the orgasm he quickly brings me to.

Crying out against his lips as it grips me, I hold him tight and have to ride it out through his steady, unwavering thrusts. He kisses my cheek soothing me, shushing my whimpers as he doesn't relent and my over sensitive nerves have to just deal. He growls as he feels his release coming, speeding up his thrusts, holding me tighter and once again searching out my tongue with his to mute his cries as he comes. I hold him tight, feeling him tense and then let it all go, kissing him down from his high. We kiss for a long time, he strokes my hair and slowly and gently keeps thrusting as we catch our breath and relax our bodies.

After one last kiss, he straightens up and picks up my underwear from beside us on the pool table. He slips them over each foot in turn and slides them back up my legs, telling me to lift when he gets to my bum. Straightening them in place, he drops a kiss just above them. He's quiet as he helps me to sit up and passes me my jeans. His actions are unhurried and affectionate, but his demeanour seems regretful. Once again an atmosphere descends on us like it did at the pool. I stand up and wander around the table collecting my things from where they were scattered.

Once my bra and top are back on, I walk over to the bar and perch on one of the stools to put my shoes and socks back on.

My mouth is so dry and I eye up the bar. "Do you have anything to drink here?" I ask quietly, as he does up the button of his jeans.

"The wine is in the house," he replies.

"I was thinking of something soft like a Coke if you have it. I'm really thirsty."

"Yeah, sure," he nods, padding over to the bar in bare feet, with no top on. I watch his muscles flex as he pulls something from the fridge and reaches for a glass. Returning to me, he hands me a glass of Coke.

"Thank you," I smile. Taking a sip, I pull a face.

"What?" he says, puzzled.

"It's Pepsi," I reply.

He rolls his eyes, "And what is wrong with Pepsi, Princess?"

"Nothing. I just wasn't expecting it. It's, in a Coke glass." I hold up the glass to show him. "See?"

"Oh, yeah," he smirks. "It's bipolar cola."

I choke on my mouthful and splutter trying to keep it in, Spencer laughs. He's really beautiful when he laughs. When there isn't a hint of sarcasm or one-upmanship, just honest, free laughter.

"That's very good."

"Thanks," he chuckles going back to get the rest of his clothes. "It just came to me." Throwing his T-shirt over his shoulder, he stuffs his socks inside his shoes and says, "You want to go back inside?"

"You're just going to go in like that?" I ask.

"Yeah, why not?"

"It will be a little obvious what we just did, won't it?"

"Where do you suppose they think we've been all this time? They're going to know we've been up to no good somewhere."

"I guess so."

"Besides, I'm going to go and shower, so there's no point in getting dressed, is there?"

"Oh. Ok." A feeling of disappointment sinks in as I realise that this evening is now over. He has had his way, it's time for me to run along.

"Come on," he says, holding open the door for me and locking up. I lead the way back up the garden and into the kitchen. Putting my glass by the sink and trying to toss up between the walk of shame into the living room alone, having missed half the film and been cast aside, or quietly going home.

Dropping his shoes by the door, he opens the fridge door between us. When it shuts, he's holding two bottles of water. He hands one to me and then takes my free hand.

MY. HAND.

What the hell? He must feel me tense and looks at me. "Shower, you coming?"

Stunned into submission for a moment, I nod.

"Good."

Then he leads the way down the hall, HOLDING MY HAND! This is waaaaaaaay too intimate for us. Have I mentioned it's my hand he's holding? Ten minutes ago his tongue and his cock were inside me, and yet it's this that freaks me out.

Pausing by the living room door, which is ajar, he squeezes my hand to get my attention and nods silently to the gap in the door. I peep in and see two pairs of feet intertwined and resting on the coffee table. I grin and he pulls me towards the stairs.

Following him up, I relax a little. This is nice, right? I haven't been finished with for the night like I thought, and he's comfortable enough to hold my hand. This is good. I smile to myself, feeling a lot better.

When we get to the top of the stairs, he turns and pulls me against his bare chest. "I think you should stay," he says.

Stay? The night? Bloody hell!

Suppressing the beginnings of a very satisfied grin, I reply, "We'll see."

He smiles and kisses me.

Jazz

MONDAY 20TH JULY

I can't help thinking the walk of shame would have been easier last night as I lay here motionless in his bed listening to him breathe. I had so much fun last night, in the shower, then in the night when he did everything he could to make me scream while I was trying to keep the noise down.

I don't know what happened to Mags, we haven't left his room; but I'm sure Will took care of her. Now I have to deal with extracting myself from his bed and slipping out, or what? Waiting for him to get up and get ready for work? That'll be nice and embarrassing, turning up at work with him. Won't they all love that? And Mags will be impossible to deal with if I roll in with yesterday's clothes on after abandoning her. No, I need to leave now, while it's still early.

He's spooning against me. He has been since we finally fell back to sleep around four. Carefully, I lift the covers and start to move myself away from him. The problem with two hot, naked bodies that have been writhing together for hours on a warm night is that they kind of stick together. So as I peel myself off him, he stirs. Feeling my absence from him as much as I feel his from me.

"Where do you think you're going?" he croaks, tightening

his arm around me.

"I've got to go."

"Why?"

"I should get home."

"What's up?" He pulls me back down to the pillow and lifts his head to study my face.

"Nothing."

"Liar."

I sigh. "Ok, I don't fancy pulling up to work with you and giving them all something to talk about."

"No problem, you can walk," he laughs.

I narrow my eyes at him. "You know what I mean."

"Princess, why should you care what anyone else thinks? You can hardly stand me, they know that. They find it highly amusing. When we pull up, get out of the car and slap me. They'll take the piss out of me all day and they won't think any less of you."

"There's Mags too, she's going to be a nightmare. I just ditched her and went to bed with you without a word. She's probably been waiting up. She'll be furious."

"The only reason Mags will have been up all night will be because Will wouldn't let her sleep. Or maybe because they could hear you scream," he grins. "She stayed, too."

"Did she?" I'm a little louder than I mean to be and drop to a whisper when I realise. "She's here?"

"Yeah. I heard them come up."

"I didn't hear them."

"No, you were...a bit preoccupied."

I try not to grin. "So, did you hear anything else? Did they do it?"

"Not that I heard, she probably had him gagged and tied up so no one could hear him scream."

I glare at him, "What makes you say that?"

I don't think anything about Mags gives away her inner domme. She doesn't come across that way at all, unless he's read her books.

"Because he loves all that. Freak."

"Will does?" I ask in disbelief.

"Yep."

"Really?" I can't imagine Will being into any of that.

"Oh, yeah."

"Wow."

"Uh huh. Now, fuck Will and Mags, let's get back to you not getting up yet."

"I still should go."

"No, you shouldn't." He shifts so I can feel him hard against me. "I've got to take care of this before I get up. You wouldn't leave me fending for myself, now would you?" The arm that's holding me slips away, and then I feel his fingers from behind me, feeling their way inside my tender folds. He groans when they slip straight in. "You are always wet, aren't you?"

"In the right company," I wince.

"Was that a compliment, Princess?"

I shrug.

"Well, it's a good thing you're always wet around me because I'm always hard around you."

"Lucky," I gasp, as he slowly replaces his probing fingers with his substantial, morning wood.

Spencer

My phone vibrates with a DM while I'm tempering chocolate on the marble. Problem is, I can't stop, I have to keep it moving. Once I'm done, I wipe my hands off on a cloth and open it. It's a link from Spencer. Weird. I pause before I open it and make sure I can see Mags sitting at her laptop. It could be porn, knowing him. I tap the link and wait while it takes me to one of those newsy, lifestyle websites. Finally, the link fully opens and I see why he has sent me the article.

'The Grapefruit Blow Job' is the title of the article. I roll my eyes. Where did he find this, and more to the point, he better not be suggesting I do it. Intrigued though, I read on. In simple terms, this YouTubing sexpert suggests that you cut the top and bottom off a grapefruit, poke a hole through the centre of the big slice you are left with and slide it on to assist you in apparently the best blow job ever. The article is funny, the journalist made her boyfriend let her try it and he said it was amazing.

'Well?'

Comes the impatient message.

'Well, what?'

'Well? How do you like the sound of that?'

'I'm not a big fan of grapefruit.'

I laugh as I press send. I can just picture his eager smile as he waits for my reply and then he gets that.

'Where did your sense of adventure go? You were fun last night.'

'I was drunk last night.'

'We should go for a drink later ;)'

'Nice try, you won't be taking advantage of me again.'

'I think it was an advantage to both of us, Princess.'

'Well drunk or not, I won't be licking grapefruit juice off any part of you. Unless there's some sugar involved. I hate the taste.'

'Sugar might be a bit gritty. What about sherbet?'

'Won't that be a bit…tingly?'

'It might be quite nice. Just as long as it's not that crackly space dust stuff.'

'Ooooh, yeah, ouch!'

'So I'm just going to put you down as a maybe on the whole 'Fruit blow job' thing.'

'Uh huh, good luck with that!'

'How about I just pick up a Sherbet Fountain too. We can throw out the liquorice and you can dip something else in it.'

'I always preferred Dib Dabs. The sherbet is a bit more effervescent.'

'I'm up for effervescent.'

'We'll see.'

'YESSSSS!'

'Oh hush, you. We'll see does not mean yes.'

'It meant yes when you said it last night.'

'No, it meant, we'll see what you can do to convince me.'

'And I was very convincing, right?'

'Maybe.'

'Maybe? It wasn't maybe you were shouting over and over.'

Oh, shit. I was so loud!

And I was embarrassed enough that Will might have heard us. But now I've had to contend with knowing looks and sarcastic comments from Mags all morning. She is determined to remind me at every opportunity that she and Will had to lay there and listen to us. I tried to point out that they could have occupied themselves to drown us out, but she still insists that nothing happened between them and that she stayed the night simply because they fell asleep on the sofa and then realised we were in bed, so it was the easiest option.

Sure. Right.

But she is having none of it. She swears they are just friends and that he was the perfect gentleman. So I'm just going to have to live with my embarrassment and hope they don't dwell on it too long.

Going back to what I was doing, I find myself thinking how it would be nice to see him later once he's finished work. Then I catch myself. Good lord, I'm thinking like he's my boyfriend. That's going to have to stop! It's fun, nothing more and it never will be.

"MAGS!" I yell into the other room.

"Yeah," she yells back.

"Fancy the flicks tonight? Just you and me?"

"Throw in a Nandos and you have yourself a deal."

I sigh with relief. There, now I'm busy later, so there won't be any time for Spencer.

Spencer
MONDAY 20TH JULY

'Whatcha doin?' I type…quickly deleting it.

I need my phone confiscated. What am I thinking? I scrub my face with my hands and turn my phone face down so that the lack of action it has seen for the last few hours doesn't bother me so much.

"What's up?" asks Will, as he wanders into the kitchen.

"Nothing's up," I snap.

His eyebrows raise. "Easy, precious, I was only asking."

"Well, nothing's up," I grumble. "Everything is tickety-boo."

"Ooooookaaaayyy." He shakes his head and puts the kettle on. "Someone's obviously a little tired from fucking all night."

My shoulders tense, and I can feel myself getting pissed off. I'm already annoyed that I've been thinking about her all day and she's practically been a ghost. I don't need him rubbing it in. "Not seeing your girlfriend tonight?" I ask, diverting the attention off me.

"She's not my girlfriend," he replies on a sigh, tired of my constant poking.

"Uh huh."

"Dude, it wasn't me all up inside a girl I'm pretending not

to give a shit about all damn night, was it?"

"So you say."

"We're just friends," he repeats for the hundredth time. "You should try it some time."

"How sweet," I groan. "Doesn't sound like much fun to me. All that effort on pleasantries and then no one sucks your dick."

"No, you're right, it's awful connecting with someone on a personal level. I don't recommend it. You stick to verbal abuse and hate-fucking, it's far safer. You wouldn't want to come down with anything nasty, like feelings." Then he shudders to illustrate his already tiresome point.

"Been there, remember? That shit and me are not designed to coexist. A giant waste of time, if you ask me."

"Oh, Jesus, Spencer, they're not all like Lucy."

I stiffen when he says her name.

"Yeah, yeah, I know, you don't want to hear it. But sooner or later you'll have to stop crashing through life like a bull in a china shop and admit that there are a few people in the world worth stopping to appreciate. Some of them, if you're lucky, will appreciate you back. They're not all self-centred bitches who'll rip your heart out, like—"

I pretend to yawn and cut him off. "So, you're not seeing your girlfriend tonight then?" I can't hear her name again.

He sighs dramatically. "If you mean Mags, then no. She and your little fuck buddy had plans. They went to the cinema."

"Oh."

He turns around and catches whatever expression that I failed to keep off my face.

"Uh oh, did she not let you know?" He smirks.

I narrow my eyes, "Now, why would she let me know? Why would I even care?"

"Mmmmhmmm." He turns back to the sink, but I see the struggle he has not to laugh at me. "It seems like she's getting under your skin, mate. How about a game of pool to take your mind off her?"

Seriously, I could kill him. It's like he's doing it deliberately. But I'm not going to show him he's winning. "My mind isn't even on her, 'mate.' Sorry to disappoint you."

Just then, my phone vibrates against the wood of the table. My eyes shoot to it, lying there face down. I can't even get a clue who it was from, and Will has turned to look as well. Shit.

A stand off begins.

Me, too stubborn to let Will see me cave.

Will, very much enjoying the torture he is putting me through, knowing I won't cave in front of him; and the longer he stares, the longer he tortures me.

His stupid grin as it vibrates again makes me want to break him.

Fuck it. I snatch my phone up as I stand and head out the door, unlocking the screen.

"I hate to tell you this, mate," he calls after me, "but it won't be her. She's up to her eyes in Channing Tatum right about now."

"Bite me," I throw back.

Of course he's right, it's not her.

But it is a bit of fun I could have. It's definitely not a good idea, I know that. But I need to do something to get my mind off Shoegirl.

Taking a deep breath, I hit reply.

Jazz

TUESDAY 21ST JULY

Aside from some flirty messaging, I managed a fairly Spencer-free day yesterday. It's not that I think for a second he would get too attached after spending one night together. He's not that type at all. I just felt like putting a little distance between us was the right thing to do.

It's either that or what?…Hang out? What next, exchange numbers and meet each other's parents? I don't think so.

I know nothing about him and he knows nothing about me. If he were interested, he would ask. But getting to know me is obviously not high on his list of priorities and that's fine. I haven't exactly tried to learn anything about him either. I'll admit, I am slightly intrigued. He's so cocky, so in love with himself, maybe he was the ugly duckling and finally becoming a swan went right to his head. Or maybe his doting mother just went overboard telling him how special he was and forgot to teach him any humility. I mean, I don't even know if he has a mother. Well, of course, he had one; I don't know if he still has one, or if so, where she is.

Quickly, I go from no interest whatsoever to wanting to know more. Damn it.

What is Spencer Ryan's story? Does he have a family other

than Will? Or was he born on Krypton after all and sent to earth to be marvellously handsome and great in bed, so that he can procreate with the swooning inhabitants and create a subspecies? I laugh to myself. It would be just my luck, wouldn't it?

Mags will know, I'm sure. But then come to think of it, she's the one who found out his name in the first place. She had no clue he was anything to do with Will.

I decide to make her a tea and do a little gentle investigation.

As I switch the fresh tea for the empty mug on the coaster beside where she is writing in the living room, I casually ask, "So, I have a question. How is it that you knew Will for years and yet didn't know Spencer?"

"Ah, well," she smiles, picking up her tea, clearly delighted I've asked. "He didn't live around here at the time. His parents live down by the coast. Will would talk about his cousin, but he would just say 'my cousin.' I think they've always been close, but I guess I just was never around when they saw each other. After they went to Australia together, Spencer moved here."

"How come they went to Australia together? It sounded like Will went in kind of a hurry."

Mags' face falls.

"I'm sure he wasn't running away from you," I add, defensively.

Mags scoffs. "Mmmhmm."

"Whatever, Mags, I've seen the way he looks at you. He did not go half way around the world just to get away from you. Open your fucking eyes."

She shakes her head, going back to her laptop.

"I'm just saying, whatever is not being said between you is clear for the rest of us to see. You need to stop kidding yourselves and sort your shit out."

She laughs, but doesn't take her eyes off the screen. "Oh, that's rich coming from you."

"My shit and your shit are not the same thing! You and Will care for each other a great deal. Just because you have unanswered questions from the past, doesn't mean you shouldn't at least explore what you have going on now. Then you can try and get some answers to put your mind at rest."

She huffs. "I've got some answers. We have been talking, you know."

She continues to stare at her screen and clicks something with the touchpad. I wait.

Oh, bloody hell! "AND?"

She jumps and turns to face me. "AND, he went because Spencer needed him."

I frown. "Why did Spencer 'need' him? What about what you needed?" I suddenly feel irritated that Mags lost the great love of her life because of that idiot. Yes, yes, that idiot I'm having fantastic sex with, but he's still an idiot. And I'm not at all surprised to imagine that he put his needs before Will's and dragged him away from his girl to go off gallivanting around Australia with him. He was probably sulking that Will spent all his time with Mags and none with him. I can picture him pulling the 'blood is thicker than water' card.

She sighs. "Look at you."

I snap out of my vision. "What?"

"I can see you getting mad with him in your head, you're

going to snap that mug if you hold it any tighter. Spencer needed Will. I accept that. It's done."

"How? How did he NEED him? Good lord, it's not all about him."

She looks around. Why, I don't know. We are inside, but I guess they are just outside. Then in a slightly more hushed tone, she starts to explain.

"Spencer had a girlfriend. They met at university and were really serious. According to Will, Spencer was besotted. They planned a year backpacking after they graduated and then they were coming back to live in London and start their careers. They both studied the same thing. He had big plans of them going to work for a few years for other companies and then set up together in business.

"Will says Spencer was so head over heels in love with her that she could do no wrong. But Will wasn't that keen on her, so while she was around, he kept his distance, which explains why I never met Spencer. Anyway, Spencer was planning on asking her to marry him on this trip. He had a ring, he was all pumped up about it. Then she just told him out of the blue one day that she didn't want to be with him any more. She had been carrying on behind his back the whole time apparently. She never got found out, but I guess because she suddenly realised she was going to be with him alone for a year and that wasn't what she wanted, she had to fess up."

I try to digest what she's saying. Trying to relate this Spencer she is describing to the arrogant, self-absorbed dickhead out there.

"It was a real kick in the teeth, there was none of that 'It's not you, it's me' crap. Just a straight up, I don't love you. Then it snowballed pretty quickly apparently. He went from begging her to change her mind and proposing, hoping it would make her see sense, to obsessively breaking apart every aspect of their relationship until he knew exactly how many times she had made a fool of him. Then he hit rock bottom."

"Shit." I say slowly and to no one in particular. I just can't imagine it's the same person. The one she's describing, I want to hug. Poor guy. But one thing I can't understand is him wanting to get married so young. "I can't imagine Spencer wanting to get married at all, never mind so young, this was all before we started uni!"

"Yeah, but Spencer is three years older, he had just finished uni remember?"

"That's still young if you ask me."

"Maybe that's why it hit him so hard, I don't know. His parents were pretty worried about him. He was in a really bad way. He wasn't going on the trip of a lifetime alone, he wasn't even getting out of bed. They called Will and asked him to try and do something to reach him." She sighs. "So he did. We had just finished college and Will wasn't going to university. He had actually been saving really hard to start his own business. But he applied for a visa, spent the savings that were for his business on a ticket, and he went down to the south coast and yelled at Spencer until he got him on the plane to Oz. He was a mess apparently and Will said he needed to get him out of the country and on some kind of adventure before he hit self destruct."

"Wow."

"Yeah."

"So, Will just gave you up to help his cousin?"

Mags shrugs. "Basically, yes."

"That...that sucks and is so sweet in equal measure."

"I know."

"I mean, if you weren't the girl he left behind, I would think that story made Will look like the sweetest guy in the world."

"Uh huh."

"So that explains the sudden departure. But why didn't he just tell you all that then? You'd have waited a year."

"That's the thing," she says, sounding defeated. "I still don't know. He's explained why he left. I get it. He needed to help his cousin. But he hasn't explained why he couldn't have..." she drifts off.

"Why he couldn't have let you down more gently? Explained that it wasn't you...Why he couldn't have come back for you?" I finish what I know is in her head.

"Yeah, that," she says quietly.

"Mags, you should ask. Because, from here, it looks like he's very much into you. So, whatever reason he had, you need to get it out there so you can get past it."

She shakes her head. "It is what it is."

"You are so stubborn at times," I huff.

"Says the mayoress of Stubbornville!"

"Pft!" She can't compare our situations, they are totally different. I need to make her see sense. "Look, me and Spencer, we're nothing. It's fun sometimes, and mildly irritating the rest of the time, and once this 'life vacation' is over and we get back home, that will be it. He's not normal. Although what you've just told me does explain a few things. But he's just a small feature on a little break I'm taking from reality. Honestly, I can't wait to get back to my life. You and Will on the other hand are something. You need to get it all out in the open and see what comes of it."

"Speaking of going back home," she says, artfully avoiding my point. "Have you thought about the shop any more?"

Laughing, I turn to leave. "I think I made myself perfectly clear about that, Mags, but nice avoidance."

Just as I get back into the kitchen and pick up my tea, the kitchen door opens and in walks the man himself. Tossing an orange from hand to hand and up in the air as he comes towards me.

"For you," he says, handing it to me with a smirk.

"Er, thanks," I look at the orange and back at him, a bit confused.

"You don't like grapefruit, so I found you a substitute," he grins.

I laugh, half in realisation and half annoyed that I didn't see it coming. "How thoughtful, thank you," I say with some considerable sarcasm, putting the orange down on the counter with a thump.

"Careful, you'll bruise it."

I shake my head, "You really think you're going to get me to do this, don't you?"

"Naturally." He looks around and goes for his fly. "We could do it now if you like."

Laughing, I push him away. "I don't think so. I'm busy."

With a distinct look of disappointment, he backs off. "Fine, well when you're not too busy, you know where to find me."

After he's gone, I wonder why that was so easy. It's not

like he normally takes no for an answer. Perhaps he's finally getting bored.

Spencer
TUESDAY 21ST JULY

The image opens on my screen. I nervously look over my shoulder at my closed bedroom door. Will isn't even home, but still, I feel guilty, which for me is a disconcerting feeling. I don't usually have the heart for guilt. I do as I please. But this feels like a bit of an abuse of trust.

Ok, it's a massive abuse of trust.

Huge.

She wasn't around earlier when I went to see her. I could hear her in the other room talking, I was going to go and listen. But her phone was right there on the counter beside her laptop. Yes, I know it was wrong. But she doesn't have a passcode on it and that photo I took of her has been on my mind. I got one glance at it as it was taken and that was it. Ok, I did get to taste the real thing, but I wanted that image of her to keep for myself.

She was never going to give in and let me have it, I'm surprised she hadn't deleted it. I'm sure she thinks I just want bragging rights. Something to show the boys. But that just proves she doesn't know me. Like I'd want anyone seeing her like that. Fuck no! Why would I do that? That was all for me and that is how that moment will always stay.

I was sure she would come back any second so I moved really fast. Straight in to her pictures, scrolled a few, amazingly, found it and hurriedly selected to send it via text. Typing my number into recipient bar, I hit send and then had an agonising wait watching the progress line grow across the screen. Finally when it was sent, I deleted the conversation.

I heard her voice coming back towards the kitchen and just had enough time to set the phone back where she left it and dash back to the door. Going out and casually walking straight back in. Smooth as always, she had no clue.

It's been killing me all day in my back pocket, but I made myself wait until I got home.

So now, not only do I have this picture that under no circumstances should I have, I've uploaded it so I can see it larger on my computer. That's right, I'm an arsehole. But, fuck me, is it worth being an arsehole!

She's just…Damn.

Every detail of the picture is perfect. I can't stop staring at it. So, obviously now I'm thinking about what happened after that. I knew I had her the moment I licked her wrist. But I never imagined this piece of perfection would be the product of what was to follow.

I've had a lot of sex in my life. I've had mediocre sex with someone I loved. I've had some pretty spectacular sex with people I didn't even know. I like to try new things, I like to push limits and I love to see a woman come undone. But in all my days, I have never had an experience that was so visually perfect.

She is just absolute perfection.

That day she was perfection all wrapped up in a ball of

anger, with a hard edge and smears of chocolate. I mean, does it get any better than that?

And now I have a serious tent in my shorts.

I could have so much fun with her. But it's getting risky. I mean, look at me, staring at her on my screen. She's not mine and that's how it should be. 'Mine' is not a concept I deal with very well. I refuse to even try. Yet here I am, thinking about her when she's not here and not thinking about anyone that could distract me.

But it's the wanting to see her that disturbs me the most. Take today, for example, I saw her for five minutes. That sucked. Will is over there probably diving in to Mags' bed right now, and I hate to admit it, but, I wish I were over there too.

Yesterday was just as bad. She woke up here, That's fine. I might not be one for relationships anymore, but I'm ok with waking up to a warm luscious body in my bed. It was after that that was the problem. That was pretty much it for the rest of the day. I sent her a few messages. She responded, but that was all. I should not care that we fucked all night and then she just got on with her life. That's what I usually WANT them to do.

It's not good. She's getting inside my head. I need to put a stop to it.

Spencer

WEDNESDAY 22ND JULY

SPENCER @TheSpencerRyan
I'm bored. Entertain me.

    I tap my foot restlessly on the floor. It's Wednesday, I've seen her for all of five minutes this week, she's only fifty feet away and still she is on my mind. I can't remember being this restless in a long time, so I've decided to try and occupy my thoughts. I'm sure the girls that follow me will be creative in their ways to entertain me, they usually are. Will it piss her off? Maybe.
    Maybe that's the point.
    The responses only take a minute to start rolling in. Some of them just take my request as an invitation to start a conversation. Some think that it's secret code for, 'I want an inbox full of boobs and pussy, STAT!'
    I start to reply to them all, I'm charming and funny as always, making sure to make it perfectly obvious that I'm getting some nice visuals in my inbox, but the thrill has gone out of it. I used to love it. I'd tweet 'entertain me' and they would, for as long as I wanted. Then I'd tell them I had work to do and leave them waiting for me to grace them with my

presence once more. But now, it's just as boring as the boredom I was already suffering.

And not a word from Shoegirl.

I guess I was hoping she might see my tweet and join in. But she doesn't even look. And it burns me up that I give a shit. She probably isn't even on. Typing in her name, I berate myself for checking. I'm starting to resemble a puppy that sits by the window all day waiting for its owner to return.

But then when her page opens up, everything changes. She has tweeted. Not to me, just to whomever is watching. I sit up a bit straighter, this needs my full attention.

JAZZ @OMGJazzyP
Attention whore!

Sent one minute after I asked for entertainment. Oh, so you don't like me getting attention, Princess? Well, since it's pretty obvious I have yours, despite the fact that you are avoiding me, maybe two can play at your air tweet game.

SPENCER @TheSpencerRyan
Stalker.

JAZZ @OMGJazzyP
Sorry did my tweet take the attention off you for a minute? Quick! Someone entertain him, or he will die of boredom.

SPENCER @TheSpencerRyan
You could always entertain me, Princess.

JAZZ @OMGJazzyP
I'm sure I couldn't do half as good a job as some of your 'Friends'.

SPENCER @TheSpencerRyan
I don't know about that. I'm sure you could come up with something.

JAZZ @OMGJazzyP
Yeah maybe, but not right now, I'm hungry.

SPENCER @TheSpencerRyan
I've got something for you.

JAZZ @OMGJazzyP
It's ok, thanks, I'm good.

I hear her laughter and turn to see her walk out onto the terrace and take a seat. Eating my orange.
Fucking bitch!

SPENCER @TheSpencerRyan
You ate my sex orange

Her wicked laugh carries across the site to me, and I feel myself getting hard immediately. Damn her.

SPENCER @TheSpencerRyan
You deserve a spanking for that.

JAZZ @OMGJazzyP
You'd have to catch me first.

Jazz

THURSDAY 23RD JULY

"You and citrus fruits! You have a weird fetish." I groan, as he strolls across the driveway, holding yet another orange. I just had to pop out to the garages, where I'm storing some of my ingredients in the cool, to check what I needed to order for the weekend.

He closes in on me fast as I find myself stepping backwards, back into the garage. Coming at me with that look in his eyes, he sets me on edge. I don't know why I've been keeping him at arm's length this week, but it has just felt like what I should do. I don't want to find myself wanting him all the time. I'm fine with just occasional hot sex. Really.

"What are you doing, Spencer? I'm busy." Ok, perhaps that was a little curt.

"Humph, fine. What are you doing anyway?"

"I'm doing an order for the market on Sunday."

"Oh, you're doing that again?"

"Yeah, I got a lot of interest, I may as well."

"Yeah, and not just in your chocolates," he snarls.

I want to confront him about his caveman behaviour at the market, but I don't think I want to poke at what that was all about, so I ignore his reference to it.

"Don't you have work to do?"

"Yeah, I just thought I'd pop over and bring you this," he hands me the orange. "And say hi. Is that a problem?"

"No, it's fine. I'm just not used to you dropping in for no reason, that's all."

That lascivious look in his eyes reappears, "There's always a reason, Princess."

I roll my eyes. "Yeah, that's what I thought. But see, I'm busy…"

"Fine. Maybe some other time," he huffs, backing off. I can't help noticing the look of frustration. What is that about? I mean, what does he want? Another tea and chat session? That's not really our style, is it?

Edging around him, I walk out of the garage and start back towards the kitchen door. He's walking with me, and although it's only a few metres, the silence is awkward. I've still got my conversation with Mags on my mind and short of anything else to say, I blurt, "What's Australia like?" Random, I know, but perhaps it will open the door to a conversation about Mags and Will and maybe give me some clue how he turned into this ego on legs.

"Hot," he replies.

"Well, thank you, Alan Wicker!" I laugh. I think I could have Googled that.

"Oh, you want more detail?" he laughs. "Sorry, ok. Let me think…" He looks to the sky. "Hot, sun kissed, flat for the most part, with a couple of notable peaks and very habitable lowlands." He pauses, thinking, "And blondes mostly," he finishes.

I gasp with mock indignation and slap his arm.

"What?" he says rubbing at my hand print. "I thought you meant Australians."

"You arsehole. I don't need to know that you slept with half of Bondi beach."

"Not just Bondi, Princess, there are some other plentiful beaches on the Gold Coast," he laughs.

I put my hand over my mouth, retching, then smile sweetly and say, "Sorry, I just threw up in my mouth a little."

He smiles. "Jealous, Princess? That's very flattering, you know."

"Oh, as if!" I huff, opening the door to the kitchen and sighing on the inside when he follows me in.

"Uh huh, ok," he smirks.

Annoyed that he always does this, I really want to get rid of him now, but I don't have the heart to just kick him out. I pick up the box of truffles on the counter and try to move around him.

"Whoa, whoa, Princess. Slow down, what do we have in here?" Without waiting for an answer, he pulls the lid off and helps himself.

Exasperated, I reply, "That's bitter sweet orange," as he takes one and has it all in his mouth in a flash.

"Aww, Princess did you make this for me to make amends for eating my sex orange?"

"Sure, why not?" I shrug, shutting the box and taking it to the cooler utility room.

"So, why bittersweet?"

Seriously, I'm ready for him to go now. "It's bittersweet because that's sometimes what they call chocolate with a high cacao content. Typically 70% or more."

"What do they call it when it's under that? Just sweet?"

"No, they call it semi-sweet."

"Semi-sweet," he laughs. "It sounds like they're describing you."

I blow out a big, long breath. I don't have the patience for this. "Ok, you can go now."

"Oh, you've finished with me now, have you, Princess?"

"Well, you only seem to be here to entertain yourself and I've got stuff to do."

"I just came to bring you a gift" he says holding out the orange.

I take it to move things along. "Well, you have and I'm grateful beyond belief, honestly," I say through heavy sarcasm. "So, why are you still here?"

Moving a little closer, he takes the orange out of my hand and puts it down beside me. "I wasn't expecting you to look so…"

"So?"

"So edible," he says, leaning in, nibbling at my neck with an animal like growl. His hand is on my boob before I can stop him, and all I can think is NO! Not my top! I know for a fact he will be filthy and I'm wearing my favourite, pristine white broderie anglaise top. I ease him off me, and we both look down at my boob, obviously for different reasons.

His hand slips away and sure enough there is a big dirty handprint on the delicate, white fabric.

I sigh.

"Whoops!"

"Awesome." I brush lightly at it to see whether it's just dusty and might brush off. But no, it's really on there. "I love this top."

"I like it too."

"Well, it's ruined now."

"You can hardly blame me for that, walking around in a top that shows all these tiny little glimpses of what's underneath. If I stand back, I can see everything."

"I'm hardly walking around taunting you, Spencer. You came to me and then followed me in here. Uninvited, I might add."

"Yeah and I got to see everything. I have no regrets."

"Not everything, I'm wearing a bra, you know."

"Yeah, I know, I can see it," he grins.

"Ok!" I say folding my arms across my chest. "I'm going to go and change."

"Spoil sport."

"Well, what would you have me do? Go about my day with your paw print on my boob?"

"Suits me fine."

"Of course it suits you." I feel the irritation building. "It's like your mark on me. A bit like when you chased off that guy at the market." Ok, now I want to poke at it. "What was that all about, huh?"

"I just don't like the guy."

"Well, I didn't exactly get the chance to decide for myself, did I?"

"There's nothing for you to decide. He's an idiot. End of. There's no way I'm having him sniffing around."

"Excuse me? 'No way you're having him sniffing around?'" Fury boils up inside me, "Now, why am I not surprised to find Spencer Ryan doesn't share his toys."

There is a flicker of something across his face. It looked like hurt. And then I realise what I've said. Of course he doesn't share his toys, he's been badly burned in the past. Only I shouldn't know that, and therefore I can't apologise. That was harsh and I feel awful about it. But before I can dwell on it further, he moves towards me, and when I can feel his breath on my lips, he whispers, "Why the hell should I?"

Then he sucks the air from my chest with a kiss that is more of a claim than any mark could ever be, leaving me breathless and with a handprint on the other boob.

Holy shit.

Letting go, he grins. "Keep the top. I like it even more now." Then he turns and leaves me leaning against the counter for support.

Just when I think the ball is in my court, he goes and steals it again.

Fucker.

Spencer
THURSDAY 23RD JULY

I think I'm going to have to invest in some new work clothes. Something with less of a vice-like grip on the crown jewels because every time I see her lately, I feel like I'm being strangled. Making another adjustment to ease the pain, I go back to what I was doing.

What was I doing?

Right now, all I can think of is what I was doing in there. Getting all possessive, that's what! Which I know full well for me is a slippery slope. See, after…the shit that happened before we went travelling…I did have a great time working my way through the beach bodies that crossed my path. It took me all of five minutes after touching down on Australian soil to decide to leave my troubles behind me and seek solace in the bevy of beauties. I'd had a full twenty four hours of Will chewing my ear off about how there are plenty more fish in the sea, in the confined space of a 747. So, just to shut him up, I decided to go for a swim.

For a few months, we barely stayed put for more than a week. But eventually, we needed money and wound up finding work as labourers on a site outside Sydney. So we did spend three months in the same place and on maybe the second or third night there, I met Cara. She was a memorable fuck and because we weren't going anywhere, she became a regular one.

The first couple of weeks, I'll admit I did get to know a few of the locals intimately, but after a succession of wild nights with Cara, I lost my taste for bed hopping. She was more than enough to satisfy me, and what's more, I enjoyed her company. She wasn't like…other girls I'd been with. This was a good thing, because my 'usual type' had proved to be able to pull the wool right over my eyes. Cara was different. She and I connected. I was in a good place, considering. I'd mended my wounds the old-fashioned way, and I was ready to give the right girl more than three nights of my time. Cara was the right girl.

Except she was just so damn hot. And I wasn't the only one who could see that. I'd sit in the bar she worked in, watching them all undress her with their eyes. As I had been made a fool of before for trusting blindly, my logic became: eyes open, high alert, don't miss a thing.

I. Got. Obsessed.

I can see now, in hindsight, that it was probably overkill. But I figured that if she never went out of my sight and no one got close, then I wouldn't have to worry. Poor girl. Yeah I can admit that now. I went too far, I became a crazy person. She stuck it out longer than was necessary, because she obviously liked me, but eventually I think I freaked her out. It finished when Will put me on a bus and dragged me a safe distance from my insanity. I beat the crap out of him, just because I was so frustrated and he was there, pissing me off. The only reason we weren't deported when the police cruised by is because he insisted some kids tried to mug him and I stopped them.

That was a low point. Things were quiet for a bit, we just put our heads down, and worked. And then slowly but surely, I found my stride again. After that fright, I decided that casual sex was far more my thing. And that's how it has been ever since.

Until Shoegirl.

Then, just then, when she said something about me not sharing my toys, I felt a little bit of that thing I felt with Cara.

Possessiveness.

And it didn't feel good.

I've avoided it since Cara by avoiding making any sort of connection with women. Other than the one obvious connection I like to make with a big part of me and a (hopefully) quite tight part of them. I keep it really simple, stay on my guard. Repeats are fine, feelings are not. I have various ways to stop myself from repeating that mistake and usually it involves fucking someone else.

I pull my phone out of my pocket and bring up Twitter. I haven't been using it like I could be lately. Fuck knows what's stopping me. I just haven't been in the mood, but it is a deep pool full of fish. Admittedly, there are some sharks and the odd killer whale, but I'm getting good at avoiding them. It's just since I started talking to Shoegirl, it's kind of lost its appeal.

I hadn't really noticed that.

This is bad.

Opening up a new tweet, I do the only thing I know how to do in situations like these.

SPENCER @TheSpencerRyan
@Bea_Have Hey angel, thanks for last night.

   I sigh.
   She comes back faster than I'm expecting her to.

BEA @Bea_Have
@TheSpencerRyan Any time handsome! It was good to have the old Spencer back ;)

   I rub my temples. Shoegirl will see that now.
   It's for the best.

When my phone beeps in my pocket a little while later, it's Shoegirl as I expected, but it's not the instant barrage I thought it would be. It's a private message.

'I keep looking at this orange. It's making me think about your cock in my mouth.'

   Holy shit. Frowning at my phone, I realise that she obviously hasn't seen my tweets or the orange would be far from her thoughts. Staring at her message, I don't know what to do. Ignore her and let her make the discovery so that she'll hate me and I can forget about her?

'You like the sound of that, don't you?'

   I stall, thinking. If I let her keep talking, it will be like I'm deliberately making a fool of her. I don't want that. But just in case it gets good, I can't make myself stop her. And what would I say anyway? 'Ummm, look at my last tweet, you're supposed to be angry with me and you're ruining it?'

'Hello?'

Shit. Ignoring her is hard.

'I know you're there. Are you hard for me?'

Taking a deep breath, I can't stop myself replying.

'Getting there.'

'Good. How do you think the orange will feel?

'Really good.'

'Why don't you come inside and see how it feels?'

I swallow. God, she really has no idea what I've done. Which makes what I'm about to do even worse. Yeah, I know, I deserve a kick in the nuts. But no sane man can turn down an offer like that. I don't wait around. If I do, I'll grow a conscience.

Opening the kitchen door, I realise straight away she's not there. I step inside with a sinking feeling, knowing she was gone before she sent that message and I walk towards the chopping board she has left out. The chopping board with the butchered remains of an orange, harpooned to the wood with a large kitchen knife. I slam my fist on the counter in frustration. Not at the aroused state she has left me in, but at what I've done.

"You idiot," Mags' voice comes from behind me.

Sighing, I just nod my head. "Is she upstairs?"

"No, she went out."

"Where?"

Mags shrugs, "No idea. She just needed to clear her head."

"Ok." Defeated, I turn to leave.

"I thought you were better than this, Spencer," she says, resigned to the reality of what I am.

I shake my head and open the door, "I knew I wasn't, Mags," I say, closing the door behind me.

Jazz

FRIDAY 24TH JULY

I'm here under duress, but that doesn't mean that I'll look beaten. Who knows if he will even turn up.

Oh, come on, this is my luck, of course he will turn up.

Just in case, I'm dressed to kill. And no, I don't mean tooled up and wearing a disposable jumpsuit. Although that's really tempting…Something about Spencer Ryan just inspires my inner serial killer. Even as I'm thinking it, my hands kind of tighten, as if somewhere in my subconsciousness I'm planning his murder.

Anyway, his possible presence in the pub tonight has, so far, ruined my night and forced me to wear a ridiculously tight skirt. There was no way I was going to be here looking sorry for myself. I want to turn a few heads, and if his head can be bothered to look in my direction, then that's fine. Let him look.

I don't remember why we're here, someone's birthday. I forget whose. I'm here for the wine.

"You alright?" Mags asks in that irritatingly sympathetic way as she watches me inhale wine number three. 'She loves me, she's worried about me, I must not bite her head off,' I repeat to myself for the hundredth time.

"Yes, I'm fine," I snap.

Her face changes. "Don't look now."

Awesome. The dickhead is in the building.

There's nothing else for it, I'm going to have to get wasted. I lean my elbows on the bar. I'm at that nice point of inebriation where I feel sexy and funny and completely invincible. But I think I'll turn up the dial on this buzz before Dickhead manages to kill it.

"Can I buy you a drink?" a voice beside me asks.

I turn to see that guy from the market, the one Spencer ran off. He's not exactly my type, but he has one quality I find absolutely irresistible: He gets right up Spencer's nose. So to hell with the high road, I smile and reply, "Why yes, that would be lovely, thank you." His face lights up.

"Evan," he holds out his hand for me to shake.

Internally, I make a face. At least, I hope it's internal. I don't like the name Evan. Which is totally not Evan's fault. It just comes off a bit drippy. Reaching out to shake his hand, I wince a little. Drippy, just like his wet, weak handshake. Oh, lord. With that, and the fact that in these heels I tower over him, it's all stacking up against poor Evan here. Not that he stands a chance anyway because I'm sworn off men forever. I'm planning to get Mags drunk later and see if she won't switch teams with me.

Then I realise I haven't said my name. "Jazz," I blurt.

"Nice to meet you, Jazz. What can I get you?"

I look at the remainder of the blush-coloured liquid in my large wine glass and reply, "I think I'm drinking the white grenache."

"That sounds nice," he says, as the barman approaches. "Two, please."

Man, oh, man. Pink wine? Way to make an impression dude. If he has been given a brief on how to be as un-Spencerlike as possible, he's nailing it! Then he starts talking….and I try, really I try, to stay tuned, but after he has asked me the cursory questions, he begins telling me about his travels. His enthusiasm is commendable, and it's not that I'm not interested, but seriously, this man must own a cardigan. Several probably. I gulp my wine and ask a pertinent question, trying to appear invested in the conversation, because it hasn't escaped my notice that a few feet behind him, Spencer has settled in my line of sight.

At first, I focus on Evan, but I can feel him watching, and eventually, I have no choice but to look over at him. He's looking directly at me, as if he has been waiting for my eyes to meet his since he arrived. I manage a look of complete indifference as my stomach churns and then turn my attention back to Evan, who is in full swing with a story about Thailand. In my peripheral vision, Spencer's beer moves slowly to his lips and then slowly back down to the bar. But his eyes never leave me.

Mags and Will turn away from the conversation they were involved in beside me, and join in. Will seems to know Evan quite well, although I can sense the arm's length he holds him at. But he takes some of the heat off me, and I quietly drink, glancing up occasionally to see if my watcher has quit.

Of course, he hasn't quit.

He never quits.

Four wines down, it isn't long before I need to pee. But of course, there is a jackass in residence right at the end of the bar, by the toilets.

I put my drink on the bar and mutter to Mags, "I'm just going to the ladies."

"You ok?" she asks, concerned

"Yeah, I'm fine, I'll be back in a sec."

Taking a deep breath, I pull myself together and try not to run, I want to strut right past him with an unaffected air. It's going well, until he reaches out and grabs my hand, pulling me so I have to take a step towards him.

"Don't do this." There is an unmistakeable plea in his voice and the sympathy that threatens inside me sparks my anger.

Yanking it away, I snap, "Do what, Spencer?"

He sighs. "Just don't—"

I cut him off. "Don't what? Enjoy myself? Because last time I checked you enjoy yourself whenever and with whomever you please. So, I think I'll do the same."

He picks up my hand again, holding it tight. "But not with him." He runs his thumb over my knuckles and I ignore the shiver that breaks out.

"What difference does it make to you who it's with?"

He opens his mouth to try and justify himself, but stops. He looks sad. I didn't notice that when I first looked over this way, but he does. His shoulders are slumped and there's an air of defeat about him. My hand slips out of his as he gives in. Unable to leave it there, even though it feels like I won that round and my conscience is telling me to drop it, I have the last word. "You're such a hypocrite. I'm not even allowed to talk to Evan, but it's fine for you to publicly thank one of your sluts for services rendered? You pathetic coward. If you're done with me, Spencer, man up and say so. I'm quite certain

I'll live."

I can't stand here and look at his sullen face a second more; he makes me sick. Barging past him, I head for the ladies.

A few moments later, I hear the door bang open, and then the lady in the stall beside me opens her door and lets out a little surprised sound.

I knew it.

Pulling my skirt back into place. I pause at the cubicle door, waiting for the lady to finish using the hand dryer and leave. When I hear the door squeak open, then closed, I reluctantly slide the bolt across and open the door.

"What do you want, Spencer?" I sigh.

He's leaning against the sinks, watching me. He mumbles something I can barely hear.

"What?" I snap.

"I said," he pushes off the sinks and stalks towards me, "I'm. Not. Done. With. You." As he finishes, he reaches the threshold of the cubicle and grabbing my face in his hands, steals a searing kiss before I can fight. As his bulk pushes me back into the stall and his foot kicks the door shut behind us, I suddenly feel claustrophobic. I need to get out. He's a piece of shit, but his tongue stroking mine is enough to make me weak at the knees. I need to get away from him. He's no good for me.

Pushing him off and gasping for air, I manage to pull his hands from my face and shove him away. "Get off me!"

"Are you going to play games again? I want you, Jazz, how's that? Maybe I was a coward, but I'll admit it. I want you."

Holy shit, he just called me Jazz.

"And look at you," he continues. "You want me too, your body is begging for it." He reaches a hand out to pull me in.

Aware that my chest is rapidly rising and falling and I have desire written all over me, I ignore him and smack it away. "This isn't a game anymore. I don't need this shit. You and your 'angel' can have each other, I'm not going to stand in your way. I hope she's worth it."

He looks at his feet, all shifty. "Nothing happened."

I scoff, "Oh, please, whatever, Spencer. You forget, I've been there, in your private VIP area. I've seen you in action. 'Nobody here but you and me, Princess,' remember? But I bet there are ten other conversations open just like it at any given time. You're cheap and I'm done." I try to push past him but he stops me.

"There was no one else. Not since I started talking to you."

"Bull. Shit."

"No lies, Princess. No one. I don't know what the deal is with that, but it's the truth."

"You'll excuse me if I don't believe a word you say."

"Your loss," he snarls, suddenly changing tacts.

"Really, because from where I'm standing, I'm the one happy to walk away, you're the one stopping me."

Without looking at me, he steps aside.

I move to the door and stop, turning to look at him. He looks up at me and sighs.

"Nothing happened with Bea. Nothing happened with anyone."

"Sure."

"She's just a friend."

"Save it. I saw you on Twitter, not two minutes after you

were standing in front of me. 'Thanks for last night, angel.' You make me sick."

"She's my parachute," he murmurs.

"Your what?"

"MY PARACHUTE!" he shouts.

"What the fuck does that mean?"

"It means that she's an old friend from home and when things get…" he gulps. "When things get too intense, I pull the cord and she helps me out."

"Huh?" I seriously have no idea what he is talking about.

"All I have to do is tweet her 'thanks for last night' and she responds with something suitable that'll make waves. It helps me put an end to things quickly when they get too much."

"Things?"

"Women. Ok? When things get too intense with a woman, she helps me get rid of them."

I can tell he's not proud right now, but I don't care. I can't believe what I'm hearing.

"You're seriously twisted, you know that? You think that you have some divine right to do what you like just because some girl did a number on you?"

The look on his face is priceless. It's like I stuck a knife in his chest. But I'm not done. I'm barely warmed up.

"Oh, yeah, I know about that. The excuse of heartbreak you use to behave how you damn well please. You didn't get your heart broken, Spencer, you don't have a heart. You were just shocked that there's a woman alive that was able to resist you. Well, breaking news, there's more than one." Shaking my head, I storm out and return to the bar, leaving him silent.

"Let's get some tequila," I announce to no one in particular when I rejoin my group.

Mags frowns at me and I shake my head, telling her no, I don't want to discuss it and no, there's nothing to worry about. I pick up my wine and swig it while I wait for the barman. This is great, I'm literally turning to drink over him now. Awesome.

I don't actually care right now, I just want to block him out.

Down his end of the bar a big cheer goes up as Spencer and the boys knock back a shot of something or other. Spencer is laughing with his mates like none of that just happened.

Twat.

Three tequilas down, I look over and he's staring at me. It's only fleeting as he is pulled back into whatever they are laughing about over there.

"Having a good night?" asks Evan beside me.

"I've had better, to be honest, Evan." I grin. I'm quite a happy drunk. You don't usually catch me crying in the corner.

"Tell Evan your troubles," he says, laying his arm across my shoulders and tipping his weight a bit too far, having to save himself from slipping off. I think Evan is a little drunk too. "You're very beautiful," he thinks out loud, not waiting for me to share my troubles. I guess we are over that now.

"Thank you," I straighten a little. Don't want to give him the wrong impression.

The next thing I know, Spencer, significantly more lubricated than before, is beside Evan. "Hands off, mate," he says in a surprisingly light tone.

"Excuse me?" Evan turns to confront him, slipping his arm off my shoulders. Little relieved, I've got to say, but still, where does Spencer get off?

Spencer looks away from Evan to me, like Evan is the least significant creature on the planet. "You don't have to do this," he says to me.

"I think you should leave the lady alone, don't you?" Evan steps between us, puffing up his chest.

"Shut up, Evan," he says, swiping him aside like a bug. He keeps his eyes and his focus on me. "Don't lower yourself to this loser," he implores.

Evan stumbles and amazingly comes back for more. "Now, look here…"

"SHUT UP, EVAN!" Spencer and I both yell in unison, not taking our eyes off each other.

Evan makes a disgruntled noise and retreats to a safe distance.

Spencer looks victorious. After all, he has seen off the competition. Again.

I stare at him. This has all been such a huge mistake.

"I wish I could delete you," I tell him quietly, my voice full of regret.

"Whatever, Princess," he says, holding up his hands in defeat. Without another word, he walks away.

I turn back to my drink and sigh. Evan has scarpered, Mags is playing pool with Will and I barely know anyone else. I chance a glance to Spencer's end of the bar and see he has joined the lads, chatting up a group of girls.

Predictably, he starts to flirt and I can't help but watch. They're nasty looking girls, probably just his type. And when he sees I'm watching he gets all touchy feely with them.

What am I doing? I need to get out of here.

While Mags is playing pool, I'm just going to slip out. I'll text her so she doesn't worry, but I can't stay and watch him maul those girls after everything that's happened. Rifling through Mags' bag for her keys, I spot another set. Will has put his keys in her bag for safe keeping. High pitched laughter carries through the bar, and I look up as Spencer pulls the girl against him and takes her mouth in a gross kiss, totally inappropriate as a PDA. More like a public embarrassment. Fucking wanker.

As he deepens his kiss, he tilts his head and opens his eyes, purposely meeting my eye. My hands tighten around the keys in my hand and my plans change. Dropping the keys into my bag, I glance around. No one is looking, so I slip out the door.

Breathing in fresh air, I can feel the effects of the tequila all the more. Why the hell did I ever have to get mixed up with a scumbag like Spencer Ryan? He's a fucking idiot, I mumble to myself, as I stomp across the road.

My foot wobbles in the gutter and I look down at my shoes. His favourites.

There was a time when they were my favourites, but they are tainted now with him.

Lucky for me, they live in a little road opposite the pub, and I'm at his door before I find something to fall over. My footsteps are unsteady in these shoes, maybe I shouldn't have had so much to drink.

Fumbling in my bag, I pull out the keys. I drop them as I try to fit a key in the lock and it's a long way down when I bend to pick them up.

With all the focus I can muster, I finally succeed in sliding a key in the front door and tiptoe in. Closing the door quietly, I bump into the hall table in the dark and shush myself. I'd make the worst cat burglar in the world. My shoes make an earth shattering sound on the hallway floor as I feel my way to the kitchen. Once there, I am on a mission. Opening cupboards, left and right using the light of my phone. I know what I'm looking for.

Tuna.

Or something equally smelly. It's an old trick I learned from an evil friend who shared a house with Mags and I at uni. Excellent for getting back at your ex when they piss you off. Tip a can of tuna somewhere it won't be immediately discovered, then let it rot. Their car, if it's their pride and joy. Their room, the bottom of the wardrobe, is my recommendation. We fed it into the hem of some curtains once. That took a while to be discovered. Basically wherever it can fester and stink.

Time for Spencer to get some of the tuna treatment, I giggle to myself. I'm getting nowhere fast and I need to hurry, so I put the light on and quickly find the cupboard with the cans in it. Bingo! Tuna. Pulling the ring pull top, I head for the stairs when my phone beeps.

I freeze.

Shit.

Looking at the screen, I sigh with relief, it's only a tweet, not Mags looking for me.

But it is a tweet from Spencer.

SPENCER @TheSpencerRyan
Out with the old, in with the new. Wonder if she plays pool?

Son of a bitch.

Spencer

That is it. Never mind his wardrobe. His precious pool table is gonna get it!

Teetering back to the kitchen, alcohol coursing through my veins, trying not to spill any tuna juice.

Tuna juice?

Do tunas have juice?

I'm so drunk.

I pull the keys off the hook by the back door, setting my stinky cargo down so I can unlock it. Half way down the garden, I have to stop and take my shoes of before I break my neck and when I reach the garage, I curse him for being so paranoid that he needs three locks. Who has three locks?

Spencer Fucking Ryan does.

Probably to stop this exact thing from happening! Well, that's what happens when you piss girls off. We find a way to fuck with you.

I hit the lights and wait a second for the fluorescent strips to flicker on. Plonking my shoes and phone down on the pool table, I take my little can of mayhem and start circling the table, merrily tipping some down each hole. My phone beeps again, interrupting me as I feel around in the slot underneath the table for the cue ball. Setting my now mostly empty can in the D and nestling the cue ball in the can on a tuna cushion. A lovely ring of 'tuna juice' forms on the pristine cloth around the bottom of the can.

I smile.

Oh, my phone. Shit. Maybe it's Mags looking for me. I don't know how long I've been.

I pick it up, but it's just him again, tweeting to whoever will listen.

SPENCER @TheSpencerRyan
http://dangerousmind.net/comments/auntie_angel I give you the grapefruit blowjob ladies! Please form an orderly line.

I don't know what I hope to achieve, I've said all I need to say to him, but he just gets to me. I open our DM conversation and send him one word that says it all.

'Classy.'

'Is that so? Maybe the world would like to see how classy you are...'

I frown at my phone. What is he going on about? Then a picture comes through.
HOLY SHIT!! How did he get that? It's the picture he took on MY phone of me standing naked in front of the mirror. He wouldn't seriously tweet that?
Would he?
Shit. I think he would.
That's it. Fuck him. Rage consumes me, and I grab a shoe from the pool table, stabbing the heel into the centre of the cloth and pulling. The world's most satisfying ripping sound occurs as I pull it all the way down to the cushion. A rush of delight and triumph fills me, and I let go of the shoe, leaving it sticking out of the cloth. I think I'll leave that as a little souvenir for him. Grabbing the little cube of chalk, I write FUCK YOU on either side of the giant rip.
I rummage in my bag for the little pair of ballet flats I keep in there for nights out like this. Pah! There are no other nights

Spencer

like this. This one will go down in history. Dropping the little slip-ons on the floor and stepping into them, I grab the other heel from the pool table and stuff it in my bag, grabbing my phone. I have to get back before they realise I'm not there. Doing it all in reverse without the heels is much easier, I have to admit. And when I slip back into the pub, I make sure to circle around and look like I'm coming back from the loos.

"I'm tired," I tell Mags as soon as I reach her. "I think I'm going to head back."

"Actually, this lot are getting really drunk, I think I'll come with you. I just need to give Will his keys."

"I'll get your bag for you." I panic.

She smiles, and when she turns to tell Will we are leaving, I slip the keys back in her bag. Phew!

Snuggling down in bed a few moments after we get home, I'm overwhelmingly tired and despite a tiny bit of room spin, I fall quickly into a deep sleep.

Spencer

FRIDAY 24TH JULY

"Dude, what are you doing?"

"I'm not doing anything, mate," I reply in as nonchalant a manner as I can, tightening my arms around the waist of this girl who is doing a great job grinding herself against me while she talks to her friend. Pity it's having no effect.

"She's gone."

I sigh with relief and let the girl go. She comes right back, but I shake my head and gently push her aside.

"Why do you do this?"

"Do what?"

He gives me that, 'don't play innocent with me' look. "You know what."

"Because I'm Spencer."

Will laughs. "You sure are."

"I'm getting out of here." I didn't want to be here in the first place, but I couldn't pass up the chance to see her. Look how that turned out.

"Yeah ok, come on."

As we walk in silence across the road, I'm replaying the whole disastrous evening. I know I fucked up. In so many ways.

"You really like her, don't you?"

I don't reply.

"That's ok, I think she really likes you, too."

"Not anymore she doesn't, trust me."

"I'm sure you can get it back. You're Spencer, remember?"

I look at him, all eager, and roll my eyes. "Your optimism is very annoying, just so you know."

He grins.

"I'm going to bed," I tell him, as I kick off my shoes. I'm so tired. The whole night has been mentally exhausting, I'm going to fall into bed and sleep all day tomorrow. Nothing to get up for.

Spencer
SATURDAY 25TH JULY

I pull the covers up and groan "fuck off" when a text comes through to my phone. I forgot to turn the sound off so I could sleep undisturbed. I close my eyes tighter and ignore it. I can get back to sleep; all is not lost. Then it goes off again. I throw off the covers and stare at the ceiling in frustration. Why? Whhhhhyyyyy? When it beeps for the third time, I growl in frustration. Grabbing it off my bedside table I take a look at what the hell is so urgent.

It's Will.

'Dude, wake up.'

'Spencer!'

'GET UP and get down here!!'

Grumbling, I type out a reply.

'Fuck off, come up here if you need me.'

'I'm out in the garage.'

'So?'

'Spencer, you need to get down here.'

I'm just about to ask why when a picture comes through. FUCK!

A few seconds later, I'm standing barefoot in my underwear beside Will, staring at the scene.

"What's that smell?"

"Tuna."

"What the actual fuck?" The stunned silence is quickly being replaced by anger.

"It's trashed mate. There's tuna down the pockets. That smell is never going away."

"She's fucking crazy."

Will stifles a laugh. "She's perfect for you."

I glare at him. "She is going to pay for this." And he and I both know I don't mean financially. My phone is still in my hand, so I take a picture. Opening Twitter.

SPENCER @TheSpencerRyan
Looking for the owner of this shoe because she's gonna fucking PAY! @OMGJazzyP we need to talk! #PsychoCinderella pic.twitter.com/gJ961tVB3x

Turning to leave, Will stops me.

"What are you going to do?"

"I'm going to find her."

"And then what?"

I look at him, indignant. The truth is, I don't know. But I'm furious and I need to have it out with her.

"Yeah, I thought so. Just stop, Spencer. Look at what's happened because you don't know where to stop. Don't you think this has gone far enough?"

"She took it too far, not me." I try to push past him and he stands firm.

"You wouldn't say she was pushed?"

"To this?" I throw my hand at the carnage she left.

"I agree, it was wrong. But if you don't stop it right here, where will it lead?" He puts his hand on my shoulder and tries to get me to look in his eyes. I'm really not in the mood for this, I just want to break something, and if he doesn't get out of my way soon, it's going to have to be his face. "Look, I know you're worried she'll turn out to be like Lucy, but—"

"She's nothing like Lucy," I roar, cutting him off.

"That's what I'm saying! Jesus, calm down."

"Just stop bringing her into this, she's in the past. Gone."

Will smiles. "I'm pleased to hear it. You've been carrying that around for too long."

"Yeah, well, Lucy isn't the problem. The problem is me."

"I could have told you this years ago," he laughs, cutting through my tension.

Sagging as I let go of the rage I'm holding, I turn and plonk myself down on the sofa. When did I become such a mess?

"You've got to sort yourself out, Spencer. You know Jazz wants Mum's shop and she won't take it because of you?" My eyes snap up to meet his. "You're screwing with her future, mate."

"Oh, please, her future will be fine, she's a spoiled little rich girl, she can probably buy a dozen shops, I'm not standing in her way."

"She's not a spoiled little rich girl."

"Sure she's not."

"No, dumbarse, I mean she's not a rich girl. Spoiled or otherwise. Mags' family has the money. Jazz is just... 'normal,' like us."

I look up at him, he is standing over me with his arms crossed.

"But she doesn't work."

"No, because she lost her job, genius. So she's thinking about a career change."

"How did I not know this?"

"Because you go around with your head up your arse. Do you even know why she came here?"

I shake my head.

"Her boss was the over familiar type, took it too far."

"What?" The rage comes flying back.

"Chill out mate, she dealt with it," he laughs. "Boy, did she deal with it. But my point is, she came here to get away from all that and decide what she wants to do. Mags has been trying to get her to see her potential. She has a passion and has dreamed of doing this for such a long time, but now she has the perfect opportunity and guess who is stopping her."

"I didn't know."

"No, well you've both been too busy playing your games. But it needs to end here. Sooner or later, you've got to trust someone enough to let them in. You can't hide from it forever. But if it's not her, then let her go so she can get on with her life."

I drop my head back on the sofa and stare at the ceiling.

"Do the right thing, Spencer," he says and then he leaves me.

So, she had a shitty time and came here to forget about it and move on. Then I came along and fucked it all up.

But she played me. Lied to me. Let me think I was dealing with two separate people. It's her that set the tone for this whole thing, not me. I just played back. But neither of us know when to stop.

It's all such a mess.

I'm basically fucking up her life, is what he's saying.

So, now I need to do the right thing.

With a resigned sigh, I drag myself up. I need to get organised.

Jazz

SATURDAY 25TH JULY

It's really light when I open my eyes, I guess it must be late. My head hurts. I had a lot to drink last night and the memories of it start to come back. Yeah I drank a lot. Ugh, maybe I'll sleep a bit longer. Closing my eyes again I try to settle back to sleep.

Wait, did I have a fight with Spencer?

I have a slight feeling something really bad happened. Shit, I shouldn't drink tequila; I can't remember exactly what happened. I know he followed me into the ladies and I yelled at him. I remember Evan and Spencer and some shoving. After that it's foggy. I was in Spencer's kitchen at one point looking for…oh, shit! Tuna! I cover my eyes. Did I break into his house and put tuna in his wardrobe? Crap.

I take a look at my phone to see what the time is. Shit. One pm.

There is a tweet notification from Spencer a few hours ago. Maybe he's discovered the smell.

SPENCER @TheSpencerRyan
Looking for the owner of this shoe because she's gonna fucking PAY! @OMGJazzyP we need to

talk!#PsychoCinderella pic.twitter.com/gJ961tVB3x

Oh.

Shit.

It all rushes back as I lay eyes on what I've done. I put my hand over my mouth. What was I thinking? Oh my God, this is so bad. Jumping out of bed, trying to ignore the searing pain behind my eyes, I run down the stairs and skid to a stop in the kitchen doorway. Mags is sitting on one of the stools at the breakfast bar and looks up from her laptop.

"Morning," she says, leaving it hanging there with no indication of her mood.

"Morning," I reply cautiously.

"How are you feeling?"

"Not good." My head is pounding, I feel awful, but that is nothing compared to how stupid I feel. I wait for her to say something and she just looks at me. I need water, so I break our stare to go and get a glass, and Mags goes back to work for a moment. After I've downed a whole glass and refilled it, I turn back to face her. She clicks a couple of things on her screen and types something.

"Oh," she says casually without looking up. "Will says he's found your shoe, just in case you were worried." With that, she turns her laptop to face me and shows me the carnage I left behind, on her full screen.

I cover my face with my hand.

"You realise you look like a mad woman, right?" she asks, but I can hear the stifled laughter in her voice.

Looking at her, I try to bring the beginnings of my own smile under control, even while the tears start to fall. "It isn't funny, Mags," I choke, caught in that very confusing place between tears and laughter.

"No, you're right it's not," she says, trying to keep her face straight. "What were you thinking?"

I shake my head, wiping my eyes and trying to get control of my emotions. Waving towards the screen, I squeak, "Clearly I wasn't thinking."

Laughter bubbles up and tears run down my face. Mags loses it. Holding her sides, she laughs until she too is crying.

"Psycho Cinderella," she manages to squeeze out between the giggles.

"Don't Mags," I half sob. "It's not funny. That's criminal damage!"

Mags pulls herself together a little. "Come here," she says, still giggling a little, but really trying to be serious, she holds out her arms. I go over to her and allow her to wrap her arms around me so I can cry on her shoulder.

With my face buried in her top, I start to think beyond the initial shock. How must he have reacted? I bet he's furious. I sigh. I'm going to have to face him now.

"How mad is he?" I ask, muffled by Mags' bear hug.

"Pretty mad," she replies, soothing me with gentle strokes of my back and hair.

I lift my head up and look at her. "What's he going to do?" Mags shrugs. "What can he do?"

I pull away and sit on the stool beside her. "Press charges?"

"Yeah, I somehow don't think he will."

"Was Will angry?"

"Shocked more than anything, I think. He didn't know you had it in you."

I drop my face into my hands. "I'm so embarrassed."

Mags rubs my shoulders in sympathy, but whispers, "Yeah, you should be." Then she laughs again.

I need to do something to fix it. Looking up suddenly, I reach for Mags' laptop. "I need to see about replacing the pool table. I can't see him until I can at least say I've got it all handled."

Typing 'pool table' into the search engine, it quickly becomes apparent that I can't just pick one. I need to find out what he had and replace that exact one.

"Look, let's go and get something to eat. You look like you could do with a proper fry up. Then we can sit and go through this."

"No, Mags, I need to apologise," I sigh. "God, this is awful, I'm never drinking again."

"You two have been pushing each other for a while. It was always going to end in tears."

"But THIS? I poured tuna juice down the holes," I cringe.

Mags bursts out laughing. "I heard!"

I let my elbows slide out from under me and bang my forehead on the cool marble. The bump rattles my sore head and then the cool soothes it.

"Why don't you call him?"

"I don't have his number."

"Are you kidding me? You've been fucking him for what? A month? And you don't have his number?"

"What would I need his number for? We aren't exactly friends."

"Jesus, Jazz," she shakes her head.

"Oh, sure, THIS you think is appalling. That I could have

sex with a guy for a month and not know how to contact him off social media. But vandalise his personal property, and you're in hysterics. Priorities, Mags."

"Right, here's what we're going to do. Go and shower and get dressed. We will go and have lunch in the village, and then we can go and see the boys. You can beg for forgiveness and I can watch." She grins.

"You're evil."

"Yes and hungry, so hurry up!"

"Text Will and let him know we're coming, ok?"

She smiles fondly. "It will be ok, don't worry."

"Hello, my dears," Will's mum greets us fondly.

As she speaks, it just hits me that given the size of the village, everyone could well know what I did by now, but if she does, she doesn't show it. I'll just have to hope that Spencer's pride makes him keep a lid on it.

"What can I get you ladies?"

"I think we both need a full English, please, Mary."

"Certainly. You go and sit down, I'll bring it over."

We find a table and Mary comes over with a big pot of tea. "I'm glad you popped in actually. I wanted to let you know that my agent has had an offer on this place."

My stomach turns over and I look around. It's like the perfect place. I could do everything I wanted to here and more probably. But there's just no way. I can't do it.

"I just wanted to run it past you girls. I know it's something you were considering, but this is a cash buyer, offering the full asking price. And to be perfectly honest with you, the new house will be ready next week, I could do with getting down there." She looks around and lowers her voice. "If I take this, we could be gone in a week. The cottage is on the market, I'm not in such a hurry to sell that, we could always rent it out for a while. I'd just like to get down and be closer to Mum as soon as possible; and if the deal is done, I can close up. There's nothing keeping us here."

Mags looks at me.

"You should take it, Mary," I tell her. "I'm not sticking around for much longer. It was a nice idea, but I'm not ready to make a go of it yet. The right place will come up."

Mags looks sad. But manages to sound optimistic when she asks Mary about the buyer.

"Oh, it's an investor apparently. They have a tenant already lined up, but they are going to renovate it first. Do all the things the old place needs."

"What's it going to be?" I dare to ask.

"Similar to what it is now, but I'm sure a bit more upmarket," she giggles. "'Artisan' was the word they used."

"Oooh! La-di-dah," I laugh.

"And they've offered to keep all the staff on, paid in full during the refurbishment, too."

"It sounds perfect." It's meant to be. She's happy, but I can stop thinking 'what if?'

Mary leaves to get our food. "Are you sure?" asks Mags.

"I'm sure," I tell her firmly.

"Ok," she says, seeming to know when to quit.

As our food is set down on the table, Will strolls in.

"Mmmmm, that looks good, Mum. Can you do one for me?"

She grins, "Of course. Anything for my baby boy," she

replies, squishing his cheeks.

"Mum!"

"Oh, hush," she says, heading back to the kitchen.

"Why is she in such a good mood?" he asks, sitting down with us.

"She found a buyer," Mags explains.

"Oh. Not…" he glances between us.

"No." Mags tells him firmly.

"Ok," he says, knowing not to ask any more questions.

There is a moment's pause in the conversation and my mortification builds.

"Will," I say with a croak. Clearing my throat, I try and lift my head and look him in the eye. "Can I just tell you how sorry I am. I'm not proud of what I did, and I will replace the pool table straight away."

Will smiles softly. "Jazz, honestly don't stress yourself out about it. The way he behaves sometimes, I'm surprised this is the first time it's happened."

"There's no excuse. I'm so embarrassed."

"Please, don't worry. Perhaps it was the wakeup call he needed."

"I'm going to go and see him after this. I know he won't want to see me, but I just need to apologise personally."

He looks uneasy as he opens his mouth to speak. "He's gone."

"Gone?" I frown.

"Yeah. I um…we had a talk. I told him to pull himself together and put a stop to all the button pushing. He's been in this place before and it only gets worse." He looks apologetic. "So he left."

"What do you mean he left?" I feel the panic rising.

"Where has he gone?"

"I don't know."

"Well, when will he be back?"

"I'm sorry, I don't know. He will be in touch eventually. He needs to sort his head out."

"Eventually?" My voice threatens to crack. "But..." I don't even know how to respond to that.

Will leans across and covers my hand with his. "Jazz, it's for the best. I've seen the person he becomes when things don't work out. Last night was just the beginning."

I look down at my plate. I can forget eating that. I need to get out of here. Pushing back from the table, I stand. "I need some fresh air...I'll meet you at home."

I know they are both watching me as I walk through the door, so I try to keep a sedate pace, but as soon as I'm out of sight I break into a run. Turning the corner into their road, my dehydrated body screaming at me to slow down, I run as fast as I can to their door. Pounding on it with my fist. Maybe this is just a ploy to make me feel terrible. It's fucking working.

"Spencer!" I yell. Banging on the door again. The house is silent. Turning round, I realise his car is gone and that's when it hits me.

He really has gone.

I sink down to sit on his door step and the tears start to fall.

Jazz

TUESDAY 4TH AUGUST

A sign went up in the patisserie window and a week later, Mary had her last day. It was a very quiet week. I spoke when spoken to but otherwise had nothing much to say. We did the market, I was there in body, but not in spirit. I kept expecting to see him walking through, all cocky and annoying. But he really has gone.

Will doesn't seem worried. But what if it's for good?

I feel just terrible, despite everything. This is his home and I have forced him out of it. I'm not even planning on sticking around. If anyone should have gone to put an end to the whole thing, it should have been me.

Since the steels went up at the house, things have been progressing quickly and every time I see Will at work, I feel awful because Spencer also ran out on him. This was their first big job and he just left. I go from upset with myself to furious with him for just leaving Will in the lurch like that.

I've tried saying to Will that it's terrible how Spencer was so inconsiderate, leaving him with half a job done, always hoping he'll agree and try calling him. But he just waves me off and says he is coping fine and that Spencer has to do this. I've asked for his number, but he won't give it up. Mags won't steal it from his phone either. She agrees with Will apparently that Spencer needs some space. Spencer hasn't even tweeted. It's hopeless. Without Will's help I have no hope of finding him. Maybe he went to the parents, I don't know. Maybe he went travelling again. Oh God I hope not.

But the fact is, he has gone. I need to accept that. He is probably waiting for Will to tell him the job is done and we've gone home. It's safe to come back.

Yesterday, I was in the village and I noticed the windows on the patisserie had been misted up and work had begun. I'm gutted. The reality that I missed out on the perfect opportunity is upsetting, but it has made me realise it is what I want. Which is why I'm sitting here looking at commercial properties.

The problem is, because I don't even know where I want to be anymore, it makes searching very difficult.

I started by searching at home, but, aside from the fact that rent is extortionate that close to the capital, the thought of going back there doesn't excite me. I thought this whole time that it was what I was waiting for, but now every time I think about it there's nothing making me want to go. I haven't talked to Mags about it yet, but I have started looking at other places like this. I can't have that shop in the village, but there are villages like this spread out for miles. Maybe we could move out here? Or nearby at least.

She's been seeing even more of Will, if that is possible. Some nights after work, he goes home to shower and then comes back and eats with us. He hasn't stayed though. I don't know what's stopping them. I need to make some head space for Mags so I can sit down with her and hash out why they aren't starting something. It's just silly that they can't take that step when they seem so right for each other. I know I've been wrapped up in my own problems too long; Mags needs her friend back.

I pick up my laptop and carry it into the living room where Mags is working. Sitting at the other end of the sofa I try to figure out how to begin. Taking a deep breath, I just go for it. "I've started looking at shops."

She looks up, "Oh?"

"Yeah, you're right, it's what I need to do and I have to start somewhere."

"Why now?" I can sense her disappointment.

"Look, I know I could have taken the shop here, but I wasn't in the right place. He may never come back now, and I might have missed out on an incredible opportunity, but at the time I didn't know that and I couldn't commit to being around him. What it has made me see is that I want this."

She smiles. "That's awesome. So, when we're done here, we can start looking around."

"No, that's the thing. I've been looking around, and rent where we live is exorbitant. Not to mention the rest of it, like wages and business rates. I really think I should look out here."

"And move here?"

"Yeah, I guess. Are you up for that?"

She thinks for a minute. "I think the right place will come along. You don't need to be in such tearing hurry."

Wait. What?

"But you are the one who has been chipping away at me nonstop about a shop and now you think I should wait?"

She gets up and puts her laptop on the coffee table and picks up her empty mug. "I think," she says, bending to kiss the top of my head, "that the right place will come up. Don't rush it. When it does, I'm with you."

She goes off into the kitchen and I throw myself back into the plush sofa. Grabbing a cushion and covering my face so I can silently scream out my frustration.

Jazz
SATURDAY 8TH AUGUST

My foot catches on the thick rug for the hundredth time and I trip and bang my hip on the mirrored dressing table.

Ouch!

I rub my hip, not too bothered about the pain. It's not as bad as the memory it triggers of tripping here and Spencer catching me...and all that happened after that.

I've never felt more desirable than I did that day. I sigh and finish getting dressed.

As I shut my wardrobe door, my lone Louboutin catches my eye, as it does every day. I get that same feeling of regret and embarrassment I do every time I see it. He was right, I am a psycho Cinderella! Leaving my shoe at the scene of the crime. It's a shame, they were my favourites. But even if I asked for it back, I don't think I'd ever wear them again. It would just bring back that memory of my lowest point.

Then again, if I had it, they would also be my reminder of him. Maybe I should just ask Will for it back.

Yes. I should ask Will for it back.

Grabbing my phone and headphones, I shout out to Mags that I'm going for a walk and set off for the village. This is what I need to do. Maybe it's the closure I need. And I'll never admit it to anyone, but maybe I just want to be in his space again and maybe smell his clean, fresh scent lingering on.

Yes, I miss him. I was so upset with myself for acting out, then annoyed with him for bailing, that I didn't have time to see the empty hole that he left. But I miss him. I miss his irritating ways, his cocky mouth, the pleasure and the way I felt about myself when he was delivering it. But the way I feel now that he's gone suggests that I had far deeper feelings than I realised. Because now, if I think about him too much, it's like I can't breathe.

It's such a cliché that you don't know what you've got until it's gone. But it is a painful truth.

Spencer is one of those things. I didn't let myself enjoy him. I fought it hard, telling myself that it wasn't what I wanted. I didn't appreciate it or analyse it, so now it's too late to realise that I was looking at it all from the wrong angle. I just have to live with it.

Much like this shop, I think, as I pass the old patisserie. I could have made a go of it here, but I was too closed minded to try. I was too busy being closed minded about the other thing I should have been giving a go. So I missed out. Big time.

Banging from inside the shop makes me stop and stare at the misted windows.

I sigh as banging again echoes around the empty shell that two weeks ago could have been my bright future. I wonder how it will look? It's probably a good thing someone that knows what they are doing is taking it on. I don't have a clue and wouldn't have the guts to make my first job ripping it all apart.

I think I need to get out of here before it is finished, for my own sake.

Carrying on the short walk to the end of the parade of shops, I turn onto Will's road. I take a deep breath as their house comes into view. I should have let Will know I was coming, not just turned up, but as I'm here, I'll see if he's home.

Waiting after I press the bell is excruciating. This was a bad idea. I'm halfway back down the path when the door opens.

"Jazz?"

I turn to find a puzzled looking Will.

"Hi."

"Are you ok?"

"Yeah, I'm sorry to disturb you. I was just wondering...it's a silly thing really..." I pause, embarrassed. After all the trouble I've caused, this is like putting someone's window through and then asking for your ball back. What was I thinking?

"What is it?"

I cover my face with my hands. "I'm so sorry. I was just wondering if I could have the shoe I left behind?" I can't believe these words are coming out of my mouth.

I hear Will's laughter and look up.

"I'm sorry, Jazz, I shouldn't laugh, but look at you. Come in," and he stands aside to let me past him.

"Do you fancy a cuppa? I was just thinking of making one," he offers.

"No, I mustn't keep you, I'm sorry, this was thoughtless."

"Stop it, Jazz, it's fine. Let me make you a tea, sit down," he insists.

"Thank you." I pull out a chair and set about winding my headphones up and putting them in my pocket.

"So, how have you been?" he asks, pulling two mugs from the cupboard.

"You mean apart from the embarrassment and disappointment? I'm fine, thanks," I laugh.

Will laughs with me, but I can tell he just feels sorry for me. "Disappointment?"

I nod as he comes to the table with the teas and sits with me.

"Not in yourself, I hope, because that was some first class crazy shit if you ask me. I'd be proud."

I screw up my face, but can't help the laugh. "Maybe one day I'll see it like that, but it's too soon." I take a sip of my tea. "The disappointment is in myself, but not for the first class crazy shit. It's because I've been so wrapped up in Spencer I've let a good opportunity pass me by. And…"

"And?"

I sigh. "And I think the shop wasn't the only thing I think I've missed out on."

"You miss him."

"Amazing, isn't it?"

"Not really, I think you were both more invested than you'd allow yourselves to believe."

"Maybe. I think I was. But I don't think he will look back."

"Jazz, I know you won't believe it, but Spencer really is a one-woman man. He has just spent so long avoiding it he has forgotten it's how he is built. He got hurt once." He holds his hands up. "I know what you're going to say, big deal, we all go through it. But Spencer loves hard and he took it so badly.

So he has completely avoided any real connection ever since." He sips his tea. "Except two slip ups that went massively wrong, he has managed it, too."

"What do you mean 'two slip ups?'"

"Twice that he's fallen off the love wagon. And neither were pretty."

"What happened?"

"One was in Australia. He and I went travelling for a year."

"Yes, I know," I blurt. He nods, realising Mags tells me everything.

"After a few months of travelling around, and shall we say, enjoying the best of what Australia could offer, we got jobs and stayed put for a while. It took Spencer all of five minutes to find a local welcoming committee, and there was this one girl who he really took a shine to. She was really feisty and a good laugh. They were quite well suited. He hadn't seen anyone that way since his relationship broke up and he felt ready."

He shakes his head recalling. "But he wasn't. Everything his ex had done to him had spawned this massive paranoia in him, and before he knew it, he was a monster of a possessive boyfriend. She couldn't take it and dumped him, which he was none too pleased about, and because she was so feisty, there was some nasty confrontation. I ended up stepping in and made him leave town and move on. He broke my nose. But he needed someone to put a stop to it because he was unable to."

I blow out a deep breath. Sounds bad. "And the other time?"

"Same story really, great girl, feisty, a really perfect match for him. But because of the other times, he was so determined not to let it be more than a bit of fun that he was ignoring the signs. See, he gets into these destructive patterns, plays games, flirts with other girls to make the point that he is still a free agent. Even has a friend that will put the cat among the pigeons if he feels he needs to get out of a situation."

"His 'parachute.' I heard."

"Yep, that's it. All so he doesn't risk getting in that situation again. And if it he starts feeling anything, the ugly green monster eventually rears its ugly head."

"So, what happened?"

"Well he started feeling something, obviously, I could see that. So he panicked and fucked it all up."

"And you had to drag him out of town again?"

"No, that time a crazy person attacked our pool table."

I look at him, stunned. "Oh."

"So, I told him he was making all the same mistakes as before and that he needed to put a stop to it before it got any worse. He left of his own volition. I'm sorry."

"Why are you sorry?"

"Because what I said made him leave."

"I think it was what I did that made him leave."

"No, he wanted to come after you. I stopped him. God knows where that would have led."

"I deserved it."

"But it wasn't going to end, Jazz. He doesn't know how to concede."

"So, you think he's gone for good?"

"I don't know. I hope he's using this time to think about this pattern he's in."

"Bet he's probably using this time to forget. And we both

know how he's going to do that."

There is silence for a moment as I know Will wants to reassure me that I'm wrong, but it's obvious he can't make that guarantee.

"I just need to go home and put this behind me."

He looks regretful, it's not his fault. "Just stick around with Mags for a couple of weeks until George gets back. Between you and me, I don't need her to be here, I just kinda like it. I strongly suspect this was a little matchmaking plan of George's. I mean, it's not like I'm some cowboy builder that needs watching. He knew what he was doing. He just didn't let either of us in on it."

I grin. "So you DO like Mags."

Will visibly blushes.

"Why is it so hard to admit?"

"It's not hard to admit. I like her a lot."

"Sooooo…what's the delay? You should be together."

He laughs. "It's not that simple, trust me."

"Hmmm." I can tell he isn't going to give me any more, so I leave it there. I think I've pushed my luck enough today.

"So, what about this shoe?" he says, changing the subject. "I've got to admit I haven't seen it since…" he pauses and glances up at me, "since you left it here."

I smirk. Bless him and his tact. How he is from the same gene pool as Spencer, I'll never know.

"Would it be in the garage still, where I left it?"

"I don't think it's there, I've been down there fixing the table and I haven't seen it around, but then again, I wasn't looking for it. Let's check." He gets up and heads out the back door and I tentatively follow.

Inside the garage, the pool table is still in place, but it has no top. I cringe with embarrassment. All the inner workings of the table are visible.

"Oh, Will, I'm so sorry. Is it salvageable?"

"Yeah, don't worry. The surface is getting a new cloth as we speak and once I got all the tuna out and gave it a clean, it was as good as new."

"Well, I insist on paying for the cloth."

He smiles. "If it helps you feel better, then ok."

"It will, thank you."

He begins searching around for my shoe and I help, but it isn't here.

"He probably threw it away."

"Maybe." He looks puzzled. "Maybe he put it somewhere in the house." He sets off up the garden again, thinking, and I follow. Stopping in the kitchen and looking around, he says, "Why don't you check his room and I'll carry on looking down here."

I stare at him. "Umm, ok."

Climbing the stairs cautiously, my stomach in knots, I almost tiptoe across the landing. His door is closed and I push it open slowly, not knowing what to expect.

The room is immaculate, but it is missing something. If a small part of me wondered if he was still around, avoiding me, this confirms he isn't. The room has a feeling of emptiness. I have only been here once, but it smelled of him before and there were little signs of his presence. A collection of skincare and hair products are notably absent from the dresser. His laptop is missing, the bed is pristine and the laundry bin is empty. The lingering smell of him I had secretly hoped for is not here.

I'm not going through drawers and cupboards, if the shoe was here, it would be out somewhere. Pausing at the door for a second, I sigh.

He is gone.

Will is still searching when I get back downstairs. "It's not here, Will. Don't worry about it. He obviously threw it away. Thank you for looking, though."

"Sorry, Jazz, if I find it, I'll bring it up to the house."

Back in my room, I take the shoe out of my wardrobe and run my fingers over the soft suede. Maybe I need to let it go?

Or maybe I shouldn't forget.

I place the shoe on the windowsill, where I can see it every day.

A reminder not to let opportunity pass me by.

Jazz

THURSDAY 20TH AUGUST

I feel her arms slip around me as I'm stirring ganache.

"Morning, sunshine."

"You got up early by the looks of it," she says, surveying the kitchen.

"Yeah, I couldn't sleep, so I'm trying out a couple of new things for the market."

"I'm so bloody proud of you," she says, letting me go and putting the kettle on.

"Why?" I frown.

"Because you're working hard at this and it's really paying off. You were really busy last Sunday, all those people coming back for more. I heard one grumble that he can only get his fix once a week. You must feel really good about how it's going."

"I do."

"And I'm so happy you haven't let what's been happening stop you."

I stiffen. If she only knew how much I've wanted to just run back home and go job hunting. Hell, I've even thought about asking James for my job back. But despite the fact that it has all got off to a rocky start, I do love the work and the feedback has been so encouraging. I am willing to accept that

Mags was right. This is what I'm supposed to do. "Yeah, you were right. This is what I should be doing."

"Sorry?"

"I said, you were right."

"Yeah, I heard you," she laughs. "I just wanted to hear you say it again."

"Cheeky bitch!"

"So are you going to keep doing the market? Or are we going to get you a shop?"

"Shop," I say with a grin.

"Good."

"How are you doing with making stuff for the market?"

"I'm pretty ahead. It's not like I've had anything else to do."

"Excellent. Can you finish it tomorrow so that you're free Saturday?"

I look around at what I still have to do. "Yeah, I think so, why?"

"Because I think we should have a day out."

"Ok. Where?"

"You leave that to me," she winks. "It's been ages since we had a day out."

Jazz

SATURDAY 22ND AUGUST

"Mags, what am I wearing?" I call across the landing when I hear her hairdryer turn off.

"Something pretty," she yells back.

I sigh. "That's not really a lot to go on."

"Why so many questions?" She sticks her head out of her room.

"If you could just give me a point to work to, somewhere on the scale between tea at the Ritz and a game of football, that would really help."

"Tea," she says and nods decisively, disappearing from view. "But not quite at the Ritz," she calls behind her.

Honestly, she's lucky I love her. I stand in front of my wardrobe and attempt to define pretty. Of course I could have asked her about this last night, but she was out with Will until all hours. She left me behind with her first draft on my laptop, and I was still up when she got home, engrossed. She looked knackered, but wouldn't give me any details. They must have done it by now.

It feels nice to dress up again. I haven't really gone all out since we've been here, and I miss it. So, I put some time into my hair and make up, and once I slip on my 'something pretty' and some heels, I feel great.

"Ready?" she calls out.

I roll my eyes. "Coming."

We pull in to the little carpark at the top of the village, "I just need to get some cash out," says Mags.

"Oh, yeah, me too," I agree, climbing out of the car.

As we turn out of the car park and the shops come into view, the first thing I notice are the tables and chairs outside Mary's patisserie. They are bright pink in stark contrast to the freshly painted black exterior. Shit. I love it. I knew I needed to get out of here before this happened. They turned it around fast, I didn't know it was opening this soon. I wish I had stayed in the car.

"What are you doing?" asks Mags from several feet ahead of me.

I realise I've stopped walking. "Nothing, sorry." I catch up with her, trying to decide if I should torture myself with a look through the window as we pass on our way to the cash machine. I think maybe not. But I know Mags will want to have a good look. As we approach, a guy comes out, carrying a chalk board sign, which says 'Opening Today' and has a big bunch of pink balloons tied to the top. He can't see where he is going at all and can't bat them out of his face because he's carrying the sign with both hands.

Eventually, he sets it down near the curb and swats at the balloons. Will's face appears. I'm taken aback. What is Will doing there?

"Morning!" he waves cheerfully with a big smile.

"Morning," replies Mags, as if she somehow expected to

see him and they kiss cheeks.

I stand there puzzled, trying to figure out why Will is coming out of this place with the sign, as if he owns it. Looking for the first time at the window, I'm even more confused.

The next few seconds are a blur.

The shop window that once was full of Mary's cakes, now just has a single shoe displayed in it. My shoe. And cascading out of it are chocolates. My chocolates. I look up at the sign.

Semi Sweet.

What the fuck?

Mags slips her arm through mine and gently pulls me towards the door, which is held open by Will.

The inside just blows me away.

Along the same wall where Mary had her counter full of cakes with all the coffee machines behind, it's all brand new.

The floor is black and white checkered and everywhere I look, things are black and white with pink accents. On the wall behind the counter is a huge chalk board with the shop's name and the menu.

It's beautiful.

I look at Mags, still totally confused.

She just nods to the other side of the room. There, where two or three tables used to be in a darker corner, is now a sleek counter. I walk tentatively towards it and there in more glory than I could have imagined, sit my chocolates. Behind them is an open kitchen area with a marble topped counter where chocolate can be tempered by hand. Behind that, the kitchen is well stocked with everything I would need to work there. On the wall, like on the other counter, is a chalk board filled with the menu of chocolates that we wrote for the market. This board is headed 'The Semi Sweet Chocolatier.'

"What the...?" I just don't have the words.

"You were never going to do it," she says.

"But..." I still can't form a sentence. How? Why? When? So many questions. But the biggest thing on my mind right now is that I don't know what I'm doing, I can't be trusted with all this. Two girls emerge from the main kitchen, making me jump.

Mags stops me freaking out by placing her hand in mine. "Don't panic," she says firmly.

She squeezes my hand so I look at her.

"I'm the investor. Ok. I could see it slipping away so I did something about it."

"But..." I stammer.

"Jazz, relax, let me explain. Over there, for now, it's going to run the same." She points at the patisserie counter.

"But I don't know how to do any of that!"

"Relax, this is Rosie and Megan, they work here." They both wave nervously and say hi.

"Hi," I reply just as nervously.

"They have been managing the shop together for three years. They know how it all works, how to make everything. Mary has left you with not only all the recipes, but also a good team of staff. The others will be here later for you to meet, but these two heroes have been baking and preparing all night. I've kept everyone on for now and provided you're happy, that's how it will stay. They will run that side of things and you can learn gradually. You can make whatever changes you want as you go. This is your baby, Jazz. I just thought it made sense to keep it going like it is, so you can take your time deciding how you want to run things." She turns to the chocolate side of the shop. "This is your domain. Focus on that for now and while you learn the ropes over there, teach the girls over here. I know they are very keen to learn."

"This is all unbelievable." I'm in shock. "I don't know what to say. It all looks amazing. Thank you so much." I look at Will, who I know must have worked his arse off. "Thank you both."

Will smirks. "Don't thank us," he says, nodding towards the kitchen doorway.

My breath catches when I follow his eyes.

Standing in the doorway, wearing the first look of uncertainty I think I've ever seen on his face, is Spencer.

Countless times over the past month, I've imagined what I would do if I saw him again. The things I'd say, how I'd react. But right now, as he looks up at me through his dark lashes, there is not a thought in my head as I move towards him. Just the pounding of my heart getting louder with each step. As I reach him, I don't hesitate. Taking his face in my hands, I kiss him.

The tension I feel in him as our lips meet, melts away instantly, and his arms wrap around me. Forgetting everyone else in the room, we finally give in to it.

Spencer
SATURDAY 22ND AUGUST

All this time spent wondering, worrying. It all falls away when she kisses me.

I had to go, Will was right, as usual. But going was the easy part. I could have kept going and not looked back. Coming back was the hard part. I had no idea how she would react. I pull her closer, making sure she is really in my arms and not just one of the countless dreams I've had where we see each other and she wants nothing to do with me.

If this is a dream, it's a good one.

Really good.

Jesus, Spencer, keep it under control, there are four other people in this room, you don't need to be having to style out a boner.

I breathe her in, not taking my lips from hers. I can't believe this is her reaction. I really thought I'd get a slap. I was ready for it. I've been psyching myself up, I thought I was in for a fight, but I was prepared to fight as hard as I needed. Will has tried to talk about her, but I kept cutting him off. I didn't want to know that she was done with me, and if she wasn't quite done, I didn't want to know that either.

This past month hasn't been about winning her back. It had

to be about getting myself straight. If I had known I'd get this reception, I wouldn't have worked so hard. I wanted that uncertainty so that I would pull my shit together once and for all. So my focus was on this place, quietly working alone. I didn't listen to music, I couldn't afford the distraction. It was just me and my thoughts. I've had nothing but time to think.

I went to see my parents for a few days first. Just a visit to get me away from here. From her. From the burning desire to retaliate and have the last word. After that, I had no idea what I'd do. Then I got a call from Will telling me that if I needed time to think, then he had a job for me.

As soon as he told me what the job was, I agreed. I needed to do this for her whether she would have me or not. I can be a dick sometimes, but this was important to her, and as I've come to realise, she is important to me.

"You disappeared," she whispers, slowly withdrawing.

"I had some thinking to do."

"But you came back."

I nod. "I wasn't sure how happy you'd be about that."

A slow smile spreads on her lips, "I can live with it."

"Is that so?" I grin, touching her nose with mine. Pulling back when she tries to brush my lips with hers. "Miss me, did you, Princess?"

"Don't get all big headed about it."

"I'll try," I laugh, trying to resist the obvious double entendre. "But it's hard, so hard."

She rolls her eyes and pulls away from my arms. Turning to look around, she shakes her head. "I can't believe you did all this for me."

I pull her back so that her back presses into my front and,

quietly, in her ear so no one else can hear, I say, "I did it for me. I wanted you to stay…but don't get all big headed about it."

She turns in my arms and looks at me intently. I know she has a boat load of questions, I can see it in her eyes. Why am I not surprised? "We'll talk about it later, Princess. I'm under orders not to disrupt your grand opening." I glance at Mags who is watching closely.

"Why don't you show her the kitchen," suggests Mags. I can't quite tell if she's giving us a moment alone, or trying to distract me. Either way, I don't care. I didn't get a slap and Jazz is still here. Today is going to be a very good day. Taking her hand, I give her a quick tour of the kitchen. "There is still some work to do in here, but it's functional. We were mainly concentrating on out front."

"I don't know how to tell you how grateful I am."

"I could think of a few ways," I smirk, pinning her against the fridge. My hand squeezing her arse as I kiss her neck, she moans.

"Ahem," comes the voice from the door.

I sigh against the skin of her neck. "Fuck," I whisper.

Jazz giggles.

"Sorry to interrupt, but we need to get moving. We open in half an hour," Mags says.

"Yeah, yeah," I say just loud enough for her to hear, reluctant to leave the lush body I'm pressed against.

"She's going to start getting shirty in a minute, we'd better do as she says," whispers Jazz.

Laughing, I concede. "Ok, Princess, let's get you ready. I'll show you where the magic is going to happen."

She follows me through the shop, not that I give her a choice, I haven't let go of her hand yet. I show her where to stash her bag and take her around to the little kitchen I've made her. I knew this part of the shop needed to be on full display. Everyone needs to see what she looks like working hard, with little smears of chocolate on her skin. It's sexy as hell. I have my seat all picked out to watch for hours.

And no, I won't be sitting here getting pissed off that other men are watching. I'm going to make her so mine that she won't see them. I'm not going to waste my time worrying about what might happen. I'm just going to work hard on making sure she's satisfied. No jealousy. No bail outs. I'm not going to fuck this up.

"Semi Sweet?" she asks me, with a quirked eyebrow, as I slip the apron over her head. She fingers the embroidered logo, while I tie the bow at the back for her.

I shrug, "Hey, I wanted to go with Psycho Cinderella. I was outvoted."

She laughs, but her face flushes with embarrassment.

I run a finger over her warm, red cheek. "You know it's hot when you blush, right?"

She does it again, closing her eyes.

"We really need to get out of here. I need to get a few things out of my system so that I can concentrate."

"That's going to have to wait, mate," says Will, sneaking up behind me, slapping my back. "Mags is going to rupture something if today doesn't go smoothly. You have your orders, for all of our sakes, you need to stick to them."

Jazz smirks and says, "He's right. Whatever she's told you to do, do it or you'll die." She looks pained, "I guess I'll see you after we close, whatever time that is."

I grin. "Oh, no, Princess, you don't get rid of me that easily. I haven't been ordered to leave, I've been ordered to stay. I'm your assistant for the day."

"Oh dear God."

Watching her get to grips with everything is funny, she's so freaked about having all this thrust at her that she's had that deer-in-the-headlights look all day. Locals have flooded in, both in relief to have a coffee shop back in the village again and in support of our latest addition. There is a lot of encouragement. People seem to be pleased that for all intents and purposes, Mary's hasn't quite gone away, but they all seem to love the new addition of the chocolates. I huff realising that Jazz is going to have to put in some considerable hours this week building up a stock of chocolates. Until she trains the other staff, that's all on her.

Her counter is busy, and I feel like a spare part, so I offer to take a plate of samples around, like Will has been doing. I have heard him talking to people about the different chocolates and making recommendations. I realise as I get to the first table, I have no clue what I'm holding.

I dash back to Jazz, "I don't know what flavours you have."

"No, that's because you don't care about anyone but yourself," Will nudges me, teasing. And takes the plate from my hands.

"Until now," I growl, snatching it back.

Turning back to Jazz, I ask, "What's the one shaped like a nipple? I'm likely to remember that one."

She just laughs and instead suggests that Will does the

rounds with the samples, and I help her behind the counter. I'm ok with that suggestion, and although I am really more of a hindrance than a help, I do enjoy being able to touch her and whisper my dirty plans to her. By the time we close the door, I'm ready to plonk her unceremoniously on the counter and drive into her, with whoever still happens to be here watching. They can hold up score cards for all I care. If I don't get her alone soon, things aren't going to be pretty.

She gives a little speech of sorts to the staff before they leave, thanking them for bearing with her and hoping they will all be happy working together. Once they leave, it is just the four of us.

Mags brings out a bottle of champagne to celebrate the first day, but I take it out of her hands. "I think we should have this back at your place," I wink at Jazz, "and some dinner, I'm fucking starving!"

"That's a great idea, I'll cook," Mags replies and I can see my evening filling up with polite dinner conversation. Oh, hell no!

"We've all had a long day, why don't you two go home, and we'll bring fish and chips after we've showered." Will nods in agreement and they agree. At least this way, we can eat and then I can get her on her own as soon as possible.

There are two things I didn't consider when I suggested this.

One, that she would be all showered with her wet hair piled up, smelling amazing and wearing little shorts and a T-shirt with bare feet. I know I'm into her shoes in a big way, but the barefoot and shower-fresh look is killing me.

And two, I have never eaten a meal with her before. I've never even made conversation with her unless it was to piss her off or get her on her knees. There's so much to talk about, but Mags and Will are here so the effect is silence. We eat and exchange glances, that's it. It's so fucking awkward. Thankfully, Will has a masters in alleviating social awkwardness and gets things going. Keeping the conversation in safe territory, kinda.

After we toast the success of the day, we get on to how much happier Jazz will be now that she will be doing what she loves.

"I'm just happy that the only fondling you'll get at work will be if Spencer calls in to see you," says Mags.

I sit up straighter. "Oh, yeah about that, who do I need to kill?" Just the thought of her getting groped by her boss has my blood boiling.

"No one, it's done. Finished. Forgotten," says Jazz, placing her hand over mine to calm me down.

"Yeah and Jazz saw to it that he won't be getting it up for a looong time," laughs Mags.

I shake my head. "Well, I don't like it."

"Well, it's over," says Jazz. "And life is better now."

"Yeah, no more supermarket sandwiches for you," laughs Mags.

Jazz glares at her.

"What? I'm just saying, you can get nice lunches prepared fresh at work."

Some private eye signal conversation passes between them that Mags finds very amusing.

"Yeah, I don't miss boring supermarket sandwiches

either," I add while I'm trying to figure them out.

Will laughs, "Whatever dude. You told me it was the highlight of your day."

Now it's my turn to glare at him. Shut the fuck up, man!

"There were always hot girls in the supermarket. I was on the phone to him one time," he tells Mags, "and this girl was literally stumbling over herself, blushing. He even followed her around."

Mags chokes on her champagne.

Jazz covers her face with her hands as Mags can't contain her laughter.

"You ok?" I ask Mags, while Will takes her glass and pats her back.

"Oh. My. God," she gets out between splutters. "Spencer, meet blushing, stumbling, hot supermarket girl."

Jazz sinks further into her chair, her hands still over her face.

"No way!' shouts Will triumphantly. "That's brilliant."

I peel her fingers away from her face. "Shoegirl, was that you?"

She gulps and gives a little wave, nodding.

"How did you not recognise her?" Will asks. "You told me what she was wearing, how fuck-me hot her shoes were, how her blush made you want to…yeah. ok, I'll stop now," he says as my face tells him he's about to get hurt. "But seriously though, dude, how did you not make the connection?"

"I don't know. Maybe I didn't pay enough attention to her face."

"Yeah, that'd be right," laughs Mags.

"And to be fair, the next time we met was under very

different circumstances." I need to get the heat off me. Turning to Jazz as it all clicks into place, I ask, "So you stalked me here? Is that what happened?"

"No!" She sits up now all defensive. "Actually, I came here with Mags. Neither of us knew you or Will were here, the rest was as much a surprise to us as it was to you."

"Damn."

"What?" She looks puzzled.

"Having a real life stalker would be hot. I've only had virtual ones before."

Will can't help his laughter.

"Yeah," she growls. "We will be having a chat about your virtual stalkers later."

"It's all in the past," I assure her.

"Mmmmhmmm."

"Are you getting jealous again, Princess?"

"Bite me," she smirks.

"Where?" I grin.

"Oh, please you two, get a room," Will groans.

I glare at him, "Dude, I've been in solitary confinement for a month!"

"Yeah, where were you?" she asks.

"I've been staying at Auntie Mary's place, but I've been at the shop most of the time."

She smiles. "I just want to say again, how grateful I am to you all for doing this for me. I know I can be stubborn sometimes but—" her words are cut off by us all laughing and making sarcastic comments.

'No! Not you Jazz! Stubborn? I'd never believe that!'

"Bastards!" She laughs. "All of you, but I love you

anyway." She gets up to take her plate to the sink completely unaware that her words left Mags and Will exchanging a knowing glance and me gasping for air.

Will comes to the rescue by scraping his chair loudly and starting to clear the table. We all help clear away the dishes and while they aren't looking, I yank Jazz out into the hallway and drag her giggling up the stairs. I've been dying to get her alone all day and I've run out of patience. I kick her bedroom door shut behind us and pull her into my arms.

"Finally," she gasps, throwing her arms around my neck and eagerly accepting my tongue as it parts her lips.

I groan, pushing her up against the wall so that I can explore her skin with my hands. But then I stop, she feels so good, don't get me wrong, but is this going to always be what we do?

"What is it?" she asks, concerned that I've stopped.

I look at her, reaching out to tuck a strand of hair behind her ear. Moving close to her, I look into her eyes. My heart pounds in my chest. She takes my breath away. I've spent so long dealing with what happens to me when I let myself feel, that now I can't remember how to tell someone what they mean to me. I know how I feel about her, but we need to take things slow.

"Spencer?" She's waiting for me to say something or do something.

"When are we going to slow it down?" Stroking her cheek, I sigh. "I'm tired of fucking you against walls. No, not tired, that's just stupid. I actually like fucking you against walls. But I want to lay in bed with you all day and stay on the brink for hours. I also want to take a bowl of your Dark and Stormy and enjoy it off each other's skin. I may even want to get out of bed some time and make you dinner."

"Make me dinner?" she says quietly, her voice strangled with emotion. "Wow."

I smile. "You know what I mean. We just fuck and piss each other off. It's getting old."

"Bored of me already?" she purrs.

"Bored of you? Never." I kiss her forehead.

"Then we don't have a problem, do we?" She pushes me back away from her and backs me over to the bed. I fall willingly and hold my breath as she lifts her top over her head. Wriggling out of her shorts, she climbs over me, settling herself so that her lace lingerie clad body is pressed against me.

"We can go as slow as you want," she says, slowly rotating her hips.

"Mmmm," is all I can say, my hands sliding over her silky smooth curves.

"Just as long as you don't disappear again."

"I had to do that."

"I know."

"I won't do it again," I promise her.

"I know," she smiles, rotating her hips again.

"I'm serious, Jazz, I'm not going anywhere."

"I know."

"I hope you're ready for that."

"I am." She lowers her lips to mine and slowly leaves an impression that I will never be able to shake out of my head.

"You sure? Because I'm going to be around a lot."

"What are you saying?" she smirks.

Man I want to wipe that smirk off her face. I flip her suddenly so that I'm on top.

"I'm saying..." I press my hips forward so that she moans with need. "That you're mine."

She stills, watching me.

"That's good," she says in barely more than a whisper, "because you're mine."

Fuck slowing it down, I need her now. I drag my T-shirt over my head and quickly stand to get rid of my jeans and underwear. My plan to ravage her is thwarted when I peel down her underwear and catch sight of her pussy. My need to taste her comes first.

I place a kiss on her thigh, lifting her leg onto my shoulder and pulling her closer to the edge of the bed. The scent of her is intoxicating. "Mmmmm." I can't help the sound I make as I lick lazily through her, her taste flooding my mouth.

She gasps.

"I love how you taste."

I run my tongue through again and she moans.

"You know, you should consider this as a flavour. We could call it the Semi Sweet Princess."

"Shhhh, concentrate!" she murmurs.

"Sorry, Princess."

She lifts her head, looks at me with that, 'you're gonna get it in a minute' face and sighs. "You're killing the moment."

"What? You don't like my idea?"

She shakes her head despairingly.

"You don't want this now?" I ask in a lower voice, with a knowing grin, playing the tip of my tongue on her clit.

"Nope, you've ruined it," she says defiantly pulling at my

Spencer

hair to remove my face from her pussy.

"Ok, Princess," I humour her, making to sit up.

She sighs, dropping her hands to the bed with an exasperated thump. "Don't call me that."

"Why not?"

"Because you only say it as an insult."

"No, I don't."

"Liar." She shakes her head. "Every time you say that to me it's in a derogatory way."

"But we're past that now, aren't we?" I watch her for a reaction.

"I don't know, are we?" She seems uncertain.

"Yes, we are. You're my princess," I tell her, hopping up onto the bed, scooping her up and laying back. Her knees come to rest on either side of my head and I grin. "And your throne is my face."

She gasps in mock indignation and slaps my arm.

"What? That's romantic!"

She grumbles, "That is the most unromantic attempt at being romantic I think I've ever—" Her words fail as my tongue takes a lazy swipe through her pussy and draws her clit into my mouth. I suck hard and feather my tongue, making her thighs tremble. "...Heard," she whimpers, when I release it.

I look up at her pussy, inches from my face and beyond that I have the perfect view of her curves, her ever begging nipples framing her face as she peers down at me. "I could lay between these thighs forever."

Her eyebrows raise.

"See, I can be romantic," I smile. "Now, pass me my phone, I have the best view, I need a picture."

ACKNOWLEDGEMENTS

To every one who read, reviewed and talked about Just Human and Still Human, from the bottom of my heart, thank you. You gave me the courage to do it again. Thank you for holding out for this one, I know it was a long wait. I promise the next one faster.

Spencer is a force of nature and he has turned my life upside down. He and I battled it out and what can I say? In the end, we did it his way. This one wasn't easy, but it was worth the highs and lows. I hope it entertains you.

To my betas, you each bring something very different to the party and I appreciate each of you and your honesty. You each helped me bring this story to a good place in your own unique way. And to Natasha, for saving the day. Thanks to all of you x

To Kel, Jen and Jojo, you girls kick butt! Mine, usually. But if you didn't make me look deeply at the important things, then where would I be? Thank you for ALL the eleventh hour butt kickings. The details may be small to most people, but you see the difference they make and force me to think hard. You don't let me settle and you stop me from being a chickenshit. Thank you…and know that I have my foot ready for when it's your turn!

To my love, Mr H, thanks for...you know.

To the 'characters' of Twitter, what can I say? Thank you for being the ever-changing freak show of inspiration that I love and loathe in equal measure. Don't ever change. I'll just sit quietly with my popcorn and keep watching.

And finally, to My Pet, you have held me together through this sometimes harrowing journey. If it were not for you, I would have turned around and gone back home. You are my safe place. You let me be me in a way only one other person ever really has and I love you. Thank you for your love, your courage and your creativity. You inspire me constantly and support me unconditionally and I thank my lucky stars every day that you are in my life. Thank you for being my best friend, my love and the family I got to choose.

Sparkles x

Printed in Great Britain
by Amazon